TWO FLAMES

A Disparate Energy Novel

TWO FLAMES

By Holly D. Morgan

Red Berry Press

Cover and dust jacket design by Benita Thompson of Kairos Book Design
Hardcover case laminate and interior illustrations design by EFA_finearts
Map of The Seven Republics by Vojin Kremic; Governor names added by Holly D. Morgan
Map of Preen by Jeremy Morgan
End paper design, postcard, and notes from Canva Pro
Publishing imprint by Christy Boughan

First Edition: 2025

Edited by Angela Morse of An Encouraging Thought
The text for this book was set in Garamond

Red Berry Press LLC

Red Berry Press

To Jeremy
I love you *all ways*
Thanks for being my love

Author's Note

The world of Disparates is full of deep, sometimes dark, emotions. Every reader has the right to know their own emotions and to choose what media they will consume. To help you know if Two Flames is right for you, a list of the darker content is below.

Content Warnings:
Anxiety and depression representation
Medication misuse
Child endangerment
Parental death
Kidnapping
Anger issues
Fire injuries

If you find yourself struggling at any point in your reading, please seek the appropriate support.

This book explores multiple points of view to tell its story. The changes can be confusing at first, so here is a guide for the point of view changes.

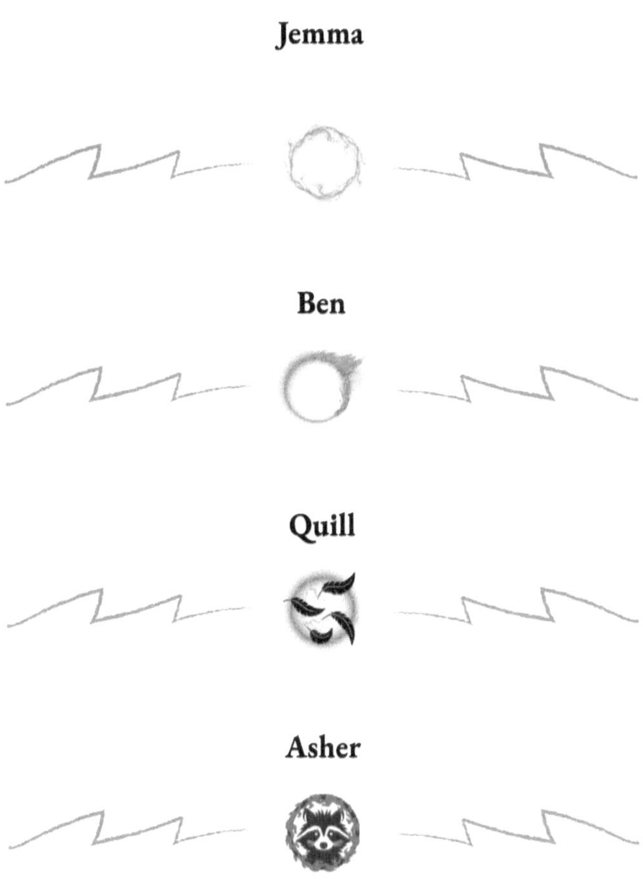

There is also a fifth bonus point of view later in the story, but I'll let you read to discover who it is and how their character symbol looks.

The Seven Republics

and their Governors

THE FIVE ENERGIES

FEAR:
YELLOW PILL

ANGER:
RED PILL

DISGUST:
WHITE PILL

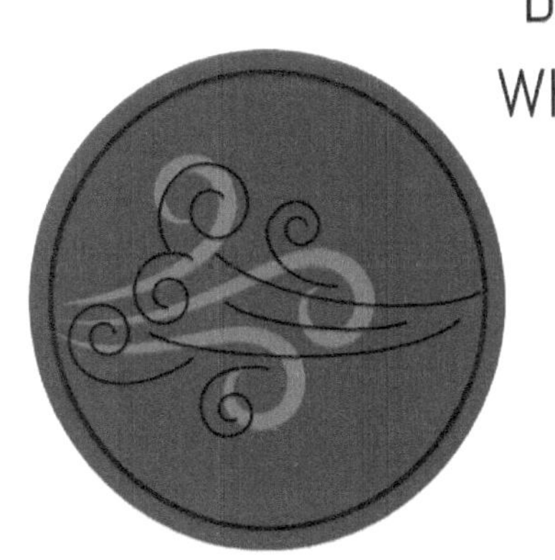

JOY:
PURPLE PILL

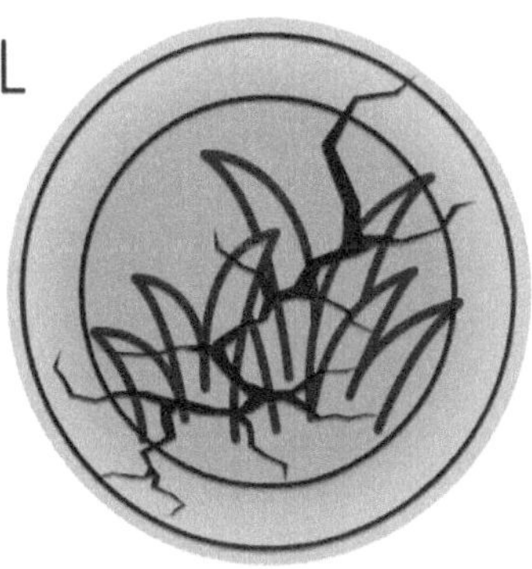

SADNESS:
GREEN PILL

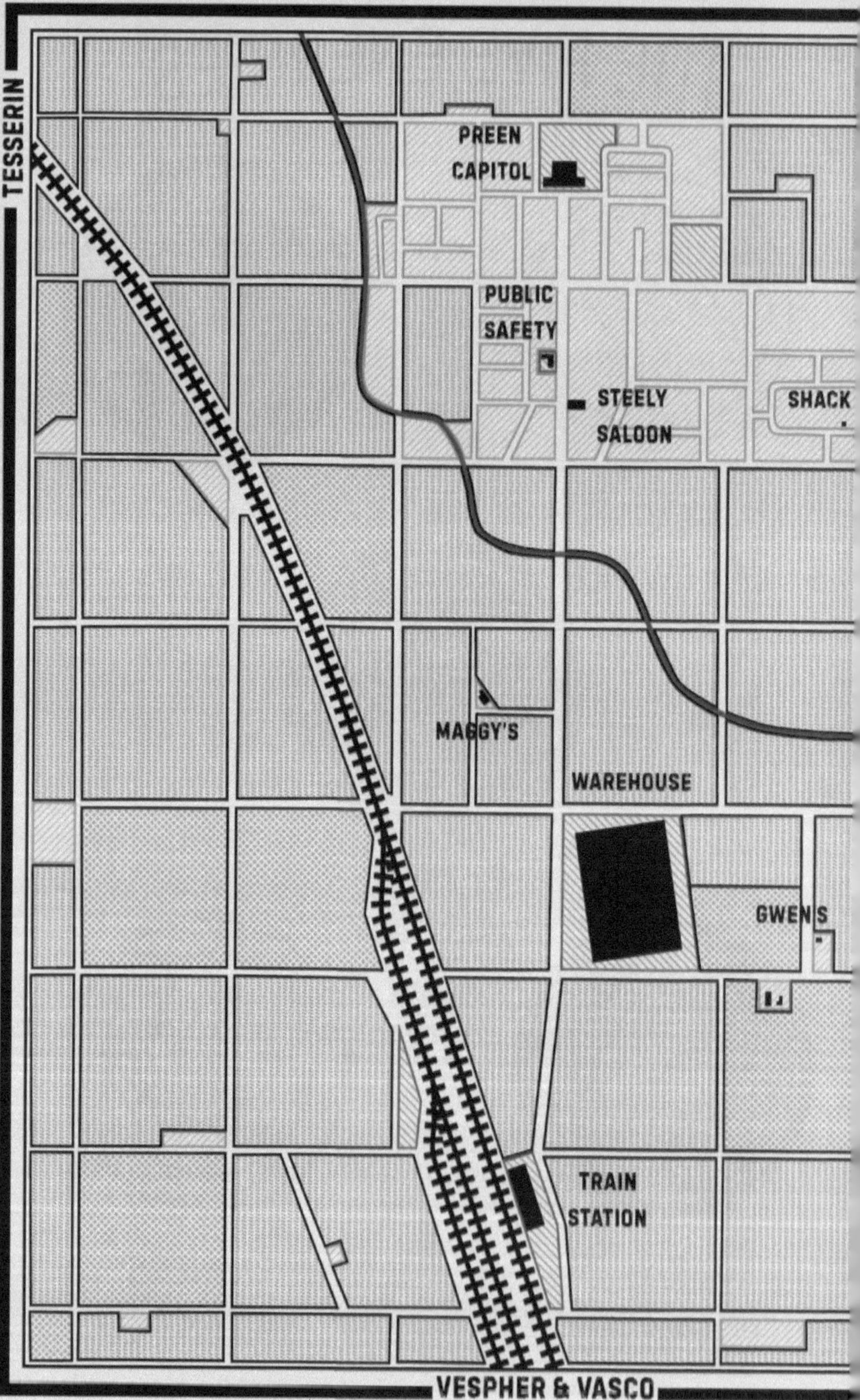

TESSERIN
PREEN CAPITOL
PUBLIC SAFETY
STEELY SALOON
SHACK
MAGGY'S
WAREHOUSE
GWENS
TRAIN STATION
VESPHER & VASCO

Outskirts Will Live
CRATER - CAUTION DO NOT APPROACH
EASTON'S FARM
REPUBLIC OF PREEN

ONE

The sunshine bounced off the red bars of the playset.

Red. Like the color of the uniform Jemma's husband had been forced to wear only a few weeks before.

Red. Like the pills he used to take to keep his fire controlled.

Red. Like the blaze in her memory that consumed her childhood home. That may rise again to devour the life she'd created if her son couldn't learn to keep his flame energy under control.

"Louie! Watch out for the tree!" she shouted, her heart thumping in her chest as static rippled through the hairs on her arms—her own electric energy. Her six-year-old stopped in time, looking up from the ant pile on the ground that had grabbed his attention and dodging the tree branch in his path.

Not that Jemma was the best example of keeping one's emotions in check, but she was trying. Her anxiety had been at an all time high the last couple months, which had led to multiple electrical issues when it came to their home wiring, but she'd kept from hurting anyone.

"You boys have half an hour left to play. Then, we'll pick up Daddy and head to a special lunch to celebrate our birthday boy." Jemma went to scrub the top of Mackie's dark brown hair; a static shock erupted at their touch. Not the way she intended to celebrate her younger son turning five.

"Ouch." Mackie pushed her hand away.

"I'm sorry," Jemma said, guilt gurgling inside her. She had caused a *little* hurt. "I didn't mean to do that."

"It's ah-kay." Mackie rubbed the spot on his head. "Can I have chicken nuggets? With lots of ketchup?"

Jemma squatted to his eye level. "Whatever the birthday boy wants, the birthday boy gets."

His face beamed with a smile, making it easy to spoil him. His fifth birthday had been a light in the darkness their family had experienced the last few weeks. Jemma almost wasn't sure Ben would be home in time. Not after the government thought he was the fire anarchist. That was actually her brother.

But that matter had been cleared up, even if Asher wasn't too happy with his current circumstances. At least he wasn't locked away in a reformation center.

Jemma sat on a wooden bench nearby as Mackie and Louie ran off to play. She pulled out her cell phone to check on Ben.

> Good luck at your interview! You've got this!

Jemma wasn't expecting a response, yet a few moments later:

Thanks, honey. Birthday good luck, right?

That only works on your own birthday.

He's got my DNA. That should count for something.

"Mom! Look at me!" Mackie yelled. He jumped up the stairs of the playset, skipping one in between each step.

"You're getting so big!"

"It's cuz I'm five now!"

Jemma smiled. The boys were safe. They were happy. Louie slid down his favorite slide, twisting in circles until he reached the bottom. A grin spread across his face as his feet landed in the sand.

Her thoughts returned to her husband. He'd only been home for two weeks. It didn't seem like long enough to start his job search, yet he insisted he was ready. Going back to Energy Watch wasn't an option for him. Not any longer, with the Republic Energy Investigators, or R.E.I., taking over.

However, that left their family in need of a source of income. And Ben insisted on being the provider.

"Mom!" Mackie shouted again. "I can do this!" He climbed onto a toy duck, all on his own. Jemma waved at him and smiled.

Governor Dunn had mentioned a position he thought Jemma would be perfect for, with her past as an Analyst and her in with Buran's group, the Dissentients. He wanted to make her the official Stillfield Disparate Liaison.

The idea intrigued Jemma, which brought a pit of guilt to her chest. She'd left the workplace to be home with her boys. She couldn't abandon them.

But then again, showing them the value of hard work wasn't abandonment. No. And providing for their family's needs—for putting Mackie on the soccer team and keeping Louie's stock of apple juice full—that wasn't abandonment.

Her phone buzzed in her lap.

This isn't a good fit. They don't employ Disparates.

Jemma sighed. This wasn't the first job interview where he'd found something he didn't like. Ben had come home... different. EnertinX had worked as Dr. Paxton claimed. He no longer had flame energy, which meant he no longer took Enertin, the pill form that subdued his anger.

And that change was highly noticeable, especially with this job search. At first, it was that the hours were awful. Which—fair point. Jemma didn't like the idea of him working the night shift either. Sleeping all day and being gone all night. But then the next job didn't allow enough breaks. Another gave *too many* breaks.

At least discriminating against Disparates was a valid reason to be upset, but they were running out of other work options.

But you're not one anymore.

It's not fair. I don't agree with this.

It is a job transporting goods from the other Republics. Like oil. That wouldn't be a safe work environment for Disparates.

I'm done.

Well, that was that. "Boys, time to pick up Dad," she said, standing.

"Help me get down," Mackie said as he slowed the duck's rocking. Jemma headed in his direction.

The flutter of light, happy music reached her ears. *Not now.* She turned her attention to Louie, who stood at the top of the playset. His face lit up as he looked in the direction it was coming from.

"Mom, there's an ice cream truck!"

"I hear it," she responded. Mackie's giggle erupted from behind her as she headed toward Louie. She'd need to keep him calm. "But it's time to pick up dad. We'll have to get ice cream next time." *Why couldn't the group obsessed with old vehicles restore a dump truck instead of one that gives away treats.*

"That's what you said last time." Louie's face fell quickly, his eyes dark. The air filled with heat.

Jemma extended her hands in front of her. "Breathe… maybe after lunch…" But she was too late to calm his quick temper.

A burst of flames erupted from Louie toward the street the truck was turning onto. Jemma twisted. Mackie floated between

Louie and the truck, suspended in midair above the duck. Not by his own powers—Mackie didn't have any—but by his brother's second energy.

Louie's excitement about ice cream had lifted his brother, and now fire from his anger at being told no was making its way in Mackie's direction.

The fear slammed into Jemma like she'd been hit by the restored truck slowly making its way to the park. Her muscles tightened as she ran to Mackie, her heart racing quicker than her legs could go.

The flames grew, extending toward Mackie like a whip. The energy in the air caused the flames to follow along its route.

Jemma screamed, her whole soul exiting her body as she jumped, reaching toward her younger son. As she did, a familiar tingling sensation spread from her heart, through her arm, and out her fingers.

The fingers that were reaching for Mackie.

Just as the flames connected with her outstretched arm, the electricity she'd released shot out as a bolt of lightning.

It hit Mackie with such force, his small body dropped, released from the air that had surrounded him. He fell limply to the ground.

With his fall, the fire stopped, leaving only smoke that rose toward the heavens.

A searing pain shot through Jemma. Her son lay motionless on the sand.

Her knees indented the ground next to Mackie and tears streamed down her face.

This wasn't right. This couldn't be real. The world around her was muffled as she held her son in her arms.

He didn't move.

He didn't breathe.

"No!" she screamed out. "No! No! Noooo!"

She placed him down, putting her hands on his chest. He needed to breathe. She pushed on him in a rhythmic pattern, watching for air to enter into his lungs.

It didn't.

Sirens echoed through the world around her.

"Mom..." Louie approached slowly.

"No," she said. That was all she could muster, all she could think.

This wasn't real.

It couldn't be.

"Ma'am," came a muffled voice over her shoulder as a pair of uniformed Responders arrived on scene. "We're here to take over."

She didn't want to stop—to let go. She could never let go of her child.

"We need to help him. You can stay right next to him." The Responder placed a hand on her shoulder.

She nodded and moved back. Mackie's lifeless body faced the sky.

No...

The Responder kept his hand on her shoulder as the other checked Mackie's neck for a pulse. "His heart is beating..."

Jemma let out a strangled breath. He was still here.

"But it's irregular," the Responder said as he grabbed the bag at his side. He pulled out a device with two paddles, then cut off Mackie's shirt and placed them onto his chest.

His small body convulsed then fell still. Unmoving.

The world around Jemma spun. She wanted to reach out and hold her boy, but that would do no good.

Mackie's body convulsed once more. As it stilled, Jemma watched.

Praying he would wake up.

The first sign that her prayer was answered was the twitch of his lips before they opened to take in a large breath. His chest swelled, his eyelids fluttering as life entered him once more.

Jemma's sobbing increased, but this time, there was relief in the tears that fell. Not entirely relief, as Mackie had been gone. She wasn't sure how long, as time had stopped during the ordeal.

He'd come back, but she wasn't sure how much.

The young boy continued to breathe. His eyes moved to look at her.

"Mom," his small voice said. The sound made more tears fall.

"Yes, sweetie, I'm here." She grabbed hold of his hand, memorizing the feel of his little fingers in her grasp.

"I'm tired," he said.

"You can't sleep yet, little man," the Responder next to Jemma said. He turned his attention to her. "He needs to go to the hospital for a full evaluation and observation. And you'll need to be checked out as well."

Jemma followed his gaze to her arm. She didn't recognize it. Bright red blisters had formed across the surface. She hadn't even noticed the burning that came from her arm; her only concern was Mackie.

"Is there ice cream?" Mackie asked. Jemma let herself smile at her boy, but it quickly turned into a gape. Someone was missing.

"Louie?" Jemma searched the area, her heart rate increasing once more. Finally, her gaze landed on her oldest son, standing a few yards away.

His face was blank, but his eyes were wide.

"Louie, come over here." A sharp pain caused Jemma to yelp as she moved her burned arm, trying to wave to him.

The pain must have been too much for Louie to see. Tears fell as he crumpled to the ground. Jemma looked at Mackie once more, who had started a conversation with the Responder getting a stretcher ready for him.

"Mom, they have ice cream at the hospital!" Mackie said to her as she nodded and headed to Louie.

She wrapped her good arm around him, snuggling her head into his hair and pulling him into a hug.

"It's okay, baby, it's okay." Her tears wet his ash blond hair.

He didn't speak. No words were needed for Jemma to understand what he was feeling.

That same shame ate at her, too.

That night, Jemma lay in her empty bed. The coldness of the sheets next to her brought back the loneliness of Ben's time on the island. Except this time he wasn't falsely accused and imprisoned. He was at the hospital with Mackie. Because of her.

Because she was dangerous.

Because she hurt their son.

The betrayal in Ben's eyes when he arrived at the hospital was burned into her mind. "I thought you were keeping it controlled," he'd said. "How did this happen?"

The blame and anger was well placed. She'd been going to Buran's training. She'd been practicing her breathing and expressing her feelings. And yet this happened.

An overwhelming fear had seized control of her body. No training session had addressed that desperation. Panic had taken over once she saw Mackie in danger. She was trying to save him, to stop the red flames that were about to consume him.

The flames that had dissipated into smoke as they reached her. As if Louie had realized what he was doing and stopped the advance. She should have been fully engulfed in his energy. If she had been, maybe her electricity would have been stopped. Maybe Mackie never would have been hit.

She should have died. Not him.

Curled in a fetal position, Jemma clutched the remains of the shirt Mackie had been wearing that day. The one that had been cut apart. Her sobbing only grew.

He's still alive. He was saved, she repeated to herself, trying to make the dread leave her body. But it refused.

She could hurt him again. And what if that time he didn't return?

If learning to control my emotions didn't result in control of my energy, there is only one other answer.

Enertin. The pills the Dissentients fought so hard against. The ones that had proven to make Disparates more dangerous in the long run... but in the short run—they helped.

She could take them, for a short time. Get her powers under control enough to learn how to use them. The alternative allowed herself to be a danger to her kids.

She didn't have any. Not any for her electric energy. No yellow pills.

But red pills.

Red pills they did have. Ben had no use for them after returning from the island energy-free. Jealousy bit at her chest as she realized this was one thing Ben never had to worry about again. Thanks to EnertinX, he'd never lose control so drastically that he'd injure another. And it was something he hadn't worried about when he took his red pills.

Maybe that was her answer. The pills each differed slightly, designed to best suit each type of energy and the chemicals the brain created to make said power. But her understanding as a former Analyst was that the individual pills relied on the same base ingredient, derived from the same plant family. Although the red pills wouldn't be best suited for her brain, they should still do the trick.

Jemma headed to their medicine cabinet. She retrieved the large bottle full of a three month supply, the weight of it heavy in her hand.

Without a second thought, she opened the lid and shoved a pill into her mouth. Turning on the sink, she placed her mouth under the flowing water and took in enough to swallow.

There. Now she was safe. Now she would no longer be a danger to her family.

A danger to her kids.

Two

Two and a Half Months Later

The grain of the wood table swirled in a tempest manner, waves filled with fury and emotion matching the atmosphere in the room. Some days, Jemma regretted her choice to be a working woman once more. Today was one of those days.

However, there was something she needed to discuss with the two men sitting at the table with her.

"I'm telling you," Buran said from his spot two chairs over, "if we don't do more to stop the reliance on Enertin, something big is going to happen."

"You've been saying that for the last three months." Governor Dunn sat straighter in his seat across from his new Disparate consultant. He'd hired Buran, along with Jemma as the liaison between the two of them, after the mall showdown last April.

"It's still as true today as it was then," Buran said. "For the safety of our town, of innocent civilians, we need to do something. And now, before it's too late."

Governor Dunn narrowed his eyes. "Is that a threat?"

Jemma's job mostly consisted of keeping discussions between these two productive and civil—which she was on the path of failing today. It may not be the right time to bring up her own problem.

"Look," Jemma jumped in, "we've been over this. Buran, you've identified the risks of continuing to produce and prescribe Enertin." Jemma's insides clenched, considering she was a fake saying this. "And Governor, you've explained how a total shutdown of the current procedures would result in its own chaos and backlash—"

"At a much smaller level," Buran interrupted.

"Yes," Jemma acknowledged, "at a level you believe would be easier to contain. But we don't know that. Something like this has never been attempted in a society before."

Governor Dunn nodded his approval. He looked back at Buran. "How have your trials been?"

Buran sighed. "We're not getting enough participants. And those who do sign up drop out at the first sign of actual feelings. It's been drilled into their heads for so long that emotions are dangerous that they don't want to open themselves up to them. But Jemma is a prime example of how it can be done! She hasn't let her anxiety get to her since... well..."

Jemma knew what he was referring to, and it hit her harder than she'd expected. She understood others' resistance. Despite seeing firsthand how dangerous it could be to not allow yourself to experience feelings, she also knew how dangerous it was to let yourself feel without restraint. Mackie's laid-out body haunted her, but Ben's pills had been helping. Too bad his supply was running out. She didn't know how to admit she needed more.

Or how to break the news to Buran that she wasn't the star pupil he thought she was. No one knew she was taking Enertin.

Of course, she still had two weeks of pills left. Perhaps that was enough time for her to get her emotions under control without them. A lot could happen in two weeks.

"I'm not sure that's enough evidence for the council meeting," Governor Dunn said. "The other governors want to see hard data that your plan works."

The mention of the other governors turned Jemma's stomach. It wasn't often the seven Republics gathered together. When they did, it usually involved new Disparate mandates, with the Republic of Stillfield leading the way.

After the Rain of Fire occurred at the beginning of the century, most of civilization had been destroyed by nuclear warfare. Those that survived rebuilt into the Seven Republics, each agreeing to focus on their own land and citizens and keep out of the business of others. It was soon after the rebuild that Disparates began to emerge, shaking up the new order that had been established. The Republics agreed together to send Disparates to Lucky Island. Stillfield, the science-focused Republic, took the lead at developing a cure.

A cure they now wanted to renounce.

The other Republics were unlikely to agree with that. And in one week, they'd learn how against the idea the others were at a meeting with the other governors.

"It will work." Buran pulled some papers out of the folder he'd placed in front of himself. "I have more case studies that have been successful." He handed the governor his evidence. "And then there's Jemma. She'll be there to testify firsthand how energy therapy is worth it. We just need to train Analysts to do this job."

Jemma was a vital piece of Buran's plan. Too bad she was a fraud.

Ben stopped to catch his breath. Chasing two young kids around was more work than it used to be, pre-island.

No. He didn't want to think about that. His time on Lucky Island, albeit short, was a period of time he didn't like to dwell on. However, his mind wouldn't let him move on, inserting reminders of that time into the simple, daily tasks of his life. Guilt hit him at the smallest moments.

He insisted on cold showers, matching the coldness inside now that his fire was gone.

Unseasoned, bland food. His taste buds rejected any intense flavor.

Laughter. It wasn't right. Not when so many islanders still lived imprisoned. Sure, they were moved off Lucky Island when Dr. Paxton was arrested, but they weren't free. Just moved to a new cell on the mainland. One near the outskirts south of

Wuslick, Watershield Prison. From the little description he got from the governor, his previous fellow inmates were essentially living in old metal shipping containers. Held far enough away to keep everyone safe from any outbursts.

At least until the old mall could be fixed and returned to its former glory of Merrytime Clinic and the islanders could be taught Buran's techniques. But to do that would require approval from the other governors since Governor Dunn was a coward afraid of change.

A small hand on his arm brought him back to the present. "You're it!" Mackie called as he ran toward the kitchen giggling.

Ben smiled. Happiness with his children was one emotion he knew he wouldn't be able to resist no matter how guilty he felt about it.

He was home, and he would get the rest of the islanders back too.

Mackie's accident due to Jemma's lack of control had frightened Ben. It wasn't that he didn't trust Jemma. He understood her struggle. He'd released his energy unintentionally before, as a teenager, and burned down half of his school. Thankfully, no one was hurt.

But having energy powers came with a responsibility to control them. Which Jemma was working on with Buran. She hadn't had any signs of an outburst since that day. Experiencing the full effects of what her emotions could do sure worked to motivate her.

He caught sight of Louie, who ran across the hallway into the master bedroom. A crash followed him. "I'm coming for you," Ben yelled as he sprinted into the room, knocking the door open. He immediately stopped.

Louie had only been in here for a moment, and yet at his feet lay the remnants of a broken object. Ben's heart sank as he realized what the broken pieces were—the glass flower vase he'd had engraved with his and Jemma's wedding date.

"What happened?" Ben demanded. His voice came out sterner than he'd meant.

"Nothing! I didn't do anything." Louie sat on the bed, his feet barely touching the ground.

"Then why is this broken?" The grief was strong, sweeping over his soul in an instant. "I bought this for your mother when we got married. Why would you mess with this?"

"I didn't."

"It was on a high shelf; it couldn't have broken unless you meant to get it." Ben's voice rose.

"I didn't break it!" Louie shouted back.

The temperature in the room warmed. The scar on the side of Ben's face throbbed. There was energy accumulating here, but not from Ben.

Louie let out a yell. A small flame pulsed above his shoulders, hungry and searching for fuel.

"Whoa, okay, okay." Ben put his shaking hands out in the space between them. "Let's both calm down. Take a deep breath."

"No! You think I broke it!" The flame grew.

"I... uh..." Ben eyed the closet on the other side of the room. He'd have to go past Louie to get the extinguisher or abandon his son to retrieve one from another room. If he was fast, he would be back before more damage was done.

Before he went out the door, someone else came through it.

"Hey Louie, you mad?" Mackie said.

Ben's heartbeat sped faster. He couldn't leave now. Not with Mackie here.

Louie growled.

"Yep. You're mad."

"Mackie," Ben said, "why don't you give your brother some space?"

Mackie slunk inward, away from Ben and his stern remark. "I wanted to see if he'd play games with me," he said timidly.

Louie's flame flickered at the suggestion.

"Maybe once he's calmed dow—"

"Yes, I want to play games!" Louie said, enthusiastically. His flame had extinguished.

"Can we play, Dad?" Mackie asked.

Ben took a deep breath and let it out slowly, his eyes focused on the mess of glass next to his bedside table. "Yes. Of course."

The boys ran out together, heading to the front room.

Ben sighed. He grabbed the tissue box Jemma had finished off the night before and plucked a larger piece of glass off the floor.

"You've had a rough day, I see." Jemma's voice came from behind.

Ben jumped. He turned to see her leaning in the doorway. "How did you know?" he asked with a shrug, trying to play it off. He didn't want her to see how frustrated he'd been, but his pulse raced.

"Try to be patient with the boys, okay?"

Ben sighed. "I'll try. Some days are easier than others."

"Mackie likes to help with Louie," she said.

"I've noticed." Ben resumed picking glass from the floor and putting them into the tissue box.

"He has a special way with him. Knows how to calm him down." Jemma moved to join Ben. She reached for a piece of glass at the same time as him, a small spark firing at their touch.

Ben drew his hand back. Jemma's voice had been calm, but clearly the release of energy reflected her insides.

Her eyes were wide. "That wasn't me! I swear. Probably from the glass rubbing on the carpet."

Ben laughed. He couldn't hold it back, and with its release, his body relaxed. "It's okay to admit you're nervous around me."

Her face fell into a glare, with the hint of a smile in her eyes. "Should I be nervous?"

"I mean, yeah." Ben gave her a smirk. "We are in the bedroom, alone. Good chance we might, you know—"

"No 'you knows' happening here." Jemma smiled as she shook her head.

"Aww, but kids are busy playing games, we could play our own..."

"It's been a long day, Ben."

There it was, shutting down any chance of intimacy Ben might've had. He understood. She was burned out after working all day. He'd been there before. But there was more to it. After Mackie's accident, Jemma wasn't the same. Although he'd never tell her she'd changed, he couldn't help but notice. She pulled away from him more than she ever had.

"I get it," he said. "Why don't you go spend some time with the boys; I'll clean up this mess."

"Thank you. I did tell Mackie I'd play with him for a bit today." Jemma placed her hand on top of his for a moment before removing it and leaving the room.

Ben picked up a piece of glass and looked at it. It was the part of the vase that had their names etched into it, but a line had broken the second half off at the plus sign that originally connected them, leaving only one name in his hand.

Ben.

THREE

Water splashed into the pond, creating a fog of mist that washed past Quill's face. The small water drops refreshed her, bringing a coolness she'd desired moments before on her hike through the dense forest. Although she'd left early in the morning, the summer sun rose much quicker than it took for her to arrive.

She'd learned about this place from Calum. Supposedly, it was a popular make-out spot for high schoolers. Quill laughed, thinking of Jemma's reaction when Calum suggested she take Ben there to "reconnect" after mentioning he'd been acting differently since the whole Lucky Island thing.

But as soon as the word "waterfall" escaped Calum's lips, Quill knew she had to find it. Thankfully, it wasn't far in the Outskirts behind the old mall she now lived in. Or rather, lived in again. As it was the same apartment she'd been raised in as a child in Merrytime Clinic.

She stepped away from the water spray before it could soak into her clothing or her backpack. Pulling the pack to the front, she unzipped it and retrieved her favorite childhood book. Being back on the mainland after all those years on Lucky Island also reunited Quill with her old belongings.

The pages fell open to the middle, where an old postcard lay. Quill held it up to the waterfall in front of her. It was about the same height. Trees surrounded it. The ones in front of her were taller than in the picture, but it had been over a hundred years since the pre-war postcard was printed. They'd have grown.

Her gaze moved to the rocks at the bottom of the falls, and her heart sank. They didn't match. There were more rocks here than in the picture. Plus, these falls flowed directly into a stream, whereas the picture emptied into a rounded pool. This wasn't the spot where her mother once stood.

She flipped the postcard over to read the back for the hundredth time.

P O S T C A R D

Toby,

I'll never forget this night. I am fully yours. Like the pond accepts the falls, I accept every ounce of you.

Gilly

P.S. Someday we'll bring our baby to the place our love began and show her the things we've learned here.

She should have known this wasn't the place. Her father never would've snuck into the Outskirts, despite the fact that radiation residue hadn't been recorded in the area around Stillfield in years. There were wild animals that likely had never set eyes on a human being in their lifetime.

Well, other than hormonal teenagers out for a rendezvous.

An image of Asher popped into Quill's mind as she stared at the flat rock in front of her. That rock had seen more action than she had in the last couple months. Her heart had expected the feelings she and Asher had developed on the island together to continue to blossom. Instead, weeds seemed to be sprouting.

Quill sighed. Asher wouldn't have been able to come here even if she'd wanted him to. Being on parole for burning down government buildings made leaving Stillfield impossible without gaining the attention of Responders.

Parole. Another form of imprisonment Asher was furious about. Did he see being in a relationship the same way? Unable to commit, as that would put another chain on his freedom.

Quill bit her lip and turned back the way she'd come. She didn't want to be a burden to Asher. Another way his freedom was limited. For herself, her feelings toward Asher made her soul feel light. Untethered. As if she could float away...

Oh shoot. She wiggled her feet inside her sneakers, meeting only air.

Asher doesn't want that, she reminded herself as she floated gently to the ground.

She fought to silence the thoughts about Asher by focusing on her surroundings as she continued her hike.

The skinny trail of trodden weeds from the light traffic of teenagers on the weekends.

The occasional rustling of a small critter disappearing into the brush at the sound of her footsteps.

The ribbons tied to tree branches, marking the way back home. She grabbed one as it blew in the wind. On it was written "A & O forever," so close to her and Asher's initials...

No. Quill shook her head and dropped the ribbon, letting the breeze twirl it once again. *Not thinking about him.*

Up ahead, the fencing around Stillfield came into view. The broken part of the old mall was visible past a large parking lot.

At least she'd made it back before breakfast was over. There was no sign of Aniyah out working on the gaping sinkhole that'd been created when the mall used to be Merrytime Clinic.

"Hi," came a voice from behind her.

Quill jumped and spun around. Her arm, with her book securely held in her hand, swung in the direction of the unexpected person as a jolt of lightning dispersed into the air.

The book made contact with Asher's cheek as Quill's energy fried some leaves in the tree just beyond the fence.

"Ow," Asher said, rubbing his face. "It's just me."

"Don't jump out behind me!" Quill crossed her arms on her chest, still holding her book, just in case.

"I'm sorry," Asher said. "Lesson learned. Next time I'll approach from the front. Get hit by lightning instead of a book. Seems safer."

"What are you even doing here?" Quill asked.

Asher glanced at the hole in the fence. "I should be asking you the same question."

Quill pursed her lips. He was right. She shouldn't be in the Outskirts, especially by herself. "*How* did you know I was here?"

"Aniyah. She told me you got up early and snuck out the back. Said you heard about makeout rock. I'm just surprised you went out there without me."

Her cheeks flushed. "It's not like you could've come with. Not with your ankle jewelry."

Asher glanced down at his leg. "Yeah, well, the thought still crossed my mind. What if you got hurt? There's wild animals."

Butterflies fluttered in Quill's stomach. "So you do care about me?"

Asher smiled, the left corner of his lips rising higher than the other. "Of course I do."

Quill swallowed. "Well, I'm glad you didn't risk R.E.I. swarming to this location by crossing the threshold out of Stillfield. You know they would've been here in no time."

"Would've been worth it if you were in trouble." Asher took a step toward her, but then hesitated.

Quill narrowed her eyes. Asher was being more flirtatious than normal. She liked it. She wanted more. But she also knew he had a hold up. Perhaps his upcoming parole hearing next week was giving him hope that he'd finally be free.

But would that be enough for him to make the move to become an official couple?

Quill wanted to test him. She took a step closer, only a couple feet away. "It wouldn't be the first time you saved me." The lighthouse rescue and the kiss at the top while island guards raced toward them was a scene she replayed in her mind often. The feel of his lips on hers.

"True. You do tend to find yourself in questionable positions."

Quill took another step, her body only inches from his. Her heart beat against the book she held to her chest.

Asher reached a hand out. This was it. He was going to make a move...

He pulled the book out of her arms and took a step back. Not the move she'd anticipated. Quill grabbed for it.

Asher twisted away. "What were you reading by the waterfall out there that's worth the risk of being mauled? Are those dead bodies? I thought you only read romances."

"They are, and I like to read a lot of different stories." It was difficult for her to get into romances at the moment, although they were her favorite to read while on Lucky Island. Now, they reminded her of Asher and how he wasn't like the love interests in her books.

"Huh. No wonder you spooked easily."

Quill stopped trying to grab the book back. "Again, *you* came up behind me. What did you expect to happen?"

He smirked.

Oh how she wished she could wipe that expression from those lips.

His lips.

The ones that touched hers three months ago.

She looked away from him. She needed to stop thinking about their kiss.

"I said I was sorry." He handed her book back. "Shall I walk you back home? I've gotta get going soon."

Quill followed him toward the abandoned mall. "What do you have planned?"

"Just meeting with my sister," Asher said. "Speaking of which, have you heard from the not-so-elite, extra forgetful, Governor Too-Biased Dunn today?"

There it was. The real reason he was stopping by—to gather information about her dad.

"It's not his fault Dr. Paxton manipulated his memories," Quill said. "But no, I haven't heard from him yet. He's supposed to be meeting with your sister and Buran. You know their meetings can go long. The two of them were made from the same cloth."

"Same, stubborn cloth. Too bad they haven't figured out how to be made into the same garment and get their goals aligned. I'm tired of waiting. If I could be at that meeting, I'm sure I'd get some action done. This lack of progress is torture."

"You know you can't be there." It seemed most of Quill's time these days revolved around keeping Asher from doing something drastic. "R.E.I. wouldn't like for you to be involved in government matters. Quick way to get locked up again."

Asher rubbed his wrists. "Maybe I can be roomies with Paxie this time. I heard she's got some sweet digs."

A shiver rolled across Quill at the mention of Dr. Paxton. Although she'd been arrested, she was kept at a high end facility. Much nicer than any room on the island. Guess that was what money and privilege got.

"At least she's locked away where she can't hurt anyone anymore," Asher said.

"How well did you know her? I mean, on the island?" Quill asked. She knew he was involved in some of the testing of the cure, EnertinX, but she didn't know the details. He didn't like to talk about it.

"Not much." Asher's face hardened. "The most interaction I had with her was when I escaped. I'm glad she's locked up."

"Me too." Quill nodded. She had known the doctor a little better, or at least longer. They met when Quill was a child at Merrytime Clinic. Her younger sister had been a friend, someone Quill had looked up to.

Quill glanced at her hands. The same power Dr. Paxton manipulated others with was within her too. Would she ever believe in something so deeply she'd be willing to hurt others in such a vulnerable way? Her father was a broken man because of what the doctor did.

They arrived at the back door of the mall. "Come on, Quill. Keep working on your dad." Asher took hold of her hands, and a wave of emotion came over her at his touch. "You may be the only one that can get through to him. You've been in control these past months. Surely that's proof that Disparates can control themselves without pills."

Quill kept quiet, her eyes glued on her fingers that rested in his. This was what she'd wanted. *Stay in control, Quill.* She glanced up in time to watch as the leaves behind Asher lowered back to the ground. The uptick of joy she'd felt was quickly replaced by the hum of electricity around her. Having two energy powers could be difficult to manage.

Because in a way, he was right. Quill could use her electricity to get her father to agree. Granted, she didn't fully know how Dr.

Paxton did it, but the capability was there. With some research and practice, she could get whatever she wanted from anyone.

Well, not anyone. Only non-Disparates.

Still, she shook her head. Manipulating another human being didn't feel right.

She took a deep breath. "I've been talking to him. He really does want to support Buran's mission, but he has a duty to make sure—"

"Citizens are safe," Asher interrupted, pulling his hands away from hers, as if he'd only blessed her with his touch to convince her to do what he wanted. "Because Disparates are *so* dangerous. We're only dangerous because—"

"We're mistreated and misunderstood. Yes, I know."

"Well, I just stopped by for an update. And to make sure you didn't get yourself in more trouble. Guess I should be going."

"Sorry I didn't have more for you," Quill said.

Asher shrugged and opened the door, holding it for Quill to walk through. "Seems to be how things are going lately. Not much being done, and not much I can do with this thing on my leg." Asher motioned to his ankle monitor.

"Do you think you'll get it off soon?" Quill asked as she walked through the opening he gave her.

"Who knows. Until then, I'm stuck being monitored. Such great freedom." While shaking his head, he let the door close between them. Leaving Quill standing on her own inside the large, lonely mall.

Sweat pooled across Asher's brow as he climbed the tree-house ladder. He was too forward with Quill; he'd seen the hope in her eyes. He'd wanted to take that last step to close the distance between them, yet the weight on his ankle monitor held him back.

It was there for a reason. He was serving time for the crimes he'd committed. Until he truly amended for the things he'd done, he wasn't sure he deserved Quill.

He plopped himself onto the wooden floor and looked at his ankle bracelet. A green light flashed to show it was on and working. A part of him wished Quill had shorted it out so he could be free. He'd gone from one type of prison to another. Of course, if his parole hearing next week went well...

A scuffling sound drew his attention up. Jemma sat at the small table, a fast food bag in front of her. He hadn't expected her to be here already. Her meeting must have ended a while ago.

"I hope you brought extra ketchup this time," Asher said as she pulled out a box of fries.

"Of course. After your lecture last time, how could I forget?" Jemma laughed.

Asher joined her at the table, dipping a fry into the ketchup Jemma had already been using. She gave him a narrowed look, but that didn't stop him. She was his little sister, after all; being separated for seventeen years didn't change that.

"Remember when Dad built this place?" he asked to keep her from reprimanding him.

Jemma's eyes widened. "Wait, Dad built this?"

Asher nodded. "I suppose you were a toddler then. He built it around my fifth birthday, after I kept begging for a treehouse. Although he said it wasn't just for me. I had to share with you."

"I didn't know, or I don't remember that." She glanced around the wooden room as if seeing it for the first time.

"It's not really something that comes up often, I guess. Plus, he built it pretty quick. I wonder how he did it."

"What do you mean?"

"He claimed the trees in our old front yard weren't strong enough for a treehouse, so he found this one near the canal. Which, thinking now, probably isn't the best place for kids to play, but it never is filled with much water." Before the Rain of Fire and nuclear weapons destroyed much of the world, the canals were full. Nowadays, they carried maybe a foot or two. Just enough to splash in. "He built it as a surprise for us. I don't recall seeing him ever carry a ladder."

"I guess he was either good at being sneaky, or you were really bad at paying attention." Jemma laughed.

"Hey, that's not fair." He let out a small chuckle. "Our powers came from somewhere. Think his was air?"

Jemma gasped. "It could have been."

How ironic that would be. Asher struggled with anger, while his dad had to restrain from feeling too happy. "So, heard your meeting went late."

"Who did you hear that from?" Jemma raised an eyebrow.

"Who do you think?"

"Quill is doing well, I take it. What is going on between you two?" she asked. Jemma was as nosy as ever. And perhaps trying to change the subject.

"I'm not sure what that's supposed to imply. We're friends." As much as he wanted more, it wasn't the right time. Quill deserved someone that didn't come with baggage.

Jemma leaned forward. "The way you two get along, there's more than just friendship there. Why haven't you made it official yet?"

Asher lifted his shackled leg. "I'm not really the finest catch."

"At least she'd know you can't run away." Jemma laughed.

The last thing Asher wanted was to dive deeper into his emotions. "The meeting. How did it go?"

Her face fell.

"No progress?"

Jemma sighed. "No. Not yet. Dunn wants to see results before jumping all in."

"Is Paxie still brainwashing him from prison somehow? What more does he need to know the medicine is harmful?"

Jemma was quiet. Too quiet.

"Out with it Jem Jam," Asher said. "There's something you're wanting to say. Say it."

"Well..." Jemma kept her eyes on the table. "A whole population taken off the drugs at once might not be the best solution either."

"It's better than no solution. Give Disparates some credit. I mean, look at you and me. We aren't on any chemicals, we're doing great."

"Are we?" Jemma questioned, her eyes locking with his.

"Yeah. I've got my energy under control. Don't really have much of a choice, thanks to my monitor. Gotta keep it from registering any sudden increase in heat. Might be tempted to smoke now and then, but I know how to smother it. And I haven't seen you have an energy release in months! Well, not since..."

His own words clued him in.

"Yeah..." Jemma said, her face downcast.

Asher didn't want to dig deeper. He knew what happened with Mackie months ago was a sensitive subject. One he wasn't sure how to talk about with his sister. Thankfully, everyone was okay. They just needed to move on.

"You've been working with Buran, right?"

"I am." Jemma nodded. "He's helped. I've learned coping skills, but even with them, I still struggle. Especially when it comes to my boys."

"So are you saying you agree with Dunn?" Asher was hurt. His face must have portrayed his pain, as Jemma winced. "That more testing should be done on Disparates before they can get the help they need?"

"Not necessarily... I'm just saying more evidence couldn't hurt."

Asher looked away from her. She was part of the problem, not trusting Disparates purely because they had emotional energy.

"Get out." He inhaled a deep breath. He couldn't risk his anger growing more and setting off the sensor around his ankle—the one there because of people who thought the way his sister was talking.

"Asher, come on."

"I said. Get. Out." Asher balled his hands into fist, extinguishing the small flames inside of him before they could escape.

The chair squealed across the wood floor as Jemma stood. "Fine. But only to keep you from doing something stupid, like burning Dad's treehouse down and breaking your parole. Maybe you should check on that energy you have so well controlled."

Asher wanted to respond, to snap back at his sister's uncalled for response. But he didn't. His silence was the best response.

Her feet hit the dirt at the base of the tree. Asher let out his breath with a growl. He didn't want to admit how close he'd been to overflowing.

Asher sat back at the table, his appetite for the food in front of him now gone. He'd bring the leftovers home and hope his mother didn't mind the space it'd take up in the fridge. Better than letting it go to waste.

His eyes wandered the treehouse, thinking about how every plank was put in place by his loving father. A man in control of himself. Who had balanced his time shaping the world as the governor and being with his family. He was everything Asher worried he couldn't be. A man so unlike the one Asher had grown to be.

His eyes roamed the display of artwork on the wall. Some new drawings done by Louie and Mackie joined the old pieces left from before the house fire. Asher smiled at the picture Louie had drawn of him. Two round ovals with lines for limbs.

Below the wall of portraits, a piece of paper lay on the floor. It must have fallen off, although Asher didn't notice anything missing. Perhaps a new piece of art Jemma brought to put up.

Asher walked over and picked the paper up. It wasn't a drawing, but rather folded to look like an owl. His memory flashed back to Lucky Island. The countless notes sent back and forth between him and Quill, although this owl shape was a new one.

He'd just seen her, and she didn't mention leaving him anything. His curiosity piqued as he flipped it over and peeled at the folds. As he unfolded the creature, it quickly became apparent that it wasn't left by Quill.

Asher turned the note over, looking for more writing. There was nothing. No name, only a threat and a demand.

Whoever left this here knew who he was and how to find him. Or at least, his hideout. His place to go when he needed to be alone. It wasn't good. He wouldn't be so easily swayed to help a stranger. For all he knew, this was another trick from Dr. Paxton and her cronies.

He'd done things on the island not even Quill knew the extent of. Change was all he wanted. But following a stranger's words blindly was not something Asher did. Not that he'd be able to go back to Lucky Island with the monitor on his leg.

He tucked the note into his pocket. Whoever left this note was too cowardly to sign their name yet brave enough to call him out. Asher wasn't sure if ignoring was the best option, but it was the only one he had.

FOUR

The outside of the old bowling alley was as run down and abandoned as ever. Except for the array of cars littered across the parking lot. Jemma counted five as her own vehicle joined them.

Counting calmed her. It was especially needed as she'd skipped taking Ben's pill the night before, since she was almost out. If they were going to meet with the other Republics, she needed to get clean. Be the example Buran expected from her.

Of course, the pill had a safe home in her pocket in case of emergency. She wasn't sure how training would go.

Speaking of which, Buran had quite the gathering today.

A bell rang as Jemma stepped inside. A line of three people with their backs to her stood facing Buran and Calum. They were only illuminated by dim emergency lights, all other power shut off.

"Looks like Jemma decided to join us today. Happy to have you here," Buran said as a larger man turned toward Jemma before facing forward again. Calum gave her a quick wave with his signature smile, his eyes narrowing as his dimples crinkled.

"You're late, but it's good practice to learn with distractions," Buran continued, turning his gaze to the students in front of him. "It will take all your focus to move your energy through you in a controlled manner."

Jemma hesitated by the doors. It'd been a couple weeks since she'd participated. She didn't like taking time away from her boys, considering she didn't see much of them while working—especially to leave them for something she was lying about. She hoped it worked for others, but trusting herself raised her anxiety instead of soothing it.

She had thirteen days to stop taking Enertin and get these techniques down.

Calum raised an eyebrow as he locked eyes with Jemma. He made his way to her and greeted her with a hug. "How are you?"

"I'm good. I guess... sorry I haven't been here lately. I've had a lot going on."

"You're a mom," he said, "and you're working with Governor Dunn to figure out the situation with Disparates, including those that were on the island."

Jemma nodded. "It's a busy life."

"Speaking of the islanders... have you heard anything about Chayse?"

Jemma shook her head. Calum's younger brother, Chayse, had been on Lucky Island, but he was taken away before the Dissentients arrived to rescue Ben. To where, they weren't sure.

Calum frowned. "Maybe he'll be on the list of names of those moved to Watershield Prison."

"Did the note from the notebook give any clues?" Jemma asked. Ben had found one left by Chayse and given it to Calum. With how they wrote in code, Jemma hadn't been able to decipher its meaning.

"It didn't give much," Calum said. "He wrote 'double the trouble, double the fun.' Not sure exactly what that's supposed to mean."

Jemma exhaled. It seemed everyone counted on her for one thing or another. "Buran and I have a meeting with the governors coming up. Maybe we can bring it up there."

"I'd really appreciate that," Calum said and returned to Buran's side, waving for her to follow him.

Enertin never completely took away her fears. Perhaps it was because Ben's pills were meant for Flame Disparates. But that didn't matter; she needed to get off. Despite the fear in the hollow of her stomach, she joined the group

As she made her way to the front, she passed a table she couldn't see from the door. The woman sitting there made her jump. "Oh, hi Keesha. Nice to see you here." Jemma had been getting to know Keesha, and she liked her. They'd had one double date, but Buran had left early when Samay, who was serving them personally at his restaurant, mentioned a possible recruit was interested in joining the Dissentients. Keesha put on a brave face as he left, but it was clear she wasn't happy about the date's abrupt end, less than half her plate being eaten. Jemma shooed Ben away and turned the night into a drinks and dessert girls night.

Keesha gave a small smile. "Took your idea to come and watch my husband at work. I want to understand why this is so important to him."

"That's great. I hope it's helping," Jemma said.

Buran was the master of keeping his schedule full. He jumped between meetings with Governor Dunn, drilling in the importance of letting Disparates learn to control their energy, and training Disparates in his methods of control. Though finding more people to train was a challenge without Energy Watch's radars.

Jemma made her way to stand with the other few Disparates. Buran looked happy, albeit a little uneasy.

"Glad you made it," an older woman named Robin said to her as she took her spot in line. "We've missed seeing you here."

Jemma smiled. Robin was one of the EnertinX-cured Disparates that was meant to go with Ben on Dr. Paxton's tour months ago before her plan was ruined. Robin's older skin wrinkled as she returned the gesture. She'd been attending Buran's class since the mall showdown. She wanted help keeping her new feelings under control, even without the threat of her electric energy flaring. The other two were unfamiliar, but both men looked to be in their mid-twenties. Perhaps they were friends of Calum's. Did he have a life outside the Dissentients?

"Alright," Buran said. "Time to work on our breathing techniques. Let's go in through our noses and out through our mouths. Ready? Begin."

Buran counted to four as the group followed. The breathing helped. Jemma's nerves settled. She didn't need the medicine. She could do this.

"Now that we're calm, we need to practice staying that way. Let's turn toward our partners."

Robin smiled at Jemma as they faced each other.

"We're going to share about the last time our energy—or feelings," he said looking at Robin, "built up. You've all been off medication for a little while now, so I'm sure you can think of something."

Guilt stabbed Jemma's heart. She was a fraud here. The last time her energy built up, she hurt Mackie.

A tingling ran through her body, her heart rate rising.

This may have been a mistake. She should take her pill, but pulling it out now would be suspicious. Perhaps she could head to the restroom. But before she could fully commit, Robin responded to the prompt.

"I was feeling it this morning," Robin said, oblivious to the inner battle Jemma was fighting. "I mean, not my energy, since that was taken, but a burst of anger. Which my powers weren't even tied to. I know it's going to sound silly. It was really just something small."

"Small things can do it." Jemma shrugged. She shook her hands to dispel some of the energy flowing through her. She could do this—stop thinking about Mackie and focus on what was happening in this moment.

Robin sighed. "Yes, they can. And this morning, small things kept adding up. First, my toast burned. Then I dropped my water bottle on my foot. My first reaction was to scream. Which I did. I'm nervous I broke it. But I'm here standing on it now, so it's likely fine."

Jemma noticed her bandaged foot.

"Not a great start to my day," Robin concluded, her eyes falling on Jemma expectantly.

Jemma tried not to begrudge Robin. The things she'd gone through were annoying, albeit minor. Nothing like the memories flowing through her mind. Plus, Robin was healed like Ben. She didn't have to worry about electrocuting anyone because she dropped a bottle.

"My last time..." Jemma paused. Her palms were clammy, energy fizzling at their surface. She wasn't going to share about Mackie. She was going to lie—again. Whatever it took to avoid this conversation and move on with the session.

But she couldn't. She held her right arm across her chest. With her other hand, she felt the rough skin left behind from the moment she'd never forget. Flames shooting out of Louie. Mackie's body on the ground. Responders dotting the playground.

The scar on her arm was an outside reminder of how she felt inside.

Broken, shriveled, and unable to return back to her old self.

Televisions flicked on, old rock music playing choppily through the speakers. Buran's gaze fell on Jemma.

She met his stare, her stomach twisting. Was that confusion or disappointment? Her anxiety grew, and so did the volume of the music. She shouldn't have come here. "I... I need to head to the restroom..." Jemma willed herself to move, but her body wouldn't let her. Her gaze darted toward the restrooms, catching sight of Keesha's open mouthed expression.

Robin took a step back, likely feeling some static being released by Jemma. "Buran..." she said shakily.

Buran's eyes widened as he looked their way. "Calum, take over for me here," he said as he headed toward them.

Jemma checked on her body. The thumping in her chest matched the staticky rhythm of the television sounds. Her breathing was short and frantic as she shook.

She needed Enertin.

"Jemma," Buran said slowly as he approached, his eyebrows knitted together. "Practice your breathing. In through your nose, out through your mouth."

She listened, trying to gain control, to hold back her energy from releasing fully.

Her throat constricted. It wasn't working. Tears puddled in her eyes as she shook her head.

The pill was in her pocket. The promise of immediate relief.

Yet the fear of Buran finding out what she'd been doing kept her from moving.

Buran opened his mouth, his forehead wrinkling before closing it again. He put a hand to his chin as if trying to think. "Calum, why don't you take our other participants out front?"

"Yeah, I can do that," Calum said.

Robin gave Jemma a small smile as she left to give her space.

Keesha rose slowly from her table. Instead of following the others out, she stopped by Jemma and Buran. "I can stay if you'd like."

Buran shook his head. "I really think you should—"

"I'm asking *Jemma*," Keesha said. "I don't want her to feel abandoned."

"*I'm* staying here," Buran said. "I need to make sure everyone stays safe. Including you."

Keesha put her hands on her hips. "And what about your safety?"

Jemma took a breath in through her nose. Their arguing wasn't going to help. "You should both go."

Buran and Keesha exchanged a look, then turned to Jemma.

"What's bothering you, Jemma?" Buran asked. "And no downplaying whatever this is. Your energy is telling you something."

"Why are you still here?" The words were strained as they left Jemma's mouth. They both needed to leave so she could take her medicine and find relief. "I could hurt you both. Stop your hearts." She wrapped her arms tighter around herself, trying to keep the electricity roaming around her from shooting out.

"Is that what this is about?" Buran asked. "I thought we came to the conclusion that what happened to Mackie wasn't your fault."

A surge of energy occurred at the mention of Mackie. She let out a yelp as she sent a bolt of lightning into the old cash register to her left.

Keesha placed a hand on Buran's arm. "He's right. You didn't mean harm. But if it'll make you feel better, I'll go. Just please don't fry my husband. I'll give you five minutes before I come back in."

Jemma nodded and Keesha headed out the front doors.

"So," Buran said. "Who's gonna break the news to Calum that you destroyed where he keeps his bottle cap collection?"

The small release of energy gave Jemma enough of an edge to allow a laugh. "Think he'll let you continue to use his place for training?"

"That boy would give the shirt off his back to anyone that asks for it."

That was true. Calum was full of hope and selflessness. Even with his younger brother missing after Lucky Island was evacuated, he fully believed they'd find him.

Just another thing that was wrong in this world. The islanders were kept locked up while she was allowed to be free. She'd done as much damage, if not more, with her own powers.

"How about I get you a drink of water?" Buran must have noticed her energy increase.

Jemma nodded. As he turned to hurry to the old break room converted into Calum's kitchen, Jemma slipped her hand into her pocket. The red pill was warm in her grasp. She quickly popped it into her mouth as Buran returned from the room with a bottle of water in his hand.

Which she was grateful for, as the pill stuck to the top of her dried out mouth. She grabbed the bottle from Buran's hand as if she were a hiker stranded in the desert for days without water. She chugged half the bottle before coming up for air.

"Feeling better?" Buran asked.

She nodded. The pill was in her; she would be okay. She took a deep breath in through her nose, releasing it through her mouth as her bottle of water slipped from her shaky grasp.

It fell to the floor, spilling water across her shoes, but she didn't mind. Such a minor inconvenience felt small to her now.

"I'll get something to clean that up," Buran said with a half smile.

The staticky music around them had stopped. Jemma was in control once more—or perhaps it was the Enertin that was truly in control.

Buran placed a small towel with the image of a bowling pin on it over the water. Standing up, he made eye contact with Jemma. "Seems you've been having a rough day, but you did it! You brought yourself back to balance."

Jemma nodded her head softly. Perhaps it was time to come clean, but the thought caused a small buzz to increase inside her. The pill wasn't fully digested yet.

"I... I forgot I need to take the boys to a doctor's appointment today." Jemma pursed her lips.

"Oh, that's okay," Buran said. "I'm glad you could stop by for a bit."

Jemma pulled her keys out of her pocket as she left out the bowling alley doors. The eyes of the other participants fell on her, including Keesha, who stood next to Calum probably telling him what had happened.

"It's safe to go back inside," Jemma said. "Oh, and sorry about your register Calum."

Calum raised an eyebrow at her. "I don't care about that, as long as you're okay."

"I will be," she said, deciding to adopt some of Calum's optimism. She wasn't sure if she believed it.

Five

The car air conditioning blasted Ben as he drove down a familiar road, his friend Anthony in the passenger seat. They'd gotten to know each other in the past couple months, bonding quickly after Dr. Paxton used both of them as test subjects for EnertinX.

And a friend that understood how it felt to be cured was what Ben needed. "How have you been doing?" he asked.

Anthony moved his neck side to side. His broad shoulders stretched wider than the seat. "You know, same old same old. Life is treating me well."

At least it's going well for someone, Ben thought. Although they'd both been cured, Ben wished at times he wasn't. When he was on Enertin, he didn't react negatively to the smallest inconvenience, but now it was like dodging flaming arrows everywhere he went. Except, without actual flames of course. That had been taken from him.

"Glad to hear that," Ben said, hiding his insecurities.

"How's life goin' for you?"

"It's great," Ben lied.

Anthony let out a chuckle. "That didn't sound very confident. Look, I know my 'smell the flowers' personality has really blossomed since not needing to keep it grounded, but your brain doesn't work the same as mine. You're a Flame Disparate. Managing anger is much different than dealing with optimism."

"Was," Ben said. "I *was* a Flame Disparate. Now I'm just a man with no control of himself." The words came out quickly, but not surprisingly. He had a hard time holding in his emotions.

"Yep." Anthony nodded. His beard had grown out in the last couple months. "No pill to control you. No island to keep you contained. You get to be *yourself* now. Your true self. It's okay if you're still finding out who that is."

Ben sighed. He didn't like who the real him was turning out to be.

"Have you thought about going to Buran's classes?" Anthony asked. "He invited all us cured ones to join. May learn a thing or two."

Buran. The man his wife found comfort from while he was gone. "I've been thinking about it." But not really. Ben was grateful for Buran's help, truly; however the way his wife talked about Buran caused a wave of anger to wash over him. He'd always felt wary of the man when he worked at Energy Watch and knowing what he was truly up to didn't completely make that go away.

"So, where are we headed tonight?" Anthony asked, interrupting Ben's thoughts.

Good thing, too, as his thoughts were going places he didn't like. Buran was Jemma's friend and that was it. He had his own wife and a hopefully happy marriage. And he was a good guy with intentions Ben believed in. He couldn't let his intrusive thoughts win.

"We're visiting a family of someone I actually knew on the island."

"Someone you knew? And there's a letter for them?"

"Not a letter," Ben said. Anthony's confusion was valid, as they'd been searching for the families of the fallen Disparates who'd left letters in the lighthouse notebook for the last couple of months, delivering those they could find. Tonight was different. "I found the family of a friend of mine that was lost."

"Oh. You've finally found Mr. Dogivan's son," Anthony said. Ben had told him about the escape attempt and the chasm that Mr. Dogivan was lost inside.

"I made a promise to him that I'd find his family."

Ben glanced at his passenger to see Anthony nodding, a small smile on his lips. "I'm glad. They deserve closure just like the rest of them."

Ben agreed, but this meeting was one he'd been putting off. He'd found out the address for Charles Lee Dogivan IV weeks ago. He'd driven past the house a few times on his own but couldn't get himself to go to the door. Although Mr. Dogivan had created the chasm that ended his life on the island, Ben couldn't help but feel responsible for his death.

He was the one that sent Mr. Dogivan to Lucky Island thinking he would be going to Merrytime Clinic for help.

He was the one that convinced the old man to stop taking the pills, the one that brought him into his escape plan.

And he was the one that let go of his wrinkled hand.

Ben put the car into park outside the small white house. A light was on inside, shining through the window onto the porch.

"So, with no letter, you got a plan for what to say?" Anthony asked.

"Sorry your dad is dead and is responsible for killing your mom?" That was blunt and Ben knew it.

Anthony laughed. "Perhaps you could ease into that information."

Warm air brushed Ben's face as he opened the car door. After standing, he noticed Anthony hadn't moved. Leaning down to look inside the car, he asked, "Aren't you coming with?"

"I didn't know Mr. Dogivan," Anthony said. "I imagine the news will be difficult to hear."

This wasn't making Ben feel better about what he had to do. "I'm sure it will be."

"But it'll be healing." Anthony nodded as he opened his door and stepped out of the car.

They approached the wooden door, Ben's palms clammy as he knocked. They stood for a moment, but no one came.

"I guess he's not home," Ben said, turning toward the parked car.

Anthony placed a hand on his shoulder to stop him. "Listen."

A soft cry came from inside the house, gradually increasing until the doorknob turned and opened to a small slit about six inches wide. On the other side of the door was a man who looked to be around Ben's age, holding a small infant whose scrunched, screaming face was barely visible. He had his father's broad nose.

"I'm sorry, now's not a good time," the man said as he bounced up and down.

"Charles Dogivan? I was hoping to talk to you about your father," Ben said, eyeing the screaming baby. As a father, he understood that babies cry, but something about the tears now grinded his gears. When his boys were young, he was on Enertin. He didn't understand when Jemma would become over-stimulated by the sound, but in this moment, he finally got it.

"I prefer to go by my middle name, Lee," the man said over the baby's cry.

"Have you tried swaddling?" Ben asked, unable to keep himself from suggesting something to quiet the cries.

"He breaks right out," Lee said. "But thanks for your un-solicited advice." The door closed with a bang.

Ben looked at Anthony, catching the amused look on his face.

"And I thought your plan to bluntly break the news about his dad to him was bad."

Ben huffed. "I was trying to be helpful."

"That man is much too sleep deprived to deal with 'helpful' advice he didn't ask for."

"I guess we go then," Ben said, his voice short. It was then he noticed the crying had stopped inside.

A moment later the doorknob turned again, Lee standing there with empty hands. "Did you say something about my dad?"

Anthony made eye contact with Ben. They weren't done here.

"Sorry if I was rude earlier," Ben said. "I have two boys of my own. Newborn days can be tough."

"Yeah, all Charlie wants right now is his mom." Dark bags outlined the bottoms of Lee's eyes.

"Charlie? That's a great name," Anthony said, joining the conversation.

"A family name. Although, if you know my name and know my dad, you likely already guessed that." Lee released a yawn. "Speaking of which, you said you have news about him? Who are you guys anyway?"

Anthony looked at Ben, giving him the space to answer Lee's questions. "Well," Ben started, "I knew your dad—"

"Knew?" Lee narrowed his eyes.

He didn't know. Ben nodded. "On Lucky Island, although we met before then."

"Lucky Island?" Lee asked. "I've seen the news about it still being in use. If my dad was there, where is he now? Is he at the prison camp everyone was taken to?"

"No, he's not there." Ben swallowed. "He didn't make it off the island."

Lee's confused expression transformed to awareness. "He caused the quake there, didn't he?"

"You knew he had powers?" Ben recalled how resistant Mr. Dogivan had been to admit that he not only struggled with depressive feelings but was also a Ground Disparate. It took a few instances of him causing small sinkholes before he was willing to go to the supposed Merrytime Clinic.

"I love my dad, but he had his own demons. There's a reason we distanced ourselves from him. He wasn't willing to accept that he needed help." Lee sighed. "At least, he hadn't been. It sounds like maybe he finally figured it out before…"

"He did," Ben said. "Before he died, he finally accepted who he was."

Tears welled in Lee's eyes. "Too bad it was too late." He shook his head, wisps of what seemed like smoke dispersing through the air.

"It was too late for him," Anthony said, joining in the conversation. "But it doesn't have to be too late for you, or your child, if he needs it."

Lee's gaze fell on Anthony. "I'm taking Enertin regularly. I don't want to end up like my dad—a danger to my family."

Ben's eyes widened. Enertin. The pill that increasingly puts Disparates at risk. "There are other ways—"

"Lee!" a voice yelled from the back of the house as a cry broke out once more. "Charlie needs a diaper change!"

Lee's shoulders drooped. "I appreciate you sharing the news of my dad. Seems it's time for you both to leave now, as I'm needed."

"Of course," Ben said hesitantly. He wanted to say more, to convince Lee how dangerous Enertin was, but there wasn't time.

Anthony nodded goodbye as the door closed. "He wouldn't have been ready to learn yet anyway," he said.

"True." Ben headed back to the car, aware not everyone was willing to accept that Enertin wasn't the miracle they all wanted it to be. The increased danger it posed when emotions became too much to handle. Like when a new baby joined the family and completely changed the dynamic.

Ben had seen the smoke rising off Lee's shoulders.

Quill grabbed onto the side of her bed to keep herself from falling over as she tugged a pair of jeans over her legs. That was one thing she missed about the island—the loose fitting jumpsuits.

"I thought your dad was on his way," Aniyah said from the open doorway.

"He is; that's why I'm getting ready." Finally, her jeans slid up, letting her button them. "Whoever decided jeans needed to be brought back from before the Rain of Fire should be the one sent to a desolate island."

Aniyah laughed. "True, but they do look good on you. Have someone you're trying to impress tonight?"

Quill's cheeks reddened. Sure, her dad was picking her up, but they were heading to Margaret's house for an extended family dinner. "I doubt Asher will notice the effort."

"Dang. He's still not making things official?"

Quill shook her head. "Maybe once he's no longer on parole. He has a hearing next week. I'm thinking he's expecting good news."

Aniyah smirked. "You think that'll be enough for him to finally commit?" Her brows turned to concern as Quill's face fell. "I don't mean to burst your bubble, but I've known boys like him. They like to keep their options open. Give their safe choice just enough attention to keep them interested. You gotta stop being his safe choice."

Asher isn't like that, Quill thought, or, rather, hoped. Aniyah did have a better understanding of how society worked. She wasn't locked up all her life... at least not away from normal society. "Have you had a boyfriend before?"

"Something like that." Aniyah sat on Quill's bed. "Nothin' very serious. Honestly, I like being on my own."

"But you're not alone," Quill said, sitting next to her and putting a hand on her knee. She'd learned about Aniyah's past in foster care and how Samay took her in. "You have Samay, and the Dissentients, and me. Who needs boys?"

"Exactly." Aniyah stood and headed for the door. "Stop giving Asher your attention. Make him come to you. If he really wants you, he will. And hey, if Asher doesn't make a move, we can eat a gallon of ice cream together."

"Share?" Quill placed a hand jokingly to her chest. "You'll have to get your own gallon."

Aniyah rolled her eyes with a smile.

Keeping her distance from Asher was going to be hard, but Aniyah had a good idea. Quill fumbled too much around Asher—those green eyes of his were easy to get lost in. But not anymore. She needed to put on a hard front around him. Let him fight for her. "You know you're welcome to come if you'd like," Quill said. "I'm sure Margaret wouldn't mind."

"Nah, that's okay. I don't do large gatherings. Plus, I'm in the mood for some Indian food."

"You're so confident in who you are—how?" Quill had meant for it to come off as a compliment, but instead it came as a question.

"I'm not sure if I am," Aniyah said. "Sometimes you gotta fake it 'til you make it. I've tried to fit into enough molds that didn't feel right in foster homes. I just stopped caring. Others can take me or leave me, whereas I'm stuck with myself. Might as well do what I like."

"Foster care must have been tough. Do you ever wonder about your parents?" Quill asked. "I mean, you don't have to answer that..."

"It's fine," Aniyah said, leaning on the wall next to the door. "I know who my parents were. They weren't the best examples of control before I was sent to the group home."

"Did they have powers like you?"

"My mom did. Ground, same as me. She probably ended up on the island at some point, but I don't really know, or care. Even with her power, she never stepped in to save me from my sperm donor."

A pit grew in Quill's chest. Her father had kept her locked away for her own safety, whereas Aniyah's father purposely chose to hurt her. And what Quill knew about her own mother wasn't much. If she hadn't died when she was young, would she have fought against her Dad's overbearance? In her mind, Quill hoped she would've. "I'm sorry that happened to you."

"Eh, it is what it is. It made me realize how much I need my powers." Aniyah shrugged. "I plan to use them for good—like getting this place back up and running."

"And you've been doing a great job at that, I see," a deep voice came from behind Aniyah. Quill stepped out of her room and into the small hallway that led into the front room.

"Dad, you let yourself in?" Quill asked.

"This used to be my home too," Governor Dunn said. "I know, it belongs to the two of you now."

Aniyah shot him a glare. "It does, and you might want to knock next time. Unless you want to risk walking in on us changing."

Governor Dunn blushed, the red of his cheeks bright against his whitening hair. "That thought had not crossed my mind. I apologize."

Aniyah crossed the hall and into her room, slamming the door behind her.

"She still doesn't like me much, does she?" The governor gave an insecure smile. He was used to being a people pleaser, considering the person he pleased the most had been manipulating his mind for years. Quill wasn't sure she'd ever forgive Dr. Paxton.

"She doesn't like most people." Quill grabbed her phone from her dresser and slid it into her tight pocket. Another downside to jeans. "Shall we go?"

"Sorry for running late," her father said. "I wanted to take a look at the work you and Aniyah have put in on the back of the building. I promise I'm working on getting resources approved to aid in the restoration."

"I know." Quill had heard all this before. She walked past him, saying, "We should probably get going."

He nodded and followed. The outer hallways of the old mall still showed some damage from their showdown a few months ago, cracks along the walls and flooring. The main lights were still busted, leaving only emergency lights along the edges to guide them. Although Aniyah had focused on the ground here first, pushing it back together, new tiles were needed to make it look seamless.

"The governors meeting is next week. If they agree to the plan of training and rehabilitation, it should be easy to increase our shipment of building materials from Hastiet and wiring from Vasco."

That was one downside to the Republics being built around their specific specialties—difficulty gaining extra supplies without approval.

Outside, the sun was barely making its descent. The summer days were longer. Quill hopped into her dad's black car, moving a pile of mail from the passenger seat. "What are—"

"Whoops, don't mind those." Her dad snatched the envelopes. His brow wrinkled as he stuffed them into the center console. Quill caught a glance at one of the open papers before he closed the lid. *Petition for resignation.*

"Are those from the protesters?" Quill asked. The recently formed group of people unhappy about the government's lies.

"Yep. Calling for me to step down."

"But you're not going to, right?" Quill asked.

Her father pursed his lips and shook his head.

It was the citizens' right to know about—and be upset by—Lucky Island. Her father was part of closing it for good after Dr. Paxton was arrested, yet not everyone saw it that way. They didn't know he had been manipulated to lie. If he were to resign, Wuslick would step in until a new election was held. If someone were to take his place, there was no guaranteeing they'd continue working with Buran and the Dissentients.

They drove in silence for a few moments. "So, Dad," Quill said, her thoughts turning elsewhere.

"Yes, honey?"

"Have you remembered anything more about Mom?"

The car slowed slightly. Quill caught the wrinkled look on her Dad's face. It was the same look he'd often get when trying to recall a memory the doctor had manipulated.

"Is this about the postcard?" he asked. "Nothing more has come back to me. I deeply wish it would."

Quill's chest tightened. "You look just like her," Governor Dunn said softly. "You got her beauty and her heart. She loved you more than anything."

That perked her up. He may not have remembered the postcard waterfall, but this was something. "Is there anything else you remember?" Quill insisted again, leaning forward in her seat. "Did she have energy powers? She had to since I do, right? What kind?"

Dad shook his head. "I... well... she grew up in Preen before we met in school in Wuslick. She was happy to move with me to Stillfield... and then we had you. She loved being a mother."

"And?"

"And what?"

"Energy powers?"

Silence settled, and Quill leaned back in her seat. There was a time he had wanted to tell her more, at least according to her mother. *Someday we'll bring our baby to the place our love began and show her the things we've learned here.* Either his memory was still blocked by what Dr. Paxton did to him, or he purposely didn't want to tell her more.

She hoped it wasn't the latter.

Six

After three months, family dinners no longer felt foreign to Asher. On the island, he ate his meals with the other inmates. There were less people at his mother's house—his house—but the surrounding sounds made it seem like more.

"I'm gonna catch you!" Mackie yelled as he chased Louie, who'd run past Asher moments before. The two were playing well... for now. According to Asher's observations of their play the last few months, they had a couple of minutes before one of them got hurt, physically or emotionally. Asher kept a side eye on Louie. If he was hurt, there was a risk of fire damage.

"Settle down," Asher's mother chastised the boys, fully in grandma mode. "I don't need you knocking over my side table. Those flowers are fresh. Dominic brought them this morning."

"That's right, Margaret." Sergeant Simmons wrapped an arm around her shoulder. "To celebrate our official three-month anniversary."

Asher shook his head with a smile on his face. His mother deserved some happiness after all she'd been through. The death of her husband. The false accusation against her son-in-law and—oh yeah—against himself as well. It was time for her to move on and let someone new into her life. He was mostly glad she didn't pick Dunn.

And Sergeant Simmons was proving himself to be a good fit, even if Asher didn't want to admit it. He was a Responder, and he played a huge role in getting Asher released from prison, but he was now his parole officer. Another person in charge of making sure Asher didn't get to make his own choices.

Specifically about the note crumpled in his pocket. Asher didn't have the desire to follow its instruction blindly, but he did have curiosity. Someone knew about his treehouse and his past, and that thought had been itching in his mind the last few days. Ignoring it wasn't as easy as he'd hoped.

But he'd never find out who the sender was while playing third wheel with his mother and Dominic. His mother only wanted to include him in as much as possible, but it was still awkward. And he sure didn't want his parole officer to know he thought about going back to the island.

Margaret turned to Asher, startling him from his thoughts. "I made your favorite tonight. Shepherd's pie with extra potatoes, since you love them so much. Just like you did as a child."

Asher smiled. Bringing up pieces of their past seemed to make her feel less guilty about the years they lost. "Thanks, Mom." It wouldn't bring his childhood back, and he didn't care much for the meal now anyway, but he wouldn't tell her that.

"And her famous brownies for dessert," Dominic said, rubbing his stomach.

Margaret nodded. "I was having a hard time deciding what to make. Thankful to have someone to bounce ideas off. I hadn't thought about brownies until he brought them up."

As cringy as these two were, Dominic kept Asher's mother from asking Asher his opinion on things, so there were benefits. And maybe they were on to something. Another point-of-view brought more ideas. But who could he ask?

"Louie, stop!" Jemma shouted as she walked out of the kitchen. Getting a second opinion on the note would also provide a lead in case Asher ended up missing. Jemma fought hard to find Ben. He could get her thoughts on the situation. Even if their last conversation had ended on contentious terms. They were siblings; that was what siblings did.

A crash sounded and crying ensued. Asher turned, expecting the flowers to have met their end. Instead, Mackie lay sprawled on the ground, Louie standing above him, his hands in fists. Putting another thing to worry about on Jemma's plate might not be the best idea.

Ben was at Mackie's side in less than a second.

Ben. Asher could share the note with his brother-in-law. The man may also be busy with the boys, but he didn't have a day job working with the governor like Jemma.

"Louie hit me!" Mackie shouted. Ben's hand moved to Mackie's arm, but his gaze was on Louie.

"What were you thinking?" Ben's words were sharp.

Asher's concern moved from the light stream of smoke growing across Louie's shoulders to the scowl on Ben's face. His brows were furrowed and nostrils flared. Perhaps Ben wasn't in the best state of mind—adding on a letter mentioning the island wouldn't help.

Asher flinched. Flames flashed across his vision, although the room was fine. Ben hadn't emitted energy. He'd been cured by EnertinX—but so had the Disparates on the island before they had an outburst that killed them. But this wasn't the island; this version of EnertinX worked. At least, so far.

Jemma was next to the fighting boys while Margaret and the sergeant turned their attention to the incident.

"Louie, we need to use soft hands," Jemma said, pursing her lips. A scowl stayed plastered on Louie's face. Ben didn't create fire anymore, but Louie could.

A knock at the door interrupted the scene. No one dared to move.

A second knock.

"Who's here?" Louie asked, his voice straight. Jemma's shoulders lowered and her attention moved toward Asher and the others.

Margaret took a deep breath in. The scene had been a bit much for her, Asher realized. She'd never liked when he and Jemma would fight as children, especially with the added stress of energy power. Asher remembered the lectures from his dad when his energy first began to show when he was thirteen. *"Calm down. Don't let your emotions win."* It was a motto that stuck with him, making him ashamed of his anger.

"I'll get it," Asher said at the third knock. He knew who would be on the other side of the door. Those blue eyes always calmed him, but he needed to be careful. Last time he'd seen Quill, he'd almost lost his resolve to keep his distance. He wanted to be with her, but she clearly deserved more than he could give her. He'd caught her sneaking under the fence to go to the outskirts. On the island, she talked about her dreams of seeing the world. The other Republics. The ruins deep in the outskirts of places she'd read about in her old books, wondering what was left of them.

Asher couldn't go with her as long as he was on parole, and he'd let the hope that he'd be freed soon lower his walls. But then the note arrived. A reminder that he may be released from parole, but he'd never be truly free from the atrocities he participated in on Lucky Island.

It would always follow him no matter where he went. Quill. Maybe he could share the note with her. She'd understand his past, help him figure out what to do...

That idea vanished as soon as he opened the door to Governor Dunn and his daughter. Quill's eyes rested on the "No Solicitors" sign hanging next to the door, keeping herself from looking at Asher. Something had put her in a bad mood.

"Sorry we're late," Dunn said as he entered.

Quill attempted to follow, cold-faced. Asher stepped into her path and closed the door behind him, stranding them on the front porch for some privacy.

"Why the grouchy face?" he asked.

Quill took a step back. "I'd like to join the rest for dinner."

Asher raised a brow. "That's it? I know you, Quill. Something is bothering you."

"I'm hungry. That's all." Quill shrugged.

It was a possibility. Wouldn't be the first time, but telling her about the note now would be bad timing. Asher would have to wait until Quill was in a better mood to steal a private moment.

Quill's gaze moved behind him. His followed to the window next to the door. Mackie's little face squished against the glass. Grinning.

Asher laughed. "Seems we have a little spy."

A smile broke across Quill's face when he looked back at her. He lost his breath for a moment. The porchlight illuminated her blonde hair, making it almost translucent against her pale skin, the blue pools of her eyes glistening.

She was stunning.

"Might be time to head inside," Quill said.

"Yes, yes of course." Asher opened the door and this time held it there for her.

He caught the smirk on Jemma's face. He stuck his tongue out in her direction, which caused her to chuckle and shake her head.

"Let's eat before the food gets cold, now that you've joined us," Margaret said, standing next to the fully set table.

"I saved you a seat, Uncle Asher," Louie said, patting the chair next to him.

Asher smiled. "As always."

The table was crowded with nine bodies sitting around it, but somehow they all fit. Asher sat across from Quill, with Jemma and Louie to his sides.

"Is there any news to share?" Margaret asked, breaking the silence that had settled after everyone served themselves food.

Her gaze paused on Asher, as if knowing about the note in his pocket.

"My new boat arrived on the train this morning," Sergeant Simmons said.

Asher relaxed, grateful for the distraction.

"A boat!" Mackie said, his little body bouncing in his seat. "I wanna go on a boat!"

Louie nodded.

"You can't invite yourself on it," Jemma said.

Dominic laughed. "I'd be happy to show them the ropes of sailing. In fact, I could show them around the *Second Chance* in the morning. She's a beaut."

Asher hid a smirk. Even the name of his boat was cheesy.

Margaret smiled at him. "Asher and I went with him to pick it out."

His mother had insisted he come, not wanting to leave him home alone. He didn't care much for boats, nor did he care to go sailing, but Dominic had tried to turn the trip into a bonding moment for the two of them, explaining all about how boats worked and how to sail. Not that Asher ever planned on using that information.

"So, will we get to have one of these dinners out on the water soon?" Governor Dunn asked. "I didn't think Margaret was a big fan of sailing."

The sergeant lowered the forkful of potatoes in his hand. "Oh, I know." He looked at Margaret. "We found some ginger drops that help for short trips, and she loved being on the water last week when we took my old boat out for one last spin."

Margaret nodded. "I get a little motion sickness, but the drops help."

Asher placed a hand over his mouth to keep from laughing as Quill's eyes locked with his. A dimple formed on her cheek as a small chuckle escaped her lips—the food was lifting her mood. Just as quick as the smile had appeared, it flattened as Quill turned to examine her food, breaking their gaze.

"Do you have something to share?" Asher's mother eyed the two of them. That was why Quill had looked away. They were caught.

Asher let out a laugh as he coughed and cleared his throat. "Um, well... just thinking of the last time I was out on the water. You know, escaping once again from Lucky. I'd rather not revisit the docks anytime soon, if that's okay with you."

His mother sighed. "No one agreed to dinner on a sailboat. But speaking of Lucky Island, how are the relocation plans going? Are the inmates still in the Watershield Prison?" She turned to Governor Dunn. "Those poor Disparates don't deserve to stay cut off from the world."

Asher raised an eyebrow. This had been a topic mostly avoided at family dinners. Why would his mother bring it up now? Perhaps revenge for Dunn's comment about seasickness.

Governor Dunn seemed equally surprised, as his fork, fully loaded with potatoes and meat, froze halfway to his mouth. "Um, well... that depends on many factors. You know that. We can't just release Disparates that have been heavily drugged, some for years, back into the world. A plan needs to be put into place and agreed upon by each Republic."

"But Lucky Island should've been shut down," Ben said, placing his own fork a bit too forcefully onto the table. It bounced against his plate, causing a clanking sound to reverberate through the ceramic. "The Republics agreed on that decades ago. Stillfield broke that agreement. The Disparates shouldn't be punished and treated like prisoners."

"That's right," Asher said. "It was meant to be closed before I ever arrived."

"I understand that," Dunn responded. "And I agree. That's what Jemma and I are working on. Making sure the island is closed, as it is meant to be, and keeping the Disparates contained in a safe manner. If we could find Dr. Paxton's notes, more might be done. It seems she kept most of the information to herself."

Asher had his own note in his pocket... *You know more than you're telling.* Could the sender think Asher knew about Paxton's secrets?

Ben grunted, sending all eyes to him. "She makes me so angry. Closing down Merrytime Clinic, sending Disparates away to an isolated island in order to experiment on them. How she's allowed to live in a fancy prison is absurd!" Ben's breathing was heavy, and his eyes darkened. His anger was fierce, which surprised Asher. But then again, he didn't really know Ben. "She should go through the same things she put other Disparates through."

"I agree, Banjo," Asher said, using the new nickname he'd recently coined for his brother-in-law. "I'd pay to see her strapped to a table. Imagine the fear in her eyes. Maybe let all those island Disparates loose on her."

"Now boys," Margaret interrupted. "She is still a person, and this is going too far. We will follow the order of law."

"The same order that landed my husband on Lucky Island?" Jemma raised an eyebrow.

"We will not talk about this anymore." Margaret laid down her own order as Dominic squeezed her hand and nodded in approval.

Dunn shifted uncomfortably in his seat.

"You're right," Ben said. "I wasn't given due process. I was unfairly judged and sent away. If we did the same to Dr. Paxton, we'd be lowering ourselves to her level. I trust justice will be served."

Jemma nodded and took a deep breath. "I wish change happened quicker, but we don't know what unforeseen consequences may occur. We are doing our best to examine every option and will be presenting them to the Board of Governors next week."

Asher shook his head. "Sounds like excuses to me. Buran wouldn't like that answer."

Jemma sulked back in her chair without arguing with Asher. There was no point anyway. They'd been arguing over this for weeks. The fact Jemma wasn't making progress resulted in many nights of Asher practicing his control to keep from triggering the heat sensor on his ankle monitor.

But Asher was getting tired of waiting for flames of change to ignite organically. He'd started the process as the fire anarchist, and yet it was stalling.

If you want change as much as we do... It's time to release your fire. The note. Whoever the sender was, they believed it took action to make change. They had that in common.

Asher studied Quill to see if she was following the conversation. If she could be trusted enough for him to share the information that resided in his pocket.

She looked at him as if he were a wounded bird, her brows knitted together. Worry? Pity? Shame?

Asher couldn't involve her. Put her at risk. Couldn't ask her to think about the possibility of returning to Lucky Island. She'd been through enough. Quill deserved a life where she could move on past the atrocities of Lucky Island. Asher wasn't in a place where he could let the past go. It would always haunt him.

Her beautiful blue eyes looked deep into his soul, as if fighting their own inner battle. He had to look away. Louie's plate was mostly empty. It seemed he enjoyed the extra mashed potatoes.

"You done already?" Asher asked, needing to break out of his thoughts.

Louie nodded. "That was yummy, but I'm full now. Mom, can I go play with Mackie?"

Jemma nodded and the boys ran off to play.

The rest of the dinner conversation lacked interest. Asher had given up the thought of sharing the note with anyone. He was the reason the note had been left, and it wasn't fair to put the risk onto anyone else's shoulders.

After everyone was done, they moved to the sitting area in the living room to relax and digest. Asher couldn't help but notice Quill sat on the opposite side of the room on the loveseat next to Jemma.

Louie suddenly shot up and ran past the blocks littering the floor, reaching Asher on the couch.

"Spider!" Louie yelled.

Mackie stayed on the floor, leaning over.

"Where?" Jemma asked, pulling her legs onto the couch.

"Over here," Mackie said. "I'm watching it." A quarter-sized spider walked into view.

Ben grabbed a shoe and smashed it. "Nothing to worry about. I got it."

Tears welled in Mackie's eyes. "Did you kill it?"

Asher turned toward Louie next to him. "So, is your brother always like this?"

"He likes bugs; I don't."

"I don't blame you. I used to not like them either. Then I lived in isolation and spent my time observing them. It's fascinating the things they do to survive."

"Maybe... I still don't like them. But... what did they do to survive?" he asked.

"Have you ever heard of the goliath bird-eating tarantula?"

Louie's forehead wrinkled. Asher took that as a no.

"Well," he continued, "they are one of the largest spiders in the world. They are fast, but their bodies aren't the strongest, so they create a hissing sound with the hair on their legs to scare away predators."

Louie's eyes widened. "Is that kind of what you had to do to survive on the island?"

Asher didn't want to explain to his six-year-old nephew the things he did to survive that place. "So, summer's halfway over, ain't it?" He changed the subject. "Are you excited to start your first year at school?"

Louie's face scrunched up.

"Ah. Nervous, I see."

He nodded.

"New place, new people. It can feel like a lot. You'll adjust."

"No," Louie said, his voice small. "I'm scared."

Asher shifted in his seat. He was still adjusting to this uncle thing, but Louie had taken a liking to him. It was easier than he thought it would be. He looked up and locked eyes with Jemma. She gave an encouraging nod.

"Hey, it's okay to be scared. We all get scared sometimes."

"What if I get mad and I'm taken away?"

Asher's eyes widened. So that was his concern. He didn't blame him. After what he'd seen happen to his dad in this past year—and what happened to himself—it was a scary possibility. He was only six; he was going to get mad.

"Well," Asher said. "If you get mad, I'll get mad with you so you won't be alone."

"You won't be there."

"Maybe not at school, but if you hold in your anger and bring it to me, then I'll get mad with you. Does that sound like a deal?"

Louie gave him a slight smile. "I'll try."

"There's my Lougie boy!"

"Ew!" Louie laughed. "Don't call me that!"

"Are they still attending preschool with Caty?" Margaret asked as she sat down next to Dominic, who wrapped his arm around her.

Dunn huffed and remained standing.

"No Mom, it's summer, remember?"

"Oh, yes, that's right."

"Caty is actually visiting her family in Vespher for the summer," Jemma said.

Asher looked incredulously between the two women. Was this how their time without him went? Jemma being on top of things while their mother was caught up in her own life. Come to think of it, life was like that before he'd been kidnapped and taken to the island. His mother would keep herself busy and leave Jemma and Asher to take care of themselves. He was used to doing things alone. He could figure out this note on his own.

"Oh, that's nice. Speaking of Caty, how's Haven?" his mother asked.

Jemma shifted in her seat. "I haven't heard from her since before Ben was taken."

Haven was one of Jemma's two best friends. Except she wasn't much of a friend at all. Asher saw pain flash across Jemma's face. Jemma had told him about her distance once she found out about Louie's powers. It was lucky he had never met this *Haven*. He'd show her what a Disparate could do.

SEVEN

J emma's nerves rose. The sight at the Capitol building was comparable to election day, with a small group of those who opposed Governor Dunn standing along the sidewalk with signs to convince voters to pick a new leader.

Except this time, instead of signs that read "Dunn is Done!", they had pictures glued onto posters with the words "Where is my brother? Daughter? Friend?" or "Disparates Deserve Deliverance." Buran's flyer slogan had caught steam with fellow hurting family members. So many people had been affected by the actions of Dr. Paxton.

Hopefully, the governors of the Seven Republics would listen to Jemma. Well, not her exactly; Buran would be doing the talking, but he'd asked her to come for support. He was presenting his plan for Disparate rehabilitation and needed things to go right.

Governor Dunn, true to his word, had gotten the rest of the Republics to agree to let Buran present his plan at their upcoming meeting. He'd given him a couple months to gather data, and Buran claimed he was ready. He didn't want to risk more Disparates by waiting longer or leave the families of those moved to Watershield Prison without answers. The more time that passed, the more questions arose about why the names weren't released.

And the crowd grew larger outside the Capitol, waiting to show their distaste in front of as many leaders as they could.

Which, today, at least three other Republics would see their display. A meeting like this couldn't be done virtually, as the pre-war satellites only supported up to five at a time before crashing. Although some governors would be attending through video chat. Preen, Tesserin, and Hastiet were the farthest from Stillfield.

And then there was Dr. Paxton. Wuslick would provide an update on her. It would be this committee of leaders that would discuss next steps: what would happen with the doctor, the Disparates from the island, and Enertin.

No one was really sure.

Governor Dunn and Jemma entered the meeting room. She'd expected to see Buran here, set up and ready to go. Yet it was empty.

Dunn's forehead wrinkled. "He's coming, right?"

Jemma nodded. "He'll be here. We still have some time before the meeting starts."

First to arrive was Governor Selah Hilsom from Wuslick, the Republic in charge of military and education. Her long black hair stretched below her hips, giving her an air of elegance as she pulled it to the side to sit. She placed a yellow binder onto the table, her solid white nails, which had been sharpened into points, resting on top.

"Welcome," Governor Dunn said, wearing his power suit of a dark blue jacket and tie. It was only him and Jemma in the room, waiting for Buran to arrive. He should have been here already. "I'm so glad you could make it."

Jemma subtly pulled out her phone.

> Where are you? People are arriving.

"Of course I'm the first here." Governor Hilsom relaxed into her chair, a smirk on her face. "Eduardo's probably stuck completing some *business* with his newest assistant."

Jemma's cheeks warmed at the insinuation as the conference room door opened. She straightened, hoping to see Buran. Instead, in walked a man who looked similar to him, except he was a few years older with shaggier blond hair that poked out from underneath a cowboy hat, the loose curls hitting below his earlobes.

"I hear you've been talking about me." Governor Eduardo Suarex of Vasco, the Republic filled with factories that churned out technology and vehicular needs, commanded the attention of the room with his presence.

Hilsom rolled her eyes as a petite woman followed in behind him, holding a briefcase against her chest. She sat behind her boss, taking one of the seats that lined the edges of the room.

"Just remarking on how reliable you are," Hilsom said. "Always true to your character." Her eyes roamed up and down his body. It was then Jemma realized he had no shirt underneath his buttoned jacket. Very unlike Buran.

"We're grateful you made it," Dunn said.

Jemma's heart raced. Buran was meant to lead part of the meeting in his role of Disparate Consultant. He should have been here half an hour ago. Jemma checked her phone—no answer.

You're on your way, right?

Moments later, one more governor entered the room: Venier Klif from Vespher. His hair was blond and shaved on the side, while the top was longer, green, and brushed backward. "My, what a techy place you've got," he said, moving to shake Governor Dunn's hand. "I would love to return your hospitality next week when the next set of supplies arrives, if you're up for a visit."

Still no Buran. Perhaps the protesters held him up. Not by force, but rather distraction. Buran was one to stop and promote his work at any opportunity.

The television screen at the end of the conference table popped on. Governor Lillierth Baswort from Hastiet gave a small smile and Governor Clairene Nesti of Tesserin waved at the full room. The leaders of the Republics greeted each other with forced pleasantries. Each Republic relied on the other, but that didn't mean they liked each other.

"How are your numbers at the factory looking this month?" Baswort asked Suarex after unmuting her mic. Her voice boomed throughout the room. "Got any extra materials you could... you know... slip my way?"

"You just received a shipment of trucks two months ago. Surely that was enough to last until next month," Suarex responded.

"You underestimate the toll mining puts on these vehicles," Baswort retorted. "It's hard to keep up with the demand for emeralds after Vespher declared gemstone green to be the new color of the year. Talk to him about why his request for minerals doubled."

"My, my," Venier Klif said, as his emerald-studded coat sleeve clinked on the table. "The people need hope. And fashion gives them hope." He smiled a charming smile at Baswort, who blushed as she looked away.

"I suppose you're right," she mumbled.

Jemma looked at Governor Dunn, who'd been quietly watching the interaction between his colleagues. His face was calm, but his eyes darted to the door and then the clock above it every few moments.

It was time to start the meeting.

Governor Dunn rose from his seat. "I'm glad each of you has arrived here today. I have some important circumstances we need to discuss."

"Wait," Nesti spoke for the first time. "We seem to be missing Preen."

The seventh and final Republic was Preen. Their specialty was arguably most important. It was a land of lush farms and dairies. They provided food and nourishment for the other Republics. Without them, resources would be scarce.

But their governor wasn't the only one missing.

Dunn's getting started.

She hoped Buran wasn't hurt. Thoughts of accidents or worse—foul play—ran through her mind. He'd wanted this meeting more than anyone. Missing it was not like him.

"They received the invitation, just as each of you did," Dunn said.

"Seems like Preen to not show up," Klif said, running a hand over the top of his green hair. "They think they're better than the rest of us. Even went so far as to refuse my last shipment of quality fur coats! Something about my designs being unfit on a farm."

Jemma could understand that. There were those in Stillfield who loved to shop and wear the newest craze. She was not one of them.

"They refused your shipment?" Hilsom narrowed her eyes as she scribbled something in her notebook. "Did you still receive your goods from them?"

"Yes. They fulfilled their end of the agreement. Although, I almost wanted to refuse, due to my hurt ego and all." Klif sighed. "But I prevailed, for my people."

"Has anyone else had this issue?" Hilsom looked around the room. The other figures shook their heads and shrugged.

Jemma's phone vibrated in her hand.

Governor Dunn coughed, gaining the attention. "It does seem strange that Preen refused new clothing. However, Governor Beecher's reasoning makes sense. He likely didn't want to waste resources that could be put to better use elsewhere. I'm sure he's too busy overseeing his farms to make it here today. There was a nasty heatwave that came through his land earlier this week."

A heatwave? Jemma hadn't heard about that. Although Preen was the farthest Republic from Stillfield and they didn't often get news from there.

"What I'd like to turn our attention to today," Governor Dunn continued, "is the issue we have with Dr. Paxton and her illegal and inhumane treatment of patients."

Jemma straightened in her seat. Getting into business was happening too quickly.

"You mean Disparates?" Suarex asked. "She was using them to develop better treatments. How was that inhumane? Without her work, people would still be catching fire on the streets."

Jemma's chest tightened. They weren't listening, and Buran still hadn't arrived. If the conversation got too far off the mark, he'd have a hard time bringing it back. Jemma needed to say something in his place. *What would Buran say?* "You don't understand," she spoke up. "She was using them against their will."

"Who is this woman?" Suarex asked as he looked Jemma in the eye.

She was too stunned by his boldness to speak.

"This is Jemma Hodgerton. She is our—" The door to the meeting room opened as Governor Dunn spoke. He immediately relaxed, and so did Jemma. "Oh, hello Buran. About time you joined us. Anyway, Jemma is our Disparate Liaison. And the man who just joined us is Buran Kuzmin, a consultant. He is here on behalf of Disparates to share his findings and ideas on how to more safely treat those with energy power."

Buran breathed heavily, as if he'd run all the way here. "Yes, thank you," he said as he straightened the bottom of his jacket. "I'm glad you were each able to be here. I apologize for my late arrival. I was inquiring about the islanders in the prison. Who do they have locked up there?"

So he had been distracted by the protesters, although that wasn't what he'd told Jemma. But then again, he couldn't tell a room full of the most important people in the world he was having issues at home.

"Did you hear anything?" Nesti asked, her voice coming over the speakers. "Is a list of names ready to be released?"

Buran shook his head.

"It's not that simple," Hilsom interjected. "Dr. Paxton used a number system. We can't find any information to line the numbers up with their names. We've been slowly going through Watershield and retrieving the names from those that remember."

"Those that remember?" Suarex asked.

"Yes. Dr. Paxton's treatments impacted memory. Many don't remember their own name."

A pit formed in Jemma's stomach. Those poor people. That could have been Ben.

"So release the ones you have," Buran said, his forehead wrinkled. "Don't their families deserve to know they're still alive?"

Hilsom's eyes widened. "Of course they do, but we don't want to give them false hope. We need to make sure our information is accurate. There are less people at Watershed than the number sent to Merrytime Clinic. Once we are sure, we'll release it."

Buran's lips pulled into a deep frown, and Jemma's shoulders fell. Disparates lost lives on Lucky Island. Their families deserved to know, to receive that closure, but all they could do was wait.

"Where were we in our discussion?" Buran regained his confidence in front of six of the most powerful people in the world.

Jemma wiped her own sweaty palms against the side of her pants before remembering she was wearing white. Hopefully it hadn't left any visible marks, which would certainly get a glare from Klif.

"We were speaking about Dr. Paxton," Hilsom said. "She's being held in our highest security Republic Prison, guarded around the clock by Disparate Responders."

Buran had looked as if he were about to interrupt but stopped at Hilsom's reassurance.

"She will need to go on trial," Hilsom continued, "before further punishment is assigned. We have to take into consideration the amount of research and progress she has offered to our cause over the years." The other governors nodded in agreement.

The temperature of the room dropped quickly. Jemma shivered. Buran was disgusted, and Jemma couldn't blame him.

"She was using Disparates for her own good," Buran interjected, his brows furrowing. "And her research has put Disparates in more danger."

Jemma sucked in her breath. This was what they had been worried about: the inability of the other leaders to understand how dangerous a woman like Dr. Paxton was.

Governor Dunn spoke slowly. "I can see your hesitation. However, I was directly affected by her ability. There are years of my life that are missing and cloudy. Years I will never get back with my daughter. Things I did because of her that I'll forever regret." He glanced toward Jemma. She understood he meant her father.

Governor Hilsom's face softened. "That may be true, but we agreed many years ago on an order of justice."

"Justice?" Jemma was tired of how she was beating around the bush. "Like the order of justice she used to send Disparates onto Lucky Island, only to be drugged, and tortured, and killed?"

Hilsom's eyes were wide. "That may be true," she said. "However, we have a choice. We can follow her lead and do unto her as she did unto others with no due process—drug her, use her as a test subject, execute..." She leaned forward, toward the middle of the table.

The other five governors followed her action.

"Or we rise above her and be an example of how justice should be served. Her wrongdoings will not justify our own."

"You're right," Buran said as he released a breath. The chill in the room subsided. "I'm confident the courts will see the danger she poses and find she deserves at least life in prison, if not more."

"You will get your opportunity to share your story." Hilsom said to Dunn. "In court next month. Her trial is set."

Governor Dunn nodded. "I'll be there. With witnesses."

Baswort spoke next, her voice coming through the speakers and drawing attention to the screen on the back wall. "That wasn't all this meeting was for, was it? I need to get back to my mines."

Governor Dunn looked at Buran and motioned his head to the side for him to take the stage.

"No, that was not all." Buran took the cue. "Part of the issue with Dr. Paxton was her research. We all know the change introducing Enertin made in our communities. However, through my own research here in Stillfield, with long term use we are seeing increased..." His voice trailed off as the meeting room door opened once more. "Risks."

In walked the head of R.E.I., Director Idris Barrett.

Jemma looked at Buran, his shoulders slumped from before. Perhaps this was part of his family issues earlier. His father-in-law was a point of contention between himself and Keesha, and now he had to present information on behalf of Disparates in front of him. The director might not even know Buran was one.

"Buran?" the director said, looking around the room. "What are you doing here?"

Seemed he didn't.

"Do you know each other?" Hilsom asked.

Director Barrett nodded. "He's married to my daughter."

Klif smiled. "Well, this should be interesting."

"I hope that won't be a conflict of interest for you," Hilsom continued. "I wanted you to be here to hear Stillfield's proposal as head of R.E.I."

The director locked eyes with Buran, noticing the file in his hands "And you're here to present the proposal?"

"I, uh, I..." Buran glanced to the side, catching Jemma's encouraging look.

She motioned for him to continue and gave him a thumb's up. Regardless of who was here, he had a dream. He needed to keep going.

Buran took a deep breath. "I'm here on behalf of Disparates. Considering I worked at Energy Watch as both a Watcher and an Intaker over the last decade, I've seen firsthand the increased risks related to Enertin usage."

"What risks?" Nesti asked, leaning forward at her desk on the screen. On the screen next to hers, Baswort scratched her ear.

"Data has shown Disparate incidents increasing in their extremity. Fifty years ago, when a Disparate had an energy outburst, they would damage items in their close proximity. Today, the same level of emotion results in a higher energy output."

"So Disparates are getting worse," Suarex said. "Which increases the need for tracking and medicating."

Buran shot him a glaring look. Cold emanated from his body.

"Not exactly," Buran said. He pulled a chart out of the large folder. "You see, this increase is only seen in Disparates that have been treated by Enertin in the last decade. The risk increases dramatically every year a Disparate is on it. Those that have relied on an alternative form of therapy have not had the same results and have been able to keep their energy under control organically."

"Do you have proof of that?" Director Barrett asked.

Jemma shifted in her seat.

"I do. Right here." Buran motioned to her and himself. "You are sitting with two unmedicated Disparates."

Jemma's eyes traveled around the room, landing on the director, who stiffened at Buran's confession. He likely didn't know much about Buran's current work either—after the outburst with Keesha months ago, it didn't seem like her father knew the full story.

That, and the fact that Jemma still hadn't told Buran how weak she was, caused her chest to tighten.

She'd taken the easy route.

She'd failed.

All eyes were on her, as if they could see right through her. Their faces showed surprise, unbelief. Disgust. As if reading her mind.

She locked eyes with Klif. His face was pale.

"You brought unmedicated Disparates into this room?" Kilf's voice was high-pitched as he stood.

"You have nothing to fear." Governor Dunn rose with him. "Take a seat and hear him out. I promise, they have their energy under control. I've been meeting and working with them for the past three months with, well, very negligible energy outputs."

"Negligible isn't none," Klif said as he slowly lowered back into his chair, glancing at his fellow leaders. "Do we all believe him?"

"Let's hear him out," Baswort said, some sort of drilling sound coming through with her voice as she unmuted herself to speak. "If there is a better way to keep our communities safe, we want that. That's why we continue to conduct research for a cure, right?"

A cure.

Like what Dr. Paxton could offer them. Like Ben.

Did they not know about it? It was rather new, and Ben was meant to go on a trip around the Seven Republics to show off the cure when Dr. Paxton was stopped. They might not know the full extent of what she did.

Buran shook his head, seemingly unsure how to answer.

What were they doing? Jemma twisted the wedding ring on her finger. This wasn't the direction the meeting was meant to go. Technically, there was a cure, but it was not the miracle people hoped for.

Jemma took a deep breath and rose from her seat. "The cure Dr. Paxton worked on wasn't without its issues. My brother was on Lucky Island and saw victim after victim die from her *cure*. My husband—" Jemma choked back a sob. The fear she had refused to acknowledge bubbled in her chest. Her husband was given the cure that killed so many. He was lucky to be alive.

"Dr. Paxton didn't do things by the book," Dunn cut in, stopping her from sharing about Ben being cured. "She took her own liberties, and it resulted in death and destruction. We need to do things the right way. That's where Buran comes in."

"Breathe," Buran mouthed to Jemma before standing to address the room. "I would like to propose a new plan of action, one less dangerous than this mad cure hunt. When Disparates are on Enertin for longer than a few years, their risk of explosion increases. And when that explosion happens, it is more dangerous and disastrous than ever. What once would have been a small, easily extinguished flame is now an inferno. Or, a small pothole"—Buran swallowed—"is now a large sinkhole."

"I know we aren't the only city experiencing this," Governor Dunn spoke up. "Governor Nesti, didn't you report a Disparate incident last week in Tesserin?"

Nesti nodded. "We're still cleaning up the mess from the gas barrels exploding. It was the poor Disparate's first day on the job, and his nerves got to him."

"And he was medicated, correct?" Dunn asked.

"That's what his paperwork showed."

"But we have no way to confirm," Suarex interjected. "How do we know they weren't flushing the medicine down the drain? Perhaps they weren't taking it as prescribed, and innocent people lost their lives because one man couldn't control his own emotions. Selfish!" He slammed a fist onto the table.

"I promise he was on his medication," Buran said. "I've been studying this for years. Enertin doesn't turn off energy power; it turns off the ability to feel it. If Disparates can't feel the energy grow, then they can't release it in a safe manner. And like a balloon at its limit, the energy bursts, causing disastrous outcomes."

"But doesn't that pose other threats?" Hilsom asked.

"What do you mean?" Buran looked at her with narrowed eyes.

"If Disparates were taught to control their energy, they could use it purposely to harm others."

"I never have," Buran said and held out his hand. An ice crystal formed in the center of it. His eyebrows frosted as the room gasped in awe. Then, just as suddenly as he brought the ice forth, it melted into a puddle on the table.

"That was a nice trick," Hilsom said. "But the truth of the matter is, if you wanted to, you could freeze this entire room. Encapsulate us all in that ice."

Buran's expression didn't change.

"Exactly," Klif said as he pulled out a handkerchief and wiped the puddle of water.

"This whole meeting, the temperature has been dropping." Hilsom's arms folded across her chest. "You didn't think we'd assumed it was the air conditioning, did you? It was clearly coming from your corner of the room."

"The temperature may be dropping, but at a harmless level," Governor Dunn said. "I promise you, I've seen the potential of Buran's words. He's been working with Disparates these last months and has a handful of success stories."

"Success?" Nesti's voice came through the speakers from Tesserin.

"Yes. Such as Jemma here."

Oh no.

Governor Dunn continued, "She's never taken a pill of Enertin in her life. Here she is, at a meeting with the highest government officials in the world, and she is showing no signs of electric energy."

The room turned their attention to Jemma.

"Alright then." Suarex leaned forward. "Let's see that control."

Jemma's pulse raced. Electricity ran through her body, but not to the point she could pull it out and demonstrate the state of control they wanted to see.

Governor Dunn gave her a quick look, seeming to catch her hesitation. "She's newer at this than Buran here, who's been practicing his powers for years. It takes time to master the control, but it is possible."

"Years?" Director Barrett, Buran's father-in-law, said. "This is the first I'm hearing about this."

Buran shrank. "Well, uh." He gathered his confidence and stood tall. "It's true. And it's something that I believe anyone can learn."

"That's amazing." Nesti's eyes were wide on the screen. "If this is true, it may be something to try here in Tesserin. What exactly is the plan?"

Buran relaxed. "I believe we can train Analysts to teach Disparates strategies to control their emotions, therefore controlling their energy. I have my entire program written out. If we continue to hand out Enertin pills, it's only a matter of time before more explosions occur."

"I'm willing to try it," Nesti said.

"This needs to be a communal decision," Baswort spoke up. "I don't believe this is the safest route. Are we stopping all use of Enertin?"

"We have to," Buran said. "It's a dangerous medication."

"I'm willing to give your plan a try as well," Suarex said. "We've had an increase in Disparate incidents lately, and if this could lower them, I'm in."

Buran smiled. Assuming they had Governor Dunn's vote, that made three.

"Shall we take an official vote?" Hilsom asked. "All those in favor?"

Governors Suarex and Nesti tentatively raised their hands. Jemma looked at Governor Dunn. His hand stayed down. Not moving to show his support for Buran. Without it, their resolution would fail...

One more hand shot up. It was Klif. Jemma hadn't been expecting that after the fear he displayed learning about unmedicated Disparates. But perhaps what Buran said got through to him.

"It's three against three." Hilsom jotted down some notes. "The resolution stalls until we can retrieve Preen's vote. The meeting is now dismissed."

Buran glared at Governor Dunn, who kept his head down to avoid his gaze.

He didn't vote for him.

Jemma wanted to know why.

Eight

Ben washed dishes while Mackie and Louie played quietly on their tablets, enjoying their screen time for the day. They were in the front room, barely visible from the kitchen, with piles of folded laundry littering the floor in front of the couch—a product of Ben's earlier productivity. He got a lot done when his mind was elsewhere.

Today it was on the people he'd left behind when he escaped Lucky Island. The injustice and mistreatment those Disparates had experienced and still did. They'd simply been moved to a new prison.

A ceramic plate slipped out of Ben's hand and hit the edge of the sink before splashing into the water. He grabbed it, a crack stretching from the edge to the middle causing him to drop it once again into the filled basin.

Ben grasped onto the edge of the sink to steady himself as a wave of nausea washed over him.

Mr. Dogivan had cracked open Lucky Island with his death. It hadn't freed those imprisoned. It hadn't freed Ben.

It'd only taken an innocent life.

Breathe, he reminded himself, closing his eyes for a moment to inhale. He opened them to see his knuckles were white. Loosening his grasp, his gaze moved in the direction of Louie and...

"Mackie! Get off that pile of clothes!" Ben's voice was elevated as he moved swiftly into the front room. Mackie had turned the clean laundry into a bed, the piles in disarray.

"Aww, but I made my own couch," Mackie said.

Ben stopped in front of him. "We have an actual couch; you don't have to mess up my hard work for that."

"Louie is hogging it!"

"Nuh-uh," Louie said. "There's space by my feet."

Mackie glared at his brother. "You keep kicking me!"

"Stop fighting!" Ben yelled. "That's all you boys ever do. That, and create messes. I can't get anything done with you two around!"

Louie pulled his legs to his chest at the reprimand.

Mackie covered his ears with his hands as his eyes widened, preparing for puppy dog tears to fall. "You're too loud," he said.

Ben sighed. He'd done it again—caused Mackie to cry. He wanted to continue ranting that Mackie shouldn't get into the clean laundry, but he'd told Jemma he'd try to be better at controlling his own emotions. And he wanted to be better. It sure was difficult some days. How anyone was able to control their emotions without Enertin, he didn't understand.

That's what Buran is trying to do, Ben thought. Perhaps he should try out his classes one of those days. But no—he was fine. He was keeping himself from yelling back right now...

"Come on boys, let's get you to Grandma's." A change of scenery might help with the rushing of blood in his ears. Plus, it was almost time for him to pick Jemma up from her meeting.

"We're going to Grandma's house?" Mackie asked, his frown straightening. "Can I bring my games?"

"Sure." Ben didn't care at this point. He needed to get them out of the house.

After searching for missing shoes, the boys clambered into the car. Ben tried to tune them out as he headed to his mother-in-law's.

"You've got different shoes on," Margaret said to Louie as they arrived. "And they are both for your left foot."

"Yeah, I don't know where my other ones are," Louie said, heading inside. Mackie followed behind him.

Ben shrugged when Margaret's gaze fell on him. "We worked with what we could find.""I see," she said.

Dominic appeared next to her in the doorway. "Did the meeting finish? I appreciate R.E.I. comin' out to help with Lucky, but I'm ready for them to take a step back. Let us handle Stillfield day-to-day."

"Meeting should end soon. They're poking around in your business?" Ben thought the Republic Energy Investigators were there solely to focus on the island Disparates.

"Tryin' to show us how to handle the protesters that've been popping up," Dominic explained. "Like we don't know what we're doing. Stepped in to help with the Fire Anarchist and think they're welcome to stay."

"Asher was doing what he thought he could to get the world's attention," Margaret said.

Dominic nodded. "And I'm proud of that boy for doing it. Just wish it didn't result in so much paperwork." He laughed.

Ben's phone buzzed in his pocket. Glancing at it quickly, he saw a message from Jemma:

Meeting's over

"Looks like it's time for me to get going," Ben said.

"Did she say how it went?" Margaret asked.

Ben shook his head. He wasn't sure what to make of her short message, but he hoped the sinking feeling in his chest wasn't a bad sign.

Ben pulled up to the Capitol. The protesters from that morning had left, which meant the increase of Responders had also dwindled. Only a few stood outside the doors as Jemma exited.

She sighed as she slid into the passenger seat. "Thanks for driving today. My nerves didn't let me sleep much last night. I'm so tired."

"How did everything go?"

She groaned. "I don't want to talk about it. Not yet, anyway."

"That bad?"

"Worse."

Ben grimaced. "Well, I guess we'll have to try and save the rest of today. Hungry?"

"I'm not sure I feel like eating much," Jemma said.

"Oh. Would you rather head home? The boys are at your mom's house…" Ben winked. Some alone time would be nice, as they hadn't had much the last couple months with Jemma working and Ben watching the kids.

Jemma side-eyed him. "No, I'm not ready to head home yet either."

Her reaction was enough to let him know the meeting truly had gone wrong. She said she wasn't feeling hungry, but there was one place that might bring her some comfort. Or at least some company to cheer her up.

"I think I know where to go."

Ben reached across the table and wiped a bit of raita sauce from Jemma's chin.

She gave a small smile in the dim lights of the Indian restaurant, still chewing the piece of naan the dip had spilled from. "Whoops." Her mood hadn't improved much from the car ride.

"Were you saving that for later?"

"Wasn't planning to, but perhaps."

"If you need more cream for leftovers, I could help you with that…"

"Benjamin!" Jemma placed a hand over her mouth to hide her smile as she shook her head. "I think I'll pass on that."

That was fine with Ben. It was her smile he'd hoped to draw out with his remark.

"Is the food helping settle your nerves?" he asked.

Her face dropped. "Buran's measure didn't pass."

"I figured as much. Didn't think you'd be so quiet in the car if it had."

"Sorry about that. I just needed a moment to..." Her voice trailed off.

"Process?"

Jemma nodded.

Ben hissed. "Buran told them about Enertin's increasing danger, right?"

She nodded again.

"And they didn't listen?" His voice rose, barely drowned out by the sound of forks clinking on plates and the muted conversations around them. "Just turned it down with no regard for life. What are they going to do when their Republics start to burn?"

"I'm not sure they care," Jemma said softly, her head and shoulders drooped toward the table. "Safety is their first priority, and as far as they've seen, life is more dangerous without Enertin. Even if it does increase the severity of an outburst for some Disparates, it keeps the majority in control. It kept you in control for almost two decades."

"But at what risk?" He couldn't understand the blatant disregard and willingness to chance a larger disaster. True, he never had an outburst. But all of this anger he'd now been feeling... it was always inside of him. It was only a matter of time before it was his turn.

"Not being on Enertin has its risks."

Jemma's words made Ben pause. "Which is why learning to control emotional energy is so important."

"But what if someone can't learn to control it?"

There it was. Her true question. Jemma hadn't been the same since the incident with Mackie, and Ben had a feeling it was because she didn't trust herself. But that was over two months ago, and she hadn't so much as caused a light to flicker since. At least as far as he'd seen.

"Everyone deserves the chance to try."

Jemma's gaze met his. "Enertin is dangerous, but I'm afraid to trust others to use their energy without harming others. How do we know another Dr. Paxton won't emerge?"

"Before Enertin was discovered, and after the Rain of Fire," Ben said, picking up one of the samosa pastries on the table, "Disparates existed throughout the Republics. They emerged from a worldwide nuclear war, scrambling for survival. Those with energy used their power to help in the process of rebuilding."

"Yes," Jemma said, "emotions were extremely high, and the few that had developed powers back then were needed. But that was a hundred years ago; society has changed. The Republics don't need Electric Disparates to power their grids now that we have the original power stations rebuilt."

"Have you ever wondered how Disparates went from being treated as a gift from above to outcasts?" Ben took a bite into his samosa, the crunchy exterior revealing the interior of potatoes and peas spiced with ginger and garlic. "The others became jealous. Why should they have such powers and not us? If we want to convince the governors of the right choice, we need to understand where their fear is coming from." A pit in Ben's chest reminded him that he was now one of the others. Was it a tinge of jealousy he felt no longer having his powers hidden inside?

Jemma's brows tightened together. "Why would anyone be jealous of Disparates? I didn't ask for this power. I don't want it;

I'm stuck with it and the knowledge that I could harm the ones I love so easily."

Ben reached his hand to cover Jemma's on the table, but she pulled it back. "You didn't mean to hurt Mackie. You were trying to help him." Ben's instant reaction at the time had been to question why she'd done such a thing. He regretted letting his anger and fear control him. The words he said now were what he believed. "And my help sent him to the hospital! It could've done worse. I killed him. He was gone." She shook her head. "You don't understand."

It was his wife's power that hurt Mackie, but she hadn't meant to. Still, the guilt was ruthless. But he did understand, more than she knew. "When I was on the island, I killed someone." Although he said it softly, the room seemed to quiet at his admission. He'd shared bits of his Lucky Island experience with Jemma, but there was a piece he hadn't been ready to admit. What he did to Markus haunted his nightmares.

Jemma wrapped her arms around her stomach, as if trying to hold herself away from him. Ben swallowed, a tightness in his throat.

The middle of a busy restaurant may not have been the best place for him to come clean. The background noise around them returned to normal as a waiter approached their table.

"I've got a paneer tikka masala, which I can assume is Jemma's, and a butter chicken," a familiar voice said.

"Samay, hi. Yes, it's my favorite." Jemma straightened in her seat, relaxing her arms as Samay placed their dishes on the table. Ben's attention stayed glued on her.

"When I heard you two were dining with us tonight, I knew a visit from the chef was in order." Samay wore his red apron, his hair shaggy and beard dotted with gray.

Jemma gave a small smile. Ben had met Samay a few times, but Samay hadn't been as involved with the Dissentients as of late. Mostly because Buran was busy with Governor Dunn. Between that and training sessions that Samay did not care to attend, the original Dissentient members were busy with their own goals.

"Well, I wouldn't want your food to get cold," Samay said. "I'll leave you to enjoy it."

"Samay, wait," Jemma said, stopping him.

Ben had said too much. His admission of being a killer was too much for her. Clearly she didn't feel safe being alone with him.

Samay paused. "Is there something more you need?"

Jemma looked right at Samay. "How do you do it?"

"I'm not giving away my great grandmother's recipes. It took a lot for her to save them during the Rain of Fire, and they are my pride and joy. Honoring our heritage."

"No, not that." Jemma shook her head. "Although that's beautiful. But you've always been so put together and organized. Your restaurant is thriving. You volunteer." She lowered her voice. "You keep your emotions in check. How do you do it all?"

"Ah, the age old question." Samay wiped his hands on his apron. "I do it messy."

Ben narrowed his eyes. Samay was the opposite of a mess in his eyes, at least from what he could see.

Jemma slumped into her chair. "I don't understand."

"You see my apron?" Samay gestured to his front. "It's covered in food spills and stains. From far away, the red hides the mess inside its fibers well. But they are still there. No one is put together. We're all hiding secrets."

"An apron can be washed," Ben said, joining in the conversation. "Stains can be treated."

Samay smiled. "Exactly. This apron will get its moment of rest. It'll get cared for in the washing machine. And it'll come out looking as if it was new, except it won't be. The fibers will break down. Some stains will stay. And the cloth will become softer."

A voice shouted from the back. Ben barely caught the word "korma" at the end.

"It seems I am needed," Samay said, nodding and heading back to the kitchen.

"Can that man be more confusing?" Ben asked, trying to process the wisdom Samay had left with them.

"I think I get what he means," Jemma said, her eyes turning to Ben. "Are you going to elaborate?"

"Elaborate on?"

Jemma gave him a glare that reminded him of the news he'd dropped before dinner had arrived. He almost hoped she'd forgotten, but how could she forget such a huge confession.

"Oh, that. It happened after I discovered 1198 and Oliver." The name caused an ache to heat inside him. His closest friend's betrayal would always hurt. "I was trying to leave, but my anger was too much. When a figure approached, I let it all out. A guard took the full force of it."

"Ben..." She put her hand on the table again, cupping Ben's that had stayed in its rejected spot from earlier. Her touch was warm; she didn't hate him. "I didn't know."

"It's not something I wanted to admit. Plus, after Mackie's accident, I wasn't sure if I should bring it up. I wanted to be there for you."

Jemma rubbed her thumb across the side of Ben's hand. "It seems we both have stains hidden inside. And you have been here for me. Clearly, I haven't returned the favor."

"Are you kidding me?" Ben shook his head. "You're keeping our family afloat right now. Working a job to pay our bills *and* helping the world become a better place. I get that the route to do so seems murky right now, but I have faith in you. You'll figure it out. And sometimes we have to try a method out before we really know if it'll work."

Jemma bit her lip and nodded. "Perhaps you're right. We'll have a better understanding of how training works once we're able to implement it. I just wish the answer was clearer."

"Don't we all?" Ben put his fork on the table. He didn't feel hungry.

Jemma didn't seem to be eating much either. "Should we take our meals to go?" he asked.

She nodded.

After boxing up their food and paying, they headed outside to the car. Ben placed an arm around Jemma's shoulders and pulled her close. "Thank you for hearing me out."

"Of course," she said. "We're partners. That's what we do."

"You're right. I'm sorry it took me so long to share." It was as if a weight had been lifted off Ben's chest now that he'd opened up about the island and Jemma hadn't run away. "I'm glad we can tell each other everything."

Jemma lowered her head. She stopped as they got to the car. Ben went to open the passenger car door for her, but she put a hand on his chest. "Wait."

Ben glanced around the parking lot. There were other cars around, but everyone seemed to be inside. He leaned over and kissed her lips. No spark erupted, a sign she'd been keeping her energy controlled. Pride swelled in his chest.

After a moment, she pushed him away softly. "That's not what I was stopping you for."

"Are you saying you didn't like it?"

She smiled. "I enjoyed it. It's just, there's something I want to tell you."

"Oh?" Ben's interest piqued. They'd shared so much tonight, what more could there be?

"Um..." Jemma fidgeted with her fingers, seeming unsure of how to tell him whatever it was she was keeping from him.

Ben stepped slightly toward her, causing her to press against the car. He whispered into her ear, "You can tell me anything."

A buzz came from Jemma's pocket. Ben gave her some space as she pulled out her phone.

"Is it your mom?" Ben asked. He hoped the boys were doing okay.

Jemma shook her head. "It's Buran. He's pretty upset. Sounds like Dunn invited him along on the next supply trip to try to make up for not agreeing. Supposed to stop in the Sister Republics, then continue on to Preen where we can talk to the governor there about his plan. He wants me to go with them. They leave on Monday."

So that was what she'd wanted to tell him. "That's a great opportunity for you."

"I'd have to leave you and the boys for a few days. I'm not sure it's good timing. They are still recovering from when you were missing."

Ben cupped a hand under her chin and lifted her face to his. "It's been three months. This is a planned trip. You can call us every night. It isn't the same and they'll understand. And if you're stopping in Vespher, perhaps you can see Caty." With all that had been on Jemma's shoulders, she deserved some time with her best friend.

"I don't know if I should go..." Jemma's gaze lowered once more.

"You're the best to go. The prime example of someone who has never taken Enertin and is able to keep your energy controlled. Sure, what happened with Mackie was scary, but if you had been on Enertin, it likely would've been worse."

Her eyes widened as if that possibility had never crossed her mind. Ben worried that perhaps he shouldn't have put such a thought there, but she had to know. If Enertin made energy stronger when it did burst, Mackie wouldn't have survived the hit.

"You're right," she said. "Enertin's not safe." Her body trembled under Ben's touch.

He placed a hand against her cheek. "You are safe now," he said. "I've got you, and I won't let anyone hurt you." He planted a kiss on her forehead.

"I should go…" Jemma said, her voice trailing off.

"You should."

"I—I need the boys to be safe."

"The boys will be safe with me. I'll make sure nothing happens to them while you're gone."

Tears welled in her eyes. Ben wiped one away as it trailed down her cheek. "And I'll keep you safe as long as I can. You must have some scary thoughts running through your head"—her eyes met his, a spark of fear inside them—"but you need to let them go. Be in this moment right now. In my arms."

This time Jemma initiated the kiss, standing on her tiptoes to reach his mouth. She wrapped an arm around his waist to pull him tighter against herself.

Ben followed her lead, pushing her against the car as he pressed deeper into the kiss. His insides swirled, a mixture of heat and desire. Although he leaned against her, he wanted to be closer. To be one with his wife.

Of course, the parking lot of Blazing Biryani wasn't the best place for that. Ben pulled away. "Shall we head home first before picking up the boys or get them and put them right to bed?"

"Did you get the back of the car cleaned out like I asked?" Jemma bit her bottom lip.

"Actually, I did." Ben's cheeks flushed. "And the back row is still down. There's almost enough space to fit a queen air mattress if we had one. Lots of room."

Jemma wasn't usually one for this type of adventure, but he felt the same heightened emotion. If they interrupted it now, those emotions could easily sizzle out and be replaced with the tiredness parenting brings.

"Well, what are you waiting for?" Jemma asked, pushing him toward the back of the car.

He let her enter first, pulling the trunk door down behind him as he configured himself above her.

At this moment, gazing down at her radiant face in the dim light from the street lights outside, he was grateful they owned a minivan.

NINE

Quill cut into her warm pumpkin pancakes with apple cider syrup. Her mom's favorite breakfast, a detail she'd finally been able to draw out of her dad the last time she saw him. She didn't care that it was the middle of summer, or that the can of pumpkin had expired a few years previously. It tasted like home.

A knock came from her front door.

"Asher," she said as she opened to his tall figure. "Nice to see you using your manners today." Had the plan to make him come to her worked?

"I'm full of surprises, I know. Plus, didn't want to anger Aniyah—"

"You better not be talking about me!" Aniyah's voice came from her bedroom. "If you are, I hope you fail your parole hearing today."

Asher leaned over and whispered, "Uhh... she's got good hearing. Was hoping she was already out for the day."

Quill shrugged. "She likes to sleep in when she can. Speaking of which, what has you up and at it so early?" *Come to confess his undying love for me? Play it cool, Quill.* "Your parole hearing isn't until later, right?"

"It's not until this evening, but you're leaving today. You didn't think I'd let you go without saying goodbye in person, did you?"

Asher followed her as she headed back to her breakfast. She had texted him the night before about the trip after her father invited her to come along. Said she couldn't pass up the chance to see where her mother grew up. Plus, her dad was clingy. Leaving for a few days without her would be hard on him.

That was part of the truth. Quill wanted to see more of the world, but there was also no better way to play hard to get than to have actual distance between her and Asher. Keeping away from him at the family dinner had been excruciatingly difficult.

Quill smiled at Asher as she took the last bite of her meal. Him showing up was a good sign he cared. At least, she hoped it was. "I was going to stop by on my way to the station. Ask if you're ready for your hearing."

"That warms my soul." Asher returned her smile. "I have high hopes. The judge was impressed by my control last month. Since I've kept it up, I might be allowed to remove the anklet and only have monthly parole hearings. Thanks for checking; you're such a great friend."

Friend. She grimaced. She used to love the attention from Asher. The notes and inside jokes. Yet, other than the kiss that night at the lighthouse, he'd never made any further moves. Him stopping by was supposed to be a good sign, yet he'd quickly *friendzoned* her like she'd read about in books.

"Hey, you feeling okay?" Asher asked. His face scrunched in concern.

She never was good at hiding how she felt. "I think I'm just a little nervous. The islands and Stillfield are the only places I know." Bringing up her feelings for him now wasn't a good idea. It would be the opposite of Aniyah's advice. Not to mention they both had a lot of stress on their shoulders.

Oh boy. Thinking about his broad shoulders right now was not the direction she wanted her thoughts to go.

"Makes sense. They're the only places I've been to as well. But honestly, that's more than most people. And I kinda wish I'd traveled less. The island isn't the best place for tourists."

Quill nodded slowly as she headed to the sink with her plate, avoiding looking at the muscles his sleeveless top showed off.

"You've seemed off the last few days," Asher said, following her to the kitchen. "Is that the only thing bothering you?"

Quill placed her dishes in the sink, then turned around. She was face to face with Asher. She hadn't expected him to be so close. The mix of smoke and cedar filled her airways as she breathed him in. Her body backed into the sink, causing a small shock. Inches separated the two.

"There's more, isn't there?" Asher asked. "That wasn't normal static."

She wasn't sure how to say the words that'd been festering in her mind these past months. The ones that flipped her mood from pure happiness, to confusion, to anger. The words neither of them had the courage to say. Nor did she know whether she should say anything at all. Aniyah's advice played at the back of her mind.

But now, she was about to leave. Not for long, but long enough. Her gaze didn't move from Asher's green eyes, the forest inside full of vines and overgrowth. Places she could easily hide and never come back out of. Her heart longed to get lost, but he made no move. Instead, the forest walls narrowed in confusion.

The moment was lost.

"I just need space," Quill said as she scooted around Asher's side. If he had come there today to make a move, surely that was his chance. "I need time to think."

"About what?"

"About us, Asher."

His eyes widened. "What exactly are you talking about?"

He didn't even realize. More evidence of Quill's delusion. "Stop the mind games. I don't know which way is up anymore!" She paced back and forth on the other side of the kitchen island from Asher. She needed that physical barrier.

"First," she went on, "you *leave* me on the island. Someone needed to escape, reveal the doctor's plan. I get that. But still, you left me."

"I came back for you…"

"Exactly! You came back for me! And then what did you do? Kiss me and rescue me and… ugh!" Quill balled her hands into fists as Asher stared at her. With those dangerous, forest eyes.

"I didn't want to leave you behind." Asher rested his hands on top of the kitchen island between them.

"But you did. And I appreciate that you came back. But then you kissed me. Asher, you know what that means to me. Surely, you must know. Did it mean anything to you?" The question she'd been so nervous about asking these past couple months slipped from her lips. No more playing hard to get.

Asher's forehead wrinkled. "We were about to be caught, right? I saw your nerves. There was no way you'd be able to lower us to the ground safely. I did the only thing I could think of at the time." His fingers tapped the counter.

"Which was to use a kiss like it was—*a tool*?" Quill shook. She understood his reasoning. It saved them at the time. But looking back at the intention of the action left only heartache. "And now you pretend like it didn't happen. Like you didn't take my first kiss away from me! That night in the cave, you told me you had to come back for me. That you missed me. I thought that meant something. You stole it, and you don't even care."

"It was just a kiss." Asher's voice was slow and quiet, but the impact was sharp. The room filled with an eerie silence as Asher's heavy breathing settled, and Quill's heart cracked as if she were a Ground Disparate and her heart was nothing more than dirt. "Fine," he said softly. "You'd rather I'd not kissed you and we were still there, as prisoners?"

"That's not what I'm saying." Tears lined the bottom of her eyelids. "I understand why you kissed me. It was brilliant at that moment. I needed to calm down, and that sure did the trick." Quill placed a hand to her chest, trying to hold together the pieces shattering inside.

"Okay..." Confusion rippled across Asher's face.

"It's not just that you kissed me. It's everything after." The tears fell. "You've been leading me on, but when I try to get close to you, you back away. This is the first time we've even acknowledged the kiss."

Asher was quiet, his face downturned at the marbled countertop between them.

Quill wiped her cheek. "I don't know if what we have is only friendship, but I'm not sure if I can continue this if it is. I want it to be more." She'd laid it all out on the table, or rather the kitchen island, between them. Now it was his turn.

"You're my closest friend..." His words fell at the end. His hands balled into fists at his side as if trying to hold himself together, or perhaps to keep his anger at Quill thinking they could be more than friends contained.

"And that's it?"

He didn't answer, but his eyes locked with hers, a sense of longing within—likely a reflection of Quill's own. *You gotta stop being his safe choice*, Aniyah's words echoed.

"You don't even give me the intimacy of a nickname," Quill said. "I've watched you, Asher. You give one to everyone. At least, everyone close to you."

"Your name is its own nickname."

Quill shook her head, willing herself to pull her broken heart together. "No. It's okay. I understand. We were two people put in the same situation needing an escape. Of course we would work together. I was foolish for thinking it was more than that."

Asher was quiet as Quill walked toward the door.

"I need to check on my dad," she said.

"Wait..." Asher ran in front of her and blocked the door. He tilted his head toward her as he spoke and grabbed her hand. There was fire in his eyes. "You have a nickname. The name I call you in my mind. In my heart. One I've been too afraid to speak out loud." He stopped and pursed his lips.

Quill's pulse raced. She wasn't sure if the blood coursing through her veins carried with it lightning or air. Right now it was a mixture of both. A storm brewing, depending on the words from the man in front of her.

"Go on," she said. She wouldn't be able to hold herself together much longer. "What do you call me in secret?"

"Multiple things, actually. A thorn in my side."

"Asher…" She'd played right into his game.

"The needle lodged in my heart. The feather that causes my soul to sneeze."

"What is that even supposed to mean?" She pulled her hand away from him. The energy in her blood quickly dissipated. In its place, she felt heat. A fire she would have aimed at Asher in this moment if only she were a Flame Disparate. "You should go."

Asher's face fell. "You're right."

With a glare and silence, Quill crossed her arms over her chest. She'd spent too much time fixated on the imaginary, on what there could be with Asher. He clearly didn't feel the same way.

"I'm not sure I can be more." He looked away from her, his chin trembling.

She no longer held the pieces of her heart together. It crumbled, the edges of each piece sharp as they pierced the inside of her rib cage, constricting her breathing. She clenched her hands into fist. She'd expected this. She knew this would happen. Asher wasn't a man of feelings; he ran from them. Always did, even on the island. It wasn't right for her to continue to chase him. At least this time, she could be the one that ran.

"I'm going to Preen. I'll be gone for a few days. When I get back, I'm not going to seek you out. I'm not going to come looking for you. I'm. Done. Chasing." She turned around and headed to her room, leaving Asher alone. This time, she was walking out on him.

Ten

A *thorn in his side. The needle lodged in his heart. The feath-*
er that caused his soul to sneeze.

Asher huffed as he headed along the sidewalk, unsure of where he was headed. It'd been over an hour since his conversation with Quill, and he had a few more before his parole hearing.

Which name could he have shared to meet the desire written across her face? None had been a lie. However, none had been fully the truth.

He was an idiot. Quill wanted answers, and he'd only left her with more questions. He crumbled the paper note in his pocket. Now wasn't the time for a relationship. Not when the weight of his prior life was upon his shoulders. He couldn't open up to her, put that on her. He didn't deserve her.

That kiss. What had it meant? They were at the top of the lighthouse, with guards closing in. All he knew in that moment was that it hurt to see her so scared—scared she might lose the one chance of true freedom she'd had in years. He'd had to do something.

But he also didn't mean for her to feel that way. To put so much meaning behind their kiss. Yet he knew he'd channeled into that moment the emotions behind their time together on the island. The secret notes. Their stolen time away dancing in a cave. She was his one good thing on Lucky. To him, that kiss was a physical depiction of what they had meant to each other—on Lucky Island.

A pain shot through Asher's chest. She was more than that. More than the island. His good thing now more than ever. And he was about to lose her.

In the distance, a train horn sounded. Asher was less than a block away from the station. All along, his feet had been taking him to the one he was drawn toward most.

Quill.

His pace picked up, now sure of the direction he was headed. He couldn't let Quill leave angry. As much as he tried not to think about their kiss, the truth was he couldn't help but replay it in his mind every time he saw her rosy lips.

All Quill asked was for Asher to be honest with her, and he'd screwed that up. He had been so close to confessing his feelings, yet they'd come out all wrong. He had to set things right.

Asher reached the red wooden doors of the train station, hoping he hadn't missed the group leaving. As he crossed the threshold, a ringing came from his ankle monitor, along with a vibration against his bone.

A loud reminder of his lack of freedom.

He bent over and tugged at the device, but there was no removing or turning it off. This was going to be great to explain at his parole board in a couple hours.

"I'm not trying to leave," Asher growled at the anklet. He was more detained by this thing than he'd realized.

The few people that sat around the small station looked in his direction, but no Quill or anyone he recognized. They must have been out on the platform boarding.

A Responder, who had been standing near the door earlier, approached. "You're not authorized to be here," he said over the alarm, his bright blond hair contrasting with his dark sunglasses.

"You think?" Asher straightened. He was a couple inches taller than the Responder. "Can you turn this thing off?"

"I'm not authorized."

"Then how do we get this ringing to stop?" Asher yelled. "I'm just here to say goodbye to some friends catching a train. I'm not trying to run away."

The Responder tilted his glasses down, his blue eyes coming into view. "I'm not—"

"Authorized. Got it." Asher's gaze moved to the glass doors that led to the train platform. He could make a run for it; certainly he'd gain Quill's attention with the noise his ankle was making. As well as everyone else's, and then he could confess his feelings with an audience.

He sighed. He couldn't do that. This alarm went off for a reason. A reminder of how wrong he was for her. How she wanted to travel the world and Asher would only hold her back.

"You'll need to leave," the Responder said, taking a step closer to Asher.

"Okay." Asher shrugged and walked backward until he was outside the train station doors. The ringing stopped.

Great. If I want peace, I have to behave. Just like his time on the island.

But this isn't Lucky Island, Asher reminded himself. This was Stillfield, his home. Yet this cuff around his ankle might as well have been around his neck, constricting tighter and tighter...

There were still a few hours until the parole hearing that might finally bring him his freedom, but until then, he needed to get out of here. He turned around and ran back the way he'd come. The train station was less than a mile from his mom's house—his house, even if it didn't feel like home.

Wind rushed past him, cooling against his sweat. It was warm outside, but not any worse than what the island was like. His breathing shortened, but he kept running.

From the train station.

From his relationship with Quill.

From the demons in his mind.

When he approached his mother's house, he didn't slow, his feet beating on the ground. He continued his sprint through the neighborhood until he passed old, familiar homes he once called neighbors. He slowed as he approached his old address, the place he'd lived as a child. The house occupying the space wasn't the one he'd known. That one had been torn down after the fire, a fresh, new home taking its place.

But the two trees in the front yard were the same trees his father said were too weak to support a wooden treehouse. After seventeen years, these trees had grown. Some limbs seemed thinner than others, but certainly they could support a hideout now.

But them being weak had only been an excuse. His father built the treehouse near the canal to hide his powers. The lectures from his father about keeping his emotions in control made sense now more than ever. Skylar Stillfield had been a Disparate hiding his full self from the world—and his family. If people knew, it was unlikely he'd have ever been elected governor. The fear of Disparates was strong in the world, and Asher didn't blame him for keeping it a secret.

The driveway was in the same spot as always. Asher stepped on it, half expecting his ankle bracelet alarm to ring. He wasn't sure why, as he was safely inside the confines of Stillfield, yet something about standing in this place again for the first time since he was fifteen felt forbidden.

"I'm sorry, Dad." Tears welled in his eyes. "I know I didn't start the fire. But I also didn't save you." He walked to the block fence that separated the front from the backyard. He placed a hand on a block next to the newer gate. It was warm under his palm. "On the island, I didn't fight to get back to Mom and Jemma. I... I let them get to me, control me, use me. I helped them test the cure on other islanders—caused their deaths. You taught me to be more than that, and I failed."

He knew he'd get no response.

"Hey! Someone out there?" a voice called from the front of this stranger's home.

Asher took off running once more, not glancing back to see who stood in the spot that once belonged to his family.

ELEVEN

The whirling of the train would be enough to lull a baby to sleep. However, it overstimulated Jemma. This supply train had survived the Rain of Fire and had since been refurbished. Just enough to keep it working—not so much the interior.

After dropping her luggage off in her room, Jemma sat in the main dining cart of the train across from Governor Dunn at one of the four-person dining booths. He quietly drank a coffee. Wood paneling lined the walls under the windows, and old maroon carpet with a swirl design decorated the floor.

Quill and Calum had been by, the latter grabbing a couple pastries to aid him on his continued tour of the place. He'd agreed to come along at Buran's insistence that he needed another Dissentient by his side—considering his trust with Dunn had been shattered. Quill stayed for a minute to chat awkwardly with her father, who answered in grunts and short phrases, before heading back to "freshen up."

Jemma stayed, knowing Dunn's poor mood was brought on by the consequences of his vote at the governor meeting. Buran had arrived to join them on the train, then promptly locked himself in his roomette.

Jemma leaned forward, eager to break the unpleasant silence that'd settled between them. "Train coffee as good as the stuff at home?"

The bags under Dunn's eyes were dark. "Not as good as the coffee place your mom and I visit... well, used to visit. She seems to cancel more often than not nowadays."

Jemma slumped back. She hadn't meant to make it more uncomfortable. "She's been extra busy at work, with her building being rebuilt after the fire and everything."

Dunn nodded. "True. And she's had other distractions." He gave a small smile. "Sergeant Simmons is a great man. I'm happy for her."

"He is." Silence settled between them once more. Jemma's fingers twitched. She'd only taken half a pill that morning and now regretted it. She was running low and figured their stop in Vespher would be enough of a mood lifter—getting to see Caty—but she hadn't figured in this feud between Dunn and Buran.

It wasn't too late to go back to her room and take the other half. She'd seen crates of supplies loaded onto the train that morning, some to be dropped off at the Sister Republics and others for Preen. All she needed was an opportunity to sneak back to the supply cart to grab what she sought.

But that opportunity was not going to be now. A disheveled Buran entered the dining cart, his blond hair swooped to the opposite side as normal, his collared shirt untucked on one side.

Dunn straightened at the sight of him, but Buran avoided looking in their direction. Instead, Buran poured himself a cup of coffee and searched the counter.

Jemma, being the Disparate Liaison of Stillfield, would need to do her job. Get these two stubborn men to clear the unpleasant air between them.

"Buran," Jemma said, "we've got the sugar over here, if you're looking for it."

His broad shoulders slumped. "I'm good."

That wasn't true. Buran liked more sugar in his coffee than anyone else she knew. As if to prove his point, he took a sip of his black coffee without flinching.

So that was how this was going to go.

"I didn't mean to make your measure fail," Dunn blurted out.

Buran set the mug down and twisted to face them, small flecks of ice dotting his eyebrows. "Then why would you vote 'no'?"

"I didn't vote 'no' exactly; just didn't say 'yes.'" Dunn shuffled in his seat.

"Same thing," Buran said.

"Why didn't you vote for it?" Jemma asked. Ben had picked her up right after the meeting, so she hadn't been there to hear his reasoning. Only his plan to hop on board this supply trip.

"He's too afraid to do his job; that's why," Buran growled.

Dunn put his hands out in front of him in defense. "That's not it. I'll admit it was a lapse in judgment at the time. I didn't fully think it through. I've been manipulated for so long, forced to go along with Dr. Paxton and her plans, I panicked in the moment. I didn't want another Republic to have an idea thrown upon them without a chance to speak their thoughts on it."

Buran leaned against the counter of the breakfast display, gripping the edge of the granite on either side of him. "He had an opportunity to do so. He chose not to come."

"We don't know if it was a choice," Dunn said. "They've been dealing with unforeseen weather phenomena that prevented him from making the meeting. You'll have your opportunity to present your plan in Preen."

"And then what?" Buran narrowed his eyes. "If Governor Beecher approves, will his vote add to the others? Or will we have to start over with a new vote and hope everyone still approves?"

"That is a good question," Dunn said.

Jemma caught the wrinkle on his forehead. "Do you know the answer?"

"I'm not quite sure," Dunn admitted. "Perhaps we should be on our best behavior with our hosts in Vasco and Vespher today."

"To keep their votes?" Buran picked up his mug. "This just gets better and better." He walked through the back door, taking another sip of his black coffee.

Dunn turned to Jemma. "Think he'll ever forgive me?"

"His energy emotion is disgust," Jemma said. "Give him time; he can't hate you forever. Wouldn't be very 'in-control of emotions' of him."

Dunn gave a weak smile as a bell rang overhead. The conductor's voice came over the old, staticky speaker system. "Supply Train arrival at Sister Republics in five minutes."

Moments later, Calum and Quill came to the dining cart, since it was next to the closest exit. Buran waited until the last minute to join the rest of them.

As the train pulled into the station, it was easy for Jemma to tell which side belonged to each Republic. Out her window to the left, the station platform was shades of brown and beige. The doors to the inside were made of worn wood, with black iron decorating the edges. The style of Vasco resembled the western style popular in this area prior to the Rain of Fire. Governor Suarex preserved its rustic charm.

They exited the train on the other side. Jemma followed behind Calum, her eyes widening as she took the final step.

Governor Klif loved changing the styles and colors he used in his creations. He employed a full design team to help in his efforts. Although the shape of the space mirrored its Sister Republic's side, the decor features were opposite: extravagant and colorful. Governor Klif had said emerald was in, but Jemma hadn't expected to be met with green neon lights brightening the white floors and walls on this side of the station. Vespher's doors were a white marble with golden designs etched across. The green lights cast an eerie glow across vases filled with tall feathers of all colors.

Calum leaned over to Jemma. "Vespher sure knows how to make an impression, don't they?"

Jemma nodded. Standing a few yards away was Governor Klif. His hair color matched his emerald coat that featured feathery edges, making him look like a bird. Governor Suarex stood next to him in a half buttoned white shirt tucked into a pair of jeans. A cowboy hat shaded his eyes.

"Welcome!" Klif said, stretching out his arms as if giving the air itself a hug. "So happy you all have graced us with your presence. Vespher and Vasco greet you with open arms!"

Klif paused and glanced at his fellow governor as if he expected Suarex to confirm his invitation.

Vespher and Vasco were first created to be one Republic in charge of all manufacturing. However, the first decade of the Republics quickly showed having an even number for voting didn't work the best. What was then Vesphco was the largest Republic, so it was split.

At first, it was feared the two Sister Republics would vote the same and have an unfair advantage, yet the opposite rang true.

Suarex nodded his head in a quick hello. "We'll be starting with a tour of my Republic. I have a car waiting."

"Thank you both for your hospitality," Governor Dunn said. "We'll happily follow your lead." He shot a look at Buran.

He'd replaced his scowl from earlier with a blank expression.

A familiar redhead walked through the marbled doors of Vespher's station. Her green eyes met Jemma's.

"Caty!" Jemma shouted, raising a hand to wave at her.

"I'm sorry, did you have other plans?" Buran asked, his expression accusing.

"I haven't seen her all summer," Jemma said, suddenly regretting not talking to Buran about her plan previously. Then again, him hiding in his room on the train hadn't given her the opportunity. "The governors here are only giving us a tour of their factories. I shouldn't be needed, right?"

"We need to make a good impression..." Buran said softly.

"Oh, so happy to see you have friends in Vespher!" Klif said, clapping his hands together. "Of course you can be excused. I'm sure she'll give you the true insider's look at our Republic."

Buran looked between Caty and Jemma as they wrapped each other in a hug.

Caty turned to Buran after letting Jemma go. "Thanks for letting me steal her."

"Gonna ditch us?" Calum interjected, standing behind Jemma next to the three governors and Quill.

Jemma flushed at the attention she was drawing. She hadn't realized they were all watching the interaction. "This is my best friend, Caty. She's been staying with family in Vespher for the last few weeks, and since we only have a little bit of time here, she wanted to get together."

"I think that's great," Governor Dunn said. "We'll meet you back here in two hours."

Quill gave Jemma a small wave goodbye as she left with the group to the Vasco side of the train station. Hopefully the group would keep it together without her.

Jemma's shoulders relaxed for the first time in weeks. She was with Caty, someone who would love her no matter what. Someone she could tell her secret to that would understand. Keeping it hidden was eating her from the inside out. If anyone would be able to help Jemma know what to do about her Enertin problem, it was Caty.

But not in the middle of Vespher's train platform.

Ben turned on music he enjoyed as he drove the boys to the outing for the day. A trip to the library. The boys played on their tablets on the drive. Anything to distract from mom being gone and to aid in Ben's mission to be the best dad they could ever have.

They passed by the docks. Rows of boats lined the area, including ships that belonged to R.E.I. The new occupants of Lucky Island. Ben was curious what type of information they were uncovering there, but he doubted he'd ever be privy to know.

The light ahead turned red and Ben stopped his car, giving another sweep of the docks. A few fishermen hung around, cleaning fish near the water. Responders, assigned to monitor the area, paced back and forth. One with dirty blonde hair caught his eye, but he didn't have time to think too much about her as the light turned green and he finished their route to their destination.

A musty scent filled the air of the library, and Ben welcomed the smell. Books had been a place of refuge for him when younger, and he hoped to instill that same love in Louie and Mackie.

"Can we look at the old picture ones?" Mackie asked as they passed the two shelves that held newer books. There weren't many; most were history textbooks that outlined the time after the Rain of Fire and how the Seven Republics rebuilt into the *thriving* communities they were today.

Too bad the Republics didn't live up to their promise of equity for all. They made Disparates the villains, convincing even the Disparates themselves that they needed to be contained.

Nothing built loyalty like a common enemy and promised change.

The woman from the docks popped into Ben's mind once more. There was something about her he couldn't quite place.

"Oooo, look at these," Mackie said, sprinting past the newer section.

There were several newer kids books, but they matched the books they had at home. Literacy was an area the Republics wanted to improve for their children, sending out a new book every year to each family household. Which meant they had dozens of copies of the same stories but not much variety.

The old books, however, provided that luxury. Mackie pulled a red spine, the hardcover book coming loose from its home. "I wanna read this one!"

Louie's eyes roved the shelves. Most of the old books that held up over the last century were hardcover, but even then, the bindings had become worn. These books weren't eligible for check out, they could only be read inside the library.

"That book does look like a good one," Ben said. He took the book from Mackie's outstretched hand and sat on a chair nearby, racking his brain as to why the woman was so familiar.

Mackie sat next to him. "Do you want to read this one with us, Louie?"

Louie shook his head. He continued to pace, his head going over every inch of the books on the shelves.

"Are you looking for something in particular?" Ben asked.

"There's a book Mom read last time…" Louie tilted his head to the side.

Ben got up from his seat and joined Louie. "Do you remember the title?"

"No."

"What was the book about?"

Louie squinted his face, as if thinking. "I don't know."

Sounded like Louie was having just as difficult a time remembering. "Well, I'm not sure I can find a book without any information. Would you like to read the one Mackie picked out?"

He didn't answer. Louie continued to browse the shelves.

"Okay then…" Ben said, sitting back in the chair next to Mackie. "I guess it'll just be the two of us."

Mackie smiled and snuggled against Ben's arm as he opened the book. "Once upon a prehistoric time…""What does prehist-ttt…ric mean?" Mackie asked.

"Pre-his-tor-ic," Ben said. "It's when dinosaurs were alive."

"Oh." Mackie nodded.

"Once upon a—"

"Where is it?" Louie said, his voice growing louder. "Where is it?!"

Ben's heartbeat quickened. Louie balled his fists as his gaze swept over the books once more, faster than before.

"I know it was here!" he shouted.

"Louie, take some breaths. I'm sure we could ask for some help."

As if on cue, a librarian approached. A man in a green vest with curly black hair walked toward them. "Are we doing okay over here?"

"My book is lost," Louie said through clenched teeth.

Ben eyed the spot on the wall where a fire extinguisher sat, ready to make a jump for it. A good father would drench his child in white powder to keep them from burning down the library, right?

Jemma used the extinguisher on him before. So it couldn't be too bad. But maybe not in a library where books could be ruined.

"It's lost?" The librarian raised an eyebrow. "What story are you looking for?"

Ben stood up. "He's not sure of the title or what happens in it. It's one he read once with his mom, but I don't know what it is. Do you know Mackie?"

Mackie shrugged. "We read a lot of books. Maybe it's the one about the pig? Did it have a pig in it?"

"No pig," Louie shouted.

"Then I don't know," Mackie said.

"Hmm..." The librarian put his hand under his chin. "Perhaps it has been brought to the book doctor. Once books become too worn, they need a little extra care."

"You hear that, buddy?" Ben asked. "The book just needs a check up, just like when you go to the doctor."

Louie crossed his arms against his chest. Although his anger had stopped growing, he didn't seem satisfied with the reason why he couldn't find this mysterious book.

Why the kid couldn't move past a minor inconvenience, Ben didn't know. It was frustrating. Ben wanted to do more for him, but his own anger was triggered at the sight of smoke drifting across Louie's shoulders.

The library was a terrible place for a Flame Disparate.

"Time to get going," Ben said. "Boys, come on."

The librarian nodded his head and turned to gather a pile of books someone had left out on the table.

Mackie groaned. "But you didn't finish reading *my* book."

Louie glared at Ben, not saying a word.

"If your feet don't get moving in the next five seconds, you'll be grounded from your tablets."

Mackie's mouth dropped open. "That's not fair!"

Louie didn't budge.

"Four... Three..." With each count Ben's nerves tightened. He was ready to grab hold of each boy and drag them out.

"Okay!" Mackie shouted, standing from his seat. "Come on, Louie." He pulled on Louie's arm, causing him to take a step.

Ben relaxed. "Thank you." The boys followed him through the library.

As they neared the front, Louie stopped. "There it is!" He pointed at a book lying on the table.

The front had a picture of two animals.

"I told you there was a pig!" Mackie said.

Louie grabbed the book. "I forgot. Can we read it?"

Ben sighed. *Be a good dad,* he told himself. A good dad would read to his child.

He opened the book and read a story about two friends having fun surprising each other, until they couldn't find where the other was hiding. Something dawned on Ben.

Why he couldn't stop thinking about that woman at the docks.

She was there. On Lucky Island. Colleen—the guard that had escorted him to his warehouse cell his first night on the island. She'd also been the guard to point Asher and Jemma to the lighthouse island when they came to rescue him. Ben figured it was to save herself. She had to have a dark heart to be a guard on Lucky Island.

Now she was at the Stillfield docks. Released from the detention center in Wuslick, where all island guards were supposed to be contained.

If she were free... no, no it couldn't be. A pain pierced the middle of his head, coldness spreading through his mind.

Similar to the animals in the book, Ben had his own "surprise" from a friend just a few months ago when Oliver showed up as a guard on the island. Little did Ben know, he'd been in a relationship with another islander—1198. The two of them worked to foil Ben's escape attempt, and he still didn't fully understand why. What was in it for the two of them? Had Dr. Paxton promised them some sort of reward?

Whatever she'd promised them, she wouldn't be fulfilling it from prison. A chill ran down Ben's spine, easing his migraine slightly as fear accompanied his anger. If they were released, out in the wild, would they seek revenge?

Ben closed the book. "Time to go."

"Aw, can't we have one more book?" Mackie whined.

Ben shook his throbbing head, which caused him to wince. "But we can grab food."

"Chicken nuggets?" Louie asked.

"Sure. Great." Ben grabbed each of the boys' little hands as they headed out of the library toward his car. He'd pick up something to eat on the way to the Capitol building. Where he knew Dominic would be representing Asher during his parole hearing. If anyone had a lead on the island guards, it would be him.

TWELVE

The governors of these two Republics were interesting to Quill. Although this was a simple side stop on the way to Preen, where she hoped to find her mother's waterfall, she relished the fact that she was a tourist exploring a new world, taking in every last word from her tour guides.

Despite the completely opposite demeanors of these two places and the fact that they often disagreed on politics, she caught moments where the governors generally seemed to like each other.

Like right now, as they stood at the front of the bus together. Although they'd been driving through Vasco, Governor Klif of Vespher took the lead in explaining historic events.

"After the Rain of Fire, this portion of land was mostly untouched by nuclear warfare. Being more central in location and low in population, it wasn't a target. However, it did provide a blank slate to build a new home on as survivors from nearby flocked together. The main draw was our proximity to rivers that birthed from a great lake."

"Yes," Governor Suarex said, "gotta have water if you want to survive. The majority of water sources had become contaminated with nuclear waste, but our rivers recovered quickly. They are central to keeping our infrastructure running."

Calum, who shared the bus seat with Quill, leaned over. The bangs of his black hair covered his almond eyes. "Who would've thought these two worked so well together?"

"Not me," Quill said.

"I would like to see these rivers though." Calum stretched against the back of his seat. "Would be nice to go for a swim. My back is killing me."

Quill raised a brow at him. "We've only been traveling for a few hours."

"True. Maybe it's all the stress."

"Have you heard anything more about your brother?" Chayse had been missing since before the island rescue. He could be with the other Disparates in the prison, but it seemed unlikely since the last time he was seen was by Quill in the lighthouse island. She didn't want to bring that up if she could help it.

Calum shook his head, his face downcast. "Buran tried to get the names ledger, but Wuslick said it's harder than just matching names with numbers or something. He was pretty upset after the governor meeting. He didn't give much to go on."

"We'll keep looking," Quill said, placing a hand on his arm. "Find out what happened to him. From what I could tell, he's a fighter."

"Thanks. That means a lot."

Quill waited for Calum to relax his shoulders before moving her attention back to the governors at the front. Instead of addressing the full bus, they'd moved next to her father. The three chatted away, with Buran sitting behind them. He leaned forward, clearly eavesdropping on the conversation, a cold mask set into his features. He was still upset with her father, and Quill couldn't blame him. All he wanted was for the Republics to agree to work on training Disparates to be in control of their own emotions, and his dream had been so close.

Hopefully, it wasn't over yet.

A few rows in front of where Quill and Calum sat was Governor Suarex's secretary. She sat with her head down, only the back of her black hair peeking over the top of the seat.

Quill turned back to her window. Outside, they passed large buildings with smoking stacks on the sides—working factories building devices that helped connect the Seven Republics together, whether through transportation or technology.

Quill soaked in all the sights. The tall buildings and cement pathways they traveled along were unlike anything she'd seen in Stillfield or Lucky Island.

Soon, they passed by the large factories and headed back toward the train station. The scenery transformed from a concrete jungle to the desert that separated the two Republics. Cacti and small shrubs sparingly dotted the ground. More buildings were up ahead, but instead of "stick to business" gray, they each had their own personalities. Vespher.

One building was covered in a rainbow of colors, each separated into its own block. At the front of the building was a large paint palette.

The next was a glittery blue. The sun glinted off it and blinded Quill for a moment.

"I see we've made it to Vespher," Buran said from his seat diagonally to the side.

Governor Klif beamed. "Why yes we have! You've got a great eye!"

The bus continued past a few equally colorful buildings before pulling into a parking lot in front of what looked like a store, the front made of windows. Behind the glass were mannequins dressed to the nines with racks of clothing behind them.

Governor Suarex's secretary perked up, her back straightening for the first time since Quill had first seen her.

"This doesn't look like a Capitol building," Buran said. "That's where the tour ends, right?"

"Your great eye strikes again!" Governor Klif smiled. His expression wavered as his eyes met with Suarex's. "The Capitol is currently undergoing renovations and is unavailable."

"Now you've set him off." Governor Suarex sank into an open seat at the front. "You all have fun; I'm fine waiting here."

His secretary collapsed back into her seat.

Were they truly stopping to shop? Quill perked up. Being surrounded by beautiful fabrics and an array of styles to choose from seemed like a dream. Although they were likely there to see how the clothing was produced... Quill tried not to get her hopes up as they exited the bus, Calum in front of her.

Before they reached the front, Calum stopped at the row the secretary sat in. "Your turn to exit, m'lady."

Quill smiled. Calum was not one to leave anyone out.

The young woman glanced up at him, her amber eyes registering what he'd said. "Oh, no, I believe we'll be waiting in here," she said in a small voice.

"Suarex there said he'd be staying, but he told the rest of us to have fun," Calum said, causing Governor Suarex to turn in his seat to see what was going on. "So, let's go."

"He's right," Suarex said, adjusting his hat. "Y'all go ahead and shop these gaudy outfits if y'all want to. That includes you, Klarissa." He turned to his secretary.

Her eyes locked with his, then she faced Calum, her pupils wide. She stood, clipboard in hand, and led them the rest of the way off the bus.

Outside, Klarissa folded her arms across her clipboard, holding it tightly against her chest. She let Calum and Quill move in front of her before joining the group.

"There you are," Quill's father said. "Was wondering what was taking you longer to get off the bus. I see you've brought a friend with you."

Klarissa blushed as Quill positioned herself next to her. "Yep. If we're truly going shopping, I'll need a woman's eye."

Calum smiled, lighting up his whole face as he looked at Quill.

"I'm not sure I'll be much help," Klarissa said.

"Nonsense!" Quill turned to her. "I love the way you paired your vest with those boots. Very up and coming."

Klarissa didn't crack a smile, but she stuck close to Quill as they approached the clothing center. One of the mannequins popped out to Quill. It wore a long, mauve dress dotted with sequins. She'd never worn a dress like that, but she imagined it'd be perfect for one of the characters in her stories to wear to a royal ball.

It wasn't something practical for her. She'd never have some-where to go worthy of the attention this dress deserved.

"You like that?" Calum asked, motioning with his head to-ward the mannequin. He must have caught her staring.

"It's beautiful," Quill said. "It's amazing the things they're able to make here in Vespher."

Calum was quiet for a moment. "Beautiful things are made in Stillfield too."

"Well, yeah..." Quill shifted uncomfortably under his gaze. She had a feeling he was talking about something other than the medical supplies Stillfield provided for the Republics. If only Asher felt the same way.

"He's right," her father said. "Stillfield has started playing with different designs to make medical care more uplifting. You should see some of the bandage options in our latest shipment."

"Oh!" Governor Klif, who had taken a few extra steps ahead when they all first stopped, now returned to the group. "I can't wait to see them!"

"Is there a reason we are stopping here?" Buran asked, his voice stoic.

Quill shuffled uncomfortably. "I'm sorry; I was just looking at this dress—"

"No," Buran interrupted, "why are we stopping at this building?"

"Because of our host's generosity..." Dunn widened his eyes at Buran. Quill knew that look well. He wasn't pleased with Buran's behavior.

"Exactly! Vespher hospitality!" Governor Klif said, waving them forward through the two glass doors that had blended into the front of the building, their clear handles barely noticeable on close inspection. "Plus an opportunity to assist in our research. Go shop, and let us know what styles and designs draw your eye the most."

Buran shook his head. "This seems pointless, but I'll play along."

Quill couldn't hide her smile. Unlike Buran, she was excited about this possibility. She'd find some new treasures to start her own souvenir collection, like people used to do in the old days. Back when there was a whole world to travel.

Her dad glanced at her before turning to face Buran. "If shopping is what our host would like us to do, then we all get new outfits."

Buran crossed his arms across himself as a deep breath puffed out his chest. A slight chill blew through the room but passed quickly.

"What do you think of this?" Calum's voice prompted Quill to turn around to see him wearing a blue jean jacket.

She caught that Klarissa had already been staring at him.

Although he didn't look bad in it, Quill shrugged. "Personally, I hate jeans. Kinda have a vendetta against them."

"Even in jacket form? Yeesh, I wouldn't want to get on your bad side." Calum removed his outer layer and glanced around the racks. "See anything either of you would recommend for me?"

"Me?" Klarissa asked.

"Of course," Calum said. "You didn't come along just to watch, right?"

"Hmm..." Quill was drawn toward a black sweatshirt. She grabbed it off its hanger and held it out to Calum. "Perhaps this is more your style."

He took it and pulled it on, running a hand through his dark hair to fix it back into place. "How do I look?"

Good. Really good—but not because the sweatshirt suited him, which it did, but because the style was familiar to her. There was someone she knew who rocked this look. Someone she was trying not to think about.

"I bet we could find something better," she said.

He glanced down at himself. "You're right, it's not quite me."

"Maybe this?" Klarissa, who had disappeared behind a rack moments before, returned with a beige suit jacket.

"I do tend to look good in earth tones." Calum took the jacket and put it on.

He was right.

Before Quill could admit how nice he looked, Calum's eyes moved to the rack next to him that was full of feminine-styled clothing. "I found something for you too, Klarissa." He pulled out a loose, flowy tank top and held it out. Large, three-dimensional flowers dotted the front of it.

Klarissa let out a laugh. "What makes you think that's my style?"

Calum grinned. "Honestly, I was hoping it wasn't, but I wouldn't know until I asked."

"Well, you've definitely got it wrong." She grabbed a silk button up shirt. "This is more something I'd wear."

"Maybe to work, but I'm sure there's a wild Klarissa inside there somewhere," Calum said. "One day, maybe I'll be able to pull it out."

Klarissa's cheeks reddened once more, a smile playing on her lips.

"So, what is it like living here?" Quill asked. "Seems like the two governors keep things interesting. I'm surprised how much they've been getting along, I always thought there was tension between them."

"That's a recent development, and it's harder for Suarex than Klif to keep up." Klarissa covered her mouth with one hand, as if to stop herself from saying more.

Calum tilted his head. "What do you mean?"

Klarissa put the shirt hanger she'd been holding with her other hand on the rack. "You asked what living here is like. Honestly, things have been getting rocky. Like when we went to Stillfield, we saw the protesters. We have them here too." She glanced around the store to make sure no one else was near. "That's the real reason we're skipping the Capitol. They're out there today."

Blood drained from Quill's face. It wasn't only people in Stillfield that wanted answers.

"And that's why Klif and Suarex are getting along," Calum said slowly. "To show unity."

Klarissa nodded.

"Smart," Calum said. He reached for something on the rack next to him. "I think I've found something Quill would love."

"It better not be a pair of jeans." After his recommendations for Klarissa, Quill was nervous. But she also appreciated the way Calum knew when to lighten a conversation.

Calum laughed and pulled a purple knit cardigan from the rack. "I noticed your goosebumps earlier. Something like this should keep you warm."

Quill accepted his choice, sliding her arms into the warm, soft fabric. The cardigan was long, stretching past her hips. The sleeves slipped over her hands easily, as if wrapped in a hug. She buttoned one spot in the middle of the front together and spun in a circle, her arms outstretched. "How does it look?"

Calum had a slight smirk on his face. "I wanna get back at you and say we could find something better, but I have a feeling you'll look good in anything."

"Yeah..." Klarissa said softly. "It looks great."

"Oh this is fabulous!" Governor Klif's booming voice filled the space. Quill twisted to see him step toward them. "You look exquisite. Purple is your color."

She blushed, suddenly feeling too warm for an outer layer.

"It's settled then," Governor Klif said. "You'll take that. I've already hooked up the two back there with proper suits, and I can get the rest of that ensemble of Calum's together for him."

"This jacket is part of a suit?" Calum asked.

Governor Klif nodded. "Absolutely! And you'll look great in it, I'm sure. I also picked out a suit for you, Quill. Same color as that cardigan; glad to see purple is one of your colors. Once my seamstress takes your measurements, we will send you all off in proper style. Oh, and Klarissa, you're welcome to pick something out and I'll bill it to Suarex."

"Wait," Quill said. "You don't have to. This sweater is enough." The thought of wearing full purple caused Quill's heart to race. Although she'd been in yellow on the island, she easily could have been placed in the purple jumpsuit of the Air Disparates, considering her two powers.

Calum's forehead wrinkled, but then he turned to Governor Klif. "I'm honored that you thought of us. I am curious about the dress on the mannequin at the front."

Governor Klif's eyes roved up and down Calum's body. "I'm not sure that particular dress would fit you, but I'm sure we could find something if that's what you'd like…"

"Oh, no. I was thinking for Quill."

"I don't need—"

"What an exquisite idea!" Governor Klif said, now eyeing Quill's body. "I'll have my associate grab it right away. It should fit you well."

"You really don't have to…"

"It would be my pleasure," Klif said.

"But…" Quill wanted to protest more, but by the smile on Klif's face, she knew he wouldn't let her leave without that dress. "What about Jemma?" She was with her friend, but if everyone else was getting something new, it was only fair that she should too.

"Don't you worry," Klif said, a sparkle in his eye. "I've got just the thing for her."

Moments later, they headed back to the bus, hangers with bagged clothing in hand. Except for Klarissa, who decided to pass on Calum's hideous top and claimed she had no need for a new work shirt.

And despite Quill's protests, Governor Klif wouldn't let her leave without the mauve dress. Holding it now, a silent thrill bounced in her chest, in and out of a hole that questioned whether she was worthy of something so nice.

"Don't worry about having nowhere to wear that," Calum leaned over to say before they climbed on the bus. "You don't need a reason to feel beautiful. Perhaps we should break in our new outfits tonight on the train?"

"Really?" Quill bit the inside of her mouth. She liked Calum. He was a good friend, and his uplifting personality was refreshing. But she didn't feel a spark with him like she did when she was around Asher.

"That is a great idea!" Quill's father boomed. He'd clearly been listening in. "A party on the train tonight after dinner. It's settled."

"Shouldn't we discuss our plan for Preen tonight?" Buran scowled.

"There'll be plenty of time for that," her father said. "And keeping our spirits up will be most important for when we get into Preen."

"I guess that's settled," Calum said. "I'll pick you up from your room after dinner?"

Butterflies fluttered in Quill's chest. Him picking her up felt kind of like a date. And they'd had an enjoyable time shopping together. He was a good person, looking out for others over himself, and made it easy for Quill to want to spend time with him.

Asher wasn't making any moves, not like Calum was now. Did a spark always have to be there from the beginning, or could one grow?

Spending more time with Calum wouldn't hurt, and his company was a good distraction. She'd only thought about Asher once today... or maybe twice. Either way, it was decided.

"Yeah, I'd like that."

THIRTEEN

Asher eyed the familiar walls of the Stillfield Capitol as he walked slowly toward it. He was here for his parole meeting, the first time he'd been back since his return from Lucky Island.

He took in a deep breath as memories flooded his mind. The place looked more or less the same as it had seventeen years ago, minus small landscaping changes. The tree that used to shed flowers onto the sidewalk he and Jemma would draw shapes on had been removed. The vines over the window two from the right of the entrance were cut in a new shape, no longer blocking the sun from shining inside the office that once belonged to a grumpy secretary. She didn't like the extra light and refused to use curtains.

Teen Asher had once slid a drawing of a possessed porcelain doll between the vines and the glass. The look on the secretary's face as she marched from her office straight to his father's desk still made him laugh.

This place was part of his childhood. A chapter of his history he'd filed away long ago. Even as the Fire Anarchist, it was never on his list of places to attack. Not because it'd be nearly impossible to hit with the amount of security—Asher could have found a way around that. But because facing his past meant Asher had to truly be ready to let it go and move on from the grief. He'd faced his old home already today; it was time to face his second one.

As he stepped through the front doors, he glanced at the anklet that reported his whereabouts and temperature levels. As much as he hated being trapped in a new way, a part of him knew he deserved it. That he couldn't be trusted to make right choices on his own. He was dangerous and could hurt again.

"Name?"

Asher looked up to see a male guard at the front desk. The courtrooms were at the back of the Capitol.

"Asher Stillfield."

The guard's eyes drifted to his computer screen. "You'll be in courtroom thr—"

"Asher, you're right on time." Dominic approached from the other side of the desk and placed a hand on the guard. "He can follow me. The board is ready, and I have a feeling we'll get some good news." He lifted a keyring on which a specially shaped bolt was attached. One that would open Asher's cuff.

Today was the day.

"Sergeant Simmons, of course." The guard nodded.

"Let's go." Dominic waved for Asher to follow him.

Dominic said the board had good news. If they removed his monitor, Asher would be free. He could hop on the next train to Preen and confess his feelings to Quill.

The thought of seeing her again brought a yearning to his chest. Even with the monitor off, there was still the matter of the mysterious note. Would the sender find him in another Republic? Until he was sure he wouldn't bring a new threat to Quill, he needed to keep away.

They entered courtroom three. A long table lined the front of the room, with two Responder's in uniforms similar to Dominic's beside it. Three stripes across the arm signified they were sergeants, visiting from other Responder Offices in Stillfield. Between the two of them, a woman wore black robes. The judge who would decide his final fate.

A desk with two chairs sat across from the front table. Dominic gestured for Asher to take one seat and he stood next to him.

"Judge Haller, I would like to present Asher Stillfield. He was guilty of starting fires on government buildings. However, his reasons were noble and his actions since repentant. We are here to release him from his parole."

Asher's eyes widened. Released was much more than he'd expected to be given so soon. The anklet removal possibly, but full release after only a few months?

Either his mother was pulling some strings or Dominic hoped to get extra brownie points for this.

"I see from his paperwork he was involved in exposing Doctor Elizabeth Paxton's misuse of Disparates on Lucky Island."

"Yes, Your Honor. He was a vital part of uncovering the island after being locked up there unfairly for almost two decades. He's served plenty of time."

"If his record is clean, that would make sense," Judge Haller said. "However, I received a call today saying his monitor alerted he was at the train station this morning. Trying to escape your hearing, were you?"

Asher swallowed. "I was there to say goodbye to my sister." He figured that might bring more sympathy than saying he was there to see the person he liked.

The judge nodded slowly. "She works with Governor Dunn, correct?"

"She does," Dominic said. "And they left today on government business."

"Hmm..."

Dominic shot Asher a look. His brows were furrowed, as if unsure how things would go.

"Before any judgment can be concluded," Judge Haller said, "I would like to hear from the defendant himself. Do you feel you have proper control of your flame energy, even without Enertin?"

That was the question. Dominic and Dunn had both advocated to keep Enertin off Asher's parole requirements, and thankfully the judge allowed it. Asher nodded his head. "Yes, ma'am. I've learned over the years how to keep my emotions in balance. I don't allow myself to produce heat simply because something didn't go the way I wanted." It was true. He'd seen the dangers of unbridled emotions and had learned to hold them deep inside.

Something the judge seemed to approve of. "That's a special ability you have. Even with your targeted attacks, you seemed to be picky on when you'd use fire."

"I didn't burn buildings down for fun," Asher said. "I did so to get away without being caught. I understand it wasn't the best method, but it did produce results."

Judge Haller's eyes narrowed. "So you believe the end justifies the means?"

Asher gulped. Perhaps he'd been too honest. Dominic gave him a worried side eye.

"Not necessarily," Asher said, searching for the words to backpedal, but more words didn't come. The phrase the judge had said was exactly why Asher made the choices he did.

He burned down government property and put guards at risk because he believed it would lead to exposing Lucky Island and saving those left alive.

Lucky Island may have been closed, but the Disparates that had been there weren't free.

But then, was Lucky Island closed? The owl note told Asher to return there. There had to be more the government was hiding.

"Would you like to elaborate?" the judge asked after a short pause.

Dr. Paxton's claws had left deep puncture wounds in the world of Disparates, and Asher had been complicit in it. "I think it comes down to intention."

Dominic tensed next to Asher as he spoke.

"Interesting." Judge Haller interlocked her hands in front of her, elbows resting on the table. "And how do you know if one's intentions are right?"

"You don't, because you don't always know what their intentions are. You can't be in their head."

Judge Haller leaned forward. "That is true. Do you believe your intentions are right, Asher Stillfield?"

Asher pursed his lips. He should say yes, that he only wanted what was good for Disparates, yet he knew that wasn't fully true. He wasn't exposing Dr. Paxton and Lucky Island to be a hero, no—he was driven by guilt, and anger, and revenge.

Dominic cleared his throat. "I believe Asher only meant to help those on the island."

Asher lowered his gaze and spoke softly, "Intentions are a fickle thing. It's hard to say if they are good simply based on results. I caused extensive damage to multiple buildings and brought a stop to an illegal operation. Was what I did right or wrong? Who gets to be the judge of that?"

"That would be me," Judge Haller said. Asher looked up to see a small smile playing on her lips. "I'd like to put your case in review and recommend you for release. It may take a few days for Wuslick to approve, but expect to have your full freedom returned to you by the end of the week. I hope you'll remember not everything is black and white. It's in the gray area we find empathy. And *that* is what will save the world."

For a moment, Asher didn't move. He was sure he'd blown the hearing by being honest with his thoughts. It didn't feel real that he'd be fully free soon.

Dominic rose. "Thank you, Your Honor." He tugged on Asher's arm.

Asher got to his feet and bowed his head slightly, unsure of what else to do. "Thank you," he said.

Judge Haller laughed. "No bowing necessary; I'm not royalty. I look forward to seeing the good you spread in the world."

They exited to the hallway, Dominic swinging his key-chain in a circle. "Soon I'll be able to use this on ya," he said, catching the bolt key in his hand. "Then you'll be able to start your life the way you want. No more locked doors, no more monitors to keep you in one place. No excuse to not join me on my boat." Dominic placed a hand on Asher's shoulder, the way a father might to show his son he was proud.

But Dominic wasn't Asher's father, and he didn't feel he'd done anything to warrant praise.

He'd finally faced the fact that his intentions weren't pure as the fire anarchist, and he wanted to fix that.

"Uh, yeah," Asher said as Dominic released his shoulder.

"I've got a few things to wrap up here, but I could give you a ride home when I'm done."

Asher shook his head. "Don't worry about it." It'd been a long day, and Asher wanted to be where he felt his father most—the treehouse.

The origami owl note crinkled as Asher put his hand in his pocket. He hadn't been back since finding the note, but he wasn't going to let them dictate his choices any longer. Whoever had written this note to him assumed he wanted to make the world a better place. They were wrong.

But they were right in contacting him, because he would do *anything* to stop Dr. Paxton's plan.

Even if it meant burning down an entire island.

The sun gleamed across Ben's windshield as he pulled into the Capitol parking lot. Thankfully his migraine had lessened after eating and calming his anger. He needed to talk to Dominic about the island guards, find out why one was back on duty—did that mean they all were? Including Oliver and 1198? Noise from the backseat consisted of chewing and soft "mmm"s. At least the boys were eating.

"Where are we?" Mackie asked.

"This is the Capitol building. Uncle Asher and Dominic are inside."

Louie spoke up. "Why?"

"Well, your uncle's hoping to get his ankle monitor off."

"Oh, his leg bracelet," Mackie said with confidence, as if he knew all along that was happening.

"He's not," Louie said.

"It probably won't happen right away," Ben said. "Things take time."

Louie grunted. "No. He's not *inside*; he's over there."

Ben glanced back to see where Louie pointed and followed his outstretched hand. Asher marched back and forth on the right side of the Capitol entrance, shaking one hand as he muttered to himself.

He didn't look happy. The parole hearing must not have gone well.

"Let's check on him." Ben unbuckled both boys' car seats while still in the car. Before he opened their door, Asher took off, walking at a brisk pace toward the edge of the building and seemingly unaware they were in the parking lot.

"Hurry, Louie!" Mackie said, his little body hopping up and down. "We've gotta catch Uncle Asher."

As soon as Louie's feet touched the asphalt, he was off, running through the parking lot with Mackie right next to him.

"Boys!" Ben hollered. "Walk! It's not safe to run through the street!" He ran after them, slowly closing the distance as they got to the edge of the Capitol building. He grabbed Mackie's arm first, pulling him back as he reached for Louie's. As his fingers wrapped around his small wrist, a loud shriek filled the air.

It hadn't come from either boy, who had stopped in place after being caught. It came from a few yards ahead, where Asher ducked with his arms over his head as an owl took flight above him, some leaves and feathers fluttering to the ground in its wake. Its long black wings flapped majestically in the air as it carried its white-and-black striped torso past the trees until it was out of sight.

"Are you okay?" Ben rushed over to Asher, the boys following behind him.

Asher straightened, brushing a stray feather off his arm. "I'm fine."

"You were attacked by an owl!" Mackie's mouth gaped.

Asher shook his head. "Nah, he was fine until you lot showed up and spooked him."

"Are you hurt?" Louie asked.

Asher twisted his arms back and forth. "I'm totally fine." His eyes grazed the ground a few feet ahead.

Ben followed his gaze, noting a piece of litter on the ground. Perhaps disturbed by the wind from the owl moments before. An owl out in the middle of the day wasn't a common sight.

Asher finally broke his stare and turned his body sideways. "What *are* you all doing here? Did Jemma put you up to support me at my hearing? You kind of missed it."

Ben shook his head. "Stopping by to see Dominic." He wasn't sure about mentioning the island guard to Asher. A reminder of trauma was not what he needed.

"He should be inside still." Asher took a step to the side.

Ben wrinkled his forehead. Asher's small movements were antsy, as if he wanted them to leave.

"Boys," Ben said, "let's see if we can find Dominic. Say goodbye to your uncle."

Louie gave a wave.

Mackie wrapped Asher in a hug. He reached to the ground as he let go and picked up the piece of litter. "What's this?"

"Garbage." Asher grabbed it from his hand and tucked it in his back pocket. "I'll throw it out."

Clearly he was trying to hide it, but Ben caught the origami shape of an owl. There was something more going with Asher.

Footsteps approached. Ben turned to see the fully uniformed sergeant walking their way.

"I heard noises," Dominic said. "Is everything okay out here?"

"Asher got attacked by an owl!" Mackie said, his eyes wide.

Asher shrugged. "It wasn't an attack. The animal was spooked. That's all."

Dominic narrowed his eyes. "Okay... is that why we're having a party on the side of the Capitol building?"

"I was actually coming to see you," Ben said. "Happened to catch sight of Asher as he was leaving."

Dominic's face lit up. "I'm honored you came to see me. Is there something you wanted to talk about?"

Ben gave a quick look around. Asher no longer seemed like a spooked animal. Instead, his head tilted to the side. Mackie had distracted himself with a stick and was drawing in the dirt. Louie tucked a rock into his pocket.

"Hey Louie," Asher said. "I'll show you a game you can play with those rocks. One I learned on the island."

"Really?" Louie pulled out the rock and followed Asher as he kneeled in the dirt and grabbed more rocks spread around them.

He was building a distraction so Ben could talk with Dominic. Surprising, but appreciated.

Ben pulled on Dominic's arm to turn away from the rest. The boys didn't need to hear about his fears.

"Have you heard anything about the island guards?" Ben asked under his breath.

Dominic's forehead wrinkled. "Nothing significant. They're being detained in Wuslick while R.E.I. continues their investigation."

"Not all of them," Ben snapped.

"That's true." Dominic's face was serious.

Ben wasn't sure what response he'd expected, but hearing he wasn't insane for thinking he'd seen one gave him some comfort. "I saw one at the docks. Colleen." Her name felt like poison on his lips.

A crashing sound drew Ben's attention to where Asher and Louie sat, Mackie now next to them. Asher leaned forward to grab a rock to place on top of his fallen over tower. "Sorry about that. I almost had more than you Mackie."

"No way!" Mackie grabbed another rock quickly and put it on his pile, bringing his height to four rocks.

Ben turned back to Dominic. "How many have been released?"

"I'm not sure how many," Dominic said. "Only those not involved in the bigger scheme of cure development. Some guards were there because it was their job."

Ben placed a hand to his chin. "Because Dr. Paxton got you to send them to her."

Dominic sighed. "It's not something I'm proud of. She was supposed to be the head of Merrytime Clinic requesting extra Responders from Wuslick to keep the Disparates there safe. I didn't realize they were brainwashed and sent to Lucky Island instead; otherwise, I never would have approved her request."

Ben took a deep breath to keep his thoughts from rehashing the anger he felt toward the doctor. "Is there a way to know who is still detained?"

"Not that I can view. I'm sure there's a list, but R.E.I. would be the ones in possession of it. Since it's not in Stillfield's jurisdiction, I wouldn't have access to those files."

Without the list, Ben couldn't know for sure if Oliver and 1198 were in Wuslick. It was a possibility they got themselves released the same way Colleen was out walking free. "If we have no data, then how do we know Dr. Paxton is actually in prison?"

Dominic pursed his lips. "We trust in Wuslick's word and the treaty that originally formed the Seven Republics. It's not our domain. There's nothing more we can do."

A pit dropped in Ben's stomach.

FOURTEEN

J emma followed Caty as a waitress led them to their seats in a rather popular restaurant. The walls were painted in shades of blue. Bubble lights dotted the ceiling above them, making her feel as if she'd been submerged inside a bubble bath, minus the actual water. The round, white tables matched the theme, and only a few were left open.

"So, what's good here?" Jemma asked, picking up the menu with a picture of a burger on the front. She flipped it open to read that the patty was made of black beans, which wasn't surprising considering the lack of meat available. Preen had a few dairy farms, but the cows were needed for milk, not food. And Vespher preferred to let the other Republics have the meat rations that were available, saying they preferred a plant-based diet.

The words on the menu blurred together as her eyes searched the page. She lowered the menu onto the table.

"I like their veggie lasagna, with extra cheese," Caty said.

"That sounds great." Saved her from having to decide on a meal. Her insides were mixed up enough with indecisions these days; even small choices felt insurmountable.

When a waiter arrived, placing two round cups of water on the table. Caty placed her order for a grilled cheese sandwich with a side of tomato soup.

Jemma went with the suggested lasagna, but she wasn't sure she'd eat much.

As the waiter walked away, Caty narrowed her eyes at Jemma. "So, how are you doing?"

"Well, my new job can be tough some days, what with not getting to spend as much time with the boys, but they like hanging out with Ben."

"Uh-huh. That's good..." Caty tilted her head, as if waiting for more.

"At least, most of the time they like Dad time. But Ben's different since he's been back home. Little things he used to ignore really get to him. With little kids, that's a lot."

"He's no longer on Enertin. That pill really does make a difference. Randy used to say it was like the way our bodies feel numb when sleepy, except on the inside."

It'd been a while since Caty had brought up her ex. He was a quick fling that had resulted in a forever change to her life when she found out she was pregnant with Lily. He tried to stick around, but he decided being tied down by responsibilities wasn't for him.

Jemma couldn't help but ask. "Have you heard from him recently?"

Caty shook her head. "Nothing at all for the last two years. But that's fine. I think I'm doing a fine job raising Lily on my own."

"You really are," Jemma said. "You're rocking this single mom thing. I wish I was as good of a mom as you."

Caty's cheeks reddened, matching the shade of her hair. "Stop. You're an amazing mom as well. Your boys love you. All three of them."

That brought an ache to Jemma's chest. An amazing mom wouldn't hurt her child. "It's hard being on this trip away from them."

"I can imagine. I'm glad I'm on vacation with Lily. I couldn't imagine leaving without her. But I'm sure *all* your boys will do great and be excited when you return."

Jemma nodded. "Speaking of Lily, where is she?"

"She went grocery shopping with her Mimi. Actually demanded to go with because she was tired of the snacks Mimi had at her house."

"That's *so* Lily." Laughter calmed Jemma's nerves. It was as if her problems melted away sitting across the table from her best friend. She didn't have to pretend to be anyone but herself.

And they always told each other everything. Everything except that Jemma was taking Enertin.

"There's something I've been needing to tell you," Caty said, beating Jemma to the phrase she'd been about to say.

Was Caty hiding her own secret?

"Go ahead," Jemma said, leaning forward. Her heart raced. There was no way Caty's secret was the same as Jemma's, as Caty wasn't a Disparate. At least, Jemma had never seen Caty emit energy, but at the same time, Jemma hadn't known she was a Disparate until just a few months ago.

"I'm sorry for not being there for you more after Mackie's accident."

Oh. It wasn't a secret she was revealing, but rather a confession. An ache stabbed Jemma's chest, the same way it did each time Mackie's injury was brought up.

Guilt. Grief. Regret.

"You did more than enough. I was a mess right after. I never would've gotten through those first days without you."

Caty was one of the first people to show up after Mackie was taken to the hospital. She brought them dinner, and picked up the house, and put Louie to bed. It was Jemma who had been a shell of herself. It was the first time she truly understood her mother's reaction after her dad died and Asher went missing.

A mother's pain sliced deeper than a knife could ever reach.

"Still, you weren't fully back to yourself before I left to spend the summer here. I mean, I thought with how quickly you seemed to recover, keeping my plans would be okay. But seeing you now..."

Jemma straightened. "What do you mean?"

Caty's gaze lowered to Jemma's hands. She hadn't realized how much she was brushing her fingers together until then.

"That's a nervous tell," Caty said. "Yet I don't feel extra electricity."

Jemma froze. Caty knew already. She saw through Jemma's façade and knew she was taking Enertin all this time. Did that mean others had figured it out as well? An eerie shadow seemed to fill the space around her, although the lighting stayed the same. Sounds muted and slowed as the realization that she was caught sank into Jemma's soul. Her hands were lighter, the hairs on her arms lifting.

She felt as if she were submerged in jello, her slight movements pushing against an invisible sludge.

Looking at Caty, she hadn't changed position. Her elbows rested on the table with her hands clamped together underneath her chin. Her eyes locked on Jemma, evaluating her, yet she didn't move other than her red hair floating slightly, as if affected by static electricity.

She wasn't feeling this mysterious force. Jemma slowly turned her head to the side to see that the others in the restaurant were almost frozen in their actions. Seeing an unmoving stream of water being poured into a cup caused Jemma to gasp.

With the quick intake of air, time resumed its normal functioning. Jemma looked at Caty, her eyes wide.

Caty didn't seem to have noticed anything had happened. "You've been working with Buran, haven't you?"

They'd been talking about how Jemma looked nervous moments before, yet no electricity was in the air. Caty didn't know about the Enertin. "I have been, yes..."

"I wanted to be able to help you with your emotions more, but clearly he's been a great influence. Just reassure me he won't take my spot as your best friend, okay?"

"He could never." Jemma gazed around the restaurant. No one else seemed to have been affected by the slowdown of time moments before.

It had only affected Jemma.

Caty smiled. "Good. Because I wouldn't let you leave me. No way."

The waiter arrived with their plates of food. Both the sandwich and the lasagna were cut in a circle. On theme. The aroma caused Jemma's stomach to growl, yet the thought of eating made her feel nauseous.

Whatever had happened wasn't normal. She'd only taken half a pill, and this strange reaction occurred. She'd left the other half on the train and would take it as soon as she got back.

She picked at her lasagna. After the first bite, she knew she couldn't eat anymore. Caty continued to talk about her mom and Lily, but after their conversation and the strange slowdown, Jemma's mind wouldn't let her bring up her own secret.

She jumped as her phone went off. It was time to head back to the train. She boxed up her leftovers and let Caty take them home. After giving her best friend a hug, she headed back to the station. Something strange had happened, and whatever had caused it, Jemma hoped it was a one time occurrence.

Fifteen

Quill tugged the mauve dress over her hips, shifting side to side. The small handheld mirror in her train room made it difficult for her to see the full picture, but tilting it at different angles gave her enough of an idea of how she looked. The way the fabric hugged her nonexistent curves caused bubbles in her stomach.

She tucked a strand of her blonde hair behind her ear, unsure of what she could do to make the mess of strings on her head look worthy of the gown that adorned her body.

Its beauty outshined any Quill could offer naturally; at least, that was what the tightness in her chest told her.

A knock sounded at her door. Calum must have been here already.

She hesitated.

She liked spending time with him, that was all. The fact that he gave her extra attention didn't mean anything. He'd stopped and made Klarissa feel important earlier during the shopping trip. That was who Calum was—it didn't mean he wanted to be more than friends with her.

That line of thinking calmed her nerves as she opened the door, only for her breath to catch in her throat. Calum wore the full beige suit, a white shirt underneath with the top button undone. He'd styled his dark, shaggy hair to the side, one strand breaking away from the rest to lay on his forehead.

He was gorgeous, and Quill fought the urge to ruffle his hair. He looked too good.

"Whoa, you clean up well," he said.

"Ha, my hair's a mess. They don't have many styling tools. How'd you get yours to stick to the side?"

"I used a bit of conditioner. Might not hold up to extensive sweat, but works in a pinch."

"Clever."

He offered his elbow, and Quill slipped her hand around it.

They headed to the dining cart. Quill hadn't expected any change, yet she walked into the usually crowded space to find that the tables and benches were missing, except for a couple at the back.

She gasped. At the front, where the tables were missing, the walls were covered top to bottom in sparkling blue fabric. Buran sat at one of the tables in the back, wearing a classic black suit. Jemma was next to him. Although she hadn't gone shopping with them, clearly Governor Klif had prepared something for her. She wore a red gown with long sleeves.

In the middle of the space stood her dad. He took a step toward her, wearing a navy suit that matched the curtains around them, minus the glitter. His shirt and tie were the same shade as his jacket, and his salt and pepper hair was perfectly styled, as always.

He reached a hand out to Quill. "May I have your first dance?"

"Of course." Quill placed her hand in his, feeling the warmth of his worn skin. It was a lot like him—a rough life on the outside but a soft, flowing heart on the inside. "I'm glad you asked, I'm not exactly sure how to dance."

He winced. "Another way I've failed as a father. I should've taught you this years ago. Place your other hand on my shoulder, and I'll keep this one here." He squeezed her fingers.

Quill listened to his instructions as he put his free hand on her hip.

"I'll lead and you follow my steps."

"Is there supposed to be music?" Quill asked after successfully shuffling around the train car for a moment.

Her father glanced behind her to where she'd left Calum. He nodded, and a soft melody played over the speaker system as they continued their waltz.

Quill glanced around the room as they completed slow twirls. "Who transformed this room?"

"That would be me," her father said. "With a little help from Conductor Jorge putting the seats away, Governor Suarex providing the curtains, and your friend back there helping to secure them to the ceiling."

Of course Calum had a hand in helping. "It's beautiful."

"Only the best for my daughter's birthday."

She locked eyes with her father. "My birthday isn't until this weekend."

"Yes, and we'll be a bit busy in Preen, so I wanted to celebrate early just in case. It's been a while since I've been able to do more than simply visit you for your important day, so forgive me if I want to celebrate leading up to it."

In a few days, she would turn twenty-six, and it would be the first birthday she'd had where she didn't have to follow a structured daily routine on the island.

What she wanted most was to know more about how her mother grew up. Learning about her mother might give her more insight into herself and what she was meant to accomplish in this life.

"That's really nice, Dad. I appreciate it."

"I'm sorry for being a terrible father. I know, I know—I've said that a lot, but I mean it. I let so many bad things happen to you because I wasn't strong enough to resist Dr. Paxton."

Quill rubbed her father's shoulder gently. "Remember how I was kept in the guard's warehouse on the island?"

"Yes, so they could keep a closer eye on you."

"So they could make sure I wasn't harmed. They didn't care if anyone else was hurt, but me, they did."

His brows furrowed. "They used you like a hostage to keep me in line."

"And why did they need to do that?"

"Because I'm a terrible father whose position of power put you in danger."

"No." Quill tilted his face so he was looking at her. "Dr. Paxton has the ability to manipulate minds, right?"

He nodded slightly into her hand.

"It didn't completely work on you. There was one thing you wouldn't let her take. Me. You *never* forgot me."

The song ended at her words, and he broke their hand hold to tuck a strand of hair behind her ear. "Nothing in the world would ever make me forget you, honey. No power could take you from my mind."

"And that's how I know we'll be okay," Quill said. "You don't have to worry so much about me. I'm a grown woman, and even if many of my growing years were locked away, I've got this. And I won't leave you behind."

Her father smiled. "I appreciate that, but I'll still be nervous about you to the day I die, and after. It's a father's job to care about their child."

"Just promise to give me some space to figure this world out for myself, okay?"

"I will." His eyes drifted to the entrance to the dining room, where Calum leaned against the wall. "Perhaps I'll start by letting you dance with a boy."

Calum caught their looks and walked over. "Do I get a turn to dance with the star?"

"I'm not famous, nor am I a giant ball of gas," Quill said.

Calum shifted his feet. "I was more thinking of a ball of light, but if that's where you want to take it..."

Her father cleared his throat. "I'll give you two youngins a chance on the dance floor." He gave her a side hug and went to join Buran and Jemma.

Calum wrapped both of his arms around her waist and pulled her toward him, much closer than she'd been with her dad. Her hands instinctively went to his shoulders, her elbows jutting out.

"You can wrap them around my neck; I won't bite," Calum said in a soft voice, his breath warm against her ear. Hints of honeyed citrus drew her toward him. "I mean, unless you'd like to dance with me like you did your dad?"

Quill had been wrong earlier about Calum's attention simply being who he was—this close touch caused a burning inside her she hadn't felt since that night on the lighthouse.

She kind of liked it, moving her arms to embrace Calum tighter. "If this is how the kids are dancing nowadays, I guess I should learn."

Calum's laughter made her blush. "I'm not sure what the kids are doing. If you could ask Chayse, he'd say I've been lame since I turned eighteen."

"So, for like a year?"

"Hey, I'm only *two* years younger than you."

"Soon to be three."

"That doesn't count. I'll catch up next month."

Silence settled as they swayed side to side. The music was slow, with a deep bass creating an almost ethereal atmosphere. Goosebumps dotted Quill's arms.

"Speaking of Chayse, I'm sorry he's missing."

"It's not your fault. Not like you left him. Dr. Paxton is behind his disappearance, I'm sure of it, and I'm going to figure it out. One way or another."

"But how? She's locked up in Wuslick."

"Someone somewhere knows something. I'm hoping I can find that person and get them to talk."

"Is that why you're on this trip?"

Calum's head brushed against her as he turned it toward the tables. "It's part of why I'm with Buran. When we failed to find Chayse, I couldn't give up. Buran has brought me the most connection to government officials. Klif and Suarex don't seem to know anything, but perhaps there is more to Preen than we realize."

"Are you insinuating there's something bigger going on than just Dr. Paxton?"

Calum shushed as they turned so his back was to the table. In a low voice, he said, "Think about it. Lucky Island has been operating almost two decades longer than it should've been. It has to take more than manipulating your dad to make that happen."

"Before Paxton took over the island, Director Wallow was in charge," Quill said. "He was a very... intense man. He fully believed Disparates were dangerous after he lost his son and daughter-in-law in a fire."

Calum raised an eyebrow. "I knew about the director, but didn't know that part of his history. I've heard rumors he had powers as well."

"I'm not really sure about that," Quill said. "But it wouldn't surprise me. Sometimes hatred for yourself spurs deeper hatred for others like you."

He nodded. "There's gotta be other pawns in this scheme. Ones other than those supposedly locked up."

Supposedly. "I've known Dr. Paxton for a long time," Quill admitted. "When I was at Merrytime Clinic she would visit her sister there."

Calum's whole face lit with surprise. "She has a sister?"

"Yes, two actually."

Their dancing paused. "Where are they now?"

"I knew Victoria while at Merrytime Clinic, but I'm not sure what happened to her after I was moved. Her other sister is much younger than her. I believe she's a half-sister. She became a guard on the island, so I imagine she's with the other island guards in a detention center in Wuslick."

"And Buran knows all of this?" Calum asked, pulling his hands away from her as they released from their dancing stance. The song had ended.

"I imagine he does... I mean, I think my dad would've told him..." She tilted to look around Calum to study her dad, letting a small gasp escape. "Although, if it's something Paxton didn't want him to know, he might not."

"Let's ask him." Calum grabbed her elbow and directed her to the table where the other three sat. "Do we know about Paxton's sisters?" he asked.

Governor Dunn wrinkled his brows. "Sisters? Why does that matter?"

"Ben mentioned something about Paxton having a sister on the island," Jemma said, leaning forward. "But he never learned anything about her. Do you have information?"

"Quill told me she has two. Do we know where they are? Are they supportive of Dr. Paxton's plan?"

Buran's eyes were wide as he scratched his chin. "That is something to look into. We need to make sure they don't believe the same as their sister, especially if they aren't in Wuslick custody already. Do you know anything about this?"

"I'm sorry, but this is something that I didn't know about." Quill's father looked at her. "Or was wiped from my memory. Which would mean she didn't want me to know about her family."

Buran hit his fist onto the table, a chill sweeping the room. "Why is her family history not something we looked into already? We need to contact Governor Baswort in Wuslick right away."

"It's getting late," Jemma said, placing a hand on Buran's upper arm. Quill imagined it was cold, but Jemma didn't flinch. "I agree we need to check with her, but it's something that will have to wait for the morning."

"She has a point." Quill's father stood next to her.

The conversation fell away from the topic of Dr. Paxton and Lucky Island. They spent time enjoying the music, food, and dancing long past an acceptable time to be calling anyone.

After dancing the last dance with Jemma and telling her goodnight, Quill sat herself next to Calum on the train bench. She yawned.

"Getting tired already?" Calum asked. His next words came out through his own yawn. "What about an after-party?"

Quill laughed. "Clearly, so are you."

Calum shook his head. "Nah, yawns are just contagious. I blame you for that."

"Am I interrupting something?" Governor Dunn approached them with a drink in his hand.

"Quill's barely keeping her eyes open," Calum said.

Quill playfully knocked into his arm, slightly regretting it when Calum responded to the touch with a perfect smile. Quill fought to keep from blushing. "I am not."

"It is late," her father said, glancing between the two of them. "The others have left. I'll walk her to her room," he said, his sight settling on Calum.

"Yes, of course," Calum said. "Hope you both have a good night's sleep." He exited ahead of them, leaving Quill alone with her father.

"It seems your early birthday party has come to an end. I hope it was enjoyable, minus the government matters that interrupted it."

"I don't mind the interruption. I like working with you and the others. We're trying to make the world a better place for Disparates so no one else has to grow up the way I did. I mean, that's a pretty great birthday gift."

"Indeed. And I hope you don't mind me keeping that young man from accompanying you to your room. I am still your father after all."

Quill blushed. "Nothing's going on between us."

"If you say so," he said, taking a sip of his drink. "Although his actions toward you seem to say otherwise."

She shook her head.

Calum was funny. He was kind. He was easy.

But he wasn't Asher.

Jemma tucked a strand of her hair behind her ear as she looked in the mirror in her small room. Her chat with Caty earlier hadn't gone the way she'd hoped. Then, Governor Dunn had almost caught her taking the other half of her pill when he brought the floor length red dress she now wore. She needed someone to talk to.

Ben. She pulled out her phone, thankful for Vespher's belief in pockets. After only one ring, her call was answered.

"Jemma!" Ben's reassuring voice came through the phone.

Jemma smiled. "How are my boys doing?"

"We went to the library. The boys were... great. They're sleeping now."

"I'm glad to hear that." Jemma missed being home but also appreciated the short break. Her chest tightened, guilt tugging at her for that thought. She took a breath in through her nose. "No problems or fighting?"

Ben was quiet for a moment. "Not much; we're doing good. How's your trip? It seems you're having a good time based on that picture from earlier. Red's your color."

They were good without her. "I thought you'd appreciate that text."

"I do. And I can't wait for you to wear it for me when you get home."

Jemma's eyes settled on the pill bottle on the side table. Two red pills sat at the bottom, taunting her.

"Yeah, of course. Just two nights and I'll be back." Jemma yawned.

"Sounds like it's time for you to get to bed. Sleep tight. I love you all ways. At home, or on a train."

"I love you, too." She hung up her phone and slipped it back into her pocket.

She needed to get to the back railcar that held the crates of supplies.

She hadn't heard noises in the walkway for the last ten minutes. Hopefully that meant everyone, including the train staff, were in bed. She pulled her room door open. The railcar walkway was empty, the red and yellow design on the floor leading to the back of the car calling to her.

Jemma slipped out and flattened the front of her dress with her hands as she headed away from the dining cart and sleeping quarters. The thought of changing had entered her mind, but her desperation to get to the pills won out. She needed to act now before her nerves got the better of her.

As she opened the door to the gangway between railcars, a burst of wind blew her hair into her face. She wiped it away, watching her step as she crossed the gap and entered the next cart.

This was the men's sleeping car, identical to the one she'd just been in. She kept her steps light to keep from waking anyone up.

Two more railcars and she should be there. She crossed the next gangway, grateful no one had exited their rooms. The chilly air caused her to shiver as she entered the observation car.

The windows in this railcar covered the full wall of the train, including the ceiling, except for a foot of metal that ran down the middle. She looked up, the sky showing off its celestial beauty.

Little did they know the world they shone upon.

"Hard time sleeping?"

Buran's voice startled her. Jemma looked to the side to see Buran sitting in one of the chairs that faced outside, his black suit jacket laid across the back. He'd rolled up the white sleeves of his shirt.

Her chest fell. There was no way she'd be able to pass him into the next railcar without questions. Not that she'd be able to get in anyway, as a lock pad was installed on the back door.

She'd have to find an opportunity in Preen to refill her Enertin.

"It's hard sleeping without Ben," she said.

Buran nodded and patted the seat next to him. "Keesha's gone on trips without me in the past. Visiting friends and family in Wuslick. It does feel different."

"Why don't you go with her?"

"Work." He shuffled his feet. He kept his eyes staring into the dark forest flashing by. "Also, her family isn't the biggest fan of mine."

"How could they not be? With your loyalty and dedication and, sometimes, intense ability to stare."

That got him to look at her. "I think that's part of the prob-lem. Her dad doesn't quite see things the same way I do. We've gotten into a spat or two. Figured it was best to let Keesha go without adding extra stress."

"You could always keep your mouth closed." That was what Jemma did, at least when they were still talking with Ben's family. Once his mom blamed him for his father's declining health; that was it. As much as Ben wanted to be there for his father, they couldn't continue going through the pain and guilt put upon their shoulders. And, as far as they knew, his father was still as healthy as ever.

Buran raised a brow. "Do you even know me?"

Jemma laughed. "You're right. You could never sit quietly."

"Maybe there are things I need to learn from you," Buran said. "I teach about staying in control, yet I can't keep my own ambitions reined in. Nor do I put my family first the way you do."

The phone call from earlier popped into her mind. Her boys were doing good without her. "I'm not so sure about that. I'm here instead of with my children."

"But you're here *for* them. That's putting them first. You wouldn't be here at all if you didn't think it was for the good of your family."

Jemma's gaze lowered to the blue floor. "Sometimes I question if that's the reason." She wasn't only talking about being on this trip but taking Enertin as well.

"What other reason would there be?"

"Being on my own, in control," Jemma said. "The feeling is freeing."

Buran put a hand under her chin and tilted her face to his. "You are still your own person, you know? It's okay to be a little selfish. Mackie and Louie are well taken care of. You're going to make a world that is safe for them to live in. You aren't selfish for enjoying alone time." His hand lowered.

Jemma's heart raced. He was right; she shouldn't let guilt eat at her. She was here for her boys. She took Enertin for her boys. And, as much as she missed them, she liked not having to clean up their messes, or change the channel on the television for the thirtieth time in a day, or do dishes. She really enjoyed not doing any dishes today.

That didn't mean she didn't love Mackie and Louie, and Ben. They were still the rock she centered her life around.

Buran stood. "Well, I should be getting to bed. Preen tomorrow is going to be a long day. We need good sleep for that. Shall I walk you to your room?"

Jemma took one last glance at the back locked door that held crates of Enertin on the other side. She wouldn't be able to get to them tonight.

"I'd appreciate that." But perhaps she could get to them in Preen.

Sixteen

Asher rolled over in bed, covering his face with his arm, trying to put out the fire that had been consuming him. Instead, a cold sweat seeped into his long sleeve shirt. It had been a dream. He turned over again; this time, the sun shining through his window made returning to sleep impossible. Not that he wanted to return to his nightmare about the island.

He'd overheard Ben yesterday—there was a reason he played with his nephews. Not that he didn't like playing with them, but he had an ulterior motive. After seeing the sweat beading on Ben's forehead, he could tell whatever conversation happening between Ben and Dominic was something he wanted to over-hear.

Colleen was unexpected.

Today, he'd slip away to confirm. If she was in Stillfield, she could have left him the note—notes, since there were two now. Although the second one the owl left behind yesterday was blank inside, though it was folded to match the first. An intentional reminder of the other? A warning?

He'd told Colleen about his dad and the treehouse during their long conversations on Lucky Island. She could have found it and left him the first one. Maybe the second was a call to come to her.

An uncomfortable scratching sound caused Asher to slowly peek toward the window. He met a pair of dark eyes surrounded by a black mask. A raccoon clawed at the slightly open window, causing it to open wider.

"Get out of here!" he yelled at the critter. The raccoon jumped back onto its hind legs and looked at him, its head tilted to the side. A small notch was cut into the animal's left ear.

"Shoo, go on." Asher pulled an arm out of his comforter, waving at the creature.

It didn't leave. Instead, its black eyes narrowed and it bared its teeth.

Asher shot up in bed. The audacity of this animal. An open bag of chips sat on the dresser under the window.

The raccoon resumed its previous break in attempt, not minding that Asher was awake and at least four times its size.

Asher grabbed the chips before the raccoon could slip through the crack. "Is that what you're looking for?"

The raccoon stood taller. It tilted its face to the side, as if watching to see what Asher would do next.

He slid the bag under the gap. "There, take it. It's yours."

The raccoon grabbed it with its small paws and seemed to nod a thank you at Asher before running into the woods.

"So much for getting a breeze at night." Asher closed the window. There was no chance of getting back to sleep now.

He headed to the kitchen, arriving in time to see his mother place two plates of pancakes on the table.

"You made me breakfast? How sweet."

"You deserve something special after your day yesterday," his mother said. "I'm proud of you."

His hearing. Of course. Any day now, they'd get the news that he was free from parole. That was, as long as something didn't go wrong between now and Wuslick approving the measure.

Finding Colleen would have to wait until he had a full stomach. No way his mother would let him sneak out. Plus, the aroma of fresh pancakes called to him. He sat and cut into the stack of syrup-covered goodness. Taking a bite, he looked to his mother, who stood next to the table. "Are you going to join me?" he asked, gesturing to the other plate.

"Oh, yes. Let me go get mine." She headed back to the kitchen.

Asher lowered his fork slowly, realizing what an extra breakfast plate meant.

"Mornin', kiddo," Dominic said from behind Asher.

He swallowed. "Good morning. I didn't think I'd see you again so soon. Does this mean Wuslick has already gotten back to us?"

Dominic laughed. "Good one. I see Margaret made her famous flapjacks. These smell delicious," he said to Asher's mother as she returned, stopping next to him for a kiss.

"I know they're your favorite, and you're a part of getting the judge to approve Asher's release. We couldn't have a celebratory breakfast without you," she said. "Of course I forgot the drinks." She set her plate down and headed back into the kitchen.

Asher lowered his head to focus on his food. He was glad his mom had found someone that treated her well, but being the third wheel in the house made it difficult for him to breathe. Moving out would be the first ankle-monitor-free step he took.

Would the next be going back to the island? Asher couldn't shake the note from his mind:

If you want change as much as we do, Find the island.

Maybe Colleen didn't leave it. She fought so hard to get him off the island the first time; asking him to go back wasn't like her. Unless there was something drastically important to show him there.

"So, Sarge," Asher said while taking a casual bite of food, the warm syrup sticking to the roof of his mouth as he continued, "I'm quite impressed by your work."

"You can call me Dominic, and thanks. Appreciate that."

"So you've been a Responder for, like, a century now?"

Dominic tilted his head slightly. "Thirty-two years to be exact."

"That's a long time," Asher said. "I imagine you know every protocol by the book."

"Even with being in the field for so long, law enforcement is always full of surprises." Dominic lowered his fork. "Like take a few months ago when we had to track down a fire anarchist. The first Stillfield had seen."

"I'm just glad you're home," his mother said as she entered the dining room with three full glasses of orange juice, "and I'm ready for you to put all of this behind you."

"I'm ready to get Asher off my parole list." Dominic shoved a forkful of pancakes into his mouth. "Would take a little bit off my busy schedule."

"Speaking of schedules," Margaret said, "so glad you finally got a day off."

"I'm excited to spend it sailing," Dominic said. "Blue skies, open water, smooth waves—as long as a summer storm doesn't pop up. But we just had one this past weekend, so we should have a few more days in the clear."

Margaret nodded. "What about you, Asher? Any plans for today? I'm happy to stay home with you if needed." She eyed him, as if unsure whether she wanted him to take her offer.

He worked up a lie. "I'm actually hanging with Ben and the boys today," he said, hiding his twitching hand under the table. Ironic—he'd also be heading to the docks. He'd have to wait for Dominic and his mother to set sail before he showed up to find Colleen.

His mother beamed. "Oh, that's great! The boys will be excited to see their favorite uncle."

"I'm hoping to get out again Sunday," Dominic said. "If your approval comes through by then, you'll have to join us."

Being a third wheel on a boat—or would it be a third sail—wasn't Asher's jam.

"Yeah, that could work." He'd have to think of something later to get out of Sunday; refusing the invite now would only open him up to more questions from his mother.

Asher finished his food quickly and pulled on the same jeans he wore the day before. Both owl notes, slightly bent, were tucked securely in his pocket.

With a wave goodbye, he headed out the door. At first, he headed toward Ben and Jemma's house before turning down the next street in the direction of the treehouse. His mother was dating a Responder sergeant after all. He'd have caught it if Asher went the wrong way.

The wind was stronger by the water. Asher shook his bangs out of his eyes, watching from the tree line as Colleen wrote on a clipboard. Next to her, a boat swayed in the water as R.E. I. Responders entered. He didn't see any boats matching Dominic's—he must have been out on the water already.

Coming to the docks was a foolish idea. If he stepped onto their wooden surface, his ankle bracelet alarm would sound the same as it did at the train station. He needed to get Colleen's attention and find out if she'd left him the letter.

"Alright, all onboard," Colleen said as she gave the captain of the boat a thumbs up. The boat accelerated forward, waves crashing against the side. Colleen was left alone on the wooden docks.

Asher picked up a rock and threw it. It bounced across the wood.

Colleen didn't notice, scribbling more notes onto her board.

He threw another, this time closer to where she stood, about thirty feet from where Asher hid. This time she heard it. She looked at the rock, a puzzled expression on her face.

Asher didn't waste time as he tossed another one, and another, trying to make a line of rocks to lead to where he was hidden. Colleen watched each rock as they landed. She gazed up toward the trees, her face quizzical but knowing.

Rocks were for more than just stacking on Lucky Island.

"That's enough," she shouted after his fifth rock. "Where are you?" She approached slowly, tilting her head side to side to catch a glimpse of her visitor. "This is government property, and we don't take kindly to threats.

Asher smiled as they locked eyes. "Hello there. Didn't mean to scare you."

Her eyes widened as she twisted her neck, searching around as if making sure no one else was near. "What are you doing here? This is too risky."

"I thought you'd be happy to see me."

"I am." She sighed, reaching down and scratching at her ankle. Her pant leg pulled up, revealing a matching anklet to the one Asher wore. "I don't want you to get caught, especially because they'll know you were here."

"They got you too, eh?" Asher shook his head. "They'll take whatever control they can get. Does yours also track your temperature?" She didn't have powers, so probably not, but he was curious if they made them all the same.

"No. Just my whereabouts." She pursed her lips, her face hardening. "Making sure I don't try to run away from working off my time for going along with Lizzie's plan. I wanted to stop her, not let her continuously murder people."

"Lizzie?" Asher asked, catching her casual use of the name.

Colleen put a hand to her mouth. "Dr. Paxton, of course. Elizabeth Paxton—"

"You called her 'Lizzie'?" Not once had he ever heard Colleen refer to the doctor in such a way.

"She was lizard-like, slithering around doing whatever she pleased." Colleen explained. "Lizard Lizzie."

A loud thud sounded behind Colleen. Asher looked past the leaves of his bush at a group of sailors unpacking boxes that were likely filled with fish.

Colleen twisted to follow his gaze, then returned it to him. "You know, it was a lot of work getting you free from the island. If you get caught about to break parole, I'm not sure I'd be able to break you out of prison."

"Why are people still going there?" Asher knew R.E.I. took control of Lucky Island, but without people there to take care of, they had to have another reason to keep going back. And if Colleen was the note writer, this bait might get her to admit it.

"Gathering information and evidence," Colleen said.

"Still, after three months?"

"It's a long process. R.E.I. isn't happy about what happened with Liz—Dr. Paxton. They've moved the old guards to a detention center. Made us all give statements about our time on Lucky Island. At first, I thought R.E.I. truly wanted to help fix the wrongs being done to the islanders, but it quickly turned into discussions about how dangerous the island Disparates were."

Asher scrunched his face. "Are they gathering evidence against Disparates?" If R.E.I. were to become convinced that Dr. Paxton's plan was the way to go, Buran's hopes would never pass.

"Well," Colleen whispered, "I'm not really sure. R.E.I . claims they want to figure out what went wrong in order to convict Dr. Paxton, but some of them seem to want to agree with her..."

Agree with a maniac who didn't care whom she hurt in her search of a "cure." A visual of bodies in a large grave popped into Asher's mind. "Are they looking into EnertinX?"

"Yeah." Colleen's face fell. "I think it's a possibility."

"Is that why you want me to go to the island?" Might as well be blunt. This time, her eyes widened. "What? The island is the last place you should be. You would definitely be caught and likely sent to Watershield Prison with the island Disparates."

She didn't send the notes. "Someone needs to do something about what is happening. If R.E.I. is on the island to gather the data for EnertinX, they need to have the right records. The one with the names of those who've died. With their faces. These people were real. They had meaning. And they were used as test subjects." A flicker of flames lit in Asher's right hand, encasing a leaf from the bush in front of him before extinguishing, leaving ashes in its wake. "But that record was destroyed."

Colleen's brows raised. "Asher! Your monitor."

A quick beeping came from his ankle, loud enough that the group of sailors a few boats down glanced in their direction. Asher took a breath through his nose and let it out quickly through narrow lips. The beep slowed slightly, but it was too late. His heat had been registered.

"What are you looking at?" Asher shouted toward the sailors. They shrugged and turned their attention back to their catch. He closed his eyes and focused on cooling himself. "Get me some water," he said, opening his eyes again.

Colleen grabbed a bucket that had been sitting nearby on the dock and dipped it into the ocean. When she returned, the beeping had slowed but was still ringing.

Asher grabbed the bucket and poured the cool, ocean water over his monitor, getting his pant leg wet. The monitor was waterproof, so it wouldn't hurt it, and the beeping slowed to a stop.

He met Colleen's drawn-together eyes.

"I'm serious when I say I can't break you out of prison," Colleen said. "So let's not test that, okay?"

Asher released a small chuckle, his body wanting to release the extra nerves that lingered. "I've avoided doing that for three months. My parole is supposed to be up in a few days; think Wuslick will approve the judge's recommendation without looking at an updated graph?"

Colleen gasped. "Asher Stillfield, if you just destroyed your chances of freedom because you thought I wanted you to return to Lucky Island, you are dumber than I ever thought."

This time, Asher broke into a full laugh.

Colleen cracked a smile. "Why did you think I wanted you to go there?"

"The way you were explaining what was happening," Asher said, hoping to avoid telling her more. "I thought you wanted me to do something about it."

"Still the same old Asher, I see." Colleen looked at the ground. "Honestly, I wasn't sure if I'd see you again after you came back to rescue Quill."

"I'm glad I'm seeing you now."

Colleen's eyes locked with his. Asher's heart quickened.

"Me too," she said. "Even if you only found me to get answers, at least you find me useful for something."

There it was. This woman, who had imprisoned him. Locked him away on an island. Forced him to take medication. Her greatest desire was to be needed and wanted.

This woman, who had talked with him. Got to know him. Who assisted in his escape and pointed him in the right direction to find Quill.

She was still the same Colleen. The one who would do anything to be relied on.

"I appreciate what you've done for me."

Colleen nodded. "I know, and I don't regret it. I know our relationship has always been complicated—a prisoner and a guard. You don't owe me anything."

"It's not like that. Now that I know you're here, I'll stop by again."

"I won't keep my hopes up. My position meant I was part of the problem. I was keeping you contained. I thought if I helped free you, it would somehow redeem me. But look at me." She motioned toward her anklet and the docks. "I'm still part of the problem."

Asher took a deep breath. "You have a good heart," he said slowly. "You're just stuck in a sucky situation, just like on the island. But without you, I wouldn't be here now."

The warmth in Asher's chest was genuine. Although Colleen would never fully understand what he'd been through, she was a good friend to have.

"I should get going," Asher said.

"Will it be another three months before the next visit?"

Asher laughed. "I'll come see you again when I know it's safe. Try not to get brainwashed while I'm gone, okay?"

"That should be easy enough to avoid. As long as Lizard Lizzie stays behind bars."

Asher nodded and turned. The leaves under his feet crunched as he headed back into the trees.

Colleen wasn't the mysterious sender.

Seventeen

Jemma pulled the Enertin bottle out of her bag. The two pills left inside rattled. A couple of days left. Jemma had hoped she'd be off them by this time, but she wasn't ready.

She took the full second-to-last pill. She couldn't risk another slow down.

Everyone else had already arrived in the dining room that morning, plates full of toast and reheated breakfast burritos in front of them. Since this was an older supply train, there wasn't a full kitchen on it, so they made do with transportable nourishment. Buran and Governor Dunn sat across from each other, talking in whispers. Jemma wasn't sure she wanted to join them. Her vision moved to Calum.

"Good morning," Calum said.

He sat across from Quill, who smiled at her and waved. She motioned at the empty space next to her.

Jemma grabbed her own food from the counter and joined them.

Although she knew Calum fairly well, she was still getting to know Quill. Family dinners made it hard to get to know each other on a more personal level, but she enjoyed her company. Plus, her brother *really* liked Quill, even if he wouldn't admit it. Jemma caught the looks he gave her when he didn't think anyone was watching.

Similar to the ones Calum had been giving her before Jemma sat down. Asher would lose Quill if he didn't wisen up and tell her how he felt.

"How's everyone back home doing?" Calum asked. "You called them last night, right?"

"I did." Although she'd only gotten to speak with Ben. The reminder that they were doing good with her gone made her chest tighten.

The last time she'd been away from her boys overnight—well, from Mackie—was three months ago when he was in the hospital. Not being able to hug him goodnight brought feelings reminiscent to that night. It had been the lowest point of her life.

The room around Jemma stilled. She placed her hand on the table to steady herself. Was the room stifling for anyone else?

Calum's mouth moved slowly. No words came out.

Quill's hair swayed as if moving underwater. But there was no water, only air. Jemma's fingers tingled.

Oh no.

Could her body's regulation of Enertin still be thrown off by splitting the last pill she took?

Jemma took a breath through her nose.

One... two... It escaped before she was ready. Her body shook.

She tried again. *One... two... three...* this time she was able to control her release.

As the air exited her mouth, the world around her came back into focus. She continued her breathing, expecting all eyes to be turned on her—except they weren't. Calum and Quill continued their conversation, unaware of what Jemma had experienced.

However, as she looked at Buran at the table next to them, his eyes connected with her and a look of understanding lit his face.

"Hey, you're working on your breathing," he said, smiling. "Nice practice."

So not aware that Jemma had experienced the world around her slowing for a moment, but at least he noticed her distress. She returned a half smile.

She'd lost some control for the second time, just like with Caty. And no one else seemed to notice. Electricity may not have escaped, but something had.

She had a sinking feeling. She'd taken her full pill that morning, yet this happened again. Perhaps taking red Enertin instead of yellow was finally catching up to her. A side effect of being on the wrong pill. She needed to get herself yellow ones—and soon.

At the table next to them, Governor Dunn and Buran sat in silence across from each other. As good a time as any for Jemma to distract herself with conversation.

"Have we heard from Governor Beecher yet?" Jemma leaned over to ask. The landscape outside the train had changed from rolling hills to flatland. Far in the distance, she could see yellow fields. The glass on the window was warm. They were approaching Preen.

Drastic weather changes were more or less normal. It wasn't uncommon for an extreme heatwave to blow in at the end of summer, especially in this northern Republic. It was, however, bad luck. Food shortage protocols hadn't been called for in the last decade, but it was looking possible. Jemma hoped it didn't come to that. Rationing food showed an uptick in Disparate incidents. Now would not be a good time for that.

"Not him directly," Buran answered. "His secretary said he would be expecting us. Hoping that's a good sign."

Governor Dunn nodded. "Floyd Beecher is an honest man. I expect he will be open to our proposal."

"Let's hope so." Buran had his folder of notes tucked under his arm. It was as if he feared it'd grow legs and walk away, and with it, all his data and proof that his plan was going to work.

Jemma still didn't know how to tell him it wasn't working for her. She didn't want to break him. Not yet.

"So, how do they do Enertin distribution in Preen?" she asked. It sounded like an innocent enough question.

"My understanding is it's similar to Stillfield." Governor Dunn wrinkled his face. "Or maybe that was Tesserin... Probably both. Anyway, they also have Analysts that prescribe the drugs. I believe they've requested a six month supply at a time."

Six months—that was a relief.

"Wow, they sound reliant on them," Calum joined the conversation. Quill leaned back in her seat, listening.

"To a degree, all of the Republics are," Buran said. "That's where we come in."

Jemma turned to Buran. "You've been researching Disparate incidents for awhile, right?"

He nodded.

"Is there a certain amount of time someone can take the pills without a risk of more extreme outbursts?"

"Well..." His eyes narrowed. "The data is a bit wonky. It seems when the drug was first put out, people could be on it long term without increased risk. In the last few years, that has changed. Mostly with ground energy. Regardless of when these Disparates started their medication, they've been having more frequent, intense bursts."

Jemma bit her lip. "What is the average length of time these Disparates have been taking Enertin?" Jemma had justified her medication use by the fact she was only taking a few months worth, even if it was the wrong kind. The problem was she wasn't ready to stop.

"Well, that's the thing. Some were on it for decades before having an outburst. Then, there were a few only on their second bottle. Some energy types don't seem to be as high of a risk, but I think any is still dangerous."

"So the risk has been increasing for only certain energies?" Governor Dunn asked. "Why wasn't that brought up at the governors meeting?"

"Well, the others still have outbursts, just not at as high of a rate. I didn't want to give the impression that any Enertin is safe, as there are still consequences. I'm sure a part of the unbalance is the fact that more things happen in life that cause sadness opposed to feeling super happy. I guess I get disgusted by enough stuff, but I don't come across those things as often. What about you Jemma? How often do you get afraid?"

Jemma's eyes widened. She was already lying about so much, she didn't want to hide another thing. "To be honest, I'm not sure if it ever leaves me. I've dealt with feelings of anxiety since I was young. Sometimes I am able to disassociate and distract myself from them for a moment, but the buzzing is still there under the surface. It never really goes away."

"Wow," Buran said. "Confirmation for my theory. You feel your anxiety without using your electric energy daily! You've learned to live with it. It's possible."

Jemma's stomach turned. If it weren't for Ben's Enertin pills, her anxiety would short out this train. Buran's trust and pride was misplaced.

"You said outbursts have increased drastically in the last two years," Calum said. "What has changed?"

"It's the pills themselves, right?" Jemma asked. Her thoughts went to when she'd first met Buran and his story about his brother who died in his own outburst. Buran was certain that if he hadn't been on the pills, his outburst wouldn't have been so strong and he'd still be alive.

"I believe Dr. Paxton was in charge of the island only, cor- rect?" Buran locked eyes with Governor Dunn. "She had juris- diction over the experimental drugs there, but not over Enertin production on the mainland."

"That's right." Dunn nodded. "She had no control over the formula for Enertin. She only had hands on EnertinX and the other drugs they were testing. Never on the formula for Enertin being used here."

"As far as we know." Quill's voice was quiet.

Buran raised an eyebrow in her direction. "Is there something more you know?"

A silence settled as the group waited for Quill to elaborate. Jemma felt an extra buzz of electricity in the air—Quill was nervous.

"It's just, the doctors on the island worked on a lot of research," Quill said. "I feel like I overheard conversations about Enertin a couple of times."

Calum leaned forward. "What did you hear?"

"Nothing for sure. Mostly rumors about formula changes, but I don't know if anything made it to the mainland."

"Did she ever meet with the head of production here?" Jemma asked, looking toward Governor Dunn. "If she had the power to brainwash you, she could have done the same to them."

Governor Dunn's face contorted. "I can't really be sure of that, can I? I don't remember it happening, but then I don't remember a lot of things Dr. Paxton did."

An eerie silence settled over the group. Jemma glanced out the window, noticing a building in the distance.

A train station.

They were almost to Preen, and in the distance, a faint alarm blared.

Eighteen

The alarm grew louder as Jemma stepped off the train, clutching her purse to her side. The rest of her luggage she left on the train, expecting to return later that evening to head back home, but she didn't want to risk being without her last pill. She'd be back home tomorrow to hug her boys—and hopefully have a new case of her correct pills to keep them safe.

Buran exited the train first, then her. Governor Dunn stepped out with Quill, who moved slowly and shakily.

Similar to the feel of the ground beneath Jemma's feet. There was a slight tremor in the earth.

Preen's station was mostly outdoors, with a wooden platform around them. To their side was a small enclosed building, likely where tickets and small snacks could be purchased. A breeze picked up papers that littered the area, as if someone had dropped them in a hurry to find shelter from the quake. One blew onto a wooden pole and flattened enough for Jemma to catch the words *Hungry for Justice* before the wind seized it once more.

"There should have been someone waiting for us," Buran shouted over the alarm, his phone in his hand. He'd been calling and messaging the governor's office since they first arrived, with no luck.

"They may be busy with other matters," Calum pointed out, being the last to leave the train. He lifted his hands to his sides to keep his balance as the shaking intensified.

"Whoa... okay yeah, feels like an earthquake," Buran said, bracing himself on a pillar nearby. "Maybe we should have stayed on the train."

The alarm went quiet as the shaking slowed to a stop, leaving the world eerily quiet. Although the ground seemed to stop moving, Jemma's knees continued to buckle. Earthquakes weren't common in Stillfield. When they did happen, it was usually connected to a Disparate—such as during the mall showdown.

She glanced around the station but saw no one nearby. The area was empty.

"Their Capitol is only a few blocks from the station," Governor Dunn said, brushing the front of his suit. "We can start walking there. See if there is anything we can do to assist. This felt like an actual quake."

The group followed his lead. Outside of the abandoned station, the landscape looked flatter than it had from the train. Jemma knew nothing about farming. Stillfield didn't have much space for gardens. Too much was covered by concrete. She took a deep breath and immediately wrinkled her nose, resisting the urge to gag. The air smelled like dirt combined with hints of manure.

To the North, a large warehouse loomed. A short drive from the train station, which would make it a good spot to store shipments. Jemma's conclusion seemed to be correct as large trucks drove to the supply car of the train to unload Stillfield's trade goods. They'd be taking Enertin away from the train, and with it Jemma's hope to grab a new bottle.

If they were going to that warehouse, she'd only need to find a way inside. Maybe it had extra supplies from the last drop right now. If it was on their way, it would be a quick stop...

But instead of turning down the dirt road to the warehouse, the group continued straight toward a cluster of buildings in the distance. Jemma hesitated, trying to think of an excuse to get the group to change direction, when an old, worn truck drove down the road ahead. It made its way toward them, stopping as it neared.

A head poked out of the window. "You lot the Stillfield group?"

"We are." Governor Dunn stepped forward. "And who might you be?"

"Well I'll be; you folks sure look to be from the city. I'm Prockter." He had a slight accent, his pitch increasing at the end of his sentences. "Gov'ner Beecher sent me himself. Sorry I'm late—had to wait for the tremblin' to stop. Hop in the back and I'll give you a ride the rest of the way." He motioned to the truck bed.

So much for figuring out a way to the warehouse. It would have to wait until they headed back to the train. She'd come up with something by then.

"Does that happen often?" Governor Dunn asked. "The earthquake?"

"Nah," Prockter said. "Only a few times in the last six months."

A few times in the last six months seemed like often to Jemma. If another one happened and they needed to take cover, the warehouse would be the closest building... too bad she wasn't a Ground Disparate.

"Let's go!" Calum was the first to lift himself into the back. Jemma raised an eye at Buran, who shrugged as he followed Calum's lead. Jemma and Quill joined them.

"Do you mind if I take the front seat?" Dunn asked. Clearly he was trying to keep an air of professionalism. Something about riding in the back of a dirty truck bed was beneath him. Jemma hid her laugh as he climbed into the passenger seat.

As the truck headed toward the Capitol, Jemma fought with her hair to keep it out of her face. The breeze from the truck's movement was warm, with a stickiness in the air making it difficult for her to tame her wild strands as they fought to stay plastered to her forehead. Her stomach churned and her head swirled.

Bodies jostled together as the truck stopped outside a building that was much smaller than Stillfield's Capitol building. Instead of white, marbled walls with pillars lining the front doors, it had a simple front: a blue wooden door with a window on each side. Nothing about it stood out to say it was an important place. Jemma took a deep breath to steady herself.

"Here we are," Prockter said, getting out of the truck. "Gov'ner Beecher is waiting for you inside." He leaned against his door.

The group slowly exited the vehicle. Jemma's hands shook as she clutched her stomach, holding it in a casual way so as not to bring attention to her nerves. Being out of the moving vehicle was helping the nausea, but it was still there. As they approached the front door, she noticed a small plaque above it.

"Preen Capitol," Quill read. "Guess we're at the right place."

"That's good; I was worried for a second," Calum whispered. "Thought maybe we were being kidnapped."

"What's that?" Prockter said, standing directly behind them.

Calum jumped. "Oh, n–nothing. I was just saying I love the color of this door."

"That's good. It's Preen's color. Matches the blue-sky view here. Inside, you'll find its companion. The green fields."

Sure enough, inside the room was covered head to toe in green. Green carpet. Green paint. Even the desk that stood in front of them had green laminate, with a fan blowing slightly cooler air as they approached. Jemma situated herself in front of it.

At the desk stood a short woman, her face wrinkled with age. She must have been older than Jemma's mother.

"Hello, dearies," the woman spoke. "I believe you're here to meet with Floyd, is that right? Don't think we've ever had so many people standing in this room at once."

Jemma could tell. The five of them, plus the secretary and Prockter standing at the back, made the room quite compact.

The fact that it only had the little air circulating from the fan didn't help. Jemma wiped some sweat from her brow, her breathing heavy.

"If you head down this hallway, you'll see the conference room on your right. Floyd is there waiting for you."

Governor Dunn took the lead. He reached a hand out as he entered, his back disappearing from her view for a moment. "Hello, I'm so glad you were able to meet with us."

As Jemma entered through the door, she saw Dunn's outstretched hand not being received. Governor Beecher's face was cold as stone. Streaks of natural orange hair were hidden within the white of his beard and fading hairline. His sun-damaged skin was wrinkled into a frown.

They filed in, taking seats at a table built for six.

Quill was the last standing. "Do you have a place I can wait?" she asked. "I don't really need to be in the meeting."

"Nonsense," Governor Dunn said. "You are welcome to join the discussion."

Quill bit her lip, looking uneasy. "I'd rather wait. I promise I don't mind."

Dunn narrowed his eyes. He looked as if he were about to protest once more.

"No problem," Beecher said. "Maggy will show you to the waiting room."

It was then Jemma realized the receptionist had followed them. As if they would get lost in a building so small.

Once Quill and Maggy left, Buran pulled out his research.

"That's a lot of fancy graphs you have there," Beecher said as he examined Buran's work.

"Yes," Buran said. "I have a few things to show you. I assume you understand why we are here. Considering you've been avoiding us."

Governor Beecher shot him a pointed look. "You're the ones who decided to come with only a couple days' notice during our toughest time of the year. Taking care of the needs of the people of Preen is my first priority. If you're not okay with that, then you're not welcome here."

"We are very understanding of that," Governor Dunn jumped in, his hands out in front of him as if in surrender. "I understand you've been dealing with a summer scorch. Hopefully you've been able to salvage most of the crop."

"We have." Beecher didn't elaborate further, his posture stiff.

"That's good," Buran said, reentering the conversation slowly. "We're here to help your people, and all the people of the Republics. There's a bigger issue that needs your atten—" There was a quiet thump under the table, and Buran stopped abruptly, glaring at Dunn.

"I'm so glad to hear the harvest is well." Dunn jumped in. "As my associate here said, your people are important to us as well. If now is not a good time, we understand."

Although Jemma sat across from the two, she quickly surmised how Dunn got Buran to stop talking. Buran crossed his legs, rubbing his right foot.

Beecher kept his gaze narrow. "I'll listen to what you have to say, but make it quick."

"Let me start by introducing you to my colleagues." Dunne motioned across the table. "This is Jemma. She is my Disparate Liaison, a new position I created after recent events."

Beecher nodded.

"And next to her is Calum, who works with my Disparate Representative, Buran." He motioned to each of them respectively. "Buran is passionate about his work and believes he has a way to not only help Disparates be functioning members of society, but also lower the risk of outbursts. I'm sure you'll find his data fascinating."

Dunn nodded at Buran, signifying that it was his turn.

Buran pointed at his graphs on the table and explained what he had observed the past few years with the increase in Disparate outbursts. Beecher slowly nodded along, showing interest with his gestures.

However, the more Jemma watched him, the more evident it was that his hazel eyes weren't showing true interest. Although they were pointed toward Buran's graphs, they were glossed over, as if not truly taking the information in.

"...as you can see, I've had successful trials. A good dozen Disparates are living drug free. Three of them are at this table."

At that confession, Beecher's eyes widened, recognition returning. "Three drugless Disparates here?" He looked at Governor Dunn.

"It's true," he confirmed. "And Quill, who's waiting in the other room."

Well, not exactly true, Jemma thought. But now was not the time to come clean.

Beecher stood from the table, as if ready to make a quick escape. "Then shouldn't she be here with us?"

"She's my daughter," Dunn said. "She tagged along to spend time with me and poses no threat. There's nothing to be afraid of. I've been working with these individuals, and each of them has a solid control of their energy."

Jemma's palms turned clammy.

"Is that so?" Beecher's eyes flicked from Buran to Calum to Jemma. It was on her they lingered. "No drugs whatsoever?"

Was he looking into her soul? It seemed as if he knew her secret and would reveal it at any moment. Her chest tightened as she took a shaky breath.

"None," Calum said. Beecher's eyes moved to him. "It's amazing what can be done when you intentionally work on yourself. I wouldn't say it's easy, and it takes time, but it is possible."

Beecher lowered back into his seat. "That is quite fascinating."

Jemma relaxed. Beecher didn't see through her.

"What would this change look like?" Beecher asked.

"It'd start with the process of weaning Disparates off Enertin," Buran explained. "It wouldn't be smart to stop everyone at once. Meanwhile, Analysts will receive new training on how to teach the skills I've been practicing with my own students. Once that training is implemented, removing the reliance on Enertin will be possible. I'm predicting the drugs will no longer be needed within the year."

Governor Dunn lifted an eyebrow at Buran. He had been advocating for a longer implementation timeline, which Buran continued to refuse.

Perhaps a year would be long enough for her. She could get off the drugs within a year, surely.

Just not right now.

For now, her secret would stay.

"And you think this will be safer than the medication?" Governor Beecher said, sounding wary. His eyes still scrutinized Buran.

"I know it will be," Buran said.

"What are your hesitations about the plan?" Governor Dunn asked.

"You, Stillfield, supply the medication."

"Yes..." Dunn said.

"Well, what will you trade if you stop that production?"

Jemma squirmed in her seat. They were pitching Disparate safety, but Beecher seemed to have other concerns.

"We will continue to supply other medical materials and research. Plus fish as needed to supplement your trade goods as well."

"But nothing will take the place of Enertin." Beecher's face was straight. "How is that fair? Our Republics are built on fair trading practices, are they not?"

"We will offer training," Buran said, "in a similar way of Wuslick. Education for your Analysts to help them best implement this new training plan."

"We're not interested in that. We don't have time to learn new tricks."

A chill filled the room as Buran's face fell. "The plan will fail without training. That is vital."

"Weren't you the one that refused a shipment of fur coats from Vespher recently?" Jemma asked, stepping in to give Buran a break to calm. Although the chill was somewhat refreshing, she didn't need it to become worse. The conversation from the governors meeting about the refused shipments made it odd Beecher would use trade as a reason to not support Buran's plan.

Beecher shot her a sharp look. "Fur coats are not useful in Preen. Imagine farming in one of them. When I say fair trade, I'd like to receive something worthy in exchange for providing nourishment for the Seven Republics. We're being cheated by Vespher already; don't need to add another Republic to that list."

"Give yourself time to think about it," Governor Dunn pleaded. "We're not trying to grift. It truly will be revolutionary. Trust me, the alternative isn't worth the risk."

"We are a farming Republic," Beecher said, working himself into a rage. "My people are busy, slaving away from dawn to dusk. And you want me to vote against the one thing that gives them comfort? Thank goodness we don't have many of them here. Do you know what happens to a field when a Disparate loses their self control?"

The room was silent.

"The crops go up in flames. Or get the leaves pulled off. Or"—he looked right at Buran—"they freeze over. And your safe, cushy Republic doesn't have to worry about that. No. Because you still get your quota. We deliver. Who do you think, though, is last on the list? Us."

Governor Dunn sat up. "I understand—"

"No, you don't. Your people don't starve. Mine do. Now leave." Beecher stood up and waved the group away.

The tension was thick. Jemma waited, watching for Buran's next move. But he had none. Defeated, he gathered his papers.

"Hold on," Calum spoke. "What if we could show you the benefit in our plan?"

"I already said there would be no benefit. Not for Preen."

"I disagree." Calum was rash, but confident. "Give us one chance to show you. Prove to you our plan works. If you're not convinced, we leave and end our campaign."

At that, Buran's eyes widened.

"But if you like what you see," Calum continued, "give it a chance. All I need is a field ready for harvest."

Everyone waited. Buzzing in Jemma's ears caused her hands to shake. She held them together to steady them.

"I'll need time to set it up," Beecher said. "Tomorrow, we will go on a little field trip."

Tomorrow? That would delay their trip by at least another night. Maybe longer if the train back to Stillfield didn't wait for them. She looked at Governor Dunn. Perhaps he would insist on going today.

"It would be our pleasure to demonstrate it to you tomorrow," Dunn said. Jemma's heart sank. She only had one pill left. "I'll discuss our extra night with the train."

Beecher shook his head. "No reason to sleep on those uncomfortable beds another night. I'll have Prockter send someone to gather your items and take them to a little bed and breakfast we have here. Treat you to some real Preen hospitality. Show you how it's done."

Jemma grabbed her shaking wrist at the thought of staying in this small, unwelcoming town for a night. But the warehouse they'd passed earlier came into her mind. If they had an extra night, that gave her time to figure out how to break into the warehouse and find the pills she desperately needed.

This arrangement might not be so bad after all.

NINETEEN

*P*ersonal Records.

Quill read the frosted door across the hall from the meeting room. If Preen kept records similar to Stillfield, there should be something about her mother in that room. It was as good of a place to start her search as any, but Quill doubted Preen let everyone have access.

Maggy led Quill to the front room and directed her to the row of three chairs against the wall next to the door. "You can wait here."

"Thanks," Quill said. This wasn't going to do. She'd be sitting in direct sight of Maggy, and something about her demeanor made Quill believe she wouldn't let her leave. Maybe she knew her mother. She could ask her directly for information.

A phone rang on the counter and Maggy frowned as she picked it up. "Uh-huh. Yep. I told you I would." She hung the phone up with a grimace on her face. "Some people don't know when to stop talking."

Or perhaps this older woman wouldn't be the best to ask about her mother. "I was wondering if you could point me in the direction of your restroom," Quill said.

"Right this way." Maggy walked her to a door on the other side of the hallway from her desk. Still near the waiting room, but perhaps close enough that this could work.

Quill waited a minute in the restroom before opening the door a crack, checking for Maggy at the front desk only to see her back a few feet away standing guard. She meant business.

Quill needed to get into the records room.

She needed to see if they had her mother's information.

Quill had a good view of the reception desk. On it, a pen sat atop a notepad. Perhaps if she could cause a distraction...

In her mind, the image of a kitten appeared. Quill smiled, the perfect memory to fuel her joy. It was her childhood pet, given to her for her eighth birthday. His name was Tangerine, after the color of his fur.

The pen on the desk slowly lifted. Her powers worked.

Quill visualized Tangerine chasing after a toy feather. Pawing her with tiny paws.

Wrapping his arms around her. No, this wasn't the kitten.

Pulling her closer. *I don't want to think about this.*

Asher's lips narrowing in on hers.

A heat rose to her cheeks as the pen fell onto the desk, rolled down the notebook, and stopped.

Quill paused, keeping her eye on Maggy.

The secretary didn't move. The pen falling hadn't made enough noise to draw her attention.

A ringing came again from the phone on the desk. Quill sighed as Maggy went to answer it. At least something was going her way.

"Hello," Maggy said with a scowl as she picked up.

Quill slipped out the door, flattening herself to the wall as she moved into the hallway. Once there, she pushed the handle on the records' room door.

Unlocked.

Luckily, a small town full of farmers didn't have much need to keep things locked up. Quill left the door slightly opened, just enough to hear the muffled sound of Maggy talking into the telephone.

Inside were shelves full of binders and dust. Quill held back a sneeze as she inspected the labels.

Outer Line

Hex Family Farm

Brighten Orchards

Little Field

The list went on. Records were clearly organized by region and farmland, in no particular order that was clear to Quill. She needed to find the name she'd recognize.

Ever Winery. There. Quill pulled the binder off the shelf. The records started a hundred years ago, right after the Rain of Fire. It listed homeowners, farm hands, maids, children born to whom and when.

Gilly Everly.

This was her.

Finally, she'd found her mother. Perhaps the waterfall from her postcard was near the winery where she grew up.

It was at that moment she realized the room was quiet. No muffled voice coming from the doorway.

She closed the binder and slipped it back into its spot. She made her way toward the exit, hoping she hadn't been found out.

She wasn't sure what Maggy's reaction would be, but she had a feeling any negative press would be bad for Buran's mission.

Sure enough, still no voice. Quill opened the door wider, trying to get a view of the reception desk. It was empty.

"Hello there." Maggy's voice made Quill jump. She was standing on the other side of the door. "Interesting place for you to sneak into. Mind if I get Floyd out here for a moment?"

"Oh no, I'm sure he's busy," Quill said as she slipped from the room. She kept her back against the wall and faced Maggy. Slowly, she shuffled toward the waiting room.

"It won't be a problem at all," Maggy said. "Floyd! Get on out here!"

"What are you hollerin' about out here." Governor Beecher opened the meeting room door. Quill saw into the room, locking eyes with her dad.

"Just this city dweller pokin' around our records room. I assumed you'd rather her be talking with you about what she's lookin' for. It could take ages for someone to find what they need."

Governor Beecher looked inquisitively at Quill. "Is there something specific you're searching for?"

"No, nothing." Panic rose in Quill's chest. "I was just curious how other Republics organized their records. It's something

I've been working on back home. You know, you can never be too organized." Quill smiled, hoping to defuse the situation.

"You coulda asked," Maggy said, giving Governor Beecher a side-eyed look.

He nodded a slow approval. "Go ahead. Maggy will accompany you, answer any questions you may have."

Quill raised her eyebrows. They were willing to let her look, and not just that, they would answer questions. She wasn't buying it, not after the reception they'd given them when they'd arrived. It might be some sort of trick to figure out what Stillfield was up to, but Quill didn't have anything nefarious to hide. Perhaps she could convince them of that by accepting their offer.

"Thank you," she said.

Governor Beecher returned to the meeting room. As the door closed, Quill caught sight of her dad once more. His piercing gaze shot through her.

She wasn't out of trouble just yet. Clearly, he would be seeking his own answers from her. Maybe something in what she found would help spark the return of his memories.

"Shall we go back inside the records room?" Maggy asked. Quill nodded.

Quill sneezed upon entering the dusty old room. A small shock jolted her nose as she rubbed it. Welp, she had built up enough energy to need a little escape. Hopefully that would be enough to keep from going overboard.

She let her eyes roam over the same binders as before, pretending she was reading them for the first time.

"Outer Line, Hex Family Farm, Brighten Orchards. How are these records organized?" Quill kept her voice friendly to sound nonthreatening.

"They are listed by location. The farthest West first and then spreading toward the Eastern Line."

Quill nodded.

"What kind of records are kept inside?" She wanted to know more about what to expect. The quick glimpse of her mother's page simply listed numbers.

"An array of things. Each field often tracks its own metrics. Growth charts, working hours, field crop output. Honestly, we probably aren't the most organized of Republics."

"That's okay," Quill said, smiling. "I find it fascinating to see how different places can be."

"If you say so."

"Do you not agree?" Quill scanned more books, purposely skipping over the area where her mother's was found.

"I don't have much opportunity to vacation." Maggy narrowed her eyes. "And from what I've heard about other Republics, I don't care to."

Her cold voice sent shivers down Quill's spine. There was more under her words. She'd need to approach this carefully.

She turned to Maggy. "Well, I'm quite enjoying my time here. Preen is truly beautiful."

Maggy nodded in agreement.

"I wish I could have come sooner. You know, my mother is actually from Preen."

Maggy raised an eyebrow. "Your mother?" She stared at Quill for an uncomfortable minute. Then, her eyebrows raised in surprise.

"You look just like her. I don't know how I didn't see it before."

Quill's mouth dropped. "You knew my mother?"

"Gilly... Gilly Everly. That's who. The prettiest young woman. Everyone was surprised when she chose to go to Wuslick College. Everyone except me. I knew that longing in her eyes. It was only a matter of time before she found a beau at school. And find a beau she did. Look at you!"

Maggy reached her hands out toward Quill.

"I can't believe you knew her," Quill said. "I have so many questions. How did you know her? What was she like?"

"I taught her in primary school. She had an energetic spirit but was always ready to learn. How is she doing these days? Still as feisty as ever?"

Quill's heart dropped. This woman didn't know her mom was gone.

Quill looked back at the binders, avoiding the question. "Where is Ever Winery?" she asked.

"Ah, she told you about her childhood, did she. That is in the middle of town, not too far from here actually. I believe her younger sister still lives in their old cottage."

"Sister?"

"So she didn't tell ya everything then." Maggy chuckled. "I can't blame her for wanting to keep Bea a secret. She's not the most sociable person."

Her mother had a sister. The thought had never crossed her mind. She'd been too busy imagining what it'd be like to have her mother in her life, Quill didn't stop to think if there were more people in her mother's life she'd never met.

A sister.

Quill had an aunt.

"Is there a way to get a message to her?" Quill asked.

Maggy thought for a moment. "I can send Prockter to deliver one to her mailbox right away."

"That would be great," Quill said as her mind raced. *What do you say to a long lost aunt?* She wasn't sure, but she'd have to think of something fast.

Twenty

Laughter bounced off the hallway walls as Ben finished putting a dish from dinner into the dishwasher and grabbing another. He sighed, exhaustion catching up to him.

If Oliver and 1198 were free, would they be after Ben for ruining what was happening on the island? Would they try to find him?

He hadn't truly processed that night on the island. When Mr. Dogivan's outburst split apart their warehouse prison, sacrificing his life for their escape, 1198 had been by his side. Helping him. Asking what the plan was once they made it home.

The words of betrayal shook him to his core. *We're friends, remember? I'll get you out of this, I promise.* Not from 1198; he hadn't known her long enough for her betrayal to cut as deep. Rather, the real betrayal came from Oliver, claiming to be his friend after being the reason he was sent to the island. It was because of him Ben was given EnertinX. He may have been cured of his flames, but his anger was stronger than ever.

In the end, Ben got him back by stopping Dr. Paxton. Did Oliver think of Ben as his friend now? Ben certainly didn't see him in that light. Oliver had hurt him once; would he do it again? He used to carpool with Ben to work. He knew where they lived. The thought shattered through Ben's head as a small body banged against a wall in the distance and crying followed.

What if they were here now?

Ben dropped the plate from his hands onto the floor. It shattered against the tile, but Ben didn't care. He rushed through the hallway to see Mackie crying on the floor outside the bathroom.

"What happened?" Ben asked. "Are you okay?" He searched the hallway; no one was there. He looked into the bathroom where Louie was at the sink, squeezing a line of toothpaste onto his brush.

"Louie pushed me!" Tears streamed down Mackie's face.

"Is that true?" Ben raised his voice as he glared at Louie.

"He was blocking the sink," Louie said.

"That doesn't make it okay to push him!" Ben shouted. "You don't ever hurt your brother!"

Louie's eyes widened as his lip trembled. "You're too loud."

Anger roared inside Ben, fighting to be released. "I could show you loud. Apologize to your brother."

"But he was blocking—"

"I said APOLOGIZE!" Ben released the anger that'd been building. Not only at Louie for not listening, but also the anger he held against Oliver, 1198, Dr. Paxton; the anger he held against himself for not being able to keep it together.

Louie's face broke as a wail came from him.

The noise irritated Ben further, his head stinging. He stepped out from the doorway of the bathroom and pointed down the hall. "Go to your room."

Louie rushed past him, his crying growing louder until he entered his room and likely threw himself on the bed.

Ben looked at Mackie, who sat cowering on the ground. The fear on his face reminded Ben of his failure. He had come to make sure his boys were safe from evil, not to be the cause of harm. The pit in his chest ached. "Are you okay?"

"You were really scary," Mackie said.

Ben took a deep breath. "I know. I'm sorry about that." Once again, he failed his resolve to be a better father. "Should we head to your room?"

Mackie nodded. "Will you carry me?"

Ben sighed and lifted his five-year-old into his arms. When they entered the bedroom, he saw Louie had wrapped himself in his comforter. Hiding from the monster that was his father. That was him.

Ben laid Mackie on his bed.

"When is Mom getting home?" Mackie asked.

Ben sat on the edge. Mackie watched him expectantly. "She'll be gone for a couple more days."

"How long?" Mackie prodded.

Ben sighed. "Well, let's see. She called us from Preen and is staying there tonight. Then tomorrow she'll hop on the train to come back to us, which will take another night. So two more sleeps." Hearing from Jemma earlier that evening about another night added to their trip had made him a bit sad, but he didn't let her know that. He needed her to feel confident that he'd handle things at home so she could focus on her work.

Mackie's eyes welled. "I miss her."

"I know buddy."

"I miss her too," Louie said from his bed, his voice sharp and strained from crying.

The tone caused Ben's heart to tighten. "She will be home soon." Ben reassured them both. "Should I read a story before bed?"

"Yes!" Mackie said.

Louie, however, kept one of his blankets over his head, rolling over so his back faced them. He held his favorite blanket, one with airplanes printed on it, in his arms.

Ben sighed. Louie was getting older, no longer as quick to forgive as he once was. Like Mackie was. Of course, part of that was in his nature.

Now that Ben was unmedicated, he also struggled to let things go. He'd give him time. Hopefully, in the morning, they could repair their bond.

"I guess you get to pick the book tonight."

Mackie smiled as he pointed at a red book with the picture of a whale on it. One of his favorites. Ben practically had it memorized.

Before he got to the last page, he heard Mackie's heavy breathing. He glanced at Louie, who hadn't moved. A sign he was also asleep. Ben turned off the lamp and tiptoed out of the room.

Louie deserves a better example, and Jemma is going to be disappointed, he thought as he plopped onto the couch. He promised he'd work on his temper, especially while she was gone. And he'd messed up. So badly that Louie still hadn't forgiven him.

But at least the boys were safe. That should count for something.

Ben's eyes closed as he willed his body to relax. *It wasn't that bad,* he told himself. *Jemma will understand—*

A rustling sound at the back door startled him. Just the wind; the weather had picked up in the last hour. A summer storm was rolling in. Unless it was something, or someone, more...

A loud crash sounded, as if his trashcan was knocked over.

He grabbed the metal baseball bat off the top of the fridge, the same one he'd used to scare away scavenging raccoons in the past. He hoped that was all it was this time, as a baseball bat wouldn't be much defense against a grown man. As he approached the door, the handle moved.

Fear pierced his chest, freezing him in place. This wasn't a raccoon. Someone was trying to break in. The door opened, and a black-hooded head came into view.

If only he had his flame energy. Scaring the intruder would be easy.

"Stop there," Ben said, making his voice as full and loud as he could. "Come closer and you'll regret it."

"Hey, Banjo." Two familiar green eyes met Ben's. Relief flooded into his body but was promptly met with a dam.

"Asher? What are you doing here?" Ben asked, putting the bat down. "And why are you breaking in through my back door?"

"You know me," Asher said. "Gotta keep things mysterious somehow. Plus the front door was locked."

The smug way he shrugged it off caused Ben to tense. "What if the boys had been in here? If you'd scared them, they'd have nightmares for weeks!"

"It's after bedtime." Asher walked over to the kitchen island and grabbed an apple. "Hence why I didn't knock. I'm a very considerate guy."

Ben shook his head. "Kids don't always fall asleep right at bedtime."

Asher's eyes widened. "Wait, are they still awake?" He tilted his head to see around Ben.

"No. They're... in bed asleep, but that's not the point. Just next time, knock."

Asher nodded and leaned against the counter.

Ben took a steadying breath, then turned and headed to the couch. He didn't care to continue the conversation in the kitchen.

Thankfully, Asher followed him. He took a bite of the apple as he sat in the chair across from Ben.

He said nothing. The munching of his snack was the only sound in the room. With each chew, Ben became more unsettled.

"So, what are you doing here?" Ben finally asked. He hadn't spent much time with Asher. After his parole hearing, he'd left rather quickly. But the look on his face when he snatched the piece of paper from Mackie's hand came to Ben's mind.

Asher swallowed his bite. "There's something going on, and you could be of help."

Ben narrowed his eyes. Asher wasn't one to share information, nor was he one to ask for help. At least as far as Ben had gotten to know him in this short time. And yet, hearing that someone needed his help? The quick-tempered Ben who no longer had Energy power? He couldn't help but feel a little special. It'd been a while since someone other than Jemma needed *his* help.

"Me?" Ben asked, still wary. "Does this have anything to do with the paper you grabbed yesterday?"

"You caught that, huh?"

"Hard not to," Ben said. "You stuffed it in your pocket pretty quick."

"Right." Asher winced. "It does have something to do with that."

"Go on."

Asher rolled the apple over in his hand. "You've been on the islands. More recently than I have."

Ben nodded.

"You helped get the islanders released..." Asher continued, eyeing Ben as if testing his reaction.

"More like moved than released," Ben said, thinking about Watershield Prison.

"Well," Asher said, "were *all* the Disparates moved off?"

Ben pursed his lips. "As far as I know, just R.E.I. are there finding and organizing Dr. Paxton's records."

Asher leaned back into the couch. "Yeah, that's what they say." After a moment, he shot forward and rested his arms on his knees. "But what if there's something more going on there... or, maybe someone else?"

A chill settled over Ben. "Like who?"

"I don't know." Asher wrinkled his forehead. He looked to be debating something in his mind, his eyes flickering side to side. "There's something I have to show you, but I need to know you won't say anything to anyone." The intensity in his eyes gave Ben goosebumps.

"What is it?"

"I'm serious," Asher said. "You can't even tell Jemma."

Ben paused. He'd assumed Jemma was an exception. She was his wife, and they shared everything with each other. That was what couples were supposed to do, right?

And now her own brother was asking him to keep something from her.

Asher looked desperate. If Jemma was in his spot, what would she say?

"I can't promise I'll keep it from her forever..." Ben said slowly. Asher's face fell. "However, if it's something you want to share with her yourself later, I can postpone revealing it."

A part of him feared Jemma would blame him if this was something serious and Asher didn't share it, but he had to be honest. He didn't want Asher to talk to him under false pretenses. He wasn't one to lie.

"Okay," Asher said. He reached into his backpack and rummaged through it. He pulled out two white pieces of folded paper. He recognized one of them from yesterday. The second matched it, both folded to look like owls.

"What are those?" Ben asked.

"Notes. This one was waiting for me in my treehouse." Asher handed Ben one.

"In it?"

"Yep. Left on the table."

"Do you know who left it?" Ben flipped the owl over, looking for writing. There was none.

"Open it."

Ben slid a finger under the bottom of the owl, unfolded it, and read the message inside.

"What do they mean, *Find the island*?" Ben asked, the words swirling in his mind.

Someone knew who Asher was. This handwriting didn't look familiar and likely wasn't left by one of Buran's gang. They wouldn't need to sneak a note.

"I don't know," Asher said. "We already found lighthouse island. Maybe the sender doesn't know that."

"That guard Colleen works at the docks. How well did you know her?

Asher smirked. "Decently."

"Maybe she sent them?" Ben wasn't sure what her angle would be doing so, but they had to come from someone.

"It wasn't her." Asher shook his head. "Talked with her yesterday. She thought I was an idiot even entertaining the idea."

"Oh. You really knew her then." Ben's hate toward her loosened. She didn't want to send Asher back into danger.

"She helped me get off the island the first time. She's one of the good ones."

"She did?" Perhaps he was wrong about her. Quick to throw the sins of all the guards onto one. He waited a moment to see if Asher was going to elaborate on his first escape, but he stayed silent. "It could be a set up," Ben said. "Did you have any interaction with a guard named Flannan or... Markus?" Ben knew Markus wasn't who had sent it as Ben had killed him on the island. But Flannan and Markus were friends. Maybe he was behind it.

"Yeah. I knew both," Asher said. "Markus was there before Paxton turned the island harsher. We had a lot more freedom. When she took over for the old Director, she brought in Flannan."

"You mean..." Ben hesitated. "Markus was nice once upon a time?"

Asher narrowed his gaze. "Well, I wouldn't necessarily say nice, but he was a reasonable guard. He understood if we needed something. Maybe he is the one who sent it. But that would mean that he wanted my help. That he knows something more is going on at the island."

Ben shook his head. "It's not him."

"How do you know?" Asher cocked his head questioningly at Ben.

Ben wasn't sure how to admit this. He felt heat in his chest, though he knew no fire would come from it. "He's dead. But maybe Flannan. He was friends with Markus, and he really hated Disparates. If it's him. It's a trap."

"He died?" Asher wrinkled his brow.

Thunder sounded outside, corresponding with a thought that dawned in Ben's head. Perfect to distract from their current conversation. "Or maybe the sender knows there's another island."

"Another one?" Asher's face paled.

"Maybe Dr. Paxton is hiding more information." Thoughts flooded quickly into Ben's mind, and he couldn't help but spit them out. "Maybe there's more Disparates there."

Heat radiated off Asher. Frankly, Ben couldn't blame him.

"That freaking fraud!" Asher yelled. A soft beeping came from his leg.

"Whoa, watch out for your monitor. They'll make you keep it if you heat up."

"Doesn't matter. I've already screwed that up."

Ben's mouth fell open. "You're supposed to be getting it off."

The beeping increased slightly. "Yeah, so much for that." Asher's nostrils flared.

"Well, you still need to calm down," Ben said. "Don't need it waking the boys. Or my house burning down."

Asher's shoulders rose as he took in a deep breath. He held it for a moment before releasing, the beeping quieting. "You're right. Letting them claim control of my emotions isn't going to fix anything they've done. My anger is mine to choose when to use."

His control brought a tinge of jealousy to Ben. Keeping himself from feeling anger was a form of rebellion to Asher; which made Ben's own struggle with it a sign that not all Disparates could be trusted to keep themselves contained. Because if he still had powers, he wouldn't have them controlled without Enertin.

Asher side-eyed him. "How are you doing in that department? The feelings one?"

"I suck at it." Ben's shoulders sank. Asher shared his secret notes with him; Ben could open up about his struggles. "I'm supposed to be an example to my boys. Instead I keep showing them what not to do."

"Can't be that bad," Asher said. "They seemed pretty happy yesterday."

"You didn't see them before bed tonight." Ben sighed. "Little things make me angry. It's like I'm a teenager again. I never learned how to deal with these emotions back then because a pill was shoved down my throat. But the pill didn't get rid of these emotions; it only froze them in time, and now they're back and raging."

"While I was on the island," Asher said, "I had time to figure it out. I mean, yes, we were being tested on. Especially the last few years. But before Dr. Paxton became the lead scientist, we weren't all overly drugged."

Ben looked at him wide-eyed. "So you're saying the island worked?"

"Not particularly. I still have my energy. I still get angry. And there are times I've heated up without meaning to. I've just learned my capacity for heat and figured out how to release it in a safe way. It's not a hundred percent, but it's better than how you blow up."

"Great. So you have noticed." Ben shook his head.

"Hey, it's hard to do something you've never done before." Asher placed a hand on Ben's shoulder. "Be patient with yourself. I'm sure you'll get better at it."

"What about that note?" Ben asked, pointing at the one Asher grabbed yesterday after the owl flew away. He was ready to refocus. "What does it say?" He reached for it, and Asher let him take it.

"See for yourself."

Ben unfolded it in the same manner as the other. Inside, it was blank, other than a small brown stain that seemed to be nothing. Likely from being in the dirt.

"There's nothing here," Ben said as he continued to inspect the paper.

"Nope. And I don't know what that means. Other than maybe whoever sent it wanted the owl to attack me."

Ben picked up the still unfolded first note. He squinted as he inspected the two.

"Wait... there's something different about this second note."

"What do you mean?" Asher scooted closer.

"When I tilt it in the light, there's a slight glimmer in some spots."

"Why would that be?"

"Are you familiar with invisible ink?" Ben asked. "Well, not quite ink. Some people use lemon juice." That was what the brown spot was from. Asher heating up earlier made it appear.

"What are you—"

Ben hopped up from the couch and moved to the stove, turning on the burner. A small flame flickered as he held the note over it.

"Don't burn it!" Asher said, reaching for the paper.

Ben pushed him back with his other arm. "I'm not. The paper, anyway; The lemon juice on it however..."

A brown design appeared as he shuffled the paper back and forth on the flame. Whoever sent this must have known about Asher's powers and hoped he'd somehow know to use them.

"There." Ben held the paper toward Asher.

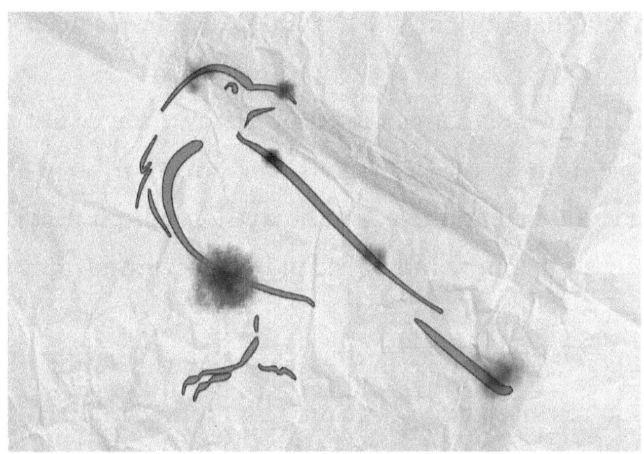

"What is it?" Asher furrowed his eyebrows as he tilted his head. "Still kinda looks like a bird."

"It is," Ben said. "Is that significant at all?"

"I don't..." Asher's eyes widened. "That's not any bird. That's a crow."

He was right. The brown lines made the shape of a large beak and wings. The side profile of a crow.

"Does that mean anything to you?" Ben eyed Asher closely. His face was hard to read.

"No." He took another bite of his apple, then passed it into his other hand. "Thanks for your help. I better get going."

"This late?" Clearly Asher had figured out more than he wanted to let on. "You could crash here for the night. Get some sleep and slip out early."

"Mom would worry if I didn't make it back."

"I could send her a message. I'm sure she'd be fine with it," Ben said.

"Nah, that's alright," Asher said. "Could use a sleep in my own bed."

There'd be no convincing him to stay. "You're not planning on running off to Lucky Island, are you?" Ben asked. Asher could be impulsive, and he wouldn't put it past him.

"Of course not. It'd be stupid to go without knowing who these notes are from."

"Okay," Ben agreed. "Just be cautious out there. Wouldn't want you to get mauled by another animal."

Asher chuckled as he walked toward the back door. "I'll try my best."

"Wait, a storm is rolling in." Ben stopped him. He grabbed a set of keys off the wall. "At least take my old car. I haven't used it since I stopped working, and it would provide you *some* shelter. You can bring it back tomorrow."

Asher stared at the keys for a moment. "Are you sure?"

Ben nodded. "If you got soaked and caught pneumonia, Jemma would be livid that I didn't let you borrow our vehicle."

"That sounds like her." Asher smirked. "Overly protective." He snatched the keys out of Ben's hand.

"Hold on," Ben said, realizing he may have made a mistake. "Do you even know how to drive?"

Asher was already headed to the garage. "Yep. Of course," he shouted over his shoulder.

Ben sighed. He wasn't sure he believed him, but if anyone could figure it out on the fly, it'd be Asher.

Ben stopped at his boys' bedroom door on the way to his room. Mackie's small body snored while Louie's was wrapped tightly inside his blanket.

He closed the door slowly. He didn't want to wake them. In the morning, they'd have their own adventure. Hopefully one that would make up for his anger outburst at Louie earlier.

The distance between them right now was too far. He needed to close the gap.

Tomorrow.

Twenty-One

Sitting behind the wheel of a car wasn't new to Asher. He hadn't lied to Ben about that, but he'd perhaps embellished the truth.

He had his driver's permit. Received it before he was kidnapped and taken to Lucky Island. Not a full license, but at least he remembered some rules of the road.

However, he'd only completed a few hours of driving. Dominic had offered to show him the ropes, but Asher was hesitant about learning from a Responder—let alone his mother's boyfriend. His lecture on how to drive a boat was enough—which, thankfully, was about to come in handy.

There was one thing Asher had lied about. He knew exactly what the crow on the note meant.

Old rock music played through the speakers. Ben's taste in music. Asher didn't mind it. Plus, the noise drowned out his racing thoughts. He could be wrong about the note being from him.

Crow was a friend he made during his time on Lucky Island. A young man with a spunky spirit—just like Asher. He was the type to call on Asher to fix the world and do so in a mysterious way.

There was one problem. A reason why Asher didn't talk about him or like to think about him much.

Crow was dead.

But then, who else would have sent him the messages?

Asher swerved as the wind outside picked up. He grabbed the wheel tighter, his knuckles turning white. That should work to keep him straight.

The light in front of him turned from green to yellow. He stomped on the break, causing his body to lurch forward. He heard objects in the back seat knock around.

Whoops. Hope I didn't break anything important.

But he kept driving. He knew what he needed to do. He'd lied to Ben about one other thing—he was going to Lucky Island. If there was a chance that Crow was alive and needed him, Asher was answering that call.

There was one person he knew with access to a boat. Well, two if he counted Samay, but stealing that man's fishing boat would certainly come with more consequences than stealing Dominic's. And there was the matter of his ankle monitor—he wouldn't get far on a boat with that thing around his leg.

He slowed as he approached his mother's house. He'd finally figured out how to be gentler with the brake during the short drive. The car came to a smooth stop next to the curb.

With it being so late, his mother was likely in bed.

He'd meant to be home sooner, before they figured out the notes were connected to Crow.

The man had been a decade younger than Asher, only fourteen when they first met. His relation to the old director of Lucky Island, Director Wallow, the one in charge before Dr. Paxton took over, had made their friendship tricky.

It also didn't help that Crow was killed during Asher's first escape.

Maybe the notes weren't from Crow. Perhaps someone else knew their background and was using it to get to him. If so, it was working.

As Asher approached the front doors, a crash from the side of the house made him jump. He looked toward the sound.

"Oh, not you again."

A raccoon scurried along the edge of the house after knocking over the trash. It stopped about a yard away from Asher, in front of the door, and stood on its hind legs. The notch in its ear told Asher it was the same animal from before.

"Shoo," Asher said, waving at the raccoon. "I need to get in the house."

The animal didn't budge.

"This is what I get for feeding a wild animal, isn't it?" Asher gently kicked toward him, which caused the raccoon to crawl a few feet away, enough to unblock the front door.

Asher used his house key to unlock it and pushed the door open.

"Ah, crap!" Before Asher could slip inside, the raccoon beat him to it, racing inside of the house. Asher followed quickly, watching as the animal ran down the hallway.

His heart raced. He just let a wild animal inside of his mother's house. She certainly would not be pleased to find that out.

Asher glanced toward the kitchen, where Dominic's briefcase sat on the table, replacing the note Asher had left for his mother earlier saying he'd be sleeping at Ben's. That had been his intention, crashing there after talking to Ben about the notes, but obviously his plan had changed.

He shook his head. Sure enough Dominic had stayed the night knowing Asher was gone. His mother was a grown woman and could do what she wanted, but he didn't want to think about it.

At least it worked in his favor tonight. The boat key might be in Dominic's bag, but there was the matter of the raccoon to attend to. He'd have to get it out first, before the animal woke up his mother and her lover.

Out of habit, Asher pulled the hood of his black sweatshirt over his head as he took soft steps down the hallway. "Here, kitty, kitty," he said softly. "Sorry for calling you a cat, but 'here, raccy, raccy' doesn't have the same ring to it."

No personally offended animals emerged.

As he neared the end of the hallway, he saw the door to his mother's room slightly ajar. His mouth widened as he froze in place, waiting to hear screams. None came. Perhaps the raccoon hadn't gone in there.

He glanced around the hallway once more. The door to the bathroom was completely shut, but his own bedroom was open halfway. He relaxed. That had to be where the raccoon went, likely searching for more chips.

Asher entered his room, his eyes adjusting quickly to the darkness. He could make out the outline of his bed, the covers still a mess on top—he wasn't used to making a bed. Dirty clothes lay on the ground. Again, he wasn't used to having so much to take care of. At least that was his excuse to his mother. She didn't seem to buy it, though, and refused to clean up after an adult man.

His gaze rested on his dresser. Nothing was there, not even old food to lure the animal in with. A layer of sweat covered his palms as he turned back toward the door, just in time to see a pile of dirty laundry on the floor move.

That's not normal. Sure, he was a little messy, but not enough to have anything growing. The notched ear of the raccoon poked out from under a shirt.

Asher grabbed the pile quickly, feeling the critter wiggle in his grasp, but the fabric of the shirt protected him from scratches. He pushed through his bedroom door with his shoulder, using both his arms to keep the animal from jumping out. As he rushed toward the front door, he lost his grip and the raccoon leaped from his arms, landing in front of him.

Instead of running away, the animal shot Asher a glare as it licked the fur on its small arms, grooming itself.

"I'm offended," Asher whispered. "I'm trying to get you back to your home outside; I don't need personal attacks about my cleanliness."

A jingling sound came from the raccoon as it continued cleaning itself. In the animal's paw was a keychain with a bolt-shaped key on the end.

Asher's eyes widened. "The monitor key. How did you get that?"

The raccoon stopped licking under its leg to meet Asher's eyes. For a second, Asher thought the animal might respond by talking, but instead it sat up and tossed the key so it landed by Asher's feet.

Asher blinked a few times in a row. This had to be a lack of sleep causing hallucinations, but that wouldn't explain how real the anklet key felt in his hand as he retrieved it. He could use it right now. Free himself from the restraint around his ankle.

But the thought of the alarm came to his mind. If he messed it up, would it sound and wake his mother and Dominic? That would be a mess to explain. Better to wait until he was far away from here. He tucked the key into his pocket.

The raccoon sat patiently on the floor.

"Guess you're my trust companion now, huh?" Asher asked.

The raccoon stared at him.

"That's one down, one to go. You didn't happen to snatch the boat key off Dominic when you grabbed this one, did you?"

The raccoon's nostrils flared as it sniffed the air. Its head twitched side-to-side before settling in the direction of the dining room table.

The briefcase. Right. Asher knew where the key was. He walked to the table, the raccoon following behind him. He wanted to tell the animal to stop, but clearly, he owed the critter something for its help. He reached into the front pocket of the briefcase first and pulled out Dominic's set of keys. He recognized the boat key from the day he tagged along on the shopping trip. He slipped the small silver key off the ring and stuffed it in his pocket.

Before heading to the front door, Asher went into the kitchen and grabbed a bag of chips from the pantry. As he turned around, the raccoon perked its ears.

"Yeah, this is for you, as long as you follow me out the front door."

The animal tilted its head to the side.

"Alright, come on," Asher said, leading the way out to the front yard.

The raccoon followed him the whole way, sitting back on its hind legs as Asher closed and locked the front door behind them. Outside, the wind had picked up. No rain yet, but it was coming. Tonight probably wasn't the best night to sail to Lucky Island, but he wasn't sure when another opportunity would come.

Asher opened the bag of chips and tossed it to the raccoon, who caught it in its small paws. "Thanks for your help."

The raccoon dug its face into the open top. Asher took that as a "you're welcome" and headed back to Ben's car. It wasn't hard to spot, as the interior lights were on.

Asher wrinkled his forehead. He didn't remember leaving any lights on, but he also wasn't fully sure they'd been off. Perhaps a button had been clicked.

He jostled around in his pocket. At this point, he had a full collection of keys. He felt the roundness of Ben's car fob and pulled it out to unlock the car.

A beep signaled his success and he climbed inside, clicking the front light off as soon as he was in. He didn't need extra light drawing attention to him, and he certainly wasn't afraid of the dark.

The drive to the docks was much smoother than his drive from Ben's to his mother's house. Turned out he should've added higher stakes to learning to drive sooner. Necessity was a great teacher.

"Unlock my monitor. Head to the boat. Get to the island." Asher repeated his plan over and over to himself to keep his focus on his goal. He looked at himself in the rearview mirror. "It'll be fine."

With it being the middle of the night, Asher didn't expect anyone to be on the water. Especially with a storm blowing in that would give him the perfect cover. If there was a Responder on patrol, Asher didn't see them. Probably hiding inside the storage shed near the Responders' section of the dock.

Still, Asher would need to be careful. His monitor suddenly felt heavy on his ankle as he stepped out of the car. He didn't worry that removing it at the docks would give away where he was going. It wouldn't take long for Dominic to realize his boat key was missing and connect the pieces. And if the alarm rang out here, there'd be no one to hear it.

"I gotta get this thing off before getting on a boat," Asher said to himself, the wind stopping his words from going far.

He grabbed the bolt key from his pocket and bent over. Before he reached his anklet, he heard a noise come from behind him, on the other side of the car. He glanced back and saw nothing, but an unease washed over him. Perhaps there was a guard patrolling nearby, or someone else sneaking to the docks at night.

Looking forward, he saw the bushes he'd hidden in when talking with Colleen. That would at least dampen any sounds.

He crouched as he rushed into the natural covering. The damp ground soaked through his black jeans as he wrestled the key into the opening on his ankle monitor. It took some fiddling, but finally, the key lined up and clicked into the hole. With a hard twist, the monitor released, making a loud beeping sound.

He held his breath, but no further sound came from the device. He peeked out of the bush, scanning the docks for movement. When he saw none, he tossed the monitor like a frisbee into the ocean. The splash it made as it sank into the water brought a strange satisfaction.

The wind had picked up, tossing boats on the waves. Asher had never driven a boat, but Dominic had explained the process to him on their shopping experience. Something about "bonding" on the water when he was released from parole.

In a way, he was fulfilling the plan of sailing when he was free. Even if he had to release himself from his monitor and he was going on his own, it still counted as a celebratory sail, right?

Asher smiled to himself. Only counted if he made it to Lucky Island alive. Although it was risky, he was already executing his plan, and he wasn't one to back off.

Unlocked the monitor. Check. Next was to head to Dominic's boat, which was a few rows down the dock. The emerald green of the bottom of the boat was black in the darkness of the night, but the name *Second Chance* plastered on the side was perfectly visible.

He untied the anchors and hopped onboard. The sail was tied down in the middle, but that wouldn't be needed. Asher wasn't taking a leisure trip, the way Dominic liked to sail. The lid of a seat at the back was open, likely blown by the wind. Asher pushed it closed and headed to the steering wheel.

He pulled out the last key he needed. It fit perfectly, the buzz of the engine waking up joined the rustling sounds around the dock.

"Get to the island," Asher said aloud as he reversed the boat from its spot. He knew the direction to go from their previous attempt at rescuing Ben. Directly west from Stillfield. He set the compass in that direction and settled in, his hands gripping the wheel tightly to keep from being blown off course.

It'd be a few hours before the island came into view. As long as the storm didn't worsen too quickly, he'd be fine.

Asher's stomach churned, but he held down what was inside. Now wasn't the time to show weakness. He'd been through worse. A little wind and rain wouldn't stop him from the truth.

He had to find Crow.

Twenty-Two

Floral wallpaper and antique clocks covered the walls in Maggy's dining room. Quill quite liked the vintage aesthetic, and she'd warmed up to Maggy, especially after her help arranging a meeting between Quill and her aunt tomorrow. The return note confirming the meeting was in Quill's pocket.

She put the last bite of her mashed potatoes into her mouth. Their meal had also included an array of fresh, roasted veggies. It was delicious.

"Thank you again so much for hosting us," her father said. "This food was divine."

Maggy gave a slight nod. "It's my pleasure as a member of Preen. Hosting visitors is a special honor bestowed to the secretary. Welcome to my bed and breakfast." Her voice was flat, giving no sign that she was actually happy.

"Such a kindness for your Republic to have accounted for," Governor Dunn said.

Calum and Buran sat next to each other across from Quill. Laughter came from their side of the table as Buran covered his mouth with his hand. Calum caught Quill's stare and brandished a large smile.

A blush filled her cheeks.

"Would you like more potatoes?" Jemma asked from where she sat on the other side of Quill, holding the bowl toward her.

"I don't know what I want," Quill said, sighing.

Jemma placed the bowl down. "That's okay. You don't have to know yet. Although I'm pretty sure dinner is wrapping up, so you might want to decide soon. At least, when it comes to eating. Other things, you've got time." Jemma gestured toward Calum, whose attention had returned to his whispered conversation with Buran.

Quill gave her a smile.

"Can I help you clean up?" her father asked Maggy.

"The kitchen is through the door behind me," Maggy said. "Soap and rags are next to the sink. I'll need a hand preparing your rooms." Maggy rose from her seat and left the room out the door opposite the kitchen. Her house wasn't large, but with two stories, it seemed plenty enough room for one old lady.

"You heard her, boys," Quill's father said. "I expect you two can take care of this?"

"Of course," Calum said, grabbing his empty plate.

"Someone should follow to help her with the rooms," Buran said, looking around.

"I can find her," Jemma said. "I'd love to be of use."

"Should I help with that too?" Quill asked, standing. She would feel awkward to be left behind.

Her father stopped her. "I was actually hoping to have a moment alone to talk." He gave her a knowing look. They hadn't had a chance to be alone since the meeting with Governor Beecher when Quill was caught in the records room. Nerves wiggled in Quill's chest.

"Good luck," Calum said with a smirk as he followed Buran through the kitchen door with his hands full of dishes.

Quill faced her father. "I was just hoping there was something there about—"

Her father put out a hand to stop her rambling. "Your birthday is tomorrow."

Quill narrowed her eyes. "Yeah, it is."

"I don't want my daughter to spend the last day as a twenty-five-year-old thinking I'm upset with her. I know you were looking for information about your mother, and I want to share what I remember with you."

"You remember more?" Quill perked up.

"Being in Preen has cleared some of the fog in my head when it came to Gilly. At times it's been a bit overwhelming, but I'm grateful."

"So you've been here with her?"

"Of course. We came to visit her family."

"What can you tell me about them? What are they like?" Quill thought about the note in her pocket. Perhaps she could tell her father about it. He might like to see Gilly's sister again.

"They did not approve of me, that's for sure." He laughed. "Sent me threats after Gilly's death, but that's not something I need to concern you with."

Quill's eyes widened. "Threats? Why would they do that?"

"They had a hard time accepting that she passed in a car accident," her father said. "Claimed they'd be conducting their own investigation into her death and would be coming after me for justice. As if I had something to do with what happened to the woman I loved!" His breathing hastened, clearly upset by the past.

Quill placed a hand on his upper arm to calm him. Even with her own doubts around her mother's passing, she believed her father. He was heartbroken by her death, even all these years later. There was no way he would've harmed her. Not by choice, anyway. Quill also used to think he'd never harm a soul, yet he'd been involved in murdering Asher's father. Was Dr. Paxton involved in her mother's death as well? "That would be difficult."

Her father relaxed. "I wanted to make sure you knew that, in case you seek out her family. They may not be welcoming, and it's not your fault."

"I appreciate that," Quill said, reaching into her pocket to pull out the note. Her father seemed to understand she'd want to talk to her extended family. He could help her figure out a plan to meet with her aunt tomorrow—

"And I need to warn you about her sister." Her father's gaze turned steely. "Avoid her as much as you can. She's not a healthy person, and she will do whatever she can to ruin anyone close to her. Do not go near Bea Everly."

Quill's brows rose as she pulled her hand out of her pocket, without the note.

"Promise me you'll stay away from her," Governor Dunn said.

Being put on the spot made Quill's anxiety rise, a light hum buzzing in her ears. She couldn't come clean to her father that she'd already been in contact with Aunt Bea. There was an urgency on his face and pleading in his eyes. Quill nodded. "Yeah, I'll stay away from her."

Relief flooded his wrinkled face.

The door behind them opened, and Jemma entered. "The rooms are ready for tonight. Boys in one, us girls in the other." Jemma smiled at Quill.

Her father smiled too. "Sounds great. Why don't you ladies head on up. We'll need our rest for our big day tomorrow." He winked at Quill.

She gave a forced smile and hugged her father goodnight before following Jemma to the staircase.

"Hey, are you feeling alright?" Jemma asked. "I can hear your nerves, with them being electric and all. I know it can feel strange staying the night in a new place, but I'll make sure you're safe."

Quill released a small breath. "I appreciate that." Her plan to see her aunt tomorrow had become complicated after learning about her father's hatred toward her, but it wasn't going to stop Quill. She needed to see the woman who cared so deeply about her mother that she was willing to fight her father for her.

That was the type of person Quill needed in her life. Someone willing to fight for her. And surely Aunt Bea couldn't be as dangerous as her father made her out to be. She lived in this small farming Republic, and, as far as Quill knew, she was the only member of her mother's family still alive.

And if she was as resentful as her father said, Quill definitely wasn't about to stand her up.

Staying an extra night meant an extra night Jemma would spend away from her boys. After helping Maggy make the beds in the room, she'd called Ben and the boys to explain the situation.

Ben hadn't sounded pleased, but there was nothing she could do about it.

She now escorted Quill to their room. Two twin beds with handmade quilts on top greeted them. Their luggage was sitting on the floor next to the door, brought over from the station by Prockter. The train had agreed to push its schedule out another day, but the conductor said they had to leave by tomorrow afternoon to make their next delivery on time.

"I'll take the one closest to the door," Quill said.

"Fine with me." Jemma placed her small purse down and sat on her bed. It was starting to get late.

The last pill inside her bag came to her mind. She tried cutting it in half; that didn't work. She'd need the full amount to get through the day tomorrow. She wasn't sure what to expect on the field.

But then that would leave her without any on the train ride home, which would be at least one more night. She'd need something to take tomorrow morning so she didn't risk shorting out the train on their journey home.

Just the thought caused a shiver to travel through her. She took a deep breath.

"So, Quill," Jemma said, wanting to get her mind off her problem. Quill's electric pulsing had lowered since they'd headed back to their room, but clearly, something was on her mind. "What were you doing in the records room earlier?"

Quill was spread out on her bed. She'd looked relaxed, but at Jemma's question, she shot up.

"I was just checking on their—"

"Organization skills? I don't think so."

Quill's cheeks reddened.

"You don't have to share if you don't want to," Jemma reassured her. She didn't want to scare her off. "But I'm here to listen if you need it. I promise I can keep a secret."

"Well..." Quill started.

Jemma sat up to give Quill her full attention, hands under her chin. "Go on."

Quill gave a small smile. "I want to know more about my mom."

That surprised Jemma. "Your mother? I thought she was dead."

"She is. That's about all I know about her."

"How old were you when she passed?" Jemma knew what it was like to lose a parent. Her heart still grieved her father.

"I was one. My dad said she died in a car accident, but something feels off about that. I wonder if he's trying to protect me. His goal is always to protect me."

Jemma nodded. She was four when Quill's mom died. Her dad worked with Dunn at the time. She remembered bringing him a meal and sending flowers, but she hadn't ever met Gilly Dunn, or baby Quill.

"I think he means well. But what were you looking for here?"

"She grew up in Preen. I want to know more about her side of the family. About *my* family."

"Did you find anything?"

Quill was quiet, contemplating. "You promise not to tell my dad any of this, right?"

Jemma was good at keeping secrets. "I promise."

"My mom has a sister. I sent her a note, asking if she'd be willing to meet with me."

Jemma widened her eyes. Why would Governor Dunn keep an aunt from Quill? "Have you heard anything back?"

Quill pulled a piece of paper out of her pocket. "She responded right away. She wants to meet with me at the local saloon tomorrow. I'm not sure how to make that happen."

"I'm sure if you explained things to your dad, he'd help you get there."

"No!" Quill's eyes widened. "I don't want him to know."

Jemma narrowed her eyes. "Because..."

"Because he asked me not to. Warned me she's dangerous even, but I don't think that's fair." Quill sighed. "He doesn't control me. I want to make my own choices."

"Even if your aunt is dangerous?" If Governor Dunn wanted to keep Quill away, there had to be a reason. But then again, he'd been brainwashed for so long, he didn't always know his own mind.

"Then I'll learn that for myself. Besides, she's an old woman. What danger could she pose?" Quill shrugged.

She had a good point. Quill was a grown woman and deserved to make her own choices. "I can help, if you promise not to go alone." Jemma wanted this for Quill. If her dad had a sibling, Jemma would want to get to know them. She'd always wanted to learn what he was like growing up. This was an important opportunity for Quill.

Quill smiled. "If you'd like to come with me, I'd appreciate that. Thank you."

It would be a good opportunity for her to get to know Quill better too. She wasn't sure what the status was between her and Asher, but she knew her brother well enough to know he was smitten with her. Although he was one who liked to keep his cards close to his chest, he couldn't shut up about Quill.

"I know you're close with my brother," Jemma said.

Quill turned her head toward Jemma. "He's an idiot."

Jemma laughed. "I can't help but agree. He likes you though." Hopefully she wasn't overstepping her bounds. She'd heard Quill and Calum laughing last night during the ball. While she liked Calum, she couldn't lie and say she wasn't rooting for Asher.

Quill sighed. "He doesn't show it."

"Has he really not made a move since the island escape?" Jemma recalled the kiss between them at the lighthouse that she had witnessed.

"Nope. We just hang out. If I try to bring up the kiss, he freaks out and leaves. Makes it hard for me to believe he likes me."

"He avoids hard things. I'd like to say the island did that to him, but it's always been in his nature."

"The island did a lot of things to a lot of people," Quill said. She wiped a tear from her eye.

"I believe he likes you. Expressing it is hard for him. Give him time; he'll come around."

"I've been giving him time."

Jemma wasn't sure what else to say. But she knew she'd be having a talk with her brother once they got back home. "Hopefully this space will be good for him." Jemma leaned back onto her pillow. She was getting sleepy. She needed energy tomorrow to figure out how to get more pills.

"Hopefully," Quill said as she yawned.

They lay quiet, the only sound coming from a branch being blown against the window in the storm outside.

Before closing her eyes, Jemma sent a message to Ben.

> Goodnight, my love. I'm sure tomorrow will be a better day. For both of us.

She tucked her phone under her pillow and waited.

A soft vibration shook Jemma awake. After tossing and turning for what seemed like forever, she'd finally gotten a wink of sleep before her alarm sounded. She grabbed her phone and turned it off, watching Quill's bed for any signs of movement.

Her blonde hair splayed out on the pillow, her breathing heavy. She hadn't woken.

Jemma slid her legs out from underneath the patchwork comforter. The hem of her pajama pants touched the wooden floor. She grabbed her shoes that she'd left next to the bed and slipped them on before sneaking out of the room. As she headed downstairs, every creak of the old wooden floor made her insides clench. If someone woke up, she'd never make it to the warehouse.

She'd seen the building on the way to Maggy's house, which was between the Preen Capitol and the train station. Within walking distance.

Outside, the sky was dark, clouds covering the moon. Camouflage to keep her hidden. The hair on her arms rose underneath her long sleeve top, though the sensation wasn't caused by the weather. The thin fabric was enough to keep her warm from the slight chill in the air. Even the heat of the day was resting.

A breeze blew through the trees around them, creating such different sounds than in Stillfield. Even the air itself felt different. As much as she hoped she'd get used to the smells of this small town, every time the wind blew, a new nauseating scent penetrated her nose. Jemma continued one foot in front of the other. The warehouse was down this road.

Finally, the large shadow of the building came into view. Tall, gray, and bigger close up than it'd looked from a distance. Jemma had a few hours before anyone should be waking up for the day. Hopefully things inside would be easy to look through.

As she approached the doors, her heart sank. A thick iron lock bolted them closed. She pulled on the chain, but they didn't loosen. Looking around the ground, she made out the faint outline of a rock just larger than her hand. She grabbed it and smashed it against the lock again and again, the sound of the crash echoing through the night. It made no difference; the lock was too thick to break. The rock rolled from her aching hand. She wouldn't be entering through the front doors.

Restlessness took over. She strode to the side of the warehouse, looking for another way in. Tall windows dotted the walls, but they were too high to reach. Along the back at the loading dock were massive rolling loading doors. She tugged on each; every one was locked.

Jemma pounded her fist against the cool metal. Tears pricked her eyes. She wouldn't be able to get inside tonight. She needed more Enertin. She had to keep her family safe.

Wiping the tears away, Jemma marched toward Maggy's house. She may not have been successful tonight, but she had another day and now knew what it would take to get inside.

Tomorrow she would find a key or a way to break apart the chain in her way.

TWENTY-THREE

Ben woke up early that morning. He knew he needed to make up for the day before, yelling at Louie during bedtime. Starting the day with chocolate chip pancakes was as good a way as any to make amends.

He piled three plates full, pouring syrup on top in a spiral. The morning was getting late; the boys were usually up by this time, but he heard no stirring. He went to their room to check on them.

Both boys were under their covers. Louie fully under his comforter, just like the night before. Not even a hair on his head poking out.

Mackie, however, rolled over in his bed. The door opening must have roused him.

"Rise and shine!" Ben smiled.

"Go away," Mackie groaned.

"It's time to get moving. We've got some fun things to do. Since mom is gone an extra night, that gives us another day just for the boys."

Mackie sat up. "What does that mean?"

Louie still hadn't moved, covered by the blankets on his bed.

"Well." Ben sat at the end of Louie's bed. "First, we are having your favorite breakfast. Doesn't that sound good?" He nudged his son then placed a hand on his hip and shook him.

Louie wasn't moving. In fact, Louie didn't feel much like Louie.

Ben pulled the blanket down. It was covering a pile of pillows.

Louie wasn't in bed.

"Where is your brother?" Ben asked Mackie.

Mackie shrugged.

Blood rushed to Ben's head. His son wasn't in his bed where he was supposed to be. He was missing—no, Ben stopped his line of thinking. Louie not being in bed didn't mean someone had taken him. He may have gotten up earlier and hidden somewhere in the house. Ben jumped up and ran into the hall.

"Louie!" he shouted, to no response. "Louie, where are you?"

He continued to call out as his head poked into his own bedroom. Then the bathroom. Then the front room, and the kitchen, and the backyard. His pulse raced quicker with each empty space.

No sign of Louie.

"Did you find him?" Mackie emerged from the hall, rubbing his eyes.

Ben stood silent. The air around him was thin as his fear from earlier came to his mind. If someone had his child, he would make them pay.

"Sometimes he likes to sleep in your car," Mackie said.

"The car..." The garage. He opened the door, his call echoing against the metal door.

No answer.

He acknowledged the empty spot where his car had been parked.

Asher took the car. Could Louie have slipped inside before Asher left with it? The pile of blankets on the bed did look to be in the same position as the night before.

He needed to call Margaret, find out if Louie was there with Asher. Ben rushed inside, searching for his phone. He finally found it, left on the kitchen counter during his mad search of the house earlier. There were no missed calls or messages. If Louie had shown up at Margaret's, she would have called.

He found her contact name and called her himself. The phone rang, then went to voicemail. Ben redialed, tapping his free hand on the countertop as he hoped for a response.

None.

He grabbed the keys to the van from the hanger and turned around to see Mackie's worried face behind him.

"Is Louie missing?" he asked.

"We're gonna find him. Grab your shoes."

Mackie quietly obeyed, as if he understood the heaviness of the situation.

The redial button was Ben's friend as they drove to his mother-in-law's house. Pulling into the driveway next to Dominic's white truck, his grasp on the steering wheel tightened.

His old car wasn't there, which meant Asher wasn't there. He hadn't passed any car accidents, but then Asher had left last night. If something had happened, it would've been cleaned by now—but also, Ben would've been called if his son was in the hospital. If they knew it was his son... if he were conscious to tell the doctors...

Maybe Margaret wasn't answering her phone because she was busy at the hospital...

Ben shook his head. He needed to get inside the house, find out if Margaret knew anything.

He unlatched Mackie from his car seat and picked him up, carrying him as he rushed to the door. It was locked. He banged on the wooden surface harder than he intended, the side of his palm throbbing.

He knocked again, and again.

"I'm coming!" Dominic's voice rang through the other side of the wood. He rubbed an eye as he opened the door. "Ben? Is Margaret supposed to be watching the boys today?"

"Is Louie here?" Ben pushed past the large man, who stepped out of the way to let him in.

"No, why would he be?" Dominic looked puzzled as Ben sat Mackie on the ground and rushed to peek into the kitchen.

Ben continued his search. "He wasn't in his bed this morning. He may have come here with Asher." Ben headed to the hallway after not seeing a trace of Louie in the front room.

Margaret exited her bedroom wearing a floral robe. "Asher was staying at your house last night."

Ben's heart stopped. "He didn't come home?"

"As far as I know, he didn't," Margaret said, heading to Asher's room across the hall from hers.

Ben joined her as she opened the door to an empty room.

No Asher. No Louie.

The notes from last night. Asher had brought them to have Ben help him figure out the message. *Go to the island*. Asher had said he wasn't foolish enough to listen—but Ben should've seen the signs. Asher was impulsive. He thought himself invincible.

"I checked his location," Dominic said. He stood at the end of the hallway, his phone in hand. "He's at the docks."

A heat unfurled inside Ben. Asher was a fool. A fool who likely had his son with him. If they were at the docks, there was time to stop them...

Dominic's face dulled. "The key is missing."

"What key?" Margaret rushed down the hall to his side. Ben followed behind her.

"For his ankle monitor, which has been at the same spot at the docks for the last six hours."

This time, Ben felt the blood leave his face. "He doesn't have a boat though. He doesn't have anywhere else to go, right?"

Dominic headed to the table, where his brown leather bag sat. Margaret's phone also lay on the tabletop. That explained the unanswered calls. Dominic tensed. "My boat key is missing."

He would kill Asher. Ben would kill Asher if he took his son to Lucky Island.

He took a deep breath in through his nose. It wasn't confirmed that Louie was with Asher; Louie could be somewhere else. He could be safe, or he could be in danger.

Would it be better for Louie to be taken by Oliver, lost wandering Stillfield, or headed to the island with Asher?

Just the thought of Lucky Island brought sweat to Ben's brow. He needed to get to the docks, see if there were clues there as to where Louie was.

"Margaret, can you watch Mackie?" he asked.

"Of course. Keep me updated if you find anything."

"I'm coming with you," Dominic said. "And I can get my squad out on a search, in case Louie isn't with Asher."

Ben nodded. That would be good.

The seriousness of the situation escalated quickly. Louie was truly missing, Ben admitted. He'd lost his oldest child while Jemma was gone, and he'd never forgive himself if they didn't find him. The thought made him nauseous. He had to find him. "We need to get going."

"I'll drive," Dominic said after finishing a text on his phone and sliding it into his pocket.

Ben was grateful for that. He was quickly spiraling, his anger and fear rising each second. Keeping his thoughts hopeful was difficult when his emotions told him to expect the worst.

Those thoughts continued on the drive to the docks. His heart leaped slightly when he saw his old, silver car parked in the lot. If Louie liked to sleep in his car, he could still be inside. And with the coolness of the night, he'd be safe there.

Ben hopped out before Dominic finished putting his truck in park. He ran to his old car and pulled on the door, which opened. Inside was Louie's extra blanket, the one with airplanes on it. He'd been here, so he wasn't kidnapped by Oliver.

Ben pulled on the blanket, but it didn't come out easily. It had gotten stuck under the front seat and Louie had left it behind. He turned to Dominic. "He was here, but he's not now."

Dominic looked toward the anchored boats. "The *Second Chance* is gone. Asher took her. Why would he steal my boat on a stormy night?"

"To go to Lucky Island, or to search for another one," Ben said.

Dominic shot him a sharp look. "What would be the reason for that?"

Ben explained his interaction with Asher the evening before, about the notes and the request for Asher to return to the island. Dominic took in the information with a studious look.

"I don't know that Asher took Louie with him on the boat, but where else would Louie be?" Ben said.

Dominic walked past Ben and onto the docks. A Responder turned from the back corner, the same one he'd seen the other day.

Colleen.

She caught sight of them as they stepped onto the wood and waved, which neither of them returned. Asher had said she was one of the good guards on the island, but then he kidnapped Ben's son.

Once they arrived at Dominic's empty boat spot, they waited for Colleen to catch up.

"Sergeant Simmons, good morning," she said. "And, Ben, right?" Her brows furrowed as she rubbed the back of her neck.

Ben didn't care to respond.

Dominic stood tall. "Were you on duty last night?"

She shook her head. "I got here about an hour ago. Traded in with Larry."

"Figures," Dominic said. "He didn't have anything unusual to report?"

"Nothing he wrote down or shared with me. I saw your boat missing, but he didn't say anything, so I figured you were out for an early sail."

"Asher's out for an early sail," Ben said. "Did you help him?" His skin crawled.

Her eyes widened. "No, I didn't know. How did he escape his ankle monitor?"

"He stole the key," Dominic said.

She gasped.

"We need to find him," Ben said. "We need a boat."

Dominic turned to face him. "R.E.I. is in charge of Lucky Island. If Stillfield intervenes, we will be breaking the agreement with Wuslick. I have no authority over this."

"Lucky island?" Colleen asked, her mouth wide.

"This is about my son!" Ben yelled. "I don't give a damn what Wuslick thinks, I'm finding *my son*."

Silence settled.

Dominic gave a strong nod. "I agree. Officer Elvene, get me the keys for Vessel Three."

No way she would help them. She was a guard on the island. She hated Disparates. Why would she help them?

Colleen shuffled in her spot for a moment before turning and heading to the Responders' shed, likely to report them to R.E.I.

Ben felt the need to run, but Dominic didn't move. "Why would she help us?" Ben asked.

"She will," Dominic said. "I've been working with her the last couple of weeks. She's not R.E.I."

Colleen returned moments later with a key ring. "I left you off the sign out sheet. If Wuslick checks, they won't be able to connect it to you."

"But they'll connect it to you," Dominic said.

Colleen nodded. "A rogue prior island guard being at fault is less suspicious than the Stillfield Responder Sergeant taking a boat out of protocol. I hope you find them."

Ben's heart softened slightly. This woman he despised was willing to put herself at risk so they could find Asher and Louie. It didn't make sense in his head, but he didn't have time to dwell. He followed Dominic onto a Responder boat and took a seat.

"We'll find them," Dominic said.

"You know the way to the island?"

"R.E.I. has been using these boats for the last couple months. A map of the route is right... here." He lifted a folded paper.

Ben nodded. The wind was light this morning, the storm from the night before having blown out.

However, the storm inside of him was brewing, breaking up as much as the water the boat sliced through.

His anger was growing.

Twenty-Four

Jemma glanced out the window of Governor Beecher's car at Prockter's truck. Buran sat in the front seat next to Prockter, his mouth moving as he chatted away. They followed them down a narrowing dirt road toward a field in the distance.

Governor Dunn sat in the front seat next to Beecher. But this time, Jemma, Quill, and Calum shared the back row instead of the truck bed. Although still tight with three adults in a row, Jemma felt less cramped than the day before. Thankfully, a cool breeze came from the car's air conditioning instead of the warm, humid air outside.

They headed in the direction of the train station before taking a sharp left, passing by the large warehouse with a lock on the door.

"Is that where you keep your supplies from the other Republics?" Jemma asked. Gathering more information about it could help her figure out a way in.

Beecher adjusted his rearview mirror until she could see his eyes in the reflection. "Yep. And the crops that are ready to send out."

"Stillfield has something similar," Governor Dunn said.

"Would we be able to see the inside?" Jemma asked.

"We'll see how things go this morning," Beecher said.

Quill squeezed Jemma's hand. Jemma hadn't forgotten about her promise last night. She'd help Quill get away at some point, a kind of birthday gift for her. Having the rest of the group tour the warehouse was a good distraction.

But right now, their focus was on this opportunity to prove to Beecher, and Preen, that Disparate energy wasn't all dangerous. That there was a reason for teaching emotion regulation. If a Disparate could control their emotions, they could control their energy and keep from having outbursts.

Calum was positive he could prove his usefulness. But Jemma was unsure. Her pulse raced. Her middle of the night adventure, and the fact that she'd taken the last of her pills that morning, didn't help her mood. Today, she *had* to find a new supply. Before tomorrow came and she caused an outburst that undid any progress they may make today.

Surely if she caused the entire electrical grid to fail in Preen, they would never approve of Buran's plan.

They stopped at the edge of a field full of corn stalks. Jemma cringed. If Calum wanted to show off his ability to harvest, corn would present quite the obstacle. Especially considering the difficulty in spotting the ready-to-harvest cobs.

At the edge of the field, an older couple stood—both farmers, presumably the owners of this land.

Calum stepped out of the car with his shoulders high. He held onto an air of confidence.

Jemma admired that. She wished she felt the same. Instead, the thought of failing today wouldn't leave her mind. And it wasn't that she didn't believe in Calum; it was that she didn't believe in herself. The image of her empty bottle wouldn't leave her mind.

"These stalks are taller than I am!" Calum said as he walked over to the field. Sure enough, they towered over him. An ear of corn next to his head was at least twice the size. "You sure know what you're doing here."

This was going to be a challenge.

"You wanted to prove your usefulness," Governor Beecher said. "This corn is ready to be harvested."

Governor Dunn whistled. "It sure is."

Jemma and Quill stayed back by the car as Buran and the governor joined Calum next to the field. They huddled together in discussion that was out of Jemma's earshot. She didn't mind; she knew this part was more on Buran and Calum than her.

Prockter joined Jemma and Quill. "You really think this will work?" he asked.

Jemma nodded.

"Absolutely!" Quill said. "Calum knows what he's doing. He's the most controlled Disparate I've ever met. You'll see." She beamed as she talked about Calum. Jemma tried to not let it bother her.

Beecher waved the farmers over to join them, which they promptly did. After a few moments, the circle stepped back. All except for Calum.

Smiling, he faced the field. He closed his eyes, concentrating on his task.

Everyone waited. Nothing was happening.

To her right, Prockter moved slightly, his coat swaying, revealing a silver Responder badge. Below it was a gun. She didn't have time to check it out further before his coat swished back to cover it.

Calum turned his head to look behind, his eyes falling on Quill. His smile widened as he faced his quest once more, raising a hand in front of him.

A single ear of corn plucked off the closest stalk and floated in the air gracefully to Quill. Governor Beecher's forehead wrinkled while the two farmers looked at each other questioningly.

The ear of corn floated in front of Quill.

"Take it," Calum said. "Count it as a birthday gift."

Quill's cheeks reddened as she plucked the corn from the air.

Calum turned to the rest of the harvest, this time raising both of his hands. Like a clip out of a ghost movie, the corn shook.

Within moments, heads of corn popped off the stalks and rose into the air. They continued to float until above the top of the corn stalks, hundreds of large, husked corn cobs decorated the sky, like stars in the daylight.

Moving his arms, Calum directed the corn to his left, next to where he'd left his huddled group. The farmers took a step back as the corn landed gently on the ground, one followed by another, creating a stack six feet tall.

Once the last corn fell, Calum sighed and bent over, his hands on his knees. Everyone rushed over. Quill was the first to greet him. She put her arm around him as she rubbed his arm.

"You did it," she said. "And, thanks, I guess." She still held the ear of corn.

Calum looked at her and smiled. A bead of sweat rolled down his cheek. "You don't think it was too corny of a gesture?"

Quill shook her head, but she smiled.

The two farmers stayed back, examining the pile. Governor Beecher had not moved. His expression was stoic and untelling.

"So," Governor Dunn said after making sure Calum was okay, "what do you think?"

"Not bad." Beecher walked over to Calum and put out a hand. Calum took it, a smile spreading across both of their faces as they shook hands.

"Think this is a skill that'd be useful for your Republic?" Buran asked.

"Absolutely." Beecher turned to the farmers. "How are the crops looking?"

This was the first time Jemma heard either of the farmers speak. "Cursed," the woman said in a shaky voice. She picked up one of the cobs and squeezed it. The insides crumbled to the earth.

Calum's face paled. "I don't understand..."

Beecher arrived at the pile of corn himself, another cob dissolving under his touch. "Is this a joke?" he asked. "Sabotage from our visitors. We welcomed you here with open hands, provided you food and shelter, and this is how you repay us?"

Jemma shot Quill a look. She held her corn delicately, like a bomb in her hands. Pulling back the husk, bits of black corn fell out.

"Could this have been done by the scorch?" Dunn asked.

"You're blaming the weather for something like this?" Beecher's face reddened. "You think we haven't seen the damage a scorch does before? This is not it."

"Look," Governor Dunn spoke. "I think there's been a misunderstand—"

"Do you see this?" Beecher picked up a cob and squeezed it to dust. "How can this be misunderstood? I've gotten your message loud and clear. I've had my suspicions about Stillfield for years. And this proves them."

Dunn's eyes widened. "What are you talking about?"

Beecher's brows furrowed. "There will be no agreement from Preen. And I ask that you all leave. Immediately. Prockter will take you back to the station."

Jemma looked at Prockter, who was no longer trying to hide his Responder badge, nor the gun on his hip. She swallowed. This was not the way today was supposed to go. Preen would never be willing to let them tour their warehouse now.

Something shiny caught her eye. Next to Prockter's weapon was a ring of keys hanging from his belt.

The Stillfield group climbed into the back of his truck. Except for Governor Dunn. Beecher wouldn't listen to any of his defenses. He climbed into his car and left as Dunn followed after him, pleading with him to listen.

"Disparates are dangerous. They are not welcome here," Beecher said as he drove away, leaving Dunn to join the rest of them in the truck.

Regardless of whatever was going on in Preen, they needed to leave. Which left Jemma less time to figure out how to get more Enertin.

Dust clouded around the truck as they drove out the same way they came in. The faces in the back were downcast, especially Buran's. Anytime someone spoke to him, he shook his head.

As they approached the main road, they passed the warehouse once again. The one Jemma needed to get inside.

She looked at Quill next to her, who held her blonde hair in one hand. Maybe there was a way to feed two birds with one corn.

They turned onto the main road, which led to the station. Thoughts ran through Jemma's head. She didn't have control of her energy at the moment, but she knew someone who did.

She scooted closer to Quill, leaning over to whisper in her ear. Quill nodded, her fierce eyes determined.

A rock the size of a baseball rolled into the path of the truck from the side of the road. Prockter swerved to miss it, but instead, he ran over a piece of metal that'd been lying on the ground, causing the truck to bounce off the road.

Jemma grabbed onto Quill's arm with one hand and braced her other against the side of the truck bed. The truck crashed into a ditch, jolting the group into the back window of the truck cab. Buran pressed against Jemma, making it hard for her to breath. Her head hit against the glass.

The world stilled. For a moment, Jemma thought it was the same phenomenon she'd experienced before, but as Buran pushed himself away from her, she realized everyone was hesitant to move because the truck was tilted forward. It took effort for each group member to right themselves.

"Is everyone okay?" Governor Dunn asked from his spot on the other side of Quill. Jemma looked in his direction to see a rip on the arm of his suit, a dark spot pooling underneath it.

Calum was near him, rubbing his leg. "I'm gonna have a nasty bruise for sure, but I don't think it's broken."

Quill nodded. She had her arms folded in front of her, one hand rubbing her bicep on the opposite arm. She'd been next to Jemma in the crash and was pressed sideways into the window.

The world spun around Jemma. "I feel a little woozy but okay."

"You hit your head; we'll need to watch for a concussion," Dunn said.

"I'm alright." Buran hopped out of the truck bed. "I'm not sure our driver is."

Jemma blinked her vision into focus and glanced through the window as she steadied herself again. Prockter was slumped over the dashboard, unmoving. Blood trickled down the side of his face.

Quill's wide eyes met hers. By her expression, Jemma imagined what she was thinking—that she'd caused this crash and possibly killed Prockter.

Jemma shook her head. "This was an accident."

Quill climbed out of the truck bed and opened the driver's door. She placed a hand on the side of Prockter's neck. "His pulse is a bit heightened, but that is expected. He likely has a nasty concussion and needs closer medical attention."

"How do you know that?" Calum asked.

Quill wiped sweat off her brow with the back of her hand. "I worked in the medical wing on Lucky Island. Picked up a thing or two."

"Should we call for help?" Governor Dunn pulled his phone out. Jemma knew before he said it that they were in the dead zone for cell service.

"Someone will need to get help." Calum joined Buran on the ground, then reached a hand out to Jemma.

She accepted it and climbed out of the truck, with Dunn following behind her on his own and standing next to Quill.

"Well, we can't leave him here like this," Buran said. "We'll need to start walking."

"Wait," Jemma said, thinking. "Walking might take too long. If we can get his truck out of the ditch, someone could drive him to the hospital." She gave a side eye to Quill, who was clenching and unclenching her fists in a rhythm.

Electricity was in the air.

"I could try to lift it out, but I don't know," Calum said. "After what happened with the corn, I might make things worse."

Buran shook his head. "I'm not sure what happened back there, but it's not your fault. You've never had anything like that happen after using your energy. I suspect a set up."

Governor Dunn stepped forward. "That's a serious allegation."

"You were there," Buran said, his voice quick. "You saw what happened. That's not something air energy would—"

"I agree," Dunn interrupted. "Calum did not cause the crop to fail. Beecher says it wasn't caused by the weather, but there has to be something."

"Beecher could be lying," Jemma said. "But if he is, why?"

Buran met her gaze. "That's the question."

"Uh, guys," Calum said. "Either way, we need to get Prockter help."

Jemma shot a look at Quill once more. This time she caught on. "I can help with freeing the truck."

Governor Dunn nodded, stepping back to give Quill and Calum room to work together. Quill closed her eyes and took deep breaths to focus, while Calum stared directly at his target until a small smirk appeared on his face. Both stuck their hands in front of them. The truck slowly shook, Prockter's body moving with it inside.

"Be gentle," Jemma said. She didn't want him to be harmed more.

"If you want us to do this," Calum said, straining, "I need quiet."

Jemma nodded and stuck to watching as the front of the truck rose a few more feet. Calum pressed his hands to the side, the truck following the motion as it moved above the dirt road.

"Alright, Quill. Slowly lower." Calum moved his arms down.

Quill followed the motion, opening her eyes once the tires touched down.

"You did it." Governor Dunn smiled. "Prockter's in the driver's seat, so we'll need to move him carefully. I can drive the truck into town; the rest of you hop in the back."

Quill's brows rose as she looked toward Jemma. She wouldn't be able to sneak away easily if they all went together.

Jemma glanced behind her. "Buran," she said, "if they set us up, could there be evidence in there?" She pointed at the warehouse, which was a short distance away.

Buran followed her line of sight. "Not sure what."

"It wouldn't hurt to check though, right?" Jemma asked. "Wuslick would want to know if Preen is lying. If we find crates of dust harvests, we'll know it wasn't Calum's energy that caused it."

Governor Dunn shook his head. "We can't go snooping around another Republic. They'll suspect us of wrongdoing."

"They already do," Buran said. "If we could figure out why, it could work in our favor. Something has put Preen on edge, and if they don't trust us enough to share what's going on, then we need to find out for ourselves."

There was Buran, the leader of the Dissentients, the standard for right. Jemma had pointed him in the direction, and he'd taken control.

"I'm going with you, then," Governor Dunn said. "I won't let you break the law without supervision."

"And what about Prockter?" Calum asked. "He needs help."

"I can take him," Quill said. "I'll get him help and meet everyone back here."

"No," Governor Dunn immediately said. "I can't have you endangering yourself that way."

"I'll be fine, Dad. I've been in more dangerous situations."

Dunn's face fell at her words. She was right. Their escape from the island was more dangerous than driving a truck back into town. Assuming she didn't get caught.

"I'll go with her." Calum stepped forward next to Quill. "That way she doesn't have to walk back by herself."

"We could use your help here," Jemma said.

Dunn's gaze speared her. Did that sound suspicious? Her hands tingled, the world around her starting to blur.

Slowly, Quill shook her head. Her voice came out as if soaked in honey, fighting to get through the thick substance. "That's okay; he can come."

With Dunn's slow nod, the world resumed its normal speed. No one else seemed to notice the disturbance.

Jemma wondered if it had all been in her head.

"Wait," Jemma said, moving to the driver's seat. Prockter's closed eyes looked almost peaceful as he slumped in his seat. She reached under his jacket, searching for the ring of keys. Her hand grazed over the cold gun before it found its target. Unhooking the clasp, she removed Prockter's keyring from his belt. As she pulled her hand back, she grabbed the gun.

"Here," she said, handing it to Calum. She tucked the keys into her pocket. Surely one would let them into the warehouse.

Calum's eyes widened. "What is this for?"

"In case he wakes up," Jemma said. "Better for you to have it than him." She walked past him and hiked in the direction of the warehouse.

Dunn and Buran shot each other a quick look as she passed, but it didn't take long for her to hear their footprints following in the dirt.

TWENTY-FIVE

The truck bumped down the road as Quill held up Prockter's body. It threatened to fall over with each turn from where Calum had gently moved it so he could drive.

This was an accident. Jemma's words to Quill ran through her mind. *He'll be okay.*

At least she'd checked on him and made sure he was still breathing before they started their drive, so Quill wasn't yet a murderer. Her time on Lucky was helpful for something; knowing how to care for wounds came in handy.

She hadn't meant for him to crash. She only wanted to add a distraction so they could think of another way to get away. Maybe a flat tire, and she would have offered to walk into town for a new one. But no. Instead, Prockter had crashed into a ditch and nearly died.

They were almost back to town. They could park Prockter's truck near a hospital—if Preen had a hospital. Maybe a doctor's office. They had to have that, right? Either way, she'd make sure he was okay before she headed to the saloon to meet with her aunt.

Maybe it was wrong of her to be contemplating going there still. A man almost died because of her, and she wasn't fully sure he would make it.

And there was the matter of Calum. She didn't need a witness to report back to her dad.

"Where do you think a hospital is?" Quill asked.

"I'm not sure," Calum said. "We can drive around and look for one."

Preen wasn't large. One long road ran down the middle of mostly unlabeled buildings. They passed one with a sign: *Steely Saloon*. This was where her aunt wanted to meet.

Small roads shot off the main street, but they seemed to wind toward farms. If medical help was down one of them, it'd take much too long to find.

Another building with a sign came into view: Preen's Public Safety Building. This could be a good spot; someone inside was bound to know how to help him. About a dozen spots lined the back of the building. They pulled over and parked.

Calum laid Prockter onto his side slowly as he let out a snore. Quill relaxed, grateful he was still breathing.

"Should we see if someone inside can help him?" Quill asked.

Calum placed two of his fingers on the side of Prockter's neck. "His pulse is strong. Hopefully, he's just sleeping off his head wound. As soon as we alert someone that we're unsupervised—well, not just unsupervised, but knocked out the Responder in charge of us—they'll round us up. Including everyone back searching through the warehouse right now."

Quill covered her mouth with her hand. "That's true. They won't like them being in there." Quill looked at Prockter's peaceful, sleeping face. "But we can't leave him out here without help. Especially in this heat."

"What if we call in a tip?" Calum asked. "There looks to be a phone number on the outside of their public safety building. Once we are safely away from here, I'll call to let them know about Prockter." He pulled his phone out and typed.

Quill gave a slow nod. "And let's make sure to leave the windows rolled down." Prockter would get help, and they wouldn't get caught with him.

Calum slipped his phone back into his pocket. "We should head back."

Quill hesitated. She glanced down the street where she'd seen Steely Saloon. "Just about," she said. "I do need to find a restroom first."

Calum smirked at her.

This excuse worked once. Why not again?

"Alright," he said. "Where do you think there is one?"

"Probably shouldn't use any inside there." She gestured to the building they were next to.

"Nope. Too suspicious."

"Maybe..." She glanced down the street as if for the first time. "I think I see a saloon that way. That could work."

"What's a saloon?" Calum asked.

Quill shrugged. She wasn't sure herself, but she knew it was where she needed to be.

They entered through two large wooden doors. Inside, the lights were dim and music filled the space. Tables and chairs were set up in an organized manner, and at the front was a bar area.

A restaurant. That was what a saloon was. Quill was grateful it wasn't something more sinister.

It was mostly empty. A couple chatted in the corner. A small group of four people sat on the opposite side, laughing.

At the bar sat a woman with curly brown hair.

Alone.

Electricity flowed through Quill. This had to be her mom's sister. The person who grew up with her. Whose blood now flowed through Quill.

"I think the bathroom might be this way..." Calum said as Quill walked in the opposite direction. "Wait..."

Quill didn't stop. Her sights were set on the stranger at the bar.

A stranger.

That made her freeze. She didn't know this woman. She wasn't sure what to expect. She didn't owe her anything. Maybe this wasn't such a good idea.

Calum was there, putting a hand on her shoulder. "Are you okay?" he asked.

At his voice, the stranger turned. Her eyes were a bright blue, holding the vastness of a clear sky. Wrinkles dotted the corners of her face.

"Hello," she said, her voice rough as leather. "I've been waiting for you."

Calum looked at Quill, confused. Quill didn't pay him any attention, as she focused it all on the woman in front of her.

"Are you…" she asked.

The woman smiled. "Bea? Why yes I am. And you must be Quill Dunn. It's about time that we met. Glad to see you're finally off that island. I have so much to tell you."

The night was cold, but it didn't bother Asher. The sun would rise soon. Plus, when he'd start to shiver, he thought about Dr. Paxton and warmed himself quickly.

There were advantages to being a Disparate.

He kept his hands on the wheel and his eyes on the moon. He knew the direction in which Lucky Island lay. Thankfully, it was right in the path of the orb above. Otherwise, he'd have no chance of finding it on his own.

The wind blew, crashing waves onto the side. A few drops of water fell from the sky. His stomach churned slightly, but he held it in and groaned.

No. Wait. That groan wasn't him. Asher glanced around the boat. Perhaps it was from the machinery inside. His heart raced at the thought. If the boat broke, he wouldn't know how to fix it.

Another groan escaped, and this time he realized it came from behind him. He turned just in time to see a small figure lean over the side of the boat and puke, the seat lid next to it open.

It took a moment for his eyes to register who the small figure was.

"Louie!" he shouted. He engaged the wheel lock, hoping he did it right from the instructions Dominic had given him, and rushed over to his nephew. "What are you doing here?"

He wrapped his arms around the small body to keep it from going overboard. Louie wiped his lips.

"I'm running away from home."

Asher widened his eyes. "Why would you do that?"

"My dad doesn't like me anymore," Louie said as he hung his head. His arms wound around his stomach.

"Really?" Asher asked. "What makes you think that?"

"He yells at me. All. The. Time."

"Hmm." Asher wasn't sure how to approach the conversation. He was in the middle of the ocean, headed to a dangerous destination. They'd been sailing for a while, now closing in on Lucky Island. But that was no place for a child.

"It's not safe for you to follow me." A new thought popped into Asher's mind. Ben's car's interior light was on when he'd first gotten in. "Were you in the car the whole time?"

"I stayed safe. I promise. I wrapped the blanket around me like a seatbelt."

"It doesn't quite work like that. And we need to get you home to your dad."

Tears welled in Louie's eyes. "I don't want to go home. I want to stay with you."

Ahead, Asher could see the outline of the island, illuminated by the rising sun behind them, despite the dark clouds. They were almost there. If he turned back now, the sun would be fully in the sky, and he couldn't be sure how long the cloud cover would keep them hidden. Rain had just started to sprinkle. Soon, it'd turn into a downpour.

He'd be seen in the daylight. And arrested, since he was breaking parole. And probably charged with kidnapping as well.

However, they could hide out on the island for the day until night fell. Sneaking Louie back home in the cover of darkness would be easier. Surely nothing too crazy would happen in one day. And a storm would be dangerous to sail in.

"Please let me stay with you," Louie begged. His wet eyes burned into Asher's soul.

The kid wanted to stay, and it was likely the safest option. At least, that was what Asher told himself.

"Okay," he said. "But you have to stay on the boat unless I tell you otherwise."

Louie beamed. Then he turned around and leaned over the edge, puking once again into the ocean.

Asher sighed. He wasn't sure what he'd just gotten himself into. Raindrops fell heavier against his skin.

About an hour later, Asher sailed to the back of the island, where they were less likely to run into any people. He was close to where they'd landed when they came to rescue Ben.

Both he and Louie were soaked from the rain that had picked up into a steady stream. It was only now slowing as they pulled onto the island.

He found some brush nearby they could dock the boat behind until night fell once again and they returned to the mainland. He couldn't risk Louie on the island.

"Is this where you were arrested?" Louie asked.

He was young and may not have understood much, but it was clear he'd been listening in on some adult conversations.

"Not where I was arrested, but where I was taken. I lived here for seventeen years, believe it or not."

"In the trees?"

"Not exactly." Asher looked at the small boy. Louie had both flame and air energy. He had all the potential to end up in the same position that Asher did.

If Asher had known of the possibility, maybe he could have been more careful. Avoided being blamed for the fire that killed his dad by remaining calm during their last interaction.

An interaction he would never be able to forgive himself for.

All he did to the people he loved was hurt them. Even if he didn't start the fire that consumed his father, his words had done damage. Pain that he would never get to apologize for and repair.

"Uncle Asher, can we go explore?" Louie asked as he stood and walked to the edge of the boat.

"Sorry, buddy," Asher said. "It's not safe."

"But I'm bored. I've been sitting all day."

"I know. Shouldn't have followed me, huh?"

Louie stuck out his tongue.

His chest tightened as he took a breath in. He released it through narrow lips.

"Look." He put an arm around Louie. "The world is a dangerous place. Especially dangerous for people like us."

"Because of our energy?" Louie looked at Asher as if he were taking in all that his uncle was saying.

"Exactly. And we have to be careful."

"Is coming to the island being careful?"

Asher was taken back by the question. Who was this six-year-old to be questioning him? But then, he was right.

"I'm not the best example to look at," Asher said, rubbing the top of Louie's head.

Louie laughed. "Yes you are. You're my favorite uncle. You're nicer than my dad."

"That's not true." Asher really needed to work with Ben more. Teach him to reserve his anger for the right time and place. He may not have had his flame energy any longer, but that didn't mean his emotions could go unchecked. He acted like a teenager instead of the grown man he was. It wasn't Ben's fault the drugs kept him subdued, but it was his responsibility to figure it out without causing more damage.

At that thought, Asher's eyes widened. Not creating emotional energy didn't let people off the hook for their emotions. They'd still have similar struggles, just maybe without as quick of a response. But damage would still be done.

Damage on little ones like Louie.

"I'm going to work with your dad," Asher said. "He's still in there. He just needs a little help learning to keep his anger under control. Just like you do."

"But he doesn't make fire anymore." Louie's face fell. "Now it's just me. And you," he said as he looked once again at his uncle, a spark of awe in his eyes.

Great, Asher thought. He didn't know how to direct a child. Thanks to his current inability to be careful and take care of the ones he loved, he was stuck on Lucky Island with a six-year-old. That certainly wouldn't earn him any uncle of the year points.

Let alone make him a viable candidate to become a father one day. He shook that last thought out of his mind. He'd accepted many years ago that children weren't on the path for him.

Safety was his path. But not for himself. Making the world safe for others like him. For Louie. And so far, he'd been failing.

Thinking about Ben, he was a good father. He would notice Louie was missing; probably already had. The freak out that would ensue when he found out what Asher did was unescapable. Asher thought he was being responsible by coming to Lucky Island to find Crow, however, Louie had thrown a wrench in that plan. Asher needed to get Louie back home. The storm has settled. They risk getting caught by R.E.I. patrols, but Louie's safety should come first.

"Hey, Lougie, I've been thinking," Asher said as he walked to the wheel, "now that the storm has passed, we can head back home."

Louie didn't respond.

"I know you're worried about it, but I'll talk to your dad," Asher continued. "Everything will be alright. I'll grab some snacks for the trip back. I'm sure you're getting hungry." He leaned over the wheel and grabbed a cooler he knew Dominic kept stocked. "What do you think? Want some trail mix?"

Asher turned around to offer Louie the bag of nuts and raisins to see the boy was missing. Louie wasn't on the boat.

Quicker than his heart raced, Asher ran to the edge. Louie had climbed over and was on the bush-covered shore.

"Louie," he whisper-yelled. "What are you doing?"

Asher jumped over the boat edge and grabbed his nephew's shoulders.

Louie's body startled. His wide eyes welled up with tears. "I saw a squirrel..."

"A squirrel? I told you to stay on the boat." Asher led Louie back toward their safe quarters.

"I... I... didn't go far..." Louie was crying. Asher had scared him.

Well, he scared me first, Asher thought, but knew he shouldn't say that out loud.

In the bushes next to them, Asher heard a scurrying. *Likely just the squirrel.* He walked faster, but then a hooting caused him to stop.

It continued. Somewhere, an owl in broad daylight was calling out.

Calling to him.

"Not now," he growled under his breath. They kept walking, but a figure stepped into their path, blocking their escape.

It was a woman wearing a Responders outfit. A silver four leaf clover was patched on her chest, although it was no longer bright. Rather, it was worn and ripped. Her hair was black, gathered in a ponytail that fell down her back.

Asher jolted back, pushing Louie behind him.

"Who are you?" Asher asked.

The woman lifted her arm out as an owl with a black face and striped white belly flew and landed onto the perch she'd made. The same owl that had dropped him the note.

"I am Leda. And I've been expecting you."

Asher narrowed his eyes. "Are there others with you?" The notes were from Crow; they had to be. Either this woman knew him or had learned about him and their history. Maybe they found records... ones that proved what Paxton was up to.

Leda shrugged. "A few."

Louie shuffled behind Asher. As tempted as Asher was to follow this woman and learn more, there was a problem. "That's cool. I'm not quite ready yet though, as you can see." He gestured at Louie. "I'll happily come back tomorrow night."

"Nonsense. There is no time," she spoke.

"Well." Asher puffed his chest. He noticed she had no weapons. "I'm not sure how you're gonna be able to keep me here."

As if on cue, two figures appeared from the bushes behind them—neither one Crow. They, too, wore old Responders uniforms, but more ripped and worn than hers. They were also missing patches.

Asher and Louie were surrounded.

"What do you want with us?" Asher asked.

"It's you we want," Leda said. "The boy can go."

"The boy doesn't have anywhere to go!" Asher held on tight to Louie's arm. Louie was shaking.

Asher wasn't about to let these strangers put him in danger. His anger was growing. He made sure to direct it through his right hand, the one currently not connected to Louie.

He released it at Leda. She didn't flinch, and with no movement, the flames that erupted toward her were met with a wall of ice. They sizzled out as steam rose into the sky. On the ground, a puddle of water was left.

Asher narrowed his eyes. "But you're a..."

"Responder? Ha," she said. "Need an extra layer of disguise here. In case we are spotted moving through the woods. Those R.E.I. people will think we are extra of them."

That wasn't a bad idea. However...

"If you aren't Responders, then who are you? And what are you doing on Lucky Island?"

"All will be explained," she said. "Once we make it to safety."

"You want us to come with you?"

"If the child truly has nowhere else to go, then yes. Both of you are welcome. I promise we will keep an eye on the youngling."

Asher looked at Louie, who had relaxed through their conversation. Asher had no more energy stored for another attack. They were outnumbered. He didn't see another choice.

"Okay. As long as you keep your promise that nothing will happen to Louie."

Leda nodded. "I assure you, nothing will. Follow." She turned to her left and headed into the trees.

Asher hesitated a moment. Behind him, the two other "guards" waited.

"Here we go, buddy," he said to Louie. "You said you were getting bored. Time for some adventure."

Louie smiled at him.

The boy's smile crushed his heart.

He'd seen that look too many times on faces he'd failed.

The look of trust.

TWENTY-SIX

In the sunlight, the warehouse seemed less threatening than the night before. This time, Jemma knew how to beat it. She pulled the keyring out of her pocket.

"It's locked," Dunn said as Jemma pushed past him. "It also looks like someone tried to break in."

Although her attempt last night was unsuccessful, she had dented the lock, the key opening smashed in. In the dark, she'd created an extra challenge for herself. If she held the correct key, it may not work because of the damage. She fumbled the dozen keys in her hands, isolating one after the other to try to insert.

"Where did you get those?" Buran asked.

"Prockter. I figured they wouldn't keep this place unlocked for just anyone to get inside." Jemma's cheeks flushed thinking about how she should have figured that last night.

Dunn walked to stand next to her. "That was some forward thinking. Glad to have you on our team."

Jemma gave a small smile as she tried the next key. No match. Another. She was able to maneuver it through the dented opening, but it wouldn't turn. She was getting close to the last option.

"Maybe he didn't have a key for this," Buran said. "He was a Responder, not a supply worker."

When the last key didn't fit inside the lock, Jemma groaned and threw the ring of keys to the ground, creating a puff of dust. "How are we supposed to get in then?" Jemma's voice was louder than she'd meant it to be.

Dunn took a step back and shrugged. "Perhaps we should head to the train station and wait for Quill and Calum."

Jemma shot a frenzied look at Buran. "We can't give up! There's gotta be a way inside."

Buran's brows furrowed as he stepped to the lock. He tugged on the chain. "Get me a rock."

The rock from last night was near her feet. It had only caused her more trouble, but there was nothing to lose now. Buran was stronger than her; perhaps he could smash it in.

"Will this work?" She held the rock out to him.

He didn't take it right away. Instead, he closed his eyes, and a scowl formed on his face as ice covered the lock. He took the rock from Jemma's outstretched hand and smashed the lock into small pieces. "Let's see what's so important in here that they needed that thick of a lock," he said.

Dunn shook his head. "I'm not feeling good about break-ing in."

"And I don't feel good about them using us as scapegoats," Jemma said, keeping up her charade as she pushed her way inside. It was true she wanted to know if Preen was hiding something from them, but her ulterior motive came first.

Stacks and stacks of boxes lined the walls. Ones from Wuslick and Tesserin. One full section was dedicated to Vespher. No wonder they sent the last shipment of clothes back. They'd barely touched the ones they had.

But why?

Jemma searched the boxes for Stillfield. Perhaps that was the resource they did use. However, Beecher's hatred toward them seemed to say otherwise.

The farther down they searched, the more Jemma sweated. If she couldn't find those pills, she wasn't sure what would happen on the train that night.

"Can you believe it?" Dunn said. "All these resources. Somehow they've been getting more than they need."

"Or they haven't been using them." Buran stopped to inspect a crate closer. "From Hastiet, full of salt."

"Didn't Beecher complain that they weren't getting enough for his people?" Jemma asked. "He must have only been referring to fresh food."

"I'm not so sure," Dunn said. "This crate is from us."

Jemma's heart skipped a beat. Was that the crate she needed?

"Full of iced fish," he finished.

Nope. Not quite, but she headed in that direction regardless.

As she searched through the boxes in that area, she noticed a door. *What is in there?* she wondered as she approached.

Thankfully, this door was unlocked. Preen must have counted on the outer doors to keep out anyone unauthorized. Inside were more crates, the tops of which met her hip. Each with a label from Stillfield.

Enertin - White 50mg

Enertin - Green 100mg

Enertin - Yellow 300mg

And on and on. Jemma glanced at the door, her pulse rising. She'd found what she was looking for, and she hadn't been followed. She pushed at the top of the crate, but it was sealed shut. It wouldn't be so easy to get her fix.

She glanced around the cluttered room for something, anything, that would give her access to what she wanted. Against the opposite wall was what looked to be a small closet, two doors wide.

She rushed to it, pulling up the lever that held the door together. It opened with a creak, revealing an array of tools hanging across the back.

There. She grabbed a crowbar and headed back to the box she needed.

This time, she'd take the correct med, full dose. Surely that would be more effective than her current one.

Ben's current ones, she corrected herself. Taking the correct medication might fix the side effect of time slowing. It had to be the medication causing the change, even if she'd been on them for three months without a problem. Buran had mentioned it took time for the risks of Enertin to build.

With some effort, the lid cracked open. It was full to the brim with bottles. Jemma pulled her small bag to her front and started stuffing pills inside. She wasn't sure when the next time she'd be able to get more would be. Besides, better to have too many and not need them than not enough if she did.

With the sound of footsteps, she froze. In her frantic packing, she hadn't noticed Buran enter the room.

She looked at him. His head moved in a sweeping motion, taking in the room.

"Are all of these Enertin?" He asked.

"Yes," Jemma said. "As far as I can tell." She slowly zipped up her purse.

Had he noticed her packing?

"Holy crap." He let out a loud breath. "All this time, they haven't even been using the meds." His face wrinkled in confusion. "If they aren't using the meds, then why did they…"

His eyes met Jemma, taking in the sight of her next to an open crate.

"What are you doing?" he asked.

Jemma saw the recognition dawn on his face as her chest tightened. She struggled to breathe as Buran's reaction came to her in slow motion.

The world spun around them, and shards of ice grew out of Buran's skin. Like sugar crystals growing in water, they spread. The ground turned to ice at Buran's feet.

Jemma wanted to move. To shout out to Buran and get him to stop his outburst. But she could barely fill her lungs.

The temperature in the room dropped. Goosebumps traveled across Jemma's arms.

Buran was now encased in ice, his scowling face placed into a tomb.

Breathe, Jemma. Breathe. Her breath came out as steam.

The ice climbed toward her. She needed to get out of there, but she felt stuck.

Glued to the spot, she stood next to the container of her yellow lifelines, the loose lid sitting on top giving access to only a small peek of what was inside. Like fighting against quicksand, she pushed through her fear and focused.

She needed to find a way out of here. Ice scaled across the ground, gaining speed. The cold tendrils were hungry for her warmth.

"Run!" she yelled, hoping to alert Governor Dunn. She, however, was trapped. Behind her were boxes. The only way out of this room was the door behind Buran. The one moments away from being frozen shut.

She backed up. The ice had barely begun to scale the boxes along the wall.

As long as the ice didn't touch her, she may yet escape it.

She took two more large steps back and then sprinted with all her might toward the slightly open yellow box. She jumped on it, the lid shifting with her weight, ready to dump her onto the field of ice.

But she was faster. She leapt onto the next box, which created a step for her to gain higher ground. Looking ahead, she grabbed the open lid, continuing along the path of boxes with it in her hand.

She was almost to the door when the boxes ended. Ice already encapsulated the ground between her and safety, sharp icicles protruding from below. She threw the lid down and hopped on it. The weight of her body caused it to slide to the narrow opening. She covered her face with her arm as broken shards flew against her.

As she approached the door to the main room of the warehouse, ice was in the process of stretching across the opening, closing her way out. Turning sideways, she sucked in her gut to straighten enough to make it through. She crashed on the other side, the cold burning her arm as the lid slowed to a stop outside the winter-encased room.

She slammed the door behind her, hopeful that would be enough to contain the glacier that threatened to form just a little longer.

"What is going on?" Governor Dunn was there, his eyes widening as he saw the frost forming on the steel door she'd just closed.

"We have a bit of a problem." She said through heavy breaths. "Buran's had an outburst."

Dunn's face wrinkled. "How is that..."

"I don't know." Jemma shook her head. "But we've got to go." The ice seeped through the edges of the door, spreading faster as it escaped.

Together they rushed toward the front door.

"Are we leaving Buran behind?" Dunn asked. "Isn't there some way we can stop him?"

At that, Jemma stopped.

Her bag contained the thing that kept her energy in control. Could it work the same, even though Buran was already releasing? She turned around. The ice covered half the warehouse but had slowed its progression.

Buran had finally run out of built up emotions.

The disgust she caused.

She needed to fix this, somehow. That is, if Buran was still alive.

She knew Disparates had some protection against their own emotional energy. At least, when no medication intervened, but this was extreme. If he stayed frozen for too long, that protection would run out. But how was she going to reach him?

"Stand back," Jemma said, waving Governor Dunn to the side.

She'd taken a red pill that morning, the same as she'd done the last three months.

The red pills worked. Kept her electricity in check. However, they didn't keep her from feeling anxious. All this time, she'd been feeling her energy build. It was escaping in small bursts, affecting the perception of time around herself in her moments of fear—at least, that was her best guess of what was happening.

But that was her trying to hold it back.

With no inhibitions, she closed her eyes.

She had to do it. She had to face that moment.

Mackie popped into her mind. Small, beautiful Mackie. Smiling as he sat on a rocking duck.

Louie was there too. Handsome, and kind. He was upset, but it wasn't his fault. His fire burst out of him. A symbol of his passion. His misunderstanding.

Jemma didn't feel fear of that. Not now. Louie's heat evaporated in the air. Her arm throbbed at the memory, but her heart steadied itself.

It knew what was coming next.

Her.

It was always her.

She wasn't afraid of Louie. Or Disparates. Or even emotional energy.

She was afraid of herself, the part that she didn't know or understand. The part that had changed as she'd grown. She was still learning it. Getting to know it.

And now, she beckoned it. That wild, unmanageable monster.

In her mind, she saw street lights on the corner raining shattered glass upon her head.

Sparks flying into Ben's mind. Not her sparks, but a representation of what she had the potential to do.

Mackie's pale face lying on the sand.

Her heart was racing, her pulse throbbing. Tears slid down her cheeks. Shaking, she raised her hands.

With all her will, she channeled her terror into the glazed glade of ice before her.

She kept her eyes closed. She didn't need to open them to know where her energy was going. She had welcomed her anxiety, and it was greeting her like an old friend.

And now she was its master.

It slithered, cracking the ice in its path until it reached the glacier that was once the door into Buran's cell.

As it crept across the block, branches reached out. The ice fell away in chunks. As the last bit hit the ground, Jemma bent over. She placed a hand on her knee to catch herself from falling.

"Wow," Governor Dunn said. His voice was right behind her.

She opened her eyes. The view in front of her was a mix of ice and water. A clear pathway stood before them.

"Let's go," she said as she rose. Together, they trudged through the icy swamp she'd created. Every other step, the water that seeped into her shoes turned from warm to cold to warm.

She'd done her job well.

She pushed against the door. The ice behind it had also melted with the shock of her lightning.

There was Buran. Still contained in his icy grave.

But he wouldn't be there for long. Jemma wasn't going to let him leave this world. Not yet and not in this way.

Buran's grimace stared back at her. The shadows under his eyes were dark under the icy glass.

She placed her fingers above his blue lips. She didn't need to close her eyes this time. Seeing her friend on the verge of death was enough for her energy to grow. Small tendrils stretched around his face.

Branches of her lightning twisted around his body, spiraling as water formed at its touch. As the ice melted, she removed her hand, taking a step back as her electricity sizzled out.

Governor Dunn caught Buran's body as it slumped. "His skin is cold."

Jemma's heart froze. She was too late.

Time around her blurred. She saw spots as Dunn slowly kneeled to the ground, placing Buran's body into the small pool of water that'd melted to the floor.

Jemma had electric power. She remembered the R.E.I. Responders at the park. The device they used.

The same element that had taken her son's life had also saved it.

If Dr. Paxton could channel it to control a person's brain, Jemma could use it for good.

The fear of Buran's dead body had sparked enough to recharge her supply. It wasn't much.

She placed her hand on his chest.

Cold as ice.

With a deep, shaking breath, she shouted. Yelled into the void of time. With the rush of her energy escape, the world around her was righted.

A burst of light seized Buran's chest. His body lifted to greet it. Dunn shifted away as the body fell back onto the ground.

They waited in silence.

Buran didn't move.

"You did good." Governor Dunn's voice was filled with sorrow.

"No," Jemma said. "No. I'm not too late." She beat her hands onto Buran's chest.

It had warmed.

"I'm trying again. Give us space."

"Okay." Governor Dunn did as he was told.

This time, with two hands on her friend, she thought about his heart.

The one that saved her when Ben had first been taken.

He believed in her. Worked with her so she could do this now.

A champion for Disparates from all walks of life. All places.

A husband. He had to get home to Keesha.

His heart was good. It would beat again.

A quick jolt. His eyes fluttered.

Not enough.

Another.

"Jemma..." Governor Dunn said softly.

"I'm not giving up." Her face, her clothes, her whole body was wet. A mix of Buran's ice energy and her own tears.

She would not give up.

Another pulse of electricity.

They waited.

Still no movement.

Jemma bent over his body. Her body convulsed in uncontrollable sobs. What she'd feared would happen to her sons had happened to her friend. A hand settled on her arm. Governor Dunn comforted her, but he couldn't stop her pain.

Except...

She looked at Dunn, who sat across the way. His hands were in his lap.

Turning, her eyes locked with Buran's. Her sobs intensified as joy flowed through her. She sat back as Buran lifted himself.

Without waiting for him to be steady, she flung her arms around his neck.

Buran lifted an arm to return her embrace. His grip was weak. "Whoa," he said, his voice croaky. "Don't knock me out again."

"I didn't think you were going to make it."

"I almost didn't. I wouldn't have, if it weren't for you." The two of them held each other in a friendly embrace.

Jemma released him.

He smiled. "Keesha will definitely insist on family holidays together now."

Jemma laughed. Relieved.

Until shouting came from outside.

"If anyone is alive in there, come out now and we promise to keep you that way. Don't, and we guarantee you won't leave this building breathing."

Responders had arrived.

TWENTY-SEVEN

T he clouds ceased their release of rain about an hour after Ben and Dominic had been on the water. The sun was bright in the middle of the sky.

"Ya doing okay there?" Dominic asked from his spot at the wheel.

Ben sat on a bench directly to the side of him, slightly behind his back. "As good as I can be when my son has been taken without my permission to an island overrun with Wuslick R.E.I. That is, if they made it to Lucky without crashing in the storm. Pretty sure Asher's never driven a boat."

"I did teach him everything I know before I bought the *Second Chance*. Granted, being taught about something and putting it into action are two different things."

Ben tensed. Asher should've known better than to have tried driving a boat in the first place. He definitely should have known better than taking Louie with him. He went to meet with some mysterious person. Asher wasn't even sure who it was.

"I'm sure they're both safe," Dominic said.

"You can't be sure."

"Nope, but I haven't seen any signs of capsized boats. Not that there would be any signs left if it sank, but I also haven't heard any sirens. If Asher had a hard time drivin', he would've crashed much closer to Stillfield."

The thought of the boat crashing wasn't very reassuring.

"Of course," Dominic said, "that's assuming he was going in the right direction. The ocean is large."

"That's not helping." Ben placed a hand on his bouncing leg.

Dominic shifted things around at the wheel and sat next to Ben. "Asher knew the way to Lucky Island well enough to direct a group there to try to save you. He knows the island like the back of his hand; I have no doubt they made it there and he's keeping Louie safe."

"Taking Louie to Lucky Island automatically voids any intentions for his safety. I thought Asher had more sense than that. I had a feeling being a prisoner influenced him too much in a bad way. I should've listened to that instead of trusting him with my children."

A buzzing sound settled in the back of his mind. Ben leaned forward and placed his hands over his ears to stop the sound. It worked, silencing the buzzing.

Ben removed his hands, and the buzzing was there once again. It wasn't in his head; it was out in the water.

Dominic must have heard it too as he jumped from his seat and returned to the helm. He set his sight straight ahead, where a matching boat sped across the water, coming their way.

These boats were currently under control of R.E.I. The people coming toward them were Wuslick Responders.

Sweat beaded against Ben's brow. Sure, the head of Stillfield Responders was driving the boat, but he had no jurisdiction over R.E.I. outside of Stillfield.

Or over the island they were sailing to. They'd be sent back to Stillfield.

"Afternoon!" Dominic shouted as their boat came to a stop. He waved his hand toward the pair of R.E.I. coming toward them. As they drew closer, Ben made out the familiar symbol of R.E.I. on their black uniforms. A large ring with six interlocking circles surrounding it.

A woman with dark hair narrowed her eyes as their boat slowed to a stop next to theirs. "Name and duty."

"I'm Sergeant Dominic Simmons of Stillfield Responder Office number 0203." He stood tall with his shoulders back and flashed his badge. Even in a t-shirt and slacks, he projected command. "Out for a sweep of the area. We had a report of a missing vessel."

"Missing vessel?" The female R.E.I. officer raised a brow after inspecting Dominic's badge. "When did this occur?"

The other R.E.I. officer was male. His curly hair swayed in the remaining breeze. "There have been no reports of a missing vessel."

"That's on me," Dominic said. "You see, it's my boat that my son took on a joyride with my grandson. He likes to do that occasionally. Tends to end up lost. Honestly, he's probably found his way back home by now. I didn't want to use up unneeded resources to track it down. I have the authority to conduct my own search. Speaking of which, present your credentials."

They each reached into their pockets and pulled out their own badges.

"Officer Hayes." He nodded at the woman, then looked at the man. "And Officer Jinkes. I appreciate your swiftness and diligence in fulfilling your duty. I'll be sure to send praise to your commanding officer. You're welcome to resume your"—Dominic tilted his head slightly, his gaze moving past the two officers on the boat—"patrol."

Ben followed his eyes, which had fallen on a pile of large duffle bags. The labels attached to the fronts were too far away for Ben to read. However, the expression that had flashed across Dominic's face told Ben they weren't something innocent.

Officer Jinkes seemed to have caught the brief look as well. He stepped to the side, blocking more of the bags from view. "This is R.E.I. water. You've crossed the barrier past Stillfield's control."

"Have I?" Dominic scratched his chin. "I didn't realize we'd gone so far out."

"You'll need to turn around," Officer Jinkes said.

An invisible darkness settled around Ben. They couldn't turn around. He had to get to the island. He had to find his boy. He shot up from his seat. "We can't do—"

"Of course." Dominic stuck his arm out in front of Ben, as if holding him back. "It's not our intention to interfere with the Republic of Wuslick's duty. If you see another ship this way, please report it, and be gentle with its occupants."

"We'll alert headquarters to be on the lookout," Officer Hayes said.

Ben shot a sharp look at Dominic. Not only were they conceding and abandoning their goal to find Louie, but they also alerted R.E.I. to the possible presence of a stray ship and who the occupants on board may be. If Asher had made it to the island without being caught, his safety was put in higher jeopardy than it already had been.

In the distance, the faint outline of Lucky Island appeared. The urge to dive into the water and swim the rest of the way to Louie was strong. But Ben knew the distance was farther than it looked. He'd never make it.

Dominic gave the officers a nod goodbye as he turned his boat around. "Try to hide your anger a bit better. You'll give us away as desperate, and desperate people can't be trusted."

There was no relaxing. "You're just giving up?" He seethed, his breathing heavy.

"Of course not," Dominic said. "But we have to be smart about this."

"Like giving away that Asher and Louie might be on Lucky Island," Ben said as he sat back down. "What if they get caught?"

"Then R.E.I. will know that they are related to the Stillfield Sergeant, who is actively searching for them, and will be less likely to make them disappear."

A cold chill rolled through Ben's body, calming the inner heat he'd been creating. "R.E.I. is as dangerous as the island Responders?"

"Those bags weren't filled with paperwork."

"What was inside them?" Ben crossed his arms across his chest as a hole opened.

"Those are specially insulated for remains."

Ben's eyes widened.

"Now," Dominic continued, "those are likely ones they've found on the island."

"Asher did mention a lot of Disparates died being tested on. Seems like evidence they would take, right?"

"It does," Dominic said. "Except there's been no reports of Wuslick doing so. Part of preparing for a trial against Dr. Paxton is full transparency of their findings. I've been suspicious of their reports, and that tells me my gut is right."

"What would they want with old bodies from the island that would keep them from reporting?" The word "bodies" created a pit in Ben's stomach. Not unlike the pit Dogivan died in. Could he be one of those bodies they now transported to Wuslick?

The thought stirred the heat inside.

"What about finding Louie?" Ben asked.

"We'll have to make a wide circle and approach after nightfall. It'll make our trip take longer but hopefully decrease the chance of being caught again. At least we know they haven't found Asher and Louie."

"How do we know for sure?" The image of the bags came to Ben's mind. Louie's small body could fit inside...

"Because they wouldn't have stopped us if they were transporting fresh bodies."

Twenty-Eight

Asher held onto Louie as they hiked through the overgrown brush. Leda and her two bodyguards continued to encircle, or rather triangulate, around them. The owl followed them with beady eyes from its perch on Leda's shoulder.

Asher lived on this island for seventeen years. Most of the Disparates that survived this place never stepped foot on this side of the island. But Asher was special. He'd been here before, his palms sweating as the memories threatened to surface.

He pushed them away as he took another step.

"Does your owl have a name?" Louie asked.

Asher shushed him, unsure if their new guides were friendly.

"Strix," Leda said. "She's my trust companion. Don't hurt me, and she won't hurt you."

Asher raised an eyebrow. "Wait, is she the same owl that dropped me a letter? She wasn't too friendly there."

"She's only mean when someone deserves it." Leda shot him a look before continuing forward.

"What's a 'trust companion'?" Louie asked.

"It's when an animal learns that a human has a good heart and chooses to bond with them," Asher answered. Like his raccoon friend helping him get the keys. Leda having one meant she'd once done something to help the owl, so her heart wasn't completely rotten. "Where are we going?" he asked. He hoped to avoid the place that held his darkest moments.

"Shhh..." Leda paused, and her entourage followed by stopping in their tracks.

Louie shuffled forward before Asher's arm stopped him, but he remained quiet.

When only the sounds of waves crashing and thunder came, Leda turned.

She looked at Asher as she whispered, "We're moving further inland and need to be quiet here on out. If you want to make it to the safehouse alive."

Asher got her point. He nodded, and she resumed their trek.

Not long after, they passed an opening in the trees. A clearing had been made, with burned leaves and cracked earth around the edge. Asher's knees wobbled.

The arena.

The place he'd taunted fellow islanders. Testing to see if the cure had worked. Witnessing their deaths in answer—the cure never worked. Not while he was involved.

He gasped as if the air had been knocked out of him. His time for reckoning had come. This group didn't call him because they wanted his help.

They wanted their revenge.

Somehow, he'd need to fight his way out of this.

"You okay?" Louie asked, his small face tilted in his direction.

Asher moved his hand to Louie's shoulder to steady himself.

Leda continued walking across the shaky battlefield. Asher didn't dare to step on the hollow ground. The two bodyguards stopped behind him and Louie.

Leda turned around. "Well, are you coming?"

Asher's breath was shallow. "What do you want from me?"

Leda looked around the clearing, as if taking it in for the first time. "Oh," she said. "You know about this place?"

She sounded genuinely surprised. Perhaps he wasn't brought here for revenge. Perhaps she didn't know about his past.

"I am aware." Asher took a step onto the uneven dirt. He tried to keep the ghosts that surely haunted this place from his mind.

He wasn't ready to face them yet.

"Where are we going?" he asked once again.

Leda smiled and stopped walking once they reached the other side of the arena. Strix flew from her shoulder, perching on a nearby tree branch. Leda bent down as if retrieving something. Instead, the bush pushed backward as she righted herself. She took a step into where the bush had been and disappeared.

Asher narrowed his eyes. One second she'd been there, and the next she was gone.

"Keep going," the guard right behind him said. He had brown hair that reached his shoulders. "The entrance is just ahead."

Asher approached the bush. There was no sign of any hidden entrance easy to spot with the eye. Loose vines covered the spot where the bush had originally been. The guard that had spoken to him took a step forward, falling through the vines. His body rushed into the earth, as if the ground itself had swallowed him.

"What just—" Asher started to say, but the last guard behind him gave him a nudge forward.

"Your turn."

Asher grabbed hold of Louie's hand.

"It's a giant slide," the guard said. "Trust me, it's fun." He winked at Louie.

Louie glanced at the guard with a look of curiosity. He faced the brush-covered hole. "Let's go." He pulled on Asher's hand.

"And don't think about running now," the guard whispered to Asher. "I'm not the only one with eyes on you."

There went the thoughts Asher had been contemplating. "Let's go together," he said to Louie, pulling him in front.

Together they sat on the ground, Louie on Asher's lap. He slid his feet forward, feeling them slope onto the slide he couldn't completely see. He wanted to push the brush back to get a better look but thought better of it.

"Ready?" he asked Louie.

Louie nodded.

Asher pushed off.

Their bodies propelled forward. Across well-smoothed ground, they rode down the almost vertical tube. Earth covered the circle around them.

Moments later, they burst through the other end of the dark tunnel. Asher's stomach lurched through his chest as his body stopped in midair. Louie was in front of him, his legs dangling free. They were suspended in the air for a moment before they slowly lowered to the ground.

Asher stood from his sitting position and brushed the back of his pants. Louie was right behind him, following his every move.

He looked at the tunnel exit, about fifteen feet in the air from where they now stood. The last guard that had been with them flew out of the exit. His body started to fall but then stopped in midair and was gently lowered.

Asher glanced to his side to see three people with their hands above them.

Air Disparates.

Together, they caught everyone who came through the tunnel.

Genius, Asher thought.

They were in some kind of underground cavern. Small lanterns illuminated the space, casting flickering shadows in the firelight. About ten yards away from where he stood, a small stream flowed through the middle. A waterfall was nearby, possibly leaking in from the ocean. Whether it was here before the Rain of Fire when this island was a mountain or formed after the water level rose, he didn't know.

"How..." Asher wasn't sure how to form the questions he had. Was this a place of nature, or an act of Disparates? This group, who were they? And what did they want?

Clearly, they had some control over their energy. They weren't previously drugged and kept from feeling. They knew what their energy felt like and how to direct it.

Like Jemma, Buran, and his group.

Like Asher and Quill.

It definitely wasn't impossible for Disparates to learn the skills they needed on their own. But it wasn't easy. Asher knew that. To gain his control, he had to do things he regretted every day of his life.

But that wasn't why he was here.

"Glad you made it down," Leda said. No wonder Strix hadn't followed. It likely didn't like being underground.

Asher couldn't blame it. "What is this place?" He grabbed Louie's hand. His eyes were wide, taking in their surroundings.

"It's a refuge. Built it with my energy as a safe place to hide."

So she was a Ground Disparate as well as an Ice one since she'd stopped his fire when they first met. Another Double Disparate, like Louie and Quill. "Okay, but where did you all come from?" The group of three that had safely softened each arrival now walked past him toward the stream and the small group of tents on the other side of it. One girl in the middle, with short brown hair, seemed familiar.

"She was an islander." Asher pointed at her. The small group didn't hear him, but Leda followed his finger.

"Yes. Many of the people here experienced this island as a prisoner. Part of why they are here now."

"But I thought she'd..." Asher's voice trailed off.

"Exploded?" Leda said. "I mean, in a way, she did. Floated into the sky, higher than the eye can see. She should be dead, but we saved her. As her body crashed to the earth, the Coats left her for dead. That's when we appeared."

"You've been saving islanders?" Asher's voice was incredulous. It gave him hope. But with his next breath, his fear from earlier returned.

No.

No one knew it was him. No one could know what he'd done. Director Wallow had promised he'd stay anonymous. But then again, he wasn't the most trustworthy person. And he was dead.

"We weren't able to revive all of them." Her face fell. "But we sure tried."

So Crow could still be alive. Asher searched around, noticing a scar across the face of the girl with the short brown hair. About a dozen people strolled around the cavern. Asher squinted, noticing visible scars on most of their arms, legs, or faces. Marks left by their outbursts. "That's almost unbelievable."

"I know," the brown haired guard said. The other guard had left shortly after they arrived inside the cave. This man was taller than Asher and at least twice as large muscle wise. "I'm Kingston, by the way. Wasn't ever a prisoner on the island, but happy to help."

"You weren't a prisoner?" Asher asked. "Then how did you end up here?"

"Came from the Outskirts, I did. Our goal is to live. And we will succeed. The Outskirts will live."

"But why the island? And what Outskirts?" Asher asked.

"Too many of our people were taken here," Leda said, tossing her long ponytail over her shoulder. "Too many." She stopped talking, her eyes wet.

Kingston took over. "We came to free them, but it wasn't so easy. Not with the amount of security and control that was here. We had to work in the background."

"I can't believe you came here undetected," Asher said. "How was that possible?"

"You did the same thing, didn't you?" Kingston looked at him. "Twice now, I believe it is. You would think they had more surveillance on this side of the island, but somehow, they missed the mark."

That was true. The old director and Dr. Paxton both believed in their mission. They didn't think they needed to worry about any opposition.

And they were right. There hadn't been any for over a decade. Not until the pieces of Ben, Buran, and Asher fell together and disrupted them.

"Why?"

"Why, what?" Kingston asked.

"Why did you want me to come back to the island?"

Kingston looked at Leda, waiting for her to take the lead. "You'll know soon enough," she said. "But for now, we need your focus on other problems. Follow me." She walked toward the tents.

A woman of secrets. Asher related to that.

His mind went to the notes he'd been sent as they walked.

"So, it's you guys that have been watching me? Somehow you go back and forth to the mainland, or what?"

"All will be revealed in time." Leda stepped over the small stream.

Asher lifted Louie into his arms. The stream was narrow enough for an adult to walk past, but Louie wouldn't reach the other side on his own without falling in.

"How are you hanging in there?" he spoke just to Louie.

"It's dark down here." Louie's arms tightened around Asher's neck. Asher didn't put him down, even after they'd cleared the water.

"That's true. The lanterns don't give too much light."

"And it's cold."

"I can help with that." Asher thought lightly about his fight with Quill to generate heat. She was always at the forefront of his mind, an easy memory to bring back.

Except, his anger wasn't at her. It was at himself. He was a fool for dismissing her advances. But if he had accepted them, it would have been wrong.

He was untrustworthy and guilty of unspeakable things.

Things this island wouldn't let him live down. Once again, here he was, and he was afraid he wouldn't be able to leave without accounting for his sins.

His temperature rose.

"It's too hot now," Louie said.

Whoops. He hadn't stopped his thoughts in time, but at least Louie wasn't burned. He placed him down so he could cool off.

They followed Leda inside the largest tent. It was furnished with chairs along the edges, and in the middle sat a table. They each took a seat.

"Are you ready to answer my questions now?" Asher asked.

"We need your help." Leda looked straight at him.

"I gathered that. But what for?"

Leda glanced at Louie for a moment before her gaze landed back on Asher. "A rescue mission."

"Haven't all the Disparates from Lucky Island been moved?"

"They have." Leda looked at the table. "The one we need to rescue is on another island."

That does complicate things, Asher thought. "Lighthouse island—"

"No."

"Then where?" Ben had brought up the question that maybe there was another island when he read the notes. It was possible. The Rain of Fire and rising water levels created a huge geographical change within the last hundred years.

"That's what we need your help with. We need to know where the other island is. The one where high profile prisoners are sent. And where highly dangerous Disparates are kept."

Asher narrowed his eyes.

"The Disparates with multiple energy types."

"You mean with two?" Asher asked. "That could be the lighthouse island." Quill was kept there after his escape.

"No." Leda shook her head again. "The Disparate I'm looking for has more than that."

Asher didn't know that was possible. The most he'd ever heard about was two energies. Like Louie and Quill. He knew a bit about what a struggle that was, trying to control two deeply feeling emotions. He couldn't imagine throwing in a third.

"The Disparate I need has all five types."

Asher's eyes widened. This was unheard of. Inconceivable. A mind that struggled with joy, sadness, anger, disgust, and fear. Life would be a walking nightmare. They would be a danger to themselves at all moments.

Someone like that existed.

Someone who was still alive and they were going to find—rescue.

"What's your plan?" Asher asked. Although it sounded dangerous and right near impossible, he needed to make restitution for his crimes. This may be one way to do so. "Wait. Before I agree to help you, where is Crow?"

"Crow?"

"Yeah." Asher studied Leda, watching for her reaction. If he were alive, she should know about him. If he wasn't, someone knew enough about him to send the invisible message.

Leda looked confused at first, but then she scoffed, a slight smile on her face. "I'll be right back."

She exited the tent, leaving Asher, Louie, and Kingston sitting in silence.

"You have a lot of hair on your face," Louie said after a minute, cutting through the quiet.

Kingston laughed. "That's what happens when you've been living underground for a while with no shaving cream. Does it look good?" He rubbed his hand under his chin.

Louie shook his head no, causing more laughter from Kingston.

Leda returned with a boy—no, a young man with dark hair and stubble on his face—behind her.

"Crow!" Asher stood from his chair and embraced his friend. They'd bonded during their time imprisoned together. He reminded Asher of himself when he'd first arrived on the island. A scared but hotheaded teenager.

"Phoenix! So you got my note." His facial hair made him look older, although he was likely around Calum's age. As they pulled away from their hug, Asher spotted the burn scars that lined his arms.

"Yeah. Bit tricky, but I did. Thinking you were dead didn't help."

"Paxton can't get rid of me that easily," Crow said. "I honestly wasn't sure you would figure out it was me."

"Okay, I may have had some help." Asher laughed. Louie coughed behind them.

"Oh, let me introduce you to my nephew. This is Louie."

"Bro, you're an uncle? That's fire."

"Louie," Asher said, "this is Crow—well, Hector."

"I'm good with Crow. Hector reminds me too much of my grandfather."

That was someone Asher didn't want to be reminded of either. Director Wallow was originally in charge of Lucky Island when Asher first went there. It wasn't until his death that Dr. Paxton took control. "So how did you end up here?"

"Well, O.W.L. found me and took me in after Paxton left me for dead. Been hiding out healing down here since," Crow said.

"Wait, Leda's owl found you?" Asher asked.

Crow laughed. "No, this organization. It stands for 'Outskirts Will Live'. They nursed me back to health and I've been here since. I thought you'd died too, but when I heard you survived, I knew you were the person to contact. I was never granted access to any of the research files, but you were. Perhaps you saw something that would be helpful."

So this group didn't have any files of information. Nothing to expose the full extent of Dr. Paxton's crimes. Her trial would have to go off the testimonies of witnesses, some of which had their minds manipulated to be on her side.

"I'm curious about that as well," Leda said. "I told you there was someone we were looking for."

"And that's the real reason why you're on Lucky Island," Asher said, filling in the blanks. "To find information about where the Disparate is."

Leda nodded. "There has to be a clue somewhere. Do you have any ideas?"

"Why should I help you find this mystery Disparate?" Asher had come to Lucky Island to find Crow, and here he was.

Leda sighed heavily. "Because she's a child. A child that was taken somewhere by Paxton."

Asher looked at Louie. His eyes were wide. If he were missing, of course Asher would do anything to find him. "What is with people thinking I have all the answers?" Asher asked. First Jemma with Buran's group, now Leda.

"Mysterious people tend to have suspicions thrown on them." Leda tilted her head. "What are you hiding, Asher Stillfield?"

Asher squirmed. He didn't care much for her direct approach.

"He'll help us." Crow stepped to his defense. "He got Dr. Paxton arrested. He wants to save Disparates."

"Hmm..." Leda folded her arms across her chest. "We'll see about that."

"Have you been able to get into Paxton's office?" Asher asked. Seemed like a good place to start if he were going to gain their trust.

"Yep," Crow said. "But it was empty. Honestly, pretty surreal seeing it that way. Gramps always kept it packed. Overheard some R.E.I. discussing how much paperwork was missing. Looks like Paxton hid it well."

"Pax did have her own sleeping quarters inside the bunker. Have you checked there?"

"We've slipped inside. Couldn't find anything."

Asher thought. "Have you been in her boat?"

Leda glanced at him. "She had her own boat?"

"Yeah." Asher had seen her arrive on a private boat before. One he'd never seen used for anyone else. One with a room in the middle instead of a cage.

"How would we find her boat? Surely R.E.I. has already confiscated it." Leda didn't sound impressed by Asher's information.

"Maybe, but I've never seen it at the docks," Asher said. "I don't think she took it between here and the mainland. It has to be her way to travel to the other islands. I imagine she'd keep it somewhere safe."

"How on earth would we go about finding it?" Leda shook her head. "Sailing around the open waters? That's already dangerous due to the amount of broken land out there, and we've already lost a boat with that strategy."

Asher's eyes widened "What?"

"That was our first plan for finding Aleeta. The boat never returned, and we lost all communication with it after an unexpected storm rolled in."

Asher was amazed they'd even tried. The waters were known for being treacherous and not sailable. There was a reason why the rest of the world was left isolated.

"Aleeta?" Asher asked.

Leda winced. "She's the Disparate we're searching for."

Asher nodded. The child with five powers. There was a lot of information to take in, but if they came to him, then they were out of other options. "Paxton's boat has to be somewhere. What about the cave on lighthouse island?"

Leda looked at him, confused. "There's a cave there?"

"Yeah, Paxton used it to bring Quill there."

Leda tilted her head. "Maybe we didn't search that island well enough. We mostly checked inside the lighthouse."

"It's on the other side, and through a narrow opening, but there is a door down there." It had been a surprise to Asher when he learned about it months ago, but he didn't realize it wasn't common knowledge. Especially to Crow. Asher looked at his old friend for confirmation.

Crow shook his head. "I've only ever been on Lucky."

Perhaps the cave at lighthouse island was truly only used by Dr. Paxton. It was small, not much on it, but it was a place to look.

Of course, if R.E.I. knew about it already, there wouldn't be any information there either.

"We haven't come across anything about it in our research. Although, we obviously know there are more places out there. Just didn't know there was one so close."

"Vicki," Leda called out, waving over a woman with blonde hair, half of it shaved. She was one of the Air Disparates who helped lower them to the ground earlier. "Do you know about the cave on lighthouse island?"

Vicki was quiet. Her eyes landed on Asher.

Does she recognize me? She seemed familiar, but he couldn't place why.

"No," Vicki said. "I didn't see any. Do we know where it is?"

"Possibly." Leda turned to Asher. "Aleeta might not be there, but there may be other information. We need to check it out. Do you remember how to get there?"

"I wasn't the one sailing that night," Asher said, "but I might be able to figure it out."

Anxiety crept over Leda's face. "You're the best chance we've got."

The pressure was on.

"Tonight," Leda continued, "we sail."

"Whoa, wait," Asher said. "I need to get Louie home. I can't take him with me to another island."

Leda eyed Louie, who stood listening next to Asher.

"You're right, he can't come with us. But we need your help. If the cave at lighthouse island isn't far, like you claim, there'll be time for both."

She had a point. If he went back to Stillfield, it would be difficult for him to leave to come back here. There were likely

Responders watching for his return, ready to arrest him. Then he'd be of no help to anyone.

But Louie would be home, so that'd be worth it. There'd also be time to make it home after Asher found the cave. He wanted to help find someone that Dr. Paxton hurt. A small form of restitution for those he didn't save.

His eyes landed on Crow. "Will you watch Louie?" He was the only person he knew there, and he trusted him enough to watch his nephew.

"Of course," Crow said. "I'll make sure he stays out of trouble."

"Can I also have a *cool* name?" Louie asked. His eyes lit up when he looked at Crow.

"A nickname is something you earn from someone else," Crow said. "I gotta get to know you a bit more first."

Louie looked at Asher. "My uncle calls me 'Lougie.' I don't like it."

"Seriously?" Crow shook his head. "That's a terrible nickname."

Asher laughed. "You be good for Crow and maybe I'll give you a better one."

Louie nodded.

It was settled then. Asher would guide Leda and her group to the lighthouse, then he'd return to take Louie home. And to give him a proper nickname.

Once back in Stillfield, Asher wasn't sure what would come of himself. At least he'd know he did something good for once.

TWENTY-NINE

She has my nose, Quill thought as she sat at the bar next to her long-lost aunt.

"Would you like some privacy?" Calum asked after being introduced to Bea.

"No, you can—"

"That would be wise, young man," Bea interrupted her.

Calum nodded. "I'll watch the door." He found a table nearby but out of earshot.

"An equally wise idea," Bea said as she turned toward Quill. "It seems you've got yourself a good guy."

Quill reddened. "Um... no, we're not..."

"You don't have to explain further," Bea said. "I saw the way he looked at you."

Quill's heart ached. Calum wasn't the boy she wanted to look at her in that way. But now wasn't the time to get into that drama with her new-found aunt.

"So..." Quill wasn't sure where to start. The space between them was heavy. Awkward. What did one say to family when you met them for the first time as an adult?'

"You want to know more about me."

Quill nodded.

"I'm happy to answer any questions you have," Bea said. "I'm sure I came as a shock to you. Honestly, I wasn't sure I'd ever get the chance to see my sister's little girl again."

"Again?" Quill didn't remember ever meeting the woman in front of her.

"Of course. I was there the day you were born. When that good-for-nothing father of yours was away for work. I wasn't gonna let Gilly give birth on her own. Which, by the way, happy twenty-sixth birthday. I've never forgotten that day."

The way Bea spoke about her father didn't bother her. Quill had her own rocky relationship with the man. However, she wrote off his behavior as being manipulated by Dr. Paxton. Had that begun even before her birth?

"Thank you, but why haven't I seen you since?"

"You did. I was around often. Until..."

"Until my mother's death," she finished the sentence for her. Bea nodded.

"What was she like?"

"Your mother was walking sunshine." Bea smiled. "She was my best friend. You look just like her." Her eyes stared intently at Quill.

Quill had been told all her life that she looked like her mother. Yet hearing it from Bea at this moment made it feel real.

"What was she like, you know, as a child?"

"The same way. Always had my back and made me smile when I was down." Her eyes darkened as she looked forward. "It's a shame what happened to her."

"The car crash?" Quill asked.

Bea whipped her head around to look at Quill once more. "No." Her eyes pierced into Quill's. She wanted to look away but couldn't.

"The sacrifice," she continued. "I don't understand why it had to be Gilly."

"Sacrifice?" The air in the room constricted around Quill at that moment. Her chest tightened as she waited for more.

Bea noticed Quill's reaction. "Perhaps this is a tale for another time. We've only just met."

"My mother was a sacrifice." It was more of a statement than a question. "A sacrifice for what? Who?" The air around her was becoming energized. A tingling sat on the surface of her arms.

"Quill..." Calum's voice interrupted their conversation. He pointed at the window. Outside was a pair of what looked to be Preen Responders, based on the guns strapped to their waists. "I think it's time we go."

"We're not done talking here." Quill looked at Bea.

"We can talk about this another time," Bea said.

"No! There might not be another time." Quill needed to delay the Responders. She needed answers. She thought about the energy flowing around her. It was different than she was used to. As if her air energy somehow mixed with her electricity.

Except, it wasn't a mix of them. It was something new.

She closed her eyes, giving in to the new feeling. She'd been so excited to meet her aunt. To hear about her mother. She was still riding that high. And yet she'd learned things she didn't expect. Didn't understand. Things that made her afraid.

Apprehension. Desperation. Eagerness.

She gave into them all.

As she did, the tingling around her body intensified. Instead of sparks flying off her, they dove inside. Through the space in her atoms, they traveled. Digging, hiding away.

"Quill..." Calum whipped his head side to side. "Where did you go?"

"I'm right here," she said.

Calum jumped. He reached out his hand, touching her chest.

"Watch it!" she shouted.

He withdrew his hand, a look of disbelief on his face. "Quill. You're invisible."

Quill held her hands out in front of her, except her gaze met the floor. She knew her hands were there, but they weren't in her vision. Her fear grew. She didn't understand what was happening. But excitement flooded her as well. A new energy flowed through her.

"Regardless of what is happening," Bea said, "I believe it's time to go. Specifically for you, young man."

The front doors of the saloon opened. The Responders from outside entered, a gun pointed at Calum. "Where is your friend?" one of them asked.

"I don't know what you're talking about." Calum raised his hands.

"We have reports from witnesses that saw you and a woman walking away from a truck with an injured Responder inside. Hands down!" the Responder shouted.

Calum listened. The look on his face revealed he wouldn't be able to use his air energy even if he'd wanted to.

Something about the girl he liked suddenly disappearing didn't bring him much joy.

Quill stood as still as she could. If she couldn't be seen, she couldn't be caught. But she wasn't sure how long this would last.

Calum seemed to be thinking the same thing. "I'll come peacefully," he said.

The Responder with the gun motioned to his partner, who approached Calum with caution. He placed cuffs around Calum's wrists.

"You're under arrest for conspiracy and terrorism against the Republic of Preen. Don't think you'll get out of this either. We've already got the rest of your friends."

Quill's invisible eyes widened. Were they being truthful or trying to shake him up?

Without further comment, they headed for the door.

Leaving Quill behind standing next to her mysterious aunt, who, for the duration of that encounter, stayed in her seat sipping her drink.

"You'll follow me to my house," she whispered. She wiped her hands and placed a coin onto the table.

Quill followed her out the door. She wasn't sure where they were going, but she didn't have anywhere else to go.

Unseen. The way she often felt on the inside was now conveyed on the outside.

And she wasn't sure how to change it.

It hadn't been difficult for Quill to keep following her aunt as she weaved through the main street despite her multiple hand checks. Each time, the space she knew her limbs inhabited was clear. She'd turned invisible, and this new energy took time to burn out.

It equally wasn't hard when her aunt swerved down a dirt road and quickened her pace. However, as they reached the end of the street, Quill paused, her mouth agape.

In the distance was the warehouse. Ice cascaded out the back window, stretching across two of the fields next to it. Two trucks were near the building as well as people too far for her to make out. That was where the rest of the group had been.

Buran—had he caused such a grand outburst? Had he survived it?

Quill glanced around herself. She'd lost track of her aunt. "Bea? Bea!" She didn't care if someone else heard her; right now, her fear was palpable. She was in a new place, her friends were in trouble, Calum was arrested. Quill didn't know what was happening with her own powers, and she'd just lost the one person who may be able to help her find answers.

Curly brown hair appeared from around a corner nearby. "Quill? Are you over here?"

"Yes!" Tears fell down Quill's cheeks. She wondered if they were invisible as well or if her emotions were on display.

"We're almost there, dear," Aunt Bea said. "Stick close to me." She held out a hand.

Quill took it, letting her guide her through a neighborhood of small homes.

When they stopped at one, Quill inhaled a sharp breath.

Her aunt lived in a shack. A place that looked as if it should have been abandoned decades ago.

Aunt Bea left the rotting front door open behind her. Quill was nervous, but she entered.

The inside was set up nicely enough. It was clean and clearly cared for. There was a rug in the middle of the eight by eight square. A chair sat in one corner, and a cot was made up on the opposite wall. A small fireplace had a pot hanging above it. Her kitchen.

Quill was used to living in small spaces. Her cell on the island wasn't much larger than this room. Honestly, to her, it felt homey.

"Close the door behind you once you're in," Aunt Bea said.

Quill listened. The door clicked as it sealed.

"Now, are you gonna stay that way or come back so we can talk face-to-face?"

"I don't know how to change back."

"Don't know how?" Aunt Bea sat in the corner chair. "I thought you Stillfield folks knew how to control your energy."

Quill cringed. She did know how to control her energy. At least, her normal energy.

"This is something new," she said. "I've never done this before. Heck, I've never heard of anyone doing this before."

Aunt Bea raised her eyebrows. "Never done it before?"

Quill nodded, forgetting she couldn't be seen.

"What were you feeling when it happened?" Aunt Bea asked.

"Well, I was feeling really great about meeting you and learning about my mother. Then, you mentioned something about her being a sacrifice and, I don't know." Quill tried to come up with the words to describe the feeling. "It was a bit of anticipation about hearing something that would make everything I'd been told growing up suddenly make sense. It was like my body knew I was on the edge of my life being changed forever. And I wasn't sure if I wanted that."

Quill looked at the floor. It was strange staring at the ground without her body to block her view.

"So you were afraid of what you were about to learn?"

"Yeah. I guess so. But I still really want to know. I need to know."

"We need to wait until you're back first. It's not common for Disparates with multiple powers to have them mixed into a new one, but it's also not unheard of."

Quill raised an eyebrow. "Really? So this has happened to others before? Did my mother have more powers?"

"Like I said, we can talk more when you're better," Aunt Bea said.

"Maybe knowing will make this feeling go away? It could fix the problem."

Aunt Bea placed a hand on her cheek and scratched her face. "That might work..."

Quill's heart raced.

"But it also might not," Aunt Bea said.

"Isn't it worth a try?" Quill hoped she'd agree.

"Possibly. However, what I'm about to tell you will definitely change your life. And you have to decide if you are ready for that."

"I'm ready." Quill didn't hesitate. She'd been waiting for this moment.

"Okay." Aunt Bea stood and walked to her cot. She lifted the rectangular bed to reach underneath it.

Quill moved to get a better look at what Aunt Bea was doing. Under the cot was a metal hatch.

Aunt Bea looked in Quill's direction, likely having heard her footsteps moments before. "It's time we take this conversation underground."

She opened the hatch, the cot falling sideways but staying attached so it would be returned to its spot once closed. Inside the hole was the top of a ladder. Quill stepped closer, seeing that it led straight down. The bottom was dark.

"Is this an old bomb shelter?" Quill asked. She'd heard stories about them. That they were common before the Rain of Fire. However, most were ineffective. The inhabitants hadn't prepared for the amount of power a super nuclear bomb held. A bomb that was strong enough to split sections of land off the edge of the country certainly was strong enough to clear fifty feet underground.

"It is indeed. Would you like to go first?" Aunt Bea asked.

"It might be better if you go first. Wouldn't want to get accidentally stepped on when you can't see where I am."

Aunt Bea tilted her head. "That is a good point. Well then, let's go." She disappeared into the hole, climbing quickly down the ladder.

Quill approached the opening and hesitated.

"Come on," Aunt Bea shouted. "The ladder is secure. It's not too far of a journey down. Well... it'll go quickly. Just pull the chain to close the hatch once you're in."

Quill climbed into the hole, her feet pressing on the metal slats. They were sturdy. A chain dangled above her, attached to the underside of the hatch. She pulled on it gently, the light from the room above disappearing with a thud.

"Glad to have you joining," Aunt Bea said from below, her feet clanking against each ladder rung she stepped on.

Quill continued her descent, unsure of what awaited her at the bottom.

She mostly hoped she didn't slip. She wasn't sure she could tap into her air powers if needed.

Solid ground met Quill's feet. Aunt Bea had been wrong; the climb had felt longer than she'd thought it would.

At one point, surrounded by darkness, she was unsure it would ever end. It was Aunt Bea's voice below her that encouraged her to keep going.

She also realized it hadn't truly mattered if she went first or not. She couldn't see Aunt Bea below her regardless.

A light turned on, illuminating the area at the bottom of the ladder.

"There we go," Aunt Bea said. "That's better. I left the flashlights at the other entrance last time. Sorry for the dark."

Quill squinted against the light. It took some time to adjust, but as they did, she took in the sight around her.

A room surrounded by concrete, a steel door on one wall. It was decorated as a homey space. Floral wallpaper and granite counter tops. It was clearly from before the Rain and larger than the shack about fifty feet above their heads. That thought caused Quill's chest to tighten.

They were under thousands of pounds of dirt at this moment. How had it not caved in?

The thought that it was over a hundred years old churned her stomach.

"Is this where you live?"

"Oh no, dear." Aunt Bea stood near the steel door. "This place isn't for living."

"Then what is it for?" Quill watched as Aunt Bea pulled the large lever that lay across the door and pulled it open. She moved to see into the next room.

Except it wasn't a room. It was a tunnel.

"Where does that lead?" Quill was already nervous about being underground, but at least she knew what was above her head. Going into the tunnel, she didn't know where it would lead. The feeling of being trapped reminded her of being on the island. But at least there, she had a small window in her cell where she could see the stars.

"To headquarters. Don't worry, I'll fill you in on the way."

Headquarters. She couldn't help but accept how unreal this sounded. Fit right in with the rest of her crazy life.

Really Quill? Getting ourselves into deeper trouble now.

She followed Aunt Bea down the pathway. There were smaller hallways that broke off and led to more steel doors. Some were clear while others had boxes and other storage materials blocking them.

"Those rooms aren't habitable anymore," Aunt Bea said.

Quill wondered if she'd seen her stare. She looked at her hands. Still gone.

Why was her mind keeping her in this state?

"Wait." Quill stopped. "I need to come back."

Aunt Bea ended her march forward. "Back above ground? Don't worry, there's another exit where we're going."

"No," Quill said. "I need to bring myself back. I'm still feeling anxious. And connected to my mother. I think that's what's fueling my energy right now. What did you mean by my mother being a sacrifice?"

Aunt Bea turned around, presumably to where she thought Quill was. Except the slight echo made her look three feet to Quill's left.

Quill moved to be in the path of her gaze. She wanted to see her face.

"Your mother was my best friend. When she met your father, she moved to Stillfield to be with him."

"They met at Wuslick College, correct?"

Aunt Bea nodded. "Your mother was learning to be an Analyst. It was an exciting opportunity. One of the first Disparates to be accepted into the program."

"Because of Enertin, right?"

"Yes." Aunt Bea looked as if she wanted to say more about the drug, but she didn't. "I was heartbroken when she moved away, but she promised to come visit and that I could come visit her. Which I did when you were born." She smiled.

"But then," she continued, "not everything was as it seemed. When Gilly was pregnant, your father met someone at work."

Quill sucked in a breath.

"This woman, she was the devil. She didn't think the Enertin pills were doing enough. Not taking away enough energy from the Disparates on them. She wanted to change them."

"Wait..." Quill was connecting the dots. "You don't mean..."

"Dr. Paxton? Yes."

The name shocked Quill. She didn't realize how long the doctor had been at the center of the story. How long she'd actually been controlling her father.

"What happened?"

"Gilly realized Elizabeth and Tobias, your father, were work colleagues, nothing more. In fact, Gilly and Elizabeth became friends. As Elizabeth explained her plan for Disparates, Gilly agreed with it. She'd felt so unlike herself those previous years, constantly causing electricity shortages and earth trembles. She confessed to shocking you one night when you wouldn't stop crying."

Quill rubbed her hands against her shoulders. Her mother had struggled with her energy. She knew what that was like.

Aunt Bea continued, "She even joined the testing for the new drug. One made with minerals from Hastiet as well as the flower from Preen.

"It worked. The earlier version of Enertin left Disparates releasing small amounts of energy because they still had some feeling. This new one took away all her anxiety. She loved it. She told me she felt free, and happy, and ready to take on the world.

"Honestly, her reaction scared me, but I tried to be happy for her. However, when she drove off the side of a cliff, I knew it wasn't her fault."

Quill had never been given details of her mother's crash. She'd always assumed it was an accident, because that was how her father had phrased it.

"She drove off a cliff?" Quill asked.

"Yes. She had no fear, remember? But the demons were still there. And this new Enertin drug that was being tested, I'm sure it's to blame."

"What do you think happened? What caused her to...?"

"Preen sent their own investigators after the crash, since she was one of our own. They found evidence that the brakes had been shorted out. Stillfield had not reported any issues with the car. They said she made the decision to drive off herself. She was a suicidal young mother. It wasn't true. She'd had an outburst in that car, one she never would have had if she'd been on the original pill. One that should have halted the testing of the new mineral formula for Enertin. But clearly it didn't, considering Lucky Island has still been in operation. The testing and experimentation only became more hidden."

"Mineral formula?" Quill asked. "You mentioned a flower before. Was that before Enertin?"

"It is Enertin," Aunt Bea said. "Or rather was. The other formula was never approved back then. Test results showed the mularium mineral increased the frequency and damage of outbursts from Disparates on it. The late Governor Stillfield made sure production of it never happened. That doesn't seem to be the case any longer."

Asher's dad had advocated for Disparates. He'd gotten approval to close Lucky Island and open Merrytime Clinic. With his death, advancements in Disparate care backtracked. Her father taking the lead under Paxton's control didn't help.

"Has Enertin changed back to this *mineral*?" Quill asked. It would explain Buran's data.

Aunt Bea nodded. "That's what is suspected by Preen. Stillfield has been requesting the same amount of the flower yet producing more Enertin than ever before. Rumor is Stillfield's warehouses are stocked with crates of the decaying flowers. Now, I don't know for sure if Hastiet is sending more of the mularium mineral, but it wouldn't surprise me. Going back to cause the same damage that was done to Gilly."

Quill's heart ached. "Why? Why, if they were friends, would Dr. Paxton want to keep the testing going?" She was almost yelling. "I don't understand; what does she want?"

"She wants all Disparates dead."

The silence reverberated off the walls of the tunnel. Quill had been imprisoned on an island by this woman. Her father manipulated. Her family torn apart. All because Dr. Paxton wanted to get rid of the people whom she was a part of.

"But why?" she asked again, trying to make sense of it all.

Aunt Bea looked directly in her eyes. "That is a question that only Elizabeth Paxton can answer."

It was then Quill realized she was visible again. Her fear and anticipation had been exchanged for hate.

She hated Dr. Paxton. Prison wasn't enough for her.

"How do we get justice?"

"That is a good question," Aunt Bea said. "That is what we are trying to do."

"We?" Quill asked.

"Come with me; I'll show you." She waved Quill forward. Together, they continued down the tunnel.

THIRTY

"What are we going to do?" Jemma asked. Buran, still weak, sat on the floor surrounded by melting ice. His face was pale and clammy.

"I don't think there's anywhere we can run." Governor Dunn looked around the room. He grabbed a crate and pushed it toward the door.

He was making a barrier to buy them more time. Jemma joined him, pulling the crate next to her away from the edge and pushing it to the door.

"What if we hide?" Jemma said, almost out of breath. Dunn had grabbed two more boxes and stacked them on top of their barricade. But there were plenty of boxes left around the room—many spots they could fit.

Governor Dunn shook his head. "They know we're here. It doesn't seem like an effective plan."

"What do you think, Buran?" Jemma asked. They needed to do something. Staying here, they'd definitely be caught.

Buran hadn't spoken much. His lips and hands were tinged blue from the exposure to his energy.

"I... I'm not sure," he finally said. "I've made it pretty difficult for us to get out of this situation, haven't I?"

Jemma bit her lip. He wasn't the only one to blame, but now wasn't the time to bring that up.

She looked at Governor Dunn. "What happens if we turn ourselves in?"

"Well," he said, his expression contemplative. "They were already upset at us. And there's the matter of Prockter. I suppose they will connect that we are to blame for his head wound as well."

Heat spread across Jemma's cheeks. She hadn't meant for him to get hurt when she'd told Quill to move the rock.

If it weren't for her, they'd be on their way home right now. But she couldn't guarantee they'd make it back alive if she didn't get more meds, which was why they—she—came to the warehouse.

She held onto her bag, knowing the pills that would suppress her emotions were inside. The puddle at her feet reminded her that she'd used her energy, her powers, to free Buran. The adrenaline of the situation led to her using her electricity for good, in a controlled manner.

Maybe she didn't need Enertin. The thought drove a sharp shock running across her arm until it reached her finger tip that was resting on a crate. The bolt caused her to snap her hand back.

Buran eyed her reaction, but said nothing.

If they got arrested, surely they would confiscate her belongings, taking away her opportunity to decide if she needed the Enertin inside. But then again, they'd give her medication behind bars, right? Whether she wanted them or not. Surely they wouldn't risk an outburst.

Like the one Buran had. Which was also her fault. He didn't seem to fully remember why he'd created an ice skating rink in this warehouse, but she was sure it'd come back to him. Just as her recollection of killing Mackie had come back to her.

It was only a matter of time.

"You're the governor of Stillfield," Jemma pointed out. "How will that affect what happens to us?"

"I'm not sure," he said. "A governor of a Republic hasn't been arrested for conspiracy and assault before."

Jemma swallowed. She had a feeling the jury wouldn't go easy on him. Not with the history of the world they lived in. Any fighting amongst the Republics would not be tolerated.

"I'm not sure that's something we can risk." When Jemma stopped talking, it was eerily quiet—no calls for surrender in the last few minutes. "We need to think of something. Now."

Buran pointed up, his hand shaking. Jemma followed it to see a small window. A stack of crates led up to it, each covered in ice, like the side of a large glacier.

It would be tricky to get to, but it may be their only escape.

"Can you melt it?" Governor Dunn asked.

"No. I don't have enough energy left." As anxious as she was about getting caught, it wasn't enough to build the level of energy it'd take to melt that much ice.

"We climb it," Buran said, his voice hoarse. Some color was coming back to his face. "We can use the crow bars. They should be sharp enough to stab inside."

Jemma looked at Governor Dunn.

"I don't think we have much other choice," he said, grabbing the crow bar Jemma had used earlier. Frost covered the metal. "If we don't make it, we'll get arrested. Which is the same outcome if we turn ourselves in."

Jemma had an uneasy feeling that there was another possible outcome if they were caught trying to escape.

Was the risk worth her life? Never seeing her children or her husband again?

They'd lived through separation due to imprisonment before. She wasn't sure if she could do that again.

And if she was killed, well, her kids would be safe from her. Maybe that was what she deserved.

All or nothing, she thought. She grabbed two crow bars and stabbed them into the ice. Small particles flew off from the impact.

"Let's go," she said as she lifted herself.

Thankfully, the glacier was sloped. It was as if she were climbing up a slide covered in soap and water. One that could give her frostbite if she touched it for too long.

She continued to climb, stabbing the ice then lifting herself up a few feet. She wiggled her feet to get some grip and pulled one crow bar out, lifting it higher. She repeated the process with the other side. One after the other. Buran and Governor Dunn followed behind.

She could tell they were physically able to climb faster than her, but they stayed back. She appreciated that they wouldn't leave her behind. Even Buran had regained his strength after being completely frozen. Dunn had helped him at first, but now he was scaling the ice on his own.

When she made it to the window, she found it was partially broken. A hole was in the bottom of the pane, though not large enough to fit through. With a crowbar in one hand, Jemma swung at the remaining window. Glass rained down upon their heads. Once the opening was large enough, she slipped through, avoiding the sharp edges of glass that remained as best she could.

She gasped.

The top half of her body rested outside the window, giving her a view of the fields below. The ones they had recently driven past.

They were now covered in ice. A shining glimmer blinded her, keeping her from seeing how far Buran's outburst had spread. She thought it had been contained inside the warehouse, but she'd been wrong. Buran's full force had continued forward and ruined Preen's crops.

This was not good.

"Are you able to get down?" Governor Dunn shouted. In the distance, clanging and banging echoed against the steel door they had blockaded before they left.

At the sound of Dunn's voice, Jemma remembered the rush they were in. She glanced back, seeing the boxes in front of the door shaking. Someone was forcing their way inside.

"Crap," she yelled as she leaned forward. At least the ice had created a slide on this side of the building as well. Head first, she slid toward the ground, picking up speed as she went. She hadn't expected to go so fast, but as the bottom leveled out, she slowed.

Looking behind her, she saw Buran already coming down. Governor Dunn was at the window behind him. A gun shot rang out as he tilted forward, allowing the weight of his upper body to carry him to safety.

Jemma sat on the ice, lifting herself carefully to her feet. Buran skidded past her, and then the Governor.

"Whoa. That was quite the ride," Buran said, holding his head. "Knocked my head on the ice as I started to come down. How 'bout you, Dunn?"

Governor Dunn remained still on the ice.

It was then Jemma noticed the trail. Bright red blood followed his path from the upper window.

Her heart stopped. She recognized his stillness.

Governor Tobias Dunn was dying.

Jemma pushed herself across the ice and shook Dunn's body. A soft groan came from him.

"Come on," Jemma said. "You're alright. We'll get out of here and get you help."

Governor Dunn rolled his head to look at her. His eyes were glossed over, and blood dripped from his mouth. "He…" he said with a strained voice, "he wasn't…"

"That doesn't matter right now. We need to get you to safety." Tears blurred Jemma's vision.

Buran arrived at their sides, placing a hand on Dunn's shoulder, above where the bullet had pierced his heart. "You've done good," Buran said. "You've proven that change is possible. That corruption can be reversed. I'll always remember you for that."

Jemma shot Buran a look. "We need to get him out of here."

Buran's face paled. He shook his hanging head.

In the distance, a siren rang.

"They're over here!" a voice called out. Jemma looked toward the road, which was half iced over, to see a group of Responders approaching, guns pointed in their direction.

"We need to move," Buran said. He carefully tried to stand on the slippery surface but slipped just as a bullet flew past him.

Jemma covered Governor Dunn with her body, warm blood seeping through her blouse.

Dunn moved his hand slowly to grip her arm. "He wasn't... meant to... die."

"What? Who?" Jemma asked, lifting herself to watch as life slowly drained from Governor Dunn's face.

"Skylar... forgive me..." he said with his final breath. Dunn's grip on her arm relaxed as his hand fell to the ground.

"No!" Jemma yelled as another bullet rang out. The Responders had already killed one of them, and they didn't seem to care if they killed more.

"We need to head for cover," Buran said, tugging on Jemma's arm. About five yards away was a grove of trees.

She didn't want to leave Dunn's body, but there was no way they could drag him with them.

Buran shuffled across the ice. It was quicker and made him a harder target. Jemma got down and followed his lead.

The Responders seemed to realize shooting from that distance wouldn't be effective. Their feet slid as they stepped onto the ice. Slowly, they made their way toward Jemma and Buran.

"They're going to get close enough to shoot," Jemma said.

"Do you have any energy back? Or is the Enertin restraining it too much?" His voice sounded bitter. Jemma let it go. This wasn't the time to fight him on it.

"I don't think I can muster any right now." Her heart was heavy. She'd lost a friend.

"Fine. I'll do all the work." Buran rolled to his side and pushed his hands out. A spray of ice flew out, creating a wall between them and Governor Dunn's body.

He grunted as he worked, occasionally glaring at Jemma. His nose wrinkled and eyebrows pulled down. He looked at her as if she were a rotten apple covered in mold with worms eating through the core.

She turned away, more determined than ever to find cover.

Behind her, Buran breathed deeply. He'd finished his defense. The ice wall between them and the Responders was a couple feet thick. She heard gunshots, but they sounded as if they were contained in the distance.

They kept moving. Once she arrived at the trees, she attempted to stand once more. Her hand pressed against the frozen trunk for balance.

Her entire body shivered, but she could no longer feel the cold. Numbness shot through her as she took a step. Then another step. She continued into the orchard, the apple trees around her unaware of her presence.

Up ahead, the ice thinned. Buran was still behind her, following in her tracks. Before long, her feet sloshed through wet grass. She could finally walk without holding onto a tree for balance.

Her body burned as it warmed. Goosebumps pricked her skin, but at least she was no longer surrounded by ice. A patch of sunlight broke through the trees in the distance. Her body yearned for the light to touch it.

The sun rays greeted her as she stepped into them. She sat on top of a large stump, its warmth bringing life back into her bones.

Buran joined her. He sighed as he lifted his face toward the sun. Light gleamed off fresh streaks of tears.

Jemma was quiet. His anger—no, disgust—earlier still chilled her insides. She waited for him to break the silence.

But he had nothing to say. Buran rubbed his hands together, likely to create heat.

Jemma shivered next to him. She wrinkled her nose, the skin on her face tingling with each movement.

"I'm not sure we're far enough away to keep Responders from finding us," Buran finally said. "They'll likely travel to this side of the ice to search for us in no time."

"Where can we go?" Jemma looked around at the trees that surrounded them. "Perhaps we could call someone?" She reached into her bag and pulled out her phone. The screen stayed black as she tried to touch it.

"Who would we have to help us out here?"

"Quill and Calum are still out there," Jemma said, trying to power on her phone. "My phone seems to be broken, or the battery died. What about yours?"

Buran patted his pockets. "I think I left it in the warehouse. I'd been taking pictures with it before..."

Jemma nodded. They were stuck on the run with no way to contact help. Great.

Buran stood. "Staying here won't be good for us. I'm heading deeper into the trees." Without waiting for a reply, he headed to the opposite side of where they'd entered the small patch of light.

Jemma hesitated. Did he even want her to follow? Her frozen heart wanted to stay put and wait for her fate. If anyone deserved to be arrested, it was her. She could explain what happened, that it was all her idea and her plan that went wrong. She was the one that deserved to be punished. She was the one that deserved to die.

She stood, hesitant for a moment before turning to face the way they'd come, the direction of the Responders.

As she went to take a step toward her doom, Buran emerged from the trees. "Let's go, Hodgerton. I believe this way is south."

He wanted her to come with him. Perhaps they could make it out of this after all.

Unlike Governor Dunn. A death that only happened because of her choices.

Her hope sank as she rose to her feet. Even if they made it back home safely, the damage had been done.

The world they'd return to would change, and a feeling of unease washed over Jemma as she thought about what was next.

For her.

For her family.

For Stillfield.

Thirty-One

The sunlight outside was bright as Quill emerged from the underground bunker. She was surprised to see the outside, considering they hadn't climbed a ladder to emerge. They'd been at least fifty feet underground.

"How are we outside?" Quill said as she squinted.

"Remember how bombs created holes throughout the Earth?" Aunt Bea asked. "Well, welcome to the Outskirts."

Quill's breath caught in her throat. The Outskirts were a barren wasteland, and yet here they were now. Her insides squirmed, still unsure if it was truly safe to be out here.

The space in front of her was bare. In the distance, the edge of land curved upward, a fence barely visible at the top. The direction of Preen and the other Republics. To the other side was flat land. Also mostly bare brown dirt, but if she looked hard enough, she could see the faint outline of green.

"That's where we're headed," Aunt Bea said. "It looks far, but it's not a bad hike."

Quill walked with her across the ground. Cracks broke across the surface. Pieces of old debris scattered throughout. The last remains of what once was.

"Is it safe to be out here?" Quill asked. She'd learned about radiation in her studies. Some atomic bombs had lasting effects, poisoning survivors in their aftermath. Others were supposedly less poisonous, but there weren't many survivors close to the impact sites to test that theory. Only the Republics had remained. Preen was closest to the largest blast.

"People have been living out here for over thirty years, so I'd say it's pretty safe."

"Living?" Quill's mouth dropped.

"We're going to the village. It's just up ahead." Aunt Bea looked at Quill, seeming to notice her disbelief. "Some places are safe for Disparates," she said.

They started their hike. The sun was hot today. Sweat rolled down Quill's face. "Exactly how far away is the village?"

"It needed to be far enough that it couldn't be seen from Preen. About two miles. I know it's a hike, but trust me, it's worth it." Aunt Bea walked quickly without breaking a sweat. "Plus, walking is good for you." She winked.

Quill wasn't too convinced. Her heavy breathing didn't feel too healthy for her. Of course, her lifestyle wasn't very active. Hard to get much exercise in while locked up.

Another thought weighed on her mind. "Are there any waterfalls out here? Or even in town?"

Aunt Bea looked at her. "Not that I'm aware of, although that would be quite refreshing after our hike."

So unlikely for her mother's postcard to be talking about a place in Preen.

As they continued their hike, the patch of green on the ground turned into an outline of trees.

"There it is," Aunt Bea said. "Just behind the evergreens."

They walked through the small grove and Quill's eyes widened. In front of her was indeed a small village. They stood next to gardens, and on the other side were small homes made of wood.

A stream of water flowed down the rows of food. It was clear, not polluted like she'd been taught. As she followed it, she noticed the water came from a block of ice that an Ice Disparate nearby created. An older woman stood next to it, her hands releasing flames to melt it as more ice formed. The two laughed after as if it were a game.

She looked closer at the other people around them. A young man was harvesting potatoes, creating holes in the ground around the starchy vegetables, while another floated them out of the holes and placed them inside bags an older child was holding. Similar to what Calum had tried to do with the corn crop, except these vegetables didn't crumble.

Quill looked at her aunt in surprise. "What is this place?"

"This," Aunt Bea said, "is the O.W.L. base. I know it's pretty unbelievable, isn't it?"

"What is O.W.L.?"

"It stands for Outskirts Will Live." Aunt Bea walked forward. "The Rain of Fire changed this land, just like it changed Disparates' minds. But that doesn't mean both are worth abandoning. Don't worry, you'll fit in and get used to it in no time."

Quill didn't follow. "What do you mean, fit in? I can't stay here." She'd just met her aunt, but now her stomach churned at how easily she'd assumed her intentions.

"Isn't that why you came to find me?" Aunt Bea asked. "To find out more about yourself? To find where you belong?"

She was right. Part of Quill never belonged in Stillfield. Definitely never belonged on the islands. But she'd only just arrived here.

"My dad wouldn't be able to stay here," Quill said. "He's the governor of Stillfield."

"It wasn't him I was inviting. Let me show you around some more," Aunt Bea said. "Give it a chance. And if you don't want to stay, you don't have to."

There wouldn't be much harm in looking. Besides, she didn't have anywhere else to hide right now. It was likely her dad had either been arrested by now or was on the train to Stillfield.

No. He wouldn't have left without her.

"Is there a way to find out where my dad is?"

Aunt Bea's eyes were soft. "I'll see what I can do."

"Okay," Quill said. "Thank you."

They meandered around the village. Aunt Bea seemed quite popular, waving back at different people as they passed. Quill counted a dozen log houses but noticed more buildings, including a larger one, farther in the village.

They stopped at a log house that had yellow curtains in the window. Aunt Bea opened the door.

"Welcome to my home."

Quill entered into the small cabin. It was larger and nicer than the shack from earlier. A light flickered on.

"How do you have electricity out here?" Quill asked.

"From batteries. Electric energy is very efficient at refilling them."

Quill thought she had control of her energy, but she never would have thought how useful it could truly be.

"We believe energy power was given to us as a blessing from above," Aunt Bea said as she sat at her table. "It is meant to help us survive, not be the cause of more suffering. That's what the Republics have wrong. They believe Disparates are dangerous and need to be contained. We believe Disparates were made for a reason. Humankind is fragile, and it has evolved to survive."

That was a new idea: that Disparates were meant to exist and had been granted their deep emotions and the energy that came with it from some greater power. It was an idea that would take some getting used to.

"What is the goal?" Quill asked. Surely there was more to what this group wanted.

"We want to live. Use our gifts for good."

"But what about the Republics?"

"The Republics are free to live how they want. As long as they allow us to be ourselves. They kicked us out, but we want to prove to them they are wrong. They want to destroy us, but we want to show them that we are the survivors. We want justice, and the way we will get it is by showing them just how well we can survive."

"So you're growing a new country? Like before the Rain?" Like before, when there were hundreds of countries, which led to mass destruction and death.

"Yes, I guess you could put it that way."

"And the Republics are okay with that?" Quill's heart beat faster. The reason the Republics existed was to keep world peace. "You aren't worried about a war?"

"We don't need to go to war. We can make what we need and live off our energy. The Republics don't even know we exist, and we plan to keep it that way. Your mother helped found this village. She was going to bring you here to raise you before she died."

"My mother did?" Perhaps that was why people stared at her. It wasn't because she was an outsider, but because she was meant to live here all along.

"Yes. And now we can go meet with Urlan. The leader of our village."

Quill swallowed. The leader of an illegal settlement meeting a Republic governor's daughter. This would be interesting.

Thirty-Two

Jemma and Buran hiked through the orchard of trees. Once they reached the last row, they examined the small farmhouse and barn in front of them.

Thankfully, they saw no signs of Responders, only a young girl leading a horse inside the barn and closing the door behind her.

"Should we find a place to hide?" Jemma asked, huffing.

"No. We should keep moving while we can. Sitting and waiting for someone to catch us isn't going to work."

Jemma's cheeks flushed. The warmth reminded her they were still thawing.

"Which way do we go?" she asked. She focused on catching her breath while they were stopped. She was more winded than usual, although the sudden shock of going from freezing to thawing under the summer heat likely played a part in her weariness. Not to mention the grief hiding under the surface. She didn't have time to think about Governor Dunn's death—or his final message.

Buran turned his head from one direction to the next. "We weren't far from the train station before we went into the warehouse. If we keep heading south, we should find some tracks that will lead us there."

The train, of course. It was supposed to wait for them before leaving. "Do you think we can sneak onto one of the train cars?"

"That, or we follow the tracks back to Stillfield. Although I imagine that would take a while walking. Not sure we could stay hidden that long. If we can sneak onto the supply train headed to Stillfield, we'd be home by tomorrow. Just as planned."

Home.

Jemma's heart fluttered at the word. Ben and Louie and Mackie were her home. Of course that was where she needed to go.

Buran continued, "As long as we make it before the—"

A whistle blew three times in the distance. The sound of a departing train.

They'd missed their ride to Stillfield.

Buran wrinkled his face then shrugged his shoulders. "It's okay," he said frantically. "There's going to be another train. There has to be. We'll just catch that one. Tomorrow. There'll be a train tomorrow."

His eyes met with Jemma's, the blue of his irises swirling like the knot in the tree next to him. She slowly nodded her approval, knowing there was unlikely to be another train scheduled for departure for a few days.

A smile spread across his face as the train faded. It'd left the station, headed away from them. Abandoning them in unsafe territory.

"We need to find a place to sleep tonight," Jemma said.

"Right, right." Buran bit his bottom lip. "Think the folks in there will let us stay?" He motioned toward the farmhouse.

"Highly doubtful." Jemma wrinkled her forehead in concern for Buran. He truly seemed to be losing his mind.

That was until he smirked at her. "Didn't think so. Considering no one has come to find us in this orchard, perhaps we find a warm spot of ground and camp out? Even have dinner here." He grabbed an apple off the tree.

Jemma was still on edge, unsure how Buran was processing the events of the last few hours. The look on his face when he'd caught her with Enertin had burned into her mind, frozen there in a way that would never defrost. "The barn might be an option."

"True." Buran tossed the apple into the air and caught it. "We'll have to make sure no farm hands are inside. Have you seen anyone exit?"

Jemma shook her head. Then again, she hadn't been watching the barn. She'd been focused on keeping herself hidden behind the trees.

"I don't think we can risk it," Buran said. "Perhaps once the sun sets, we can return. No one should be inside overnight."

Movement near the barn drew her attention. It wasn't the girl from earlier, but rather a young man with dark, curly hair. He moved slowly, hiding himself behind a tractor before popping his face over the side to search the space in front of him. Once he seemed satisfied that it was empty, he rushed to the side of the barn, knocking on the door.

The girl from before opened. Jemma just made out the smile on her face before the boy slipped inside. They looked to be on some teenage rendezvous.

"Or maybe someone will be there all night," Jemma said, shooting Buran an amused look.

He ran a hand through his blonde hair. "Well, that answers that. We haven't heard any Responders searching through here in the last half an hour, so I bet they've cleared it. Let's head deeper inside though—more warning if someone is trooping through the woods."

They headed back to a small clearing they'd passed earlier, one deep enough inside the grove of trees to not be seen but with just enough space to lay down for sleeping. Buran gathered wood and laid it in the center. Then he took a step back and stared at it. Jemma raised an eyebrow, once again worried about his state of mind.

"Well," he said, "I seem to have forgotten we don't have any flame energy between the two of us."

Jemma couldn't help but release a laugh. "You also seem to have forgotten that we're trying to *not* be caught. Smoke would be a dead giveaway."

Dead. The word rang in her ears.

"Instead of laughing at me, why don't you think of another way to stay warm tonight. Maybe use that electricity you have? You can create heat without smoke..." He trailed off as his eyes darkened, landing on her purse. "That is, if you can use your energy."

She grabbed it defensively. "I mustered enough to save you. I can probably create some warmth if we need it."

"Go ahead."

The sun was setting, and a new chill filled the evening air. She recalled the way Quill had control of her electricity in the mall months ago. The strings of lightning had danced around her. If Jemma could emulate that command, she wouldn't need to worry about the cold. Jemma's body craved warmth. She closed her eyes and focused on her current situation.

Governor Dunn was dead. The thought hit her first, causing her chest to buckle. It didn't make her uneasy; it only opened a deep crevice in her soul. Thoughts of her father poured out, reminding her that Governor Dunn had been his friend and had taken on a bit of a fatherly role to her these past months.

He wasn't supposed to die. Those had been some of Dunn's last words. He'd mentioned her father's name. If her father wasn't meant to die, then why start the house fire in the first place?

It was Dr. Paxton that had wanted him dead. At the time, however, she wasn't in charge of Lucky Island. Director Wallow was. Asher had been there during the transition. There had to be more to this story.

Her heart ached, but she pushed it aside. She needed to think of something else. Now wasn't the time to dwell on sadness.

She opened her right eye slightly, just enough to catch sight of Buran. He stood nearby, watching her expectantly. Waiting for her to show her power. Not unlike the times in training, when he expected her to keep her energy in control. He'd looked at her during those times with pride. A teacher helping his pupil succeed.

Except then, the teacher didn't know the student was cheating. But he knew now, and that knowledge changed the expression on his face. Instead of hopefulness, he looked spiteful. He didn't expect her to be able to do it.

Fine. *If you can use your energy*. His challenging words flowed through her mind.

She wanted to be indignant. Prove him wrong. Her stubbornness was coming to the surface.

No, Jemma, wrong emotion. She shook her head. She needed to focus on her fears. Even with the red pills, she'd still felt them. Why couldn't she do so now?

She felt light headed. She opened her eyes to see the ground in front of her ripple. She glanced at Buran, who tilted his head. But he did so slowly, as if pushing against the air to get himself to move.

Jemma glanced at the leaves; the wind had all but stopped. A leaf next to her face hung in the air, not attached to the branch but not following the force of gravity to the ground.

This was it. Time around her had slowed, as it had with Caty and on the train. As it did during Buran's frost. She figured it was a side effect of taking the wrong Enertin for too long.

Jemma tried to stand, but her body was stuck. The most she could do was move her eyes and think.

She didn't like that. The fear she was looking for rippled through her. It flowed from her mind, down through her heart, and spread across her chest. As it crawled its way through her arms, it intensified, heading for her hands, which were currently sitting on her lap.

Sweat rolled down her face as she lifted her hands out in front of her. A scream escaped as lightning plowed into the ground.

Buran jumped backward and fell onto the ground, the slowing spell somehow broken. Jemma's breathing was heavy as the last of her electric energy left her.

"Whoa," Buran said as he scrambled to his feet. The sticks he'd so meticulously gathered were now black ash. "Where did that come from?"

"I don't know," Jemma said. "But I felt every inch of it as it flowed through me. Everything else had slowed." She looked at him, her eyes widening to match his.

"What do you mean?" he asked.

"Time has been slowing around me. Well, at least that's what it looks like to me." Jemma glanced at the leaf that had landed on her arm. How it'd stayed there after her motion, she wasn't sure. She blew on it, watching as it drifted the rest of the way to the ground.

Buran's eyebrows met in the center of his face. "How long has this been happening?"

"The last few days, but it doesn't happen very often."

"How long have you been taking Enertin?"

"Um..." The conversation Jemma had been afraid of was here. Buran had put two and two together when he caught her in the warehouse and now she'd need to explain herself.

Instead of feeling afraid though, she felt lighter. As if the secret had been the heavier burden to bear.

"Since that day with Mackie," she confessed. She took a deep breath. "Since I killed my baby. I couldn't be trusted. I didn't trust myself. What if it happened again?" Tears streamed down her face as she locked eyes with Buran. "I couldn't risk hurting him, or Louie, or anyone else like that again."

Buran was quiet. The silence was more hurtful than any words he could have said.

"I'm so sorry," Jemma said, looking away. "I didn't mean to hurt you either or cause an icy reaction. And now I'm responsible for Dunn's death as well. I'm a danger to everyone around me—with or without Enertin."

"I get it," Buran said. He looked at the burned sticks in the middle of the trees. "It's too dangerous with pills. It's too dangerous without them."

Like a wasp to her heart, Jemma's chest stung. The thing she'd been hiding for so long was now accepted, but it didn't feel as freeing as she'd hoped.

Of course, he didn't know the full truth. That she wasn't taking *her* Enertin. She was taking Ben's.

Buran lowered himself onto the dirt, placing his head into his hands. "I was foolish," he said. "My plan never would have worked."

Jemma wanted to move to him, place a hand on his shoulder to give him comfort, but it felt too intimate of a gesture. Especially after admitting she'd been taking Enertin all these months.

She stayed where she was, watching the man break and having no words to put him back together.

"What do you think will happen now?" Jemma asked as she lowered herself to sit across from Buran, his weary face illuminated by the light of the stars and waning moon.

"I told you. A train will come tomorrow, and we will be on it."

"As long as it's heading to Stillfield, right?"

Buran looked at the ground. "Yeah..."

"You do want to go home, don't you?" His unsure attitude made Jemma wonder if there was more. And then the thought hit her. If people didn't know already, they would soon find out about Governor Dunn. She could only imagine the fear that would run through Ben's mind when he heard about it. Too bad she didn't have a way to contact him. "Keesha must be worried about you."

At the name of his wife, Buran straightened. "Maybe. Although I imagine she's glad to be rid of me."

Jemma's eyes widened. "What do you mean?"

"Things haven't been going well at home." Buran sighed. "Keesha's been wanting things I can't give her."

"Like what?" Jemma pried. She felt her face warm; perhaps she was being too forward. She'd listened to some of Keesha's concerns when they'd had their drinks and dessert girls' night, but most of them went back to wanting to spend more time with Buran. "I mean, if you want to talk about it."

"She wants to have a baby."

"And you don't?"

"I don't right now." Buran stared at the ground. "This isn't a safe world for children. No offense."

Jemma didn't take any. After everything she'd been through and put her children through, she agreed.

"But also," Buran continued, "she's been begging me to spend more time at home. She doesn't fully understand my work, even with attending my classes. She sees it as a side hobby. It's nice, but she doesn't realize how important it is. That I'm doing it so that we can start our family. Make this world a place where it's possible for Disparates to grow up in peace. I want to be a father. That's why I work so hard."

"That's beautiful," Jemma said. "Have you told her that?"

"I've tried, but she says I'm using that as an excuse. That I've been using it as an excuse for the last seven years of our marriage. She doesn't believe there will ever be a perfect time to have children."

"Well, she's right." Jemma let out a small chuckle. "There is no right time, and there's no way to fully prepare. Your desire is admirable. I get it. Even more now than I ever had before. But at the same time, I'd never take back having my children. They are a huge part of what keeps me going. If you don't want kids, that's fine. Not everyone does. But if you have the desire to be a father, don't let fear stop your dreams."

A small smile spread on Buran's face. "You may be right."

"So, will you talk to Keesha about it when you get back?"

"Depending on if we get out of this mess, I'll take your words into consideration."

"I look forward to meeting baby Kuzmin in the future."

Buran laughed. But the word kept floating in her mind.

Baby.

Would it be irresponsible to bring another life into this world? She shook off the thought.

"Besides, work won't be much of an issue anymore."

"What do you mean?" Jemma raised an eyebrow. Buran was work, and work was Buran.

He huffed a small laugh. "You were there. You saw what happened. Clearly, I'm not the person to preach staying in control. All this time, I was telling Disparates they could handle their emotions on their own. That they didn't need pills. They just needed to breathe and count fingers." He shook his head. "Yet this whole time, the progress I thought my students were making... the progress I thought you were making..."

Jemma's chest tightened. He wasn't as okay with her actions as she'd thought.

Buran's dark eyes turned toward her. "How did you do it?"

"What do you mean?"

His gaze was a spotlight fixated on her. "Use your energy. If you're taking Enertin, you shouldn't be able to use your energy with such control."

"Oh..." Jemma took a deep breath. "That's the thing. I'm not taking the right kind of Enertin."

"Jemma, I saw you take the bottle." A light bulb went off as Buran's eyes widened. "Jemma, no. Don't tell me you were taking the wrong kind."

Jemma gulped, although her mouth was dry. "I've been taking Ben's. It's all we had, and I was desperate. Buran, I needed something to keep from having an explosion. And it worked."

"There's a reason they formulate the pills differently." Buran looked as if he were trying to find the words to explain the concept to Jemma. One she already knew well. "Taking the wrong one is dangerous. It could make your powers unpredictable. You could light up without feeling anxious. By trying to make yourself safer, you did the opposite."

"But I didn't. And I was able to use my electricity in the warehouse. It came in handy." Jemma regretted the words as they came out. Perhaps she was being too indignant, bringing up his outburst.

She knew she was projecting. He'd hit a nerve, as the side effects of taking the wrong drug had finally caught up to her. She shook off the thoughts of terror she had an hour ago, frozen in her own skin.

The hurt on his face was evident. "You're right; I'm not one to judge. You made the choice because you felt it was the best one you had. Same as me. Too bad we were both wrong." Buran's gaze moved to the bag lying next to Jemma.

Instinctively, she placed her hand on top of it. The pills inside rattled.

"Those are the proper ones, right?" Buran asked.

Jemma nodded.

"Good. Did you happen to grab any white ones?" He looked at her with a sad hopefulness.

She wanted to tell him yes, but she knew that'd be a lie. She shook her head.

His face fell back toward the ground. "Figures. Have enough of the yellow ones to share?"

Jemma's body froze. She wanted to believe Buran was joking, but his tone told her otherwise.

"Look, you've kept your energy under control for years," Jemma said. "I think you can continue to do so a little bit longer. At least long enough to get the medication that's made for Ice Disparates."

Buran responded with a sigh as he laid down in the dirt and closed his eyes.

Looked like Jemma would be taking the first watch of the night.

THIRTY-THREE

The water was rougher than the night before, the storm from then had returned with a vengeance. Asher's knuckles whitened from his grasp on the steering wheel.

When he'd learned that O.W.L. sailed to Lucky Island on kayaks, he didn't believe them. That was until he saw the small boats with his own eyes. He insisted right then to take Dominic's boat. He'd already stolen it—might as well get his use out of it.

He needed to make it back home. And those kayaks would not have preserved his life long enough for that.

The sky was dark, as the moon was waning and taking its light with it. A skilled navigator would use the stars to guide them. Asher was not. Having spent most of his nights inside behind barred windows, his knowledge of the stars was limited.

"Do you recall anything that could help guide our path?" Leda yelled over the wind.

Asher shook his head. "I'm pretty sure we sailed straight."

"Straight in what direction? We're on the ocean. Straight could take us anywhere." Leda stood next to the captain's chair, her arms folded across her chest. Her eyes searched the darkness in front of them.

"I'm trying my best to remember," Asher grunted. As frustrated as the darkness made him feel, at least it hid the smoke rising from the small space between his fingers.

"We've been out here for hours," Kingston said. He sat on the side seat near the two. "The winds are getting stronger. I don't think we're finding the lighthouse tonight. We should turn back to Lucky Island."

"No, we have to keep searching," Leda said. "You know how important this is."

"Is it worth risking our lives?"

Leda crossed her arms. "I'd risk anything for her."

Kingston stood from his seat and placed a hand on Leda's shoulder. "We're not giving up on finding her. We're making sure we're still around to do so."

After a brief silence, Leda answered, "You promise we'll try again?"

Kingston held his hand up, making the shape of an 'O' with his fingers. "O.W.L.'s honor."

"Fine," Leda said. "Asher, turn us around."

"One problem," Asher said. "I'm not too sure where Lucky is either. I mean, I have an idea. Not a solid one, but it's there."

The sigh that escaped Leda could rival a lion's roar. "Move over," she said as she pushed Asher away from the wheel.

"Yesterday was my first time driving a boat." Asher willfully stepped back, his hands raised in surrender. "All yours. I do believe we need to sail in..." He looked around then pointed at the back of the ship. "That direction."

"Watch it," Kingston said, sitting back down. "She once overcooked a pot of porridge simply because she was told she needed to stir it more often. She's more keen to do the opposite of what she's told. Considering much more is at stake in this situation than some burned breakfast, I suggest you take a seat and let her lead."

"Really?" Asher raised an eyebrow with a smirk. "Guess that's one thing we have in common."

Leda rolled her eyes as she turned the wheel of the ship. "Hopefully we make it back before morning."

Asher sat, or rather fell, onto the seat next to Kingston. His stomach churned with the sudden sharp pivot. Leda held her strong posture at the wheel, barely swaying from the motion.

The wind became stronger the longer they sailed. Asher gripped the rail of the ship, his eyes searching the distant darkness for a sign of land. Just as the sun's fiery first rays breached the horizon, Lucky Island came into view.

"We're almost there!" Leda shouted over the roaring waves. The ship bounced on the water, as if the ocean were a predator playing with its prey. If they didn't make it to land soon, the water's hunger would win.

Yet the distant shore seemed to bring its own threat. There, on the small beach they were headed toward, between the bushes and overgrown trees, Asher made out the shape of a person.

"Are you expecting someone to be waiting for us on land?" Asher asked.

"Not that I know of." Kingston placed a hand over his eyes as he followed Asher's gaze. "They aren't expecting us back at least until tomorrow, assuming we had found Lighthouse Island."

"It's too dangerous to be on the surface in the daytime," Leda said. However, she didn't falter.

"Should we change our course?" Asher yelled. Although he could see the rest of the island edge was covered in sharp rocks. Not a safe journey for a boat, especially in this weather.

"It's only one person. They can be easily dealt with." Leda's voice had softened, barely heard over the crashing waves.

Asher wiped water off his brow after an especially tall wave hit the side of the boat. He understood her plan. He'd need to fight his tightened chest and turn his trepidation into vexation. Whoever was standing at their landing spot would be met with a challenge.

Especially if it happened to be a member of R.E.I.

As they sailed closer, the rising emotion for the encounter Asher was anticipating waned. The anger he wanted to feel all but disappeared as the fear returned when he saw the face on the shore.

He was seething.

"Where is he?" Ben shouted once the boat was closer to shore. "If he's hurt... I swear, Asher. If you hurt my son..." Ben's head shook violently.

Both Leda and Kingston looked wide-eyed at Asher.

"You know this guy?" Leda asked.

"He's okay," Asher shouted back. "He's safe, don't worry."

Kingston hopped out of the boat first to anchor it to shore. Asher followed him. Ben waited on the edge of the water, his arms folded across his chest.

"Where is Louie?" Ben glared at Asher, his nostrils flared.

"Relax." Asher regretted his word choice as soon as he'd said it. Ben's face tightened. "Whoa, whoa. I get it, you're upset. But he's safe. He's with a friend." It was true. Crow was a friend.

"Friends? On the island?" Ben's voice was sharp. "Look where we are!" he shouted. "And you have the audacity to leave my six-year-old out of sight? Not to mention the fact you brought him here in the first place. Absolutely unbelievable." Ben's mouth gaped and his hands tangled in his hair.

"Shhh, keep it down," Asher said. The sun was rising behind the heavy gray storm clouds. R.E.I. officers certainly were beginning their day. Ben's shouting would easily draw their attention.

But instead of quieting, Ben glared at him. His face was red, and a vein underneath his scar bulged. Sweat poured from his brow line.

It was then Asher noticed the warmth. Despite the chill of the wind and the mist from the raging sea behind them, heat pulsed from the man in front of him. Like a fever that wouldn't break.

"I WILL NOT KEEP IT DOWN," Ben shouted. "NOT UNTIL MY CHILD IS IN MY ARMS." Ben threw his hands down in front of him, lighting a spark. A flash of flames blinded Asher, who threw his body to the ground.

He waited for the intensity of the heat to lessen, for the flame energy to be used up, giving a break from the burning he felt on his skin through the clothes on his back.

It didn't let up. The heat continued to burn. Asher glanced over his arm. Flames danced around him, encasing him in their glow. Through the blaze, he made out the forms of Leda and

Kingston. They both squatted, their bodies facing away from Ben.

"Get up!" Asher yelled. "The forest is on fire!" All around him, the world burned. Leda and Kingston rose at his exclamation.

Leda coughed. "We have a clear path next to us if you can make your way here." She covered her mouth with her arm as Kingston held her elbow and motioned her forward.

They were about three yards away. Three yards that were covered in an inferno.

Asher turned around, toward where Ben had stood. His body lay on the sand of the small beach. His eyes were closed, his clothes covered in burnt ash with holes in spots that burned. The exposed skin Asher could see on his arms was wrinkled and dark.

This shouldn't have happened. This shouldn't be happening. Ben wasn't a Disparate any longer.

And yet, Asher wasn't too surprised that EnertinX had failed. He'd seen this happen time and time again, with each new version of the cure. Each time being promised that it would finally work. But it didn't. Each round he had tested resulted in another outburst.

And just like those other times, he was to blame for this outburst as well.

He looked back at Ben. After a burst like that, it was a wonder his flesh still clung to his body. Images of past islanders flashed into his mind. Bodies burned and mangled, or crushed by the very Earth they'd moved. Faces with death frozen behind glaciers. Bodies ripped apart, floating in the air in pieces.

Asher had seen Disparates destroyed by their own energy. Their own emotions. Ben was dead. He had to be dead. But Asher couldn't leave his body behind. He needed to know for sure.

He jumped through the fire that burned between him and his brother. Asher patted out the flame that had caught onto his pant leg. He wasn't ready to burn, not today.

Ben's chest lifted. Relief flowed through Asher. He was still breathing. Somehow, he was still breathing.

He knew it wasn't good to move the injured, but in this situation, with the island burning around them, it wasn't an option to leave him. Carefully, he slid his arms underneath his back and legs. Asher grunted as he lifted Ben's limp body.

"Need some help?" Kingston's voice rang through the crackling fire.

Asher turned toward his voice. He'd made it through the inferno and now stood where Asher had first fallen only a few feet away.

Just as Asher was about to leap over the flames to join Kingston in his small, clear space, a loud crack rang out. A rush of heat pelted Asher's face as a large tree trunk fell between him and Kingston. He leaped back, moving out of the way just in time.

Unfortunately, he stepped into a burning bush. The flames licked at his legs as he fell against the bark. Ben's body collapsed onto the sand at the base of the fallen tree trunk.

"If we can bring him up here, we should be able to use this tree to get to safety," Kingston said. He had climbed on top of the trunk and now stood about four feet above the ground.

Asher grabbed under Ben's arms and lifted his body, using the trunk to stabilize himself. Kingston leaned over and grabbed hold of Ben, pulling him the rest of the way to temporary safety.

"Get him out of here," Asher yelled at Kingston. "I'll be right behind you."

Kingston nodded as he lifted Ben into his large arms. "Sorry I can't be of more help. Electricity wouldn't stop this fire." He turned, taking large strides across the log.

A sharp heat bit at Asher's leg. The fire had indeed caught hold of his jeans, which had now incinerated to his knee. Asher grabbed handfuls of sand and buried his burning leg until the flames ceased.

Breathing heavily, he assessed his situation. Flames bellowed around him, other than on the trunk at his back. But even that would soon be consumed. His leg continued to throb under the cool sand, but he had no other choice. He had to keep moving.

He tried not to look at his melted skin as he braced himself on the trunk and stood. His whole body winced as he put weight onto the limb. He coughed and doubled over, his lungs filled with smoke. He fell once more on the sand.

Fire flashed across his vision. Even with eyes closed, it raged underneath his eyelids.

He couldn't walk. Couldn't move. Almost poetic that his life was ending by the fire of someone he'd hurt instead of his own flames.

"Get up!" A voice broke through the sizzling all around him. "Use your energy!"

Without opening his eyes, Asher winced. His fire wouldn't help him against this blaze. It'd only add to it.

"You're not going to let a fire get the best of you, are you?"

Asher opened his eyes to see a figure walking past the flames toward him, dodging each hungry flicker. An angel, no—a demon. Come to welcome him to his afterlife in hell.

Except as it crept closer, he recognized the face.

"Dominic?" he croaked before another fit of coughing began.

"Use your flames as a protectant," he said. "It won't last for long but hopefully enough for us to get out of here."

"I don't…"

"Asher, do it! Get mad. For your own good!"

For one thing, Asher didn't like to be interrupted. He also didn't like to be told what to do—especially by Dominic Simmons. He leaned into those impulses, throwing the thought of confusion from his mind. He didn't have time to question why Dominic was there.

He needed to be angry.

Angrier than those simple pet peeves. This required the big guns.

He'd been taken from his home as a teenager, forced to be on Lucky Island.

"There you go!" Dominic's flickering smile competed with the brightness around him. Let's go!"

Asher was tested on at first, forced to take medication to keep his true self hidden.

He felt his body warming, this time from within.

His father was murdered. His mother lied to. His sister forced to grow up too soon.

Each thought grew in his mind. Each one he refused to acknowledge previously, knowing that recognizing his hurt wouldn't change the things he'd done.

The things he was forced to do.

"No, Asher. Keep your focus, boy." Dominic was still there. He must have seen the way his energy flattened as guilt overtook his thinking. Behind him, a tree crashed to the ground, engulfed in flames. "I'm counting on you getting us both out of here."

Asher hated when Dominic called him "boy."

As much as he wanted to fight it, he thought about Quill. Her desire to be with him—something he wasn't good enough to fulfill.

His energy flowed through his veins, heading toward his palms. Instead of letting it release that way, he focused on bringing it to the surface of his skin.

He let his anger fester over himself. He let out a screech as his frame exploded in heat. He raised from the ground, his burned leg no longer fighting against his adrenaline.

He was angry. Furious. Ready to burn the whole world down, if it hadn't already been on fire.

"Good," Dominic said. "Now make us a path."

"What?" Asher yelled. Covered in his own flames, Ben's didn't hurt him.

"You think I can get through this fire on my own? It's too large now. I'll follow your lead."

Asher took a step forward, his fire licking at Ben's flames. He took a few more steps, looking back to see that Dominic had positioned himself behind him, walking in the burned path his fire had left behind.

His anger was creating a safe space for Dominic. Something good came from releasing his fire.

He continued forward, followed by Dominic each step of the way. He clung to the hate in his heart. The betrayal between him and Quill. It wasn't until they burst through the edge of the trees that he allowed his fury to transform into self pity as he fell onto his knees in the dirt.

The hate he felt wasn't for Quill. Wasn't for the way she pressured him or questioned his loyalty.

No, his rage was for himself. For leading her on, putting her through the range of emotions that led to her confusion.

"Nice work," Dominic said, placing a hand on his shoulder.

"You were part of getting us here," Asher said. "How did you know I could do that?"

"I've responded to many calls where I needed to deescalate the situation," Dominic said. "I've seen what the powers can do."

"Who is this?" Kingston asked, moving to stand next to Asher. Ben was no longer in his arms.

Asher's breathing quickened, his eyes blurring, and he didn't move. In the blurriness, he caught sight of Ben's body a few yards away on a patch of grass.

"I'm Dominic Simmons. I came here with Ben to find Asher and his son Louie. Where is—" His voice stopped before he rushed past Asher and fell to the ground next to Ben. "He's still breathing, but he needs help. We need to get him help!"

"We need to keep going," Leda said. Asher looked up. Her face was covered in soot. "Get into the hideout before R.E.I. shows up. There's help there. A fire on the island will definitely get the wrong attention."

Dominic lifted Ben's body into his arms. His broad shoulders hunched over as he walked.

Leda reached a hand out to Asher. "You can't dwell on it. You can't let the flame consume you."

Asher nodded as he accepted her help. However, his agreement was empty. He didn't know how to keep from dwelling on it.

How to keep from hating himself.

THIRTY-FOUR

Birds chirped outside the small hut. Quill stirred on the couch, relieved by the rays of light that shone through the curtains. *Finally*, she thought. She'd had a rough night sleeping as thoughts of those she cared about ran through her head.

Calum was sitting in a jail cell somewhere in Preen. Was he alone, or did the rest of the Stillfield Representatives share it with him?

If they didn't, then what had happened to her dad? Likely back in Stillfield, she told herself. He ran to save himself. Although he'd shown effort to repair their relationship the past few months, his record still showed who he cared most about. Himself.

The last person on her mind was Asher. Not because she cared about him the least. No, the opposite. He was the one she fought most to not think about because she knew her thoughts would only bring anger, and hurt, and hope.

A small hope that wherever Asher was now, he was thinking about her.

She shook the thought out of her head as Aunt Bea entered the kitchen area.

"How'd you sleep?" she asked. "Hope that old couch wasn't too lumpy."

"I slept well," Quill lied unintentionally. "The couch wasn't too bad." Years of telling island guards exactly what they wanted to hear was hard to break.

"You can be honest with me." Aunt Bea grabbed a box out of her cabinet. "That couch was rescued from the dump outside Preen. They complain about limited resources yet create so much waste."

Quill chuckled. "Okay you're right. It was terrible." Her back cracked as she stretched and stood up. "What's on the agenda for today? Any news about my dad?"

Aunt Bea continued grabbing items out of the cupboards and setting them on the counter, including a bowl with a large chip around the edge and a metal spoon that Quill imagined was once a shiny silver, but was now spotted with black.

"After breakfast, we'll check in with Urlan. Last I heard, he sent some scouts to intercept the Stillfieldiens."

"Stillfieldiens? Is that what you call us?" Quill sat on the lone stool next to the island and watched as Aunt Bea stirred the floury mixture from the box with some water. A frying pan sat next to the bowl, but Quill didn't see any stovetop or oven inside the small kitchen.

"Came up with it myself just now. You like it?" Aunt Bea smiled at Quill, who mirrored it. Despite the unexpected and unknown circumstances she now found herself in, Quill couldn't help but like this woman in front of her.

"I hope you like pancakes," Aunt Bea said as she poured some batter into the pan. "Don't have any syrup to go with it, but I've always found them to be sweet enough without any." She picked up the pan and held it on top of her right hand. Her fingers stretched out below it, a small flame bouncing across her palm.

Quill's eyes widened.

"Don't worry, dear," Aunt Bea said. "I take my turn cooking in the mess hall kitchen as well. Happens to be my day off today."

"The mess hall? Was that the large building we passed yesterday?"

"Yep. Built around remains of an old bomb shelter. Being this far from the impact of the nuke led to more materials being salvageable." She held up the spoon. "Almost the entire shelter was intact out here. The people inside certainly didn't make it, but steel is stronger than flesh." Aunt Bea placed a steel plate in front of her, three pancakes stacked on top.

Quill winced. "Aren't there side effects to worry about? Bomb poisoning?" This plate had the same black spots as the spoon. She wasn't sure she trusted it.

"After this long? Highly unlikely. However, Urlan makes sure to test each piece of salvage before we are allowed to reuse it. Been out here for decades and not one case of bomb poisoning."

That was convincing enough for Quill. She picked up her fork and sliced into the rounds on her plate. "So Urlan was the first to find this place?" She took a bite and chewed slowly, waiting for her aunt's response.

"One of the first."

"How many were there?"

"Urlan came with five others. It was during the time that Enertin pills were first developed. It was an answer to prayers. Finally, something to help with the rise of Disparates. Urlan was one of the first people to take them." Aunt Bea's eyebrows squished together as she sat her own plate down. The food on it was half eaten. "Um, actually, I take that back. He wasn't one of the first people to take it. He was *the* first one. And he took it against his will."

Quill slowly lowered her own fork; she knew where this story was going. "He was on the island."

Aunt Bea nodded. "Yes, and he was the first Disparate to ever be released. Right around when Merrytime Clinic was opening, thanks to Enertin. Finally, Disparates could receive treatment off of Lucky Island. And those who struggled most would still have a safe place to stay until they got a handle on their emotions. That's why the late Governor Stillfield created Merrytime. It was a compromise for the other Republics to agree to shut down Lucky Island and cease the dangerous testing that was going on there in the search for a cure."

Quill wrinkled her brow. "I thought Enertin was dangerous. Isn't that why all of you are out here?"

"It didn't start that way," Aunt Bea said. "At first, the pills did what they said. They helped Disparates control their energy. It wasn't perfect by any means, but it gave Disparates the little edge they needed to keep from having complete meltdowns. In fact, I remember how it made me feel." Aunt Bea closed her eyes as she drew in a breath. With its release, a smile formed.

"So the pills were good?" Quill asked. "What about the mularium mineral? You said Preen thinks the formula has changed."

"That's true," Aunt Bea said. "As time went on, Enertin started cutting off my ability to feel my emotions. I was no longer bothered by every little thing. My anger was in check. No—my anger was gone. It made me think of the experimental drug and I stopped taking Enertin. Of course, when I got off it, my anger came back just as it had been before, if not worse."

"Wait, you also participated in the experiments?" Quill asked.

Aunt Bea's face fell. "It's something I regret, but Gilly was so adamant that it would work. I agreed to participate as well. I stopped after her accident."

Quill nodded. "And that's why Enertin is more dangerous now, isn't it?" She'd never taken Enertin. It was one thing her father spoke out against trying on her as a child, especially with her double powers. No one could convince him it was safe, as they'd never had a Disparate with two powers to test them on, and Governor Dunn refused to let his daughter be a guinea pig. Even with Paxton's brainwashing, he never changed his mind about that. He always put her safety first, and now Quill didn't know where he was. The glacier of ice protruding from the warehouse came into her mind...

Stop, Quill, he's safe. He has to be.

Aunt Bea placed a cup of water in front of Quill. "Drink. It'll help calm the nerves."

Quill picked up the cup and raised it to her lips. Her hand shook as she took a sip. The coldness of the water traveled through her chest and into the pit in her stomach.

She was in a new place with a woman she'd only met the day before. She claimed to be related, but Quill didn't know that for sure. The people she cared about were currently out of her reach and she didn't know if she'd ever see them again.

Nothing was guaranteed.

Quill looked past her aunt and noticed a figurine on the counter behind her. "What is that?" Quill asked, hoping to distract her mind. She rubbed her hand on her pant leg, causing a small shock, when her aunt turned around.

"Oh, that?" Aunt Bea picked it up and brought it closer for Quill to see. It was a piece of wood with the figures of two women carved into it. "Your mother made it for me."

"Can I see it?"

Quill looked into the faces of the two women. Neither stared back, as they were smooth. No features were carved onto the faces, but strands of hair were carved above each. They sat next to one another. She turned it over. On the bottom was carved the name *Gilly*.

Quill's heart slowed. This woman was indeed who she said she was. Right now, Quill needed to have trust. Letting her emotions get the better of her would only keep her from finding out the truth.

"I think it's about time we go see Urlan," Aunt Bea said as she cleared the empty plates off the counter.

"Oh." Quill's eyes widened. "We're meeting with him directly?" She didn't understand why that felt surprising. Her dad was a governor. She'd met the other Republic leaders. Yet meeting someone in a position of power she never knew existed was something else.

"He prefers to be involved in all the operations of this camp. Especially when welcoming a new member."

New member.

Quill tried to shake the thought from her mind. Certainly her aunt didn't expect her to stay here permanently. She was visiting. Once the mess with her dad, Calum, and Preen was cleared up, she'd return home.

A quiver in her stomach, like a feather faintly falling, greeted her as she stood.

Outside, the sun had risen, casting morning shadows across the ground. Quill followed Aunt Bea toward the center of the village.

Past the neighborhood of houses, larger buildings were made of mismatched materials. The one in the middle looked to be the biggest. The back was metal, the remains of whomever first lived in this area. The other two thirds were patched together with wood and steel panels.

"That one there is where we're headed," Aunt Bea said. "The community kitchen and mess hall. At the back is the meeting room, which happened to be an almost fully standing structure that survived the Rain. That's where the first group of Outskirters lived. But now, it's where Urlan likes to conduct important business."

Quill's stomach churned. "Do you think he has an update on my group?"

"If anyone has information, he's the one they'd bring it to."

The metal door opened as they approached. A teenage boy walked through, nodding solemnly at the pair, his black curls bouncing with the movement. "He went in the back to grab breakfast, but he's expecting you. Should be back shortly."

"Thank you, Teddy," Aunt Bea said.

Teddy held the door open for them to enter before he left. The room was empty. The wooden desk in the center of it felt misplaced in its metal surroundings. On the back wall was a door that likely headed into the mess hall.

"That young boy lost his parents on the island."

Quill looked at her aunt with sad eyes. "When were they there? Perhaps I knew them?"

"Unlikely. It was a decade ago. They were Ground and Air Disparates. As opposite in personality and disposition as they were in energy. But they sure did love each other and that boy."

Quill felt the heaviness in her voice. "You knew them?"

Bea nodded. "His mother was a neighbor of ours. Gilly and I used to babysit her, before her energy showed."

Another piece of her mother's past.

"They contacted the Outskirts about ten years ago for refuge," Aunt Bea continued. "We were too late for them, but Urlan took in their seven-year-old boy. Raised him as his own."

"And he's been a pain in my side ever since." A deep voice startled Quill. A man had entered from the back door, a plate of biscuits drenched in gravy held in his hands.

"You know that's not true, Urlan." Aunt Bea gave him a stern glare.

He laughed, his long beard almost dipping into the food on his plate as it moved up and down. He placed his meal on the desk as he sat. "Of course not. I'd do anything for that boy. Just as I would for anyone here."

"He thinks of everyone in the Outskirts like family," Aunt Bea explained.

"In the Outskirts, in the inskirts. All Disparates of any ability deserve to be wanted. And to have their wants taken into consideration, which is something so often ignored in the Republics. Please, take a seat." He motioned to the scattering of chairs around the room.

Aunt Bea nodded along, truly smitten with this man as she sat in a leather chair across from him at the desk. Quill took the one next to it: a thin metal folding chair. There were other, more comfortable chairs nearby, but she didn't want to bring extra attention to herself by dragging one over. She wasn't sure yet what to think of the man in front of her, let alone the rest of this place.

She was hesitant to trust. She'd heard words like this before from someone who turned out to be the opposite of what they'd said. Dr. Paxton truly left her mark.

"So, Miss Quill Dunn, what is it that you want?" Urlan's cloudy eyes focused on her. Quill wanted to sink into the cold back of her seat, but something about his gaze enticed her. There was meaning behind his dark eyes. Signs of age and weariness.

Pain.

Her heart quickened. "I need to know what happened to my dad. Where is he?"

Somehow, his irises darkened. "We'll get right to it then. Governor Dunn is dead."

The words rang in her mind. *Dead.*

"No," she shook her head, blood rushing to her ears. "He can't be. What do you mean?"

"He was shot by Responders trying to escape the storage warehouse."

He had been headed to the warehouse when she and Calum left them yesterday, but it must have been a mistake. Urlan had to be mistaken. "How? How was he caught? Why would he need to run?"

The pieces were not lining up in her mind. Her father was invincible. He was a leader. Why would Preen risk upsetting the balance of the Seven Republics by killing him?

Responders did show up at the saloon to arrest her and Calum. She thought they must have seen them driving Prockter to the parking lot earlier. Had their poor job of hiding him led to her dad's death?

"Half the harvest of carrots were destroyed in a frost outburst. One that came from the warehouse. He was caught trying to escape with two others when he was killed."

Buran and Jemma.

She'd seen the frost outburst with her own eyes. Surely something more must have gone wrong for him to use his power in such a way.

"What about the other two?" Quill asked. Nothing felt real.

"They're being blamed for his death," Urlan said.

Quill clutched her chest. Her father was dead. Her friends were on the run. And she was far away from home in an unfamiliar place.

With the woman her father had warned her about.

"I know this must be hard to hear." Aunt Bea placed a hand on Quill's shoulder. A spark caused Bea's hand to draw away.

"Where are Jemma and Buran now?" Quill asked.

"They got away, but we aren't sure where. We have members of O.W.L. scouting for them, but so far no luck."

"Outskirts Will Live, right?" Quill asked, remembering what her aunt told her. She wasn't sure if she was relieved that Buran and Jemma got away or angry that her father hadn't. The news needed time to settle.

"That's right," Urlan said. "It's our group of trained personnel with the goal of recruiting as many Disparates to the Outskirts as needed."

He continued speaking, but Quill barely listened. It didn't really matter to her now.

"Why haven't I heard about you?" Quill asked. Her suspicions mixed with the grief in her heart. These people could still be lying... they could still be wrong... her father could still be alive...

"We keep a low profile. Don't want to draw attention to ourselves." Urlan sat back in his chair. "Especially in the busier cities. We have very few recruits from Stillfield due to its distance and size. However, I guarantee you, your father knows we exist. Well, knew." His face was truly empathetic.

His correction stung Quill's heart. They weren't lying. She'd come on this journey to learn about her mother, but she'd also wanted time to get to know her dad, to grow their bond that had been corrupted by Dr. Paxton.

And now, he was gone.

"Will you let me know as soon as you track down Buran and Jemma?" Quill asked, her stomach queasy. They were the two people that would be able to give her details. Right now, she needed to lie down.

"I will," Urlan said.

"I'm sorry for your loss." Aunt Bea's face wrinkled in Quill's direction once they exited the office. "Quill, I'm losing you again."

Quill looked at her hands. They wavered in and out of visibility, but she didn't care.

She wanted to run. To get away from this place, this news. If she could escape it, perhaps it wouldn't be true. She could go back to her home and wait for her dad to visit after work. They'd sit on the couch and watch a movie together, likely an older romcom that Quill missed while she was imprisoned on the island. They wouldn't say much, but they would laugh together when the protagonist misunderstood the meaning of her love interest and swoon when they finally came together at the end for true love's kiss.

Of course, her dad would say it was a silly representation of love. That it scratched the surface of how he'd felt about her mother, but it didn't touch the depths of the hole her absence had left.

That was one thought that brought Quill comfort as she lay down on Aunt Bea's couch. Although she didn't know what she believed about an afterlife, she couldn't shake the feeling that now, finally, her parents had been reunited.

Thirty-Five

The sun rose quicker than Jemma would have liked. She'd stayed up for the first watch last night and woke Buran up to take her place once her eyelids would no longer stay open. It seemed as if the sun was switched on as soon as she laid her head on the cold, hard ground.

She stretched, yawning as her body ached. It had been through a lot in the last twenty-four hours. It almost didn't seem real that it was just yesterday they were traveling to the corn field to demonstrate Calum's power.

Right before everything went wrong.

Her stomach growled, reminding her that it needed nutrients. She looked at the apple trees around her and gagged. That was not going to work.

It also was time to take Enertin. Jemma's bag was strapped across her body, safe from the day before. Enertin was in there, yet her desire to take it had waned. She had caused a lot of pain and death, but she'd also demonstrated control. It was just her and Buran now, and after his reaction the day before, taking a pill in front of him seemed like the riskier move.

She could always take one when he wasn't looking.

"Buran," she said. He was sitting on a rock nearby, drawing swirls in the dirt with a stick.

"Good morning." He smiled.

She sat up. "Morning." She was going to ask about breakfast, but the reality of their current circumstances swept over her as she recognized the sound of a vehicle driving over a dirt road. It was more important to make it out of Preen alive. "Do you hear that?"

"Yeah," Buran said, resuming his drawing. "The farm wakes up early, but no one has headed in this direction. Although, that sounds more like a car than a tractor. Maybe a delivery?"

"We should check it out," Jemma said. He was being too calm about their situation. The Responders saw them run into the orchard. Sure, they'd avoided being caught yesterday, but that didn't mean Responders wouldn't be back.

Buran tossed his stick down. "Alright, lead the way."

Jemma rose to her feet and wiped dust from her pants. Her jeans were extra uncomfortable after sleeping in them all night.

The sound of the vehicle had stopped, but Jemma followed their path from the day before toward the farmhouse. She stepped softly, listening closely for anyone coming their way. Instead, there was a knocking followed by voices.

As they neared, Jemma was able to make out some of their conversation.

"...heard and seen nothing?"

"Nope. You're welcome to search again."

"We'll do that."

Buran nudged Jemma's arm and pointed to a truck blocking the front of the farmhouse. It looked like Prockter's, except this one also had "Responder" written across it in spray paint.

A man in a uniform appeared from the front of the truck. He opened the door to the cab and two dogs jumped out.

The Responders were continuing their search to find them, and this time, they brought backup.

Jemma's heart thumped. "We need to hide."

"The trees worked last time," Buran said, "but I don't imagine it'll fool those dogs."

"So what do we do?"

"We run and hope they don't catch our scent."

Jemma's stomach gurgled. She hadn't eaten breakfast, but that wasn't why.

Buran headed swiftly back into the trees, along a different path than they'd taken before.

"Do you know where to go?" Jemma asked.

"No, but we can't go down the same path. The dogs will sniff it out for sure. If we make a new one, perhaps the first will buy us some time."

As they got farther away from the house, they picked up speed. Nothing seemed to be following—yet.

Jemma's breathing shortened and her chest tightened, making it hard for her to get a full breath. All this running was taking its toll. She stopped and bent over, her hands on her knees. She was winded and needed to gain control of her shallow breathing.

Buran didn't notice at first, but after continuing past a few trees, he slowed and glanced back. He circled around those trees and stopped by Jemma. "We need to keep going."

"I'm not... sure I can." The world spun around her.

A rustling in the woods behind them spiked the small rest her heart had been given.

"Crap. They're onto us," Buran said. He searched around them frantically, then his sights landed on Jemma. "I need you to do it again."

"What?" Jemma took a deeper breath.

"You need to use your energy. Shoot it out as far as you can. You pushed quite a bit out last night—now do it again, except in a straight direction."

The idea went off in her mind. "You want to throw them off by spreading out my scent."

Buran gave a smirk. "Exactly."

Jemma straightened and faced away from Buran. Her electricity was there, easily on the surface. Especially since she hadn't taken Enertin yet that day.

She lifted her hands in front of her, breathing deeply through her mouth as the spinning blurred the trees around and the sound of the dogs in the distance slowed.

It was happening again. The world around her slowed, but she didn't let it faze her. She tapped into that fear of the unknown. The fear of being caught. The fear that she was a danger to everyone around her.

And she focused that fear in front of her. If it was going to be there, she was going to use it for good.

A burst of electricity exited her hands, a bolt frying all bark and leaves in its path. It extended farther than Jemma knew, until she felt the last of her anxieties exit through her. She slumped forward, breathing heavily.

Buran grabbed her arm and pulled her away from the path of destruction she'd created. Time had resumed its normal speed. A sizzling joined the sounds around them.

"That was it, Jem!" Buran's voice was victorious. "You did that flawlessly. Had to have burned at least half a football field length in a line! If that doesn't throw off those dogs, I don't know what else would."

Pride swelled inside her. She'd used her electric energy exactly as she'd wanted. She didn't let her fears take control. She guided them. Used them.

She kept up with Buran, his hand releasing her once she was conscious enough to follow. To where? She wasn't sure. But they had to keep moving.

After a few minutes, Buran abruptly stopped, putting an arm out to block Jemma.

She was about ready for another break, but following Buran's gaze, she realized they hadn't stopped to rest.

The young woman from the barn last night stood between two trees, her hand paused in midair after picking an apple. She wore a pair of overalls with long sleeves underneath and gloves on her hands. A basket was hooked on her elbow.

Buran immediately stretched out his arms, ice forming on his palms. The woman dropped the apple and basket and raised her hands above her head.

"Wait," Jemma placed a hand on Buran's shoulder. The woman's eyes were wide and terrified. Jemma didn't want them to be the cause of more pain. "She's just a farm hand, not a threat."

"We don't know that," Buran said, his hands still in front of him.

"Wait," the woman squeaked. "Are you the fugitives from Stillfield?"

"And what if we are?" Buran asked.

The woman's eyes shifted to the side—perhaps she was thinking about running—then returned to the pair of Disparates in front of her.

Jemma took a slow step toward her, hoping to not scare her away. "Are you going to turn us in?"

The woman shook her head. "I need your help."

"Our help?" Buran questioned, his hands lowering slightly.

She nodded. "There's more going on than Governor Beecher wants to admit. If we don't get help soon, everyone will starve."

The dissolving corn came to Jemma's mind. If that crop failure wasn't from Calum's power, it'd come from somewhere. "So you want help from Stillfield," Jemma surmised. Governor Dunn was dead; perhaps she thought they were next in line to run the government.

"We should talk about this elsewhere." The girl glanced around the trees. "Someone will likely head this way soon, but I know a place."

"We don't even know your name, but you want us to follow you?" Buran was still skeptical.

"Name's Gwen. And I know these aren't the best circumstances to meet, but I promise you, I hold no loyalty to Preen." At that, her face went dark. She picked her basket off the dirt.

Buran grabbed Jemma's arm. His touch was ice. "Are you sure we can trust her?" he whispered.

"Not sure we have another option," Jemma said. If this were a trap, they'd figure a way out of it. And if not, they'd be in a safer spot than hiding in a grove of trees.

"Okay," Jemma said. "Lead the way."

They walked cautiously out the other end of the trees. A field spread before them, with a row of colorful small cottages in the middle. They headed toward a red one.

Jemma glanced in the direction of the train station and warehouse. She could see it in the distance, the ice long melted. Buran's outburst certainly hadn't aided in the crop concern.

"Don't worry," Gwen said, her basket now full of apples she'd picked while they'd walked. "Everyone is in the west fields planting today."

"Is that where you're supposed to be?" Buran asked. He was clearly still cautious about their new friend.

"Well... kinda. But I had an epic case of cramps this morning. Got me a rest day. Was just goin' for a walk to replace our apple supply when I ran into you two." She opened the door and motioned Buran and Jemma inside.

Cautiously, Jemma stepped over the threshold. The humble home was ill-furnished. A loveseat pressed against the wall, the space in front of it open to the kitchen, which consisted of a small oven and sink. "Hope you're feeling better. Cramps can be a pain."

"Oh I'm feeling much better now, more of a dull ache, but I can deal with that. It was nice to sleep in." Gwen headed toward the back of the house.

"Because of your late night in the barn?" Buran asked. Jemma bumped his arm. Calling out someone who was trying to help them probably wasn't a good idea.

Gwen twisted sharply to face them, her cheeks red. "How do you know about that?"

"The secret is safe with us," Jemma said.

"He's just a friend," Gwen said quickly.

Buran met Jemma's gaze with a half smirk.

Jemma shook her head. Wasn't worth pushing. She remembered the early days of falling in love. The butterflies and excitement and the insecurity that came at the start of a relationship.

It hit her that she hadn't felt that way with Ben since he'd returned from Lucky Island, and especially not since Mackie's accident. Their connection had been there before all the extra stress. It was what carried her when Ben was gone. What motivated him to get back to her. Yet now it was gone.

Had their flame burned out?

Or was it simply fighting against the wind of change to catch fire once more?

Gwen headed to the small two-person table and placed her basket on top of it. "You can hide here for a couple hours before everyone finishes up their work. Then we'll find you somewhere new to hide."

"So what's really going on?" Buran asked, sitting on the loveseat against the wall. "What's with the crops being ruined?"

Gwen held her hands behind her back. "Would either of you like a snack?"

Buran scowled. "Are you trying to distract us?"

Gwen shook her head sharply. "No! You both just look exhausted, and I thought maybe some food would help the information I have go down easier."

"We haven't actually had anything to eat yet today," Jemma said, stepping forward. "I, for one, would very much appreciate something."

Gwen smiled and went to the small counter in the kitchen. "I made some fresh berry compote yesterday. Would toast be okay with both of you? It's what I usually have for breakfast. We don't really have other options. Honestly, you're lucky we still have some bread left. Have to wait until next week's rations to pick up more."

"Toast sounds great," Jemma said. "If it's not too much of an inconvenience." She didn't want to take food they were in need of, but at the same time, her stomach hadn't settled down since she first woke up. All their running didn't help, and she felt bile threatening to surface.

Buran didn't hide the annoyance on his face, which only made Jemma more willing to wait for answers. Sure, she wanted them too, but being impolite to the young woman that was providing them food and shelter wasn't the way to get it.

Gwen placed a pan on the stove and threw two pieces of bread on it. "Back to your questions about what's going on—well, uh, we don't really know."

Jemma sat in one of the chairs at the table, glad that Gwen wasn't avoiding the question completely. "You said you wanted our help. What is there that we can do?"

"Governor Beecher won't admit we need it." The words spilled out quickly. "His pride is keeping him from asking the other Republics for help, even though that's what they are there for, right? We are supposed to rely on each other, but Beecher thinks we can figure it out on our own. He doesn't even like using resources the other Republics send."

"That explains the crates in the warehouse," Jemma said.

Buran nodded. "So is no one using Enertin here?"

Gwen took in a sharp breath through clenched teeth. "He especially doesn't trust Enertin."

Buran and Jemma locked eyes once again, this time sharing in their confusion.

"So Disparates here are living without any type of medication?" Buran sounded incredulous.

"Not exactly..." Gwen said. "There aren't very many Disparates in Preen. Most have been chased out... come on you old Bertha." She kicked the side of her small stove.

Jemma looked at her with wide eyes.

"Sorry," Gwen said. "This stove doesn't like to stay on for longer than a couple minutes at a time. A new one would be really great."

"Disparates are just leaving?" Jemma asked. "Or are they being sent away?"

"A little bit of both." Gwen used a spatula to flip the bread. "Preen isn't very kind to Disparates. Doesn't like the threat they pose with their powers. And Beecher doesn't trust the other

Republics. There's nothing those of us with sense can do about it. Beecher is going to isolate Preen to its death."

"If Beecher doesn't trust the other Republics, why does he continue to send food you clearly need to everyone else?" Buran asked.

"That's the thing," Gwen said. "At least he hasn't stopped that yet. If he did, he might as well declare war on the other Republics. And there's no way Preen would defeat everywhere else. But honestly, I wouldn't put it past him. Beecher has been getting more and more unpredictable."

A trade was only good if both parties received something they needed from it. The papers from the train station popped into Jemma's mind. *Hungry for Justice.* They didn't mean justice for Disparates—they meant for Preen, which was literally hungry. Food was one of the most valuable assets. If Preen cut themselves off from the other Republics, they'd have to fall back on whatever resources they currently had in reserves. Stillfield had access to fresh fish but certainly didn't have enough to provide for all the Republics.

"How would Preen survive without the other Republics?" Jemma asked. "Don't you all need oil, vehicles, and clothing?"

"We do. But Beecher doesn't care." Her eyes narrowed. "As I said, he's been getting less and less sensible the last couple months." She grabbed two plates and flipped a piece of toasted bread onto each. With a knife, she scooped a bright red mixture from a mason jar and plopped some on top of each piece. "Like his brain is turning to mush." She pressed down a pile of berry compote and spread.

The idea of someone declining in such a way brought a thought of Governor Dunn and how wishy-washy he'd been when he was brainwashed.

"So where are the Disparates going?" Buran asked.

Gwen bit her lip and shrugged.

Jemma got the impression she was hiding something, but she wasn't sure accusing her directly was the best move.

"Where are they?" Buran asked, leaning forward.

"I can't say," Gwen said. "It's not my place." She set a plate of toast in front of Jemma and looked out the window near the door. "Oh shoot, my housemates are heading home for lunch already. We need to get you two a better hiding spot."

Jemma glanced out the window to see three figures headed their way. They were laughing and pushing against each other, unaware of the fugitives inside their home eating their food. Her eyes met Buran's, and he slowly leaned back, accepting that Gwen wasn't going to give more information. But Disparates missing for a whole Republic was definitely something he wouldn't be letting go of.

"Do you have any ideas?" Buran asked.

Gwen smiled. "I think I have just the place, and here—take your breakfasts with you."

Thirty-Six

Back in the underground cavern, Asher scrutinized Ben's still body. He laid motionless on the small cot next to Asher, his back against the plastic wall. On Ben's arms and down his right side were wrapped towels of mud, mixed with other herbs Kingston had explained to Asher before he quickly forgot them. Ben would have burn scars that matched his face along his arms, but he was alive. Somehow, he'd survived the point of no return.

His feelings were caused by the fear he had for Louie. The anger he had for Asher for bringing him to the island.

Dominic placed a hand on Asher's shoulder, causing him to jump. "He'll be okay."

"How do you know?" Asher asked. It wasn't his plan to bring the child along. He would have preferred to come alone.

He always preferred to be alone.

"He has a lot to live for," Dominic said. "The outburst didn't kill him right away, which means he has a chance to fight for his life. Ben's a fighter."

"I want to see him," a small voice came from outside the tent's door. Louie had been there when the group had returned that morning. His wide eyes, set on his unmoving father, was a picture that would not leave Asher's mind.

He'd caused the surprise.

The hurt.

The pain.

Ben was vulnerable after being given EnertinX. In a perfect world, the shot would have done its job. Kept him contained and controlled.

Asher was part of testing that drug, bringing many Disparates to the very edge of tolerance. He knew how to get under a person's skin. To find what made them tick and set it off.

That was why Dr. Paxton had forced him to do what he did. To bring the Disparates they'd tested to their very last nerve.

And he was good at it. Always had been.

The tent swooshed open. "Is Daddy okay?" Louie asked as he stepped toward Ben's cot.

Leda and Crow entered behind him.

"Sorry," Crow said. "I couldn't get him to wait longer."

"That's okay," Asher said.

Louie reached a hand out to touch Ben, then quickly drew it back.

"He should be okay," Asher said, glancing at Dominic. "If he lives through the night."

Louie let out a gasp.

Dominic shook his head.

"It seems you have a poor bedside manner." Leda said from the back of the tent. "Can't say I'm surprised. But he'll be alright."

Asher wasn't sure how Leda could be so optimistic. Surely it was better to be honest with the boy than to lie about what could be. This world was cruel enough; adding in broken trust at such a young age wasn't worth the risk of causing him extra worry.

He'd dealt with enough secrets and lies in his lifetime, especially around his father's death.

"Your dad will be okay," Dominic said, standing next to Louie. "He has some burns, but they're being treated. His body needs rest right now, but he'll wake up. We just need to hold onto hope." He glanced at Asher.

"Yeah," Asher said, meeting Dominic's gaze. "He has a lot to live for. He'll make it." He groaned as he stretched his legs. His left one was wrapped in a towel bandage that matched Ben's.

Louie looked at it. "You're hurt too?"

"Observant, I see," Asher said. "Just a minor injury. Should be better in no time."

Asher fought the feeling of hypocrisy that popped into his mind. Why he was so insistent on being honest about Ben's state when he downplayed his own.

He wasn't on the brink of death, he reasoned. He didn't deserve any extra worry.

Louie was quiet, his eyes glued to his father.

"You're welcome to stay here, little guy," Leda said. She looked at Dominic. "I have some chores I need to help with. Are you good to supervise these two? Not sure I should leave the kid alone with Asher."

Asher sneered. "He's my nephew. We'll be fine."

"I'll keep an eye on them," Dominic said.

She nodded. "Crow, follow me. I'll need your help getting the fires started for dinner."

Before exiting, Crow eyed Ben. "I'm sorry about what happened to your dad, Louie. If you want to go for a swim in the creek again later, just let me know."

Louie didn't respond. Once the two members of O.W.L. were gone, tears welled in his eyes. "Did I do this?" Louie whispered.

Asher cocked his head to the side. "What do you mean?"

"I was mad. I didn't want him to be my dad anymore. I wanted him gone." A tear streaked down his dirt-ridden face.

Asher's heart beat in his ears. This was what Dominic was talking about, darn it. He was right. He shouldn't have been so disheartening about Ben's condition. He met Dominic's eyes once more.

"You've got this," Dominic said. He wanted Asher to take the lead in comforting Louie.

Asher didn't know what he was doing. He was used to things going wrong. Used to expecting the worst. It'd become a survival mechanism at this point. "No, look. He's going to be okay. See his chest? It's still moving. He's still breathing." Something about these words came out empty. Hollow.

Louie's sobs stabbed Asher's heart. A boy mourning his father.

A boy taking the blame.

Asher turned away from his hurting nephew. The boy he saw himself in. He cleared his throat to keep from joining Louie in his sobs.

He closed his eyes, the image of his own father rising in his mind. Fire. Smoke. Anger. He'd been so upset at his father, and why? Over a silly concert he wouldn't let him attend. Louie wasn't the only son who'd wished his father was different.

Gone.

Asher had been granted his foolish, emotional wish. He wiped his eyes as he turned once again to Louie. "Your dad is not going to die," he said, confidence in his voice. "I refuse to allow it."

Asher winced as the boy bumped into his leg, wrapping his arms around his shoulders.

"You mean it?" Louie said into his ear.

Asher looked once more at the cot. *Come on, Ben. You have to wake up. You can't make me a liar. Your family needs you.*

"I mean it," he said. Louie's grasp tightened around him.

Dominic smiled, nodding his head in approval.

It stirred a feeling of warmth inside Asher, even in such terrible circumstances.

A small show of hope and kindness had a way to lift a situation. They still didn't know if Ben would make it or not, but Asher knew what he wanted the outcome to be. He wanted Ben to be okay. And he had faith that he would be.

The world swirled. Dirt and smoke clogged his airways as Ben lay still. He heard faraway voices, muffled within the sound of crackling.

He coughed. It came out as a wheeze. His throat was dry and tight. Light danced across his still-shut eyes.

"Dad?" a small voice fought through the roaring hiss of fire. His boy. "Daddy, are you awake?"

"Ben?" a deeper voice said. Dominic's.

As the talking continued, the sound cleared.

"Daddy, wake up."

This time Ben fought against the heaviness of his eyelids. Slowly, they lifted, the light stinging his corneas. He promptly closed them once more.

"Dad's awake!" Louie yelled. "I saw him open his eyes!"

The sound of scuffling came from the floor nearby.

"Ben? Is that true?" At the sound of this voice, Ben's muscles tightened. His eyes stayed closed.

"Please, wake up. You have to be okay," Asher continued. "I'm so sorry. I didn't mean for Louie to come here. I should have brought him home as soon as it was safe."

Ben tried to respond, but it came out as a rasp followed by more coughing.

"Water. Get him water, Louie," Asher said.

"I'll get some—" Dominic said.

Louie's little voice cut him off. "No! I want to!"

Moments later, the coolness of a cup pressed into his lips. He opened them, accepting the offering. It wasn't until this moment that he realized how thirsty he was. With difficulty, he swallowed a small sip. His throat welcomed the coating.

"I..." Ben began, "don't..."

"You don't have to say anything right now." Asher's voice sounded hasty. It was clear he expected Ben's next words to be about him.

"I don't," Ben said again, "think that... was... water." Ben opened his eyes once more just in time to catch Asher's confused face, while Louie glanced into the cup in his hand.

"It's brown," Louie said, handing it to Asher.

"Oh no." Asher swirled the cup. "You grabbed the salve made for our burns." He looked at Ben with raised eyebrows.

"I tasted some honey, vodka, and, I believe, mud?" Ben started coughing once more. "Water... for real... please."

Dominic approached with a new cup.

"Glad to see you're okay," Ben said, reaching to take the cup. Before his arm moved much, pain shot through it. He let out a yell, his mind now aware of the state of his body. His eyesight, once again, began to swirl.

"Hold on, Ben. I've got the water right here..." Dominic's voice was fading.

"Dad," Louie said. "Dad! Stay awake!"

Ben tried to fight the incoming darkness, but he knew he'd fail. His body was in control and wanted rest. Begged for rest.

"I love you all ways, Dad."

The last sound he heard was Louie's sob.

THIRTY-SEVEN

Louie's chest hurt. More than when he was told he had to leave grandma's house. More than it hurt saying goodbye to his mom on his first day of preschool. His chest hurt more than it had the day the ladder broke off his toy firehouse.

"We need to get Ben to a doctor," Dominic whispered to Leda, the boss. They must have thought Louie's curled body meant he was asleep. "Back to a hospital in Stillfield. He could die."

"Going back to Stillfield might not be a safe option," Leda said.

"Why wouldn't it be?" Dominic said, his voice rising. "Ben needs expert care. I'll take him back myself."

Leda paused. "Perhaps we should discuss this outside. Wouldn't want to wake anyone."

Shuffling ensued as the tent flap opened and closed.

Louie had never felt this much pain, looking at his dad's small breaths as he laid on the cot next to his.

Asher was wrong about Dad being okay. He looked at his uncle, who lay on the ground at his feet with his eyes shut. Asleep.

Louie was told he should try and get some sleep as well, but rest didn't come. He couldn't help but think of how it was his fault his dad was here now. Louie had been wrong to think he wanted his old dad. Sure, after his dad came back from Lucky Island, he could be mean. But he also played with Louie. They'd go to the park together, the library, and watch movies together.

Truth was, his dad was his hero. He understood what it was like to be a Disparate. To be different as a child. And although Louie had never seen him use his flame energy, he still knew he had it because he'd always been honest with him about that. And that meant the world to Louie.

He suppressed a sniffle, wiping his nose with the back of his arm.

He wanted to hug him, to wrap his arms around his dad, but he knew he couldn't. Not without causing him more pain.

"Hey, kid," Vicki, one of his new friends, whispered as she entered the tent. She sat next to him.

He didn't try to hide that he was awake, but he gave no response.

"Rough day, isn't it? I understand if you can't sleep. I've been there."

Louie looked at her curiously.

"I lost both of my parents when I was young."

His eyes widened.

"I'm not saying your dad isn't going to make it," Vicki said quickly. "But I've been in this waiting zone before. Unsure of what the outcome was going to be."

A silence settled for a moment.

"Would you like a bedtime story?" Vicki asked.

Louie wasn't sure. He wanted to sleep, but he also feared closing his eyes. He didn't want to open them to a dead father.

"I'll keep an eye on your dad today. I know it's weird sleeping during the day, but tonight we'll take him to the mainland. There's a doctor there that will be able to help him. Does that sound okay to you?"

Louie liked that she was asking for his opinion. Giving him a say, since he was responsible for his dad's accident. He nodded.

"I think that's an excellent choice you've made. Now, you do need to get some rest. We have a long night of travel ahead of us."

Louie was tired after the long night sailing to the island and then staying up to help his body adjust to the schedule underground. He hadn't minded it much. He explored more of the cave system with Vicki. She'd even shown him a small cave covered in stalactites.

He yawned. "Can I have a story now?"

"Of course." Vicki smiled. "I'll tell you a tale of two sisters who were in a similar set of hard circumstances and how they made it through."

"I have a brother," Louie said.

"You do? So maybe you'll relate to these siblings. You see, these two were sisters, but they didn't have much in common. At least, that's what the older sister thought. Her younger sister was quiet and shy, while the older one enjoyed others' company and often sought out new friends. They lived with their mother in the mountains. Their favorite time of year was in the winter, when the snow would fall.

"One day, a knock came at their door. They opened it to see a bear."

"A bear?" Louie interrupted. "Like in the zoo?" He hadn't been expecting that.

"Yes, a bear." Vicki ruffled the hair on his head. "But this bear wasn't kept in a cage to keep his species from dying out. This one lived in the woods. And he showed up, half frozen."

"Whoa."

"The bear told them not to be afraid. That he merely wanted to warm up inside their cabin then he would be on his way. The girls looked at each other, unsure, but their mother let him in. He warmed himself by the fire, and in the morning, he left.

"Later that day, the older sister was outside gathering sticks for the fire. She came across a little old elf. His beard was long and white, and glasses sat on the tip of his nose.

"'You met the bear, didn't you?' the little elf asked. She nodded. 'Do not be quick to trust him, as he is still a beast deep inside. One that cannot be tamed.'

"With a poof, the elf was gone."

Louie looked at Vicki. "Is this a scary story?" He wasn't sure he'd be able to sleep if so.

"Part of it is, but that's how the best stories are written. The ending wouldn't be as sweet if it came easily."

Louie nodded. "Okay."

"Each night," Vicki said, continuing the story, "the bear returned to warm himself once again. The family grew fond of him, especially their mother. She'd grown attached to the beast, welcoming his presence each night.

"However, the older girl became wary. The beast began to arrive at night earlier and linger longer in the morning before leaving. She watched the way her mother and sister flocked to his side, yet when she'd get a look in his eyes, they were as dark as the moonless night outside. They fixated on her mother.

"One day, the bear arrived while her mother and younger sister were out harvesting in the garden for dinner. When the older sister insisted on the bear returning later that night, he refused and pushed himself into the cabin. 'Go and get your mother,' the bear growled. She listened and obeyed quickly, as the gruff sound of his voice scared her."

Louie's heart quickened. He, too, was spooked.

"Her mother was pleased to hear that the bear had come so early that day. She saw it as a sign of luck. The older sister begged her mother to tell the bear to shoo, but she didn't listen. Instead, her mother left, demanding she stay to help her younger sister finish gathering the carrots.

"On their way back home, they encountered the elf once again. 'Your home is gone,' he said. 'The bear has destroyed it.'"

Louie's eyes widened. Under his thin blanket, the hairs on his arms raised.

"Are you okay?" Vicki asked, placing a hand on his shoulder. A spark jumped from their touch. She withdrew her hand and tilted her head.

"I don't like the bear," Louie said.

"Me either," Vicki shook her head. "Shall I continue the story? We are getting close to the end."

Louie nodded. "Only if they are going to be okay."

"Well, they will be, but first, the two girls were shocked. The younger sister didn't believe what the elf had said. After all, she'd come to admire the bear. Thought of him as a protector, coming to them during the coldest parts of the night.

"However, the older sister knew what the elf said was true. She saw the bear for the predator it was. And now, he'd consumed their mother in a fit of rage. The elf offered his home for them to stay. They passed their cabin on the journey, the wooden walls turned to ash."

Louie gasped.

"Maybe this wasn't the right story to get you to sleep."

"It's okay. I want to know the ending. Is the bear gone? Are the girls happy with the elf?"

Vicki wrinkled her forehead. "No. The bear is not gone. He returns to knock at the elf's door. But the elf doesn't answer. He shoos it away, blocks the door with boards, and warns the girls each day to never go near the beast."

"Do they listen?" Louie asked. He hoped they did.

"The older sister, yes. The younger, however... that's a story for another day."

Louie yawned once more. He wanted to know more about these sisters, but he could hardly keep his eyes open.

That day he dreamed of a closed door. A knocking came from the other side.

THIRTY-EIGHT

Jemma placed a finger under her nose to keep from sneezing. Dust surrounded her as she lay flat on her stomach under Gwen's queen sized bed. A plate with her toast on it sat next to her, but she'd lost her appetite.

Buran was next to her, his thicker body barely able to fit under the low frame.

"I didn't expect a flashback to my school days on this trip," Buran said.

Jemma released a snorted laugh. "I can only imagine the trouble teenage Buran got into."

"Look, Keesha's dad didn't like me back then. Doesn't mean I was trouble."

"So, what does it mean that he still doesn't like you?"

"That he's a prick."

Jemma placed a hand over her mouth to catch her laugh. "Wait, so you and Keesha are high school sweethearts? I don't think I knew that."

"We were, but then we split for a number of years before reconnecting," Buran said. "I won't lie and say she wasn't on my mind those years we were apart."

Jemma smirked. "You're going soft on me, Buran Kuzmin."

"What can I say, I'm just a teddy bear at heart." The sound of a door opening cut him off. A couple of new, laughing voices entered the main room of the house. A soft voice asked, "How are you feeling, Gwen?"

Gwen's groan reached through her closed bedroom door. She knew how to pull out the dramatics.

"Dang, that bad? I'll have Poppy make you a sandwich," the voice said. Ruffling and clanking sounds ensued.

"By the way," Buran whispered, "how are things going with Ben? I know it's been an adjustment for him."

"He's trying." Jemma's heart ached. It was true, even if it was hard to see progress. Ben loved Jemma and their family more than anything. He fought against a whole island of guards and Paxton's brainwashing to make his way home. The love they had for each other had always been a fairytale. It hadn't taken long for each of them to fall for each other, and they'd stuck by each other's side ever since.

And that love was still there, but more in the background. Like a hidden memory rather than a burning passion.

"He's finally able to feel his emotions fully again," Buran said. "That takes time to adjust."

"But it's been months now," Jemma said. "It's like his anger is his default. Always on edge. Sometimes it feels like walking on eggshells trying to keep the boys from upsetting him again."

"Change doesn't have a timeline," Buran said. "But at the same time, the safety of you and your boys is important."

Safety. Jemma's breath caught in her throat. Ben may have gotten angry quickly, but she'd never had the thought that he would hurt them. Not the way that Jemma could and did. Then again, the mental exhaustion of keeping him happy didn't bring that feeling of safety.

"I can have a talk with him when we make it back," Buran said. "It's not just Disparates that could benefit from therapy and emotion management."

"I think that would be good." With Jemma knowing Ben the way she did, he'd be willing to give it a chance.

"Grief also doesn't have a timeline."

Buran's words stabbed into her chest.

"I know you've been struggling after the accident with Mackie," Buran said. "I should have seen it sooner, and I'm sorry. I haven't been a good friend; focusing so hard on changing the Republics for good, I missed the signs. It's the same thing I do with Keesha. Focus so hard on my work, I miss the things right in front of me."

"Forgiveness can take time too." Jemma smirked. "She'll get there. Give her space and continue to show her you're trying."

A loud knock sounded over the muffled sounds of lunch being prepared. Silence settled for a moment as the front door of the cottage creaked open.

"Hello, officer," a roommate's softened voice said. "Is there something we can help you with?"

"We are doing a search of the premises. There are two suspected fugitives on the run."

"Fugitives?" Gwen's voice took over. "I haven't seen any-thing."

"Then this should be quick," the officer said.

"Oh, yeah," Gwen said. "Hope our food preparation doesn't distract your dog." Her voice increased in volume at the end.

Jemma met Buran's shadowed eyes. They were searching the house with a dog that would surely sniff them out.

"That shouldn't be a problem." The officer was getting clos-er.

Jemma shuffled toward the edge of the bed. They needed to run. Maybe escape out the bedroom window.

Buran's hand on her arm stopped her. "Wait," he whispered.

The bedroom door knocked against the wall, signifying that it had been opened.

Feet shuffled toward their hiding spot, barefoot and covered in dirt. Gwen's face popped down. "They're in the front room right now," she said. "If you two can get out the window, meet me tonight at the barn you saw me at, okay?"

Jemma nodded before freezing. A flash of fear crossed Gwen's face.

"Is everything okay here?" the officer's voice from earlier said. The sound of soft paws padded across the wooden floor. His dog started searching the room.

"Yeah..." Gwen moved a hand to scratch her lower leg before straightening, her face disappearing from view. "It's just that I've had really painful cramps all day today." She moaned. "I was hoping to lie down for a bit."

Although Jemma only had a view of her feet, she imagined Gwen grasping her stomach.

Heavy footsteps moved closer as dirt-covered boots appeared. "We'll clear the room quickly for you then."

"That's appreciated—" Gwen released a deep groan and plopped onto the bed, causing the frame to dip in front of where Jemma was.

Jemma pressed herself against Buran as they both huddled under the middle of the bed to be as hidden from view as possible. The dog's snout appeared near the head of the bed where Jemma's feet were. The dog's nose tucked under deeper...

"I need a heated bag!" Gwen yelled out, her moans continued. The dog ignored the outburst as his head pushed under the bed, his dark eyes meeting her with a soft growl. "Please, can you get me one from the kitchen?"

"Is there something under your bed?" The officer's boots neared.

Gwen stood, moving herself in front of the officer. "I just want this pain to stop." She sobbed. "Please..."

The dog snapped his face back out from under the bed for a moment and growled toward Gwen. Jemma imagined she must have put a hand on the officer and the dog wasn't liking that.

The officer took a step back. "I'll see what I can get you—once we're finished here."

The bed creaked as Gwen fell on top of it, perhaps pushed by the officer? Black boots stood next to the bed as the dog's snout faced Jemma once more.

Sweat beaded on her brow. Electricity raised the hair on her arms. They'd have to fight their way out of here.

"Breathe," Buran whispered, snaking his arm between her side and the top of the bed frame. With it wrapped around her, he reached for the plate of toast Jemma had forgotten about and pushed it toward the dog.

The dog took his bait, snatching the berry-covered toast and pulling it out from under the bed.

"Toast?" the officer said. "You dumb dog. Always have led with your stomach. Come on, this room is cleared."

Gwen released another groan.

"And I'll get your housemates to check on you," the officer said. His heavy steps left the room.

Jemma released a breath. Buran's arm wrapped around her was comforting, the weight of it putting pressure on her side helping to clear her mind of the electric energy that'd been growing.

And it made her miss Ben. Her busy work schedule the last months hadn't left them much time to be in each other's arms. Other than their date night, which still made Jemma blush whenever she drove their minivan.

Buran didn't give her that same feeling. It was a gesture by a friend, not by the man she loved and desperately wanted to get back to.

"You needed this?" The voice of one of Gwen's housemates came from the doorway.

She approached the bed, brown leather shoes appearing by the bedside. "What were you doing with food in your room anyway? That's a house rule, and you're a stickler for them."

"It's my cramps," Gwen said. "I thought a snack would help."

"Hmm," the housemate said. "You're sure it's cramps and not guilt from sneaking out to meet with that Outskirts boy last night?"

Gwen gasped. "Poppy! You said you wouldn't speak of that."

"It's just us in here," Poppy said. "No one will overhear your secret."

Buran's arm tensed. He'd clearly heard and felt a similar surprise as Jemma.

Were the Outskirts a real place?

"Still, I don't want to risk it," Gwen said.

"Do you think they'll catch the Disparates that attacked the Eastons' farm?" Poppy's voice was filled with excitement. "Not gonna lie, I've been watching over my shoulder all day. I know they say they were from Stillfield, but were they really? Or did your boyfriend have something to do with it?"

"He knows nothing about it." Gwen's spot on the bed shifted.

"Yeah, that's probably true," Poppy said. "Rumor is the Stillfield Governor was killed in the attack. Can you believe it? They attacked a governor!"

Jemma bit the side of her cheek. So Preen was blaming Governor Dunn's death on them. However, if the world believed it, Buran and Jemma may have more trouble to deal with after they made it back to Stillfield. It was enough work clearing her husband's name; Jemma wasn't sure how to go about it for herself.

At least she had a close connection to another important figure in charge. Dominic would never believe that Buran and

Jemma killed Dunn, even if Jemma felt some responsibility over what happened. She wasn't the one that pulled the trigger.

"That is unbelievable," Gwen said. A whistle sounded in the background.

"An emergency train is coming for his body tomorrow," Poppy said. She hopped off the bed, her feet touching the ground once more. "We'll have to watch for it from the fields! Maybe it'll arrive at the same time as the northern supply drop. Two trains in the station at once! That'll be a unique sight!"

"Poppy!" a new voice came from the doorway. "Lunch break is over, We need to head out."

"Bye Gwen! Feel better soon!" Poppy's feet walked away. Some shuffling came from the front of the house and then the front door opened and closed.

Gwen's face popped into view in front of Jemma's. "The coast is clear. You two can come out now."

Jemma had worried learning about Dunn would change the way Gwen treated them, but her demeanor was the same as ever. Jemma shuffled her way through the dirt and dust, allowing herself to cough out the residue that'd made it into her mouth as she stood.

Buran exited the other side and looked right at Gwen. "What's this about the Outskirts?"

Gwen's face reddened. "You heard that?" She looked at Jemma, as if expecting to be saved.

Jemma nodded. "We did. Is that where the Disparates are hiding? Is that safe?"

"It's safe. The radiation died off years ago, although it's not the easiest place to thrive, or so I've heard," Gwen said.

"From the boy," Buran said. "So they've made a settlement in the Outskirts. It can't be far from here. Can you take us there?"

Jemma shot him a worried look. They needed to get back to Stillfield, not the Outskirts.

Buran caught it. "We need a place to hide out. If it's close, it might be our safest option."

Gwen shook her head. "I don't know where it is. Teddy always comes to me. Ran into him one time when he was visiting Preen to restock supplies. I chose not to turn him in when I caught him stealing apples, and he promised to come back to see me. I really didn't expect him to, but he's a man of his word."

"Do you think he would take us there?" Buran asked.

"It's a possibility, but I can't promise." Gwen shrugged. "He's supposed to come back again tonight. You could ask him."

Jemma's stomach rumbled, her mouth filling with saliva. More was waiting to follow it. "May I use your restroom?"

"Yeah, of course. It's at the end of the hall." Gwen stepped to the side as Jemma rushed past her and down the small hallway into her restroom.

She made it to the toilet in time for the little contents in her stomach to expel.

They were wanted for murder. Fugitives on the run.

It wasn't the Outskirts she wanted to go to, it was Stillfeld. Knowing Buran, he wouldn't be able to resist the pull of a whole community of Disparates. It was his dream. And Jemma would have to be honest with him that it wasn't hers.

Her dream was to hug her boys and never let go.

"Quill!" her aunt's voice boomed through her home. "Quill, at least let your aunt know you're safe. Gosh, if you're not in here, I sound like I'm losing my mind."

"I'm here," Quill's voice squeaked out. She wiped invisible tears from her eyes. She wasn't sure how long she'd been crying. Time didn't feel real.

"What are you doing in the corner?" Aunt Bea said. "There's a perfectly good couch for you to sit on.

"It's too soft. I'm used to sitting on concrete." On the island, Quill's bed was a concrete slab. Even though she had been in the third warehouse where the guards lived, she didn't have a much grander room. A little larger. A blanket and pillow. But she was locked up at night like everyone else.

Right now, it seemed fitting to revisit the hard ground. Things were different on the island. It was dark. Terrible things happened. But there was someone there who made her day better—she wished Asher was with her. She wished Asher *wanted* to be with her.

And it wasn't like Quill would be capable of feeling comfortable at the moment anyway. Not when her heart had shriveled and died with her dad's death. She sat, hugging her knees to herself.

Aunt Bea shuffled slowly toward her. Once her foot bumped into Quill's feet, she squatted and reached a hand out until it connected with Quill. "Are you going to stay invisible forever? That's okay with me, I only request you wear a bell so we don't bump into each other."

Quill didn't respond. Her aunt was trying to cheer her up, but her body was too heavy.

"I can't see you, but I hope the thought made you smile. And if it didn't, then maybe learning that your mother loved cats will?"

"She did?" Quill asked with a flutter of curiosity. "I had a cat. His name was Tangerine. My dad took care of him while I was on Lucky Island."

Another memory. Another sign her father loved her.

Quill released a sob.

"Oh dear," Aunt Bea said, patting the side of her calf. "I didn't mean to upset you. That was mighty kind of Tobias. As much as I hold a grudge against him, he certainly loved you."

Quill wiped her nose on her arm. "Why don't you like him?"

Aunt Bea sighed. "He took Gilly away from me, and then he took you away."

"Jealousy?" Quill shook her head. "Is that all?" Her father had warned her about her aunt, but that couldn't be the only reason why.

"It's not," Aunt Bea said. "Are you sure you're in the right state to hear more about my history? Might be a better story once you're visible."

Fear bubbled inside Quill once more. She didn't know how to bring herself back. Last time, her aunt had explained more about her mother's death. She'd told her how Dr. Paxton was involved, and her fear turned to hate.

"Tell me," Quill said. "It might help me return."

"You can't rely on me being there to tell you an upsetting story every time your emotions cause you to hide."

"How do I come back? Do you know?" Her aunt hadn't been fazed by Quill's unusual power the first time it happened.

"You've got to make the decision there's something more important you're ready to face."

Like Dr. Paxton. Quill had been so ready to blast the doctor from existence. She could tap into that feeling again...

Dr. Paxton had locked her away since she was a child.

She manipulated her dad, keeping him away from her. Keeping him from being the father he wanted to be. Dr. Paxton killed the father Quill never had and now never would.

She took a sharp breath in through her nose, releasing it with the thought of how she'd make sure the doctor paid for the pain she'd caused.

"There." Aunt Bea smiled. "Happy to see you again."

"What aren't you telling me?" Quill demanded, an edge to her voice. She was tired of being out of the loop. Of being perceived as too fragile to be told the truth.

Aunt Bea moved her hand to Quill's upper arm. "Your father was a good man at heart, but he was an easily influenced man, as we know."

Quill nodded. It was true, but not his fault.

"The problem is"—Aunt Bea squinted for a moment, as if picking her words carefully—"he knew your mother was going to die and he did nothing."

Quill's eyes widened. "What do you mean?"

"I told him." Aunt Bea shook her head. "I told him not to let her leave in that car. I told him to not let her take those pills. I saw her death before it happened, but he wouldn't listen to me. She wouldn't listen to me."

"I don't understand..."

"You're not the only one with an unusual talent," Aunt Bea said. "Yours is invisibility, mine is flashes of the future."

Quill's mouth fell. It didn't make sense. Something like that was impossible. It had to be.

"It has its limits. I have to be in the place to get any glimpses, and they only come under certain circumstances. The vision of Gilly's death was one of my first, but one I felt strongly about. My vision didn't show how it was going to happen. Only the Responders that showed up at our door and the pain and mourning that hit my family at that moment. Your father ignored me, then ran away after it happened. And I don't think it was Paxton making him do that, as she was back in Stillfield at the time in an internship."

It was unbelievable. Her father would have a hard time believing Bea had psychic powers... although, the things Disparates could do were pretty unbelievable at first. People were afraid of things they didn't understand.

"How do you—we—have these extra powers?"

"Mularium is seen as the catalyst that created energy powers. Experimenting with it created new ones."

Dr. Paxton's testing. "But so many people are on Enertin. If it's inside of the pills, wouldn't everyone develop a new power?"

"That's a valid point," Aunt Bea said. "But not everyone has two powers. A new one seems to develop when a body already evolved to have more."

Quill didn't understand how she had two powers in the first place, but now she had a third from being experimented on when her father worked so hard to keep her from being a test subject.

"Someone is about to get in trouble," Aunt Bea said, standing to look out the window. One of her visions?

"Teddy!" a loud voice boomed outside.

Nope. An observation.

"Told you," Aunt Bea said. "I'll be right back."

Quill rose from the floor as her aunt exited the room. Out the window was the O.W.L. leader, Urlan. His large shoulders tensed as Teddy approached him slowly.

"You snuck out, again?" Urlan yelled. "With the increase of Responders around? Are you trying to get caught?"

"He's a young man," Aunt Bea said. "Go gentle on him."

Urlan snapped his face to her. "Did you know what he's been up to?"

"She's not involved at all," Teddy said. "I was staying safe. See? I'm here."

"Thankfully." Urlan's shoulders relaxed slightly. "You can't be leaving like that."

"I'm old enough to go to Preen on my own. No one knows I'm from the Outskirts."

"Not even the young lady you've been seeing?" Urlan asked. "You need to stop seeing her before you blow our cover. I didn't take you in so you could run back to Preen."

An overprotective father. But he was right. There was a lot of danger in the world, and Urlan clearly cared about Teddy. With almost the same intensity that her father loved her.

"You'll be staying in my room tonight," Urlan said.

Teddy's face widened. "What? No, you can't babysit me like I'm a child."

"You are a child!" Urlan's fists were tight.

With a glare, Teddy turned and marched away.

"You really should be more gentle with the kid," Aunt Bea said. "He won't stay here if he doesn't feel valued."

"I promised his parents I wouldn't let any harm come to him," Urlan said. "And I intend to keep that." He shook his head as he headed back to the middle of the village.

Quill forgave her father for the pain he caused in her life. He'd only been doing what he thought was best for her. It wasn't his fault his thoughts had been messed up.

It was because of Dr. Paxton, and Quill promised to watch her burn.

THIRTY-NINE

Hands on Asher's shoulders shook him awake.

"Night has fallen," Leda said, a foot from his face.

Asher hadn't expected to sleep for so long. He moved to a stand but was quickly reminded of his injury.

His gaze moved to Ben. He was lying on the cot, eyes closed. The up and down movement of chest was shallow; sweat rolled down the side

of his face.

"Vicki has volunteered to carry him," Leda said.

"Thank you." Asher met Vicki's eyes. "Are you sure you've got him on your own? Can I help hold some of his weight?"

"If anyone were to help, it'd be me," Dominic stepped forward. "You're in no condition to be lifting extra weight."

"And risk either of you touching his wounds and opening them more? Not a chance. I'm stronger than I look." She smirked. "My energy can handle it."

Asher nodded. It was best to have an Air Disparate transporting Ben, even if he wasn't used to trusting energy to be used efficiently. So far, something always seemed to go wrong.

"Where's Louie?" he asked, searching the tent.

"He went with Crow and Kingston to get some food," Leda explained. "Wasn't about to let a child go hungry. He's got a long journey in front of him."

Asher thought for a moment. He wasn't sure if taking Louie into the Outskirts would be the safest choice. With Ben's reaction to Asher allowing Louie to stay with him on the island, he could only imagine the response for letting him go to dangerous, uncharted Outskirts that were said to be full of scattered poison and debris. Perhaps that was something to talk to Dominic about. Once they made it to the mainland, he could take Louie to Margaret's house.

As they headed toward the ravine entrance, Crow met up with them. Louie ran to his father's floating body.

"Careful," Vicki said, and Ben's body bounced slightly. "One touch and I might lose my hold on him. But you're welcome to take a look at him, see that he's still alive."

She lowered his body enough for Louie to take a good look. Asher recognized that guilt still plagued his eyes, but it softened as Ben took an unusually deep breath.

"Let's go," Louie demanded, looking to the hole above them.

"Not that way." Asher wrapped an arm around Louie's shoulders. "Thankfully, there's an easier route out of here." He pointed toward the little stream that they'd followed out the night before. It exited closer to the ocean, to their boats.

"We don't like to let new people know about this entrance." Leda knelt to be eye level with Louie. "Only people we trust." She winked.

"To keep bad guys out?" Louie said.

"Exactly."

"Hey, so it was good to see you again, Asher," Crow said. "I hope you make it to the mainland again. This will make, what, escape number three? And look at me, still stuck here."

"Do you want to come with us?" Asher asked.

Leda raised a brow.

Crow's face lit up. "I... uh, maybe... could I go?" He turned to Leda.

"You helped us get Asher here," Leda said. "You've been quite the asset, but I understand if you're ready to leave."

"I've wanted to see what life is like off the island since I was a boy." Crow smiled. "Thank you."

The group of seven followed the stream, Crow holding Louie's hand. They'd bonded in their short time together.

"Thanks for letting him come with," Asher said to Leda.

"An extra hand might be helpful." Leda stepped on a large stone within the widened stream to get to the other side.

"There's already seven of us, if you count Louie."

"Six. I won't be going with you. I'm going to find lighthouse island and see if I can find anything important there. I gave Vicki the keys to the truck we have hidden on the mainland. She knows the way back."

Asher looked at Leda with raised eyebrows. He barely knew Vicki, yet he was supposed to trust her to get them to the Outskirts.

"Don't worry, I know what I'm doing," Vicki said, as if reading his mind. She followed Leda across the stream.

"Okay," Asher said. He leaned over to pick up Louie. Water rushed past the stepping stone, which was within a stride's distance for an adult, not so much for a child.

"I got this," Louie protested.

"Yeah you do," Crow said. "Just like we've been practicing."

Louie closed his eyes and stretched his leg out. His shoe was about to be immersed in the water, which wasn't deep enough to sweep him away just enough to leave him uncomfortably wet for the rest of the journey.

However, before the water made contact, Louie's body lifted slightly in the air and levitated to the stone. Asher smiled. His nephew had done it on his own, used his own air energy. Louie brought his legs together to stand on the stone before hopping to the other edge.

"Well done." Crow smiled at him. "Knew you could do it."

The brightest smile lifted Louie's mouth.

"So you've been helping him practice using his powers, huh?" Dominic asked.

Crow tensed. "Just a little bit. Needed something to do while we waited. I showed him what I could do with my fire, and he wanted to know how to do something similar."

"That's great," Dominic said.

Crow relaxed.

Helping Louie use his energy in a healthy way wasn't a bad idea. Asher also had to learn to use his powers on his own in a controlled manner.

"And Vicki's been helping too!" Louie said.

Vicki looked back, her cheeks reddening. "He's a quick learner."

Maybe Vicki wasn't so bad. Asher joined the rest of them.

Dominic crossed last, his protective nature taking the tail end.

It was a short trip to the exit. Steam filled the air as they emerged behind a waterfall. The mist was thick, but as he squinted, Asher saw an R.E.I. Responder making his rounds near the shore.

Of course.

After Ben burned a good portion of the island and a boat was found near it, security would be on patrol. He looked at Leda.

She seemed deep in thought, glancing to the side. She motioned them into a huddle.

Vicki lowered Ben onto a smooth, rocky surface. "Keep an eye on him for me, okay?" she said to Louie. Once Louie sat next to him, she joined the adults.

"Our plan to take the sergeant's boat back isn't going to work," Asher said. "Got any more of those kayaks?"

"Not sure those will be the safest option," Leda whispered.

Asher shrugged. "It might be our only one."

"I may have an idea," Vicki said. All eyes turned to her. "While patrolling last week I found a boat."

Leda's mouth gaped open. "What? Where?"

"Down the beach, away from R.E.I."

"Why didn't you say something sooner?" Leda asked, her face pained.

Vicki rubbed the back of her neck. "I knew you'd insist on taking it out to search for the lighthouse island without having any direction as to where it is. After losing so many kayaks, I kept it quiet to use in case we needed to evacuate."

Leda's chin trembled, but she gave a slow nod.

"How do we know R.E.I. hasn't found it already?" Dominic asked.

"We don't," Leda said. She looked worriedly at Ben. Louie had placed his hand on Ben's head, wiping his hair to the side. "But it's the best chance you have right now to save his life."

"And if they *have* found it?" Asher asked.

"There hasn't been enough time to move it. It's not a simple sailboat that can be towed."

Vicki didn't actually answer his question.

"When you get back, you can send recruits for us. I feel like we're close to finding Aleeta." Leda sounded confident. Vicki nodded, approving of the terms.

"Thank you," Asher said.

Leda shooed off his thanks. "Now get going. Vicki knows where this boat is. She'll lead the way."

Vicki took a deep breath and lifted Ben's body once more. It floated through the gap in the waterfall. Following behind him was the group of people willing to put their own lives at risk to save him.

Water washed over Asher's body as he pressed through it. The cold shocked his system, a burning reemerging from his wounded leg. He pressed forward, no time to stop and recover. They had to get Ben help in time.

FORTY

Jemma followed Gwen as she headed in the direction of the farmhouse and barn. Buran was right next to them both, keeping up in the darkness of the night. They'd hidden in the cottage until it was almost time for Gwen's housemates to return, then made their way slowly toward their destination.

"And you're sure this Teddy is going to show up tonight?" Buran asked.

"He promised me he would," Gwen said. "He hasn't let me down yet."

Jemma held her tongue. She hadn't explained to Buran her apprehensions yet, but she also wasn't sure if she needed to. If the Outskirts were close, they could hide there for the night and return to catch the train the next day. At least that was what Buran claimed was the plan. If he would actually leave or not, Jemma wasn't sure.

If the Outskirts were truly a community of Disparates working together to live, would Buran be able to resist that?

Gwen stuck a hand out and hid behind a tree trunk. Jemma and Buran found their own trees to hide behind next to each other.

A man with a straw hat rode a horse past their spot and into the barn.

"Shoot," Gwen said. "The farmer took one of his night rides. He shouldn't be long, though. He likes to take them a couple times a week. Usually when he's fighting with the missus. We can hide out here for a few minutes to wait for him to come back out."

A cool breeze ruffled the treetops, sending a shiver down Jemma's spine.

"You know Keesha must be missing you," Jemma said. "Even with the issues you've been having, I know she loves you."

Buran looked at her, his forehead wrinkled. "I miss her too, but not sure why you're bringing her up now?"

Jemma shrugged. "We're heading home tomorrow. Haven't you thought about what it'll be like to hold her again?"

"Ah, I see what's happening," Buran said. "You're missing Ben and worried about what the Outskirts are like."

Jemma sighed. "If it's a community of Disparates using their powers to run it—that sounds like your dream."

"And it's not yours?" Buran asked. "Imagine it. Disparates allowed to be themselves. To *feel* and use their feelings for good. To create a life without others trying to control them and use them."

Jemma's heart sank. Buran was already infatuated with the place.

"But no," Buran continued. "I'm not going to leave my family behind. I'd want her there. And if the Outskirts is truly as great as it seems, I'll find a way back—with my wife."

"Do you think Keesha would move there?" Jemma wasn't so sure. Keesha wasn't a Disparate, and her dad was part of R.E.I.

"I... well, I hope," Buran said.

Gwen shushed them and pointed toward the barn. The farmer exited out the wooden doors, closing them behind him as he huffed toward the farmhouse. Once he entered, Gwen waved them forward.

Once safely inside the barn, Jemma glanced around the earthy smelling space, scrunching her nose when whiffs of manure hit. The farmer's white horse was in a stall to the right with two other horses next to it, both with shiny brown coats. Stacks of hay sat on the opposite side. Wooden beams crossed below the triangular roof. It wasn't a large barn, but it had enough places to hide.

"When does Teddy show up?" Buran asked.

"He usually doesn't take long once he sees me enter." Gwen glanced toward the front door.

Jemma twiddled her fingers. The barn was warmer than outside, but there wasn't much to do while waiting. She looked at the horses again. She'd never been this close to one before. She'd seen them on occasion, mostly during special parades that celebrated the creation of the Seven Republics, but they were not a daily thing in Stillfield.

She approached the farmer's horse. His snout fit over the small metal gate in front of him. His large nostrils twitched as he took in her scent.

Jemma reached a hand out slowly, waiting to see if he'd allow her to pet him or if he'd pull away. The horse lowered his head and Jemma stroked the side of his neck.

"His name is Lightning," Gwen said, approaching from behind. "He's usually pretty unsure of new people, but he seems to like you."

"Hello, Lightning." Jemma brushed his mane. "New people make me nervous too sometimes. Actually, a lot of things make me nervous." Petting this animal calmed Jemma's nerves, the electricity she'd felt growing simmering out.

Lightning nudged the top of Jemma's arm when she paused her hand for a moment.

Jemma laughed. "Okay, no stopping."

"It's been at least half an hour now," Buran said. "Is Teddy usually this late?"

Gwen shook her head. "No. If he's taking this long, I head back home."

"So he has stood you up before." Buran's gaze narrowed.

"Only once!" Gwen said. "When Urlan was sick and needed extra care. As far as I know, Urlan is well."

"Who is Urlan?" Buran asked.

"He's kind of like his father figure," Gwen said. "He took Teddy in after his parents died."

Jemma caught Buran's gaze. He seemed to be thinking the same thing as her. So much hurt spoken about so matter-of-factly. There was too much pain in this world.

"Could something else be holding him up?" Jemma asked.

"There are a lot of Responders out looking for you two," Gwen said. "Perhaps it was too dangerous for him to come."

Buran crossed his arms in front of him. "If he doesn't show up, where do we go?"

"You can stay in here for the night," Gwen said. "As long as we sneak you out before the sun rises, you won't be caught."

"And we can head to the train station then," Jemma said, wanting to remind Buran about their plans to go home. He'd wanted to see the Outskirts, but it wasn't worth risking missing the train.

Buran nodded. "Yeah. We can head to the station early so we're ready when the emergency train shows up."

Lightning nuzzled his nose against Jemma's ear, causing her to wince but smile at the same time. She'd get to spend the night with his sweet soul and then tomorrow head home.

She couldn't wait to hug her babies.

Floating on a cloud, Ben called out to Jemma. He was flying, and he wanted his wife to experience it with him. She stood on the ground a few yards in front of him, her back to him, her brown hair blowing in the breeze he sailed through.

He called to her again, this time catching her attention. She turned around to face him. Half the skin on her face had melted off, as if burned by fire, spots of bone exposed beneath the charred flesh.

Ben screamed, the sound rolling from his chest and out his mouth. It startled him, causing him to fall from the sky. Down... Down... Do—

"Ben!"

He shook as he hit the earth.

"Ben! Wake up!"

His eyes opened to reveal Asher kneeling above him. He lay on grass, the needles poking against his bandages. A scream continued to sound. It took him a moment to realize it was coming from him.

Silence settled like a dark mist.

"Ben, you're scaring Louie," Asher said.

"Sorry, I didn't mean to cause him any pain," an eerily familiar female voice said.

Ben's world was blurry. It was too dark to make out anyone around him, and his eyelids were heavy. He closed them.

"It's not your fault." Dominic's voice. "We needed to get him off the boat, and this hill is a soft spot. We'll need to lift him into the truck next."

"Will it hurt him again?" Louie's voice was shaky. Ben's screams had scared him.

Ben wanted to speak out. Tell Louie he was sorry and that he was going to be okay, but he couldn't. It was as if he were trapped in his own body, in a land of wavering consciousness. He didn't know how long he'd be present before he'd slip away again.

"I'll try my hardest not to hurt him," the female said again. Her voice had a sharpness to it, although she'd spoken softly. Something in his soul told him not to trust her. His floating had drawn attention to the burning in his body.

No. He didn't want to focus on that. Didn't want to give the pain power to shut him down. He needed to fight. He needed to stay.

"Wow. So this is what the mainland looks like?" This was an unfamiliar male voice.

"Yeah, Crow," Asher said. "What do you think?"

"Honestly, not that different from the island," Crow said. Laughter sounded.

"That's because we're only at the beach," Asher said. "As we move inland, you'll see how much it changes. Speaking of which, we should probably get to the car."

"About that," Dominic said. "We're not too far from Still-field. I was thinking I should get back. Take Louie with me. It's dangerous traveling to Preen through the Outskirts, and I don't know what your little community is like out there, but I'm sure Ben would want his little boy safe at home."

Ben tried to nod his head to agree, but had no control.

"I don't want to leave my dad!" Louie sounded frantic and scared.

"It's for your safety," Asher said. "He'd want you to be safe."

"But you're strong and can watch me." Louie's voice wavered. "I don't want to go."

Dominic's voice came next. "I'll take you back to your grandmother, and they'll send word as soon as—"

"He's right," Asher said. "I'm capable of keeping an eye on him."

No, Ben thought to himself. He wanted Louie in Stillfield. Margaret's house was a place he knew. He knew Mackie was safe and spoiled there; Louie would be the same.

Footsteps neared Ben's position.

"Are you sure you can handle Louie?" Dominic whispered. "Not let him out of your sight?"

"You're considering it?" Asher's voice matched Dominic's, but with a bit of surprise.

"Governor Dunn is dead," Dominic said. "I'm not sure what Stillfield will be like with Wuslick stepping in. It's not safe for Ben to show up to a hospital there in this condition without leading to questions, and I don't know what the rest of the city will be like. It might be better for him to stay with his dad."

"Dunn is dead?" Asher's astonishment matched Ben's. "How?"

"Things happened in Preen... Leda didn't have the details, but something went wrong."

"What about my sister? Is she okay?"

Ben's chest tightened, his head swirling, unconsciousness threatening to return as his thoughts of Jemma in danger increased his heart rate.

He needed to stay awake. He needed to know Dominic's answer.

"Last Leda had heard, she's on the run with Buran. They're searching for them now to bring them to the Outskirts."

Jemma's on the run... words slipped through Ben's mind as he fell back into an uncomfortable blackness.

FORTY-ONE

Quill wasn't sure how much time had passed when she was startled awake by the sound of a horn. She sat up on her aunt's couch.

"Good to see something rouses you," Aunt Bea said from the kitchen.

Quill groaned, lying back down and pulling the blanket over her head. "What is that for?"

"Vehicle in the distance."

Quill's heart skipped a beat. "Vehicle? Is someone coming?" Aunt Bea had insisted that hiking was the safest way to get to the Outskirts when they made their journey. They needed to keep from drawing attention to themselves, plus the bomb shelters provided a safe route to get outside the walls. A vehicle felt like a bad sign.

"No worries," Aunt Bea said, sensing Quill's apprehension. "The vehicle is one of ours." Aunt Bea put a dish into her cupboard. "You'll need to get up. Clean your space. Make it presentable."

Quill wiped a crumb from her sleeve. It'd been a full day since she learned she was an orphan. She was not adjusting well. "Are they coming here?"

"Not all of them, but my daughter better be, if she's with them."

Quill glanced at the picture on the table next to her. The smiling face of a young girl in her teens with dark hair sitting amongst wildflowers, holding a baby wrapped in a pastel pink blanket. The girl looked similar to Bea, yet with a darker complexion. "Is this her?" Quill asked.

Aunt Bea picked up the picture with a forlorn smile. "Yes. With her daughter Aleeta."

"Oh, she has a daughter. Will she be with her?"

"I sure hope so." Bea stared at the picture a moment longer, then returned it to the table and headed back to cleaning the kitchen.

"So I'll get to meet my cousin." More relatives she never knew existed, more connection to her mother's side of the family.

"Possibly. If she's with them." Aunt Bea stopped in the middle of wiping the counter with an old, ripped piece of fabric. Her face lit up. "I've imagined this moment since the day Leda was born. My daughter and my sister's daughter meeting. And now it's about to happen."

She shook her head and went back to cleaning. "...If this is Leda's group. It's just as likely to be one of the other ones."

"How many groups are there?" Urlan had mentioned special O.W.L. groups were scattered around the Republics to gather resources and help other Disparates in need.

"I can't tell you that. Even if I knew." Quill caught the small smile that formed on her aunt's face for a moment. Though this was the most alert Quill had been, the fog she'd let herself dwell in was still there. Hanging around, waiting for her to lie back down.

But she couldn't do that. Like a busy bee, her aunt gathered the mess around her, grabbing a plate out of Quill's hand that she had picked up, hoping to muster the energy to help.

"You can head to the bedroom. Make yourself presentable. We don't know what state those returnin' will be in. We need to be prepared for anything."

A splash of cold water jolted Quill's thoughts to this moment. There was no mirror in this small bathroom, but she didn't care. She knew her grief was plastered across her pale face. She grabbed a less wrinkly, unstained red shirt from the wardrobe of clothes her aunt had given her. She hesitated before putting it on. It used to be Leda's. Hopefully it wouldn't make things weird when they met.

She hadn't felt such a trivial worry since the news. She threw the shirt on. Nothing mattered; her dad was dead.

"Ready to head out?" Aunt Bea said as she returned to the front room.

Quill followed her, heading in the opposite direction from the middle of the village. They passed a few other makeshift homes as they walked. Soon, they spotted a small group of villagers waiting. Past them was an expanse of wasteland unlike anything Quill had seen before.

In Stillfield, she was used to trees and buildings blocking her view. None existed here. At least, no buildings that were whole.

Instead, a scattering of metal debris was swallowed by over-grown weeds.

Urlan was among the crowd waiting, along with Teddy and a few others Quill hadn't yet met.

"Glad you could make it," Urlan said. He turned to Quill. "How are you holding up?"

Quill steadied herself. The question brought a new wave of grief, washing over her as tears threatened to fall.

"That good, huh?" Urlan locked eyes with Aunt Bea. Quill caught her shrug through her blurry vision.

As she blinked away the tears, she saw a truck in the distance, the cab bouncing across the uneven ground. She focused on the incoming new arrivals. Anything to keep the cloud in her mind away.

The sun glared across the truck's windshield. Quill squinted as the truck barreled closer, believing her vision now deceived her. But with each second it neared, the person in the passenger seat became clearer.

She gasped as she recognized him.

Asher.

He was smiling toward the middle seat before turning his vision forward. Quill paid attention to no one else in the car as Asher swiped his medium length hair to the side and faced forward.

He was here. The man she'd longed for more than anyone after she heard the news of her dad. She sought comfort, and Asher was the one who had come to her mind. But to be truthful, her yearning for him had existed for much longer.

The truck stopped, and Asher hopped out without looking in her direction. His leg wobbled for a moment before he regained his balance. "We need help," he said. "Is there a doctor here?"

Quill's chest tightened. Asher was in the Outskirts asking for a doctor.

Aunt Bea raised her hand and headed in his direction. "I'm trained. Where—" She paused, her eyes growing wide as the back door of the truck opened. "This looks worse in person than I expected, but I've got this. He'll be okay. I've *seen* it. Now, can I get a hand with moving him to the infirmary?"

People from the Outskirts descended on the truck and followed Aunt Bea's commands. A flash of a woman with blonde hair was in Quill's peripheral vision, but her focus was elsewhere.

A body was floated out of the truck feet first, covered in cloth. Glimpses of burnt skin peeked between the rags. Ben's head was last to emerge.

Quill's eyes went wide. She moved her gaze back to Asher. A young man with dark facial hair stood next to him. Something about him seemed familiar, but she couldn't place what. They must have arrived together, as his mouth moved, saying something to Asher.

Asher didn't seem to be listening. The moment his eyes locked with Quill's, the world stopped. He was covered in dirt with dark circles under his eyes, yet seeing her, they brightened just a spark, and so did her soul. The heaviness was there, the curiosity, the fear of whatever happened to Ben. But Asher was here—the one she'd trust with her heart over and over again.

He wouldn't break it. Not with something so heavy on the line.

Asher turned back to the man and motioned to the crowd surrounding Ben as his body moved toward the building to the left. "Can you keep an eye on him? Get me immediately if anything happens."

The man nodded and followed the group.

Asher turned again to Quill and limped in her direction.

She rushed forward, crashing against his chest without a second thought. She wrapped her arms around his thick body, not even caring about the mix of dirt with his smoky scent. She rather liked his smoky odor. It was Asher, and he was in her arms.

Asher shook slightly at her embrace but returned it. His warm arms accepted her. "What are you doing here?" His rough voice sent shivers down her spine.

"I could ask you the same question."

Asher pulled back but kept his hands on her upper arms. "I asked first."

"What happened to Ben?" She couldn't shake how frail he looked. Her aunt had mentioned she'd seen that he would be okay, but in what exact way, Quill wasn't sure.

"Turns out EnertinX still has its faults."

Quill winced. "He had an outburst?"

Asher nodded. "Because of me. I sort of took Louie to Lucky Island."

Quill's mouth gaped. "What? Why?"

"It's a bit of a long story..."

"I don't have anything better to do."

He explained about receiving mysterious notes, about stealing keys from Dominic, about Leda—

"Leda!" Quill exclaimed, looking around for the cousin she'd never met. "Is she here?" She tilted to search behind Asher.

"No, she's still on the island searching for hints about Aleeta."

"Aleeta? Did something happen to her daughter?"

"Aleeta is Leda's daughter?" Asher asked. "That checks out, honestly. With how desperate she is to find her. Part of why a group is on Lucky Island. They're searching for her."

Aunt Bea hadn't mentioned Aleeta was missing. Worry bubbled in Quill's stomach for the missing child. Speaking of children...

"Wait... is that?" Quill moved around Asher to head to where Louie sat outside the infirmary, next to the young man from earlier. "Louie?" she half asked, half shouted. It then dawned on her who sat next to him. "And Crow!" Both their heads lifted.

"Quill!" Louie bounded to her and wrapped his arms around her waist. "My dad is hurt. He's being seen by a doctor."

Quill knelt to his eye level. "That doctor is my aunt, and she said he's going to be okay."

Crow gave a small wave. "Hey, Quill."

She nodded her head at him, still taking in the fact that he was here, alive. A part of her past on Lucky Island she'd never expected to see again.

"Your aunt?" Asher stood behind her.

"You asked why I'm here," Quill said. "That's why."

"I'm glad he's getting help," Louie said.

Quill nodded. "Me too. I see you've made a new friend. He's a good one." She looked at Crow.

"Ha, if you say so," he said, reaching out a hand.

"Your hair's a lot longer than it used to be." Quill pulled him into a hug, a spark escaping at their touch, but Crow didn't flinch. They held on for a few seconds before letting go.

Asher put a hand on her shoulder. "I saw that. You holding up okay, Little Raccoon?"

"Little Raccoon?" she asked, truly puzzled. She didn't hate the name, but she didn't know where it had come from. "Like the black masked animal?"

Asher ran a hand through his hair. "I heard about what happened to your dad..."

The reminder that her heart was shattered stabbed deep.

"Aw crap." His eyes widened. "Raccoon was a bad comparison. I didn't mean to say your eyes are dark."

His meaning hit her, making her wish she were invisible. For a moment, she'd forgotten that her dad was gone. Asher was here, and Louie. And they were having a conversation together without Asher walking on eggshells. A conversation that didn't revolve around the loss of her father or how she was feeling.

Reality hit her as the tears responsible for the dark bags around her eyes once again threatened to fall.

He'd managed to remind her of her grief for her father as well as her anger toward him from the last time they spoke. As much as she cared for this man, words were not his strong suit. There was no stopping the tears this time.

She didn't want to cry in front of Louie. His dad was hurt, and it didn't feel like the right time to explain that her dad was dead.

"I'll be right back," she choked out before turning around and heading toward her aunt's house. She kept her pace brisk as she wiped tears from her eyes. They wouldn't stop coming, no matter how desperately she willed them to.

Forty-Two

A soft knock sounded on her aunt's door. Quill sat on the couch, hugging her legs to her chest.

"Quill," Asher said from the other side of the door.

She didn't respond.

"Quill, I'm sorry." His apology fell flat. Quill didn't have the energy to move, to respond. She'd let herself empty out her emotions after Asher's reminder of her pain. She didn't want to feel, and seeing his face would bring all the emotions she was detaching from flooding back.

And that was exactly what they did as Asher opened the front door. She buried her face into her knees.

"I'm an idiot," Asher said, standing above her a few feet away. "I'm so sorry about your dad..." The couch shifted as he sat next to her.

Of course, she thought. *Everyone's sorry about my dad. That doesn't bring him back.*

Quill sniffled, unsure how to respond.

"This week has been one of the hardest of my life. And that's saying a lot." He let out a soft chuckle to defuse the tension.

"Your whole life has been pretty rough."

"That's true." Asher reached to take Quill's hand, and she let him. "Not as rough as yours, though."

The betrayal she felt at herself for not pulling away melted at his touch. The warmth of his palm on hers traveled to her heart. It didn't fix it, more like wrapped a broken vase in a blanket, but at least it was something.

"The thing is, I messed up," Asher confessed. "Again. I wanted to be a better person off the island, prove that I could do good, and I've created this mess. I don't even know if Ben will survive. I don't think I could ever forgive myself if he doesn't."

"He will," Quill said. "I was being truthful when I said my aunt knows. She sees glimpses of the future."

Asher's brow furrowed. "How is that possible?"

"I'm still figuring that out myself. Something to do with Paxton and her testing."

"Paxton is involved here too?" Asher shook his head. "She has her hand everywhere."

Quill nodded.

Asher rubbed a finger along the side of her palm. "I'm sorry I haven't been open with you."

She tilted her head. "You mean before everything hit the fan and was torn to shreds?"

Asher laughed. "It's hard to believe we can be in a dark situation off the island, isn't it?"

"I used to dream about getting off the island," Quill said. "This was definitely not what I imagined."

"I mean—" Asher shifted his legs to touch hers. "There is one thing here that I never dared to imagine yet plagued my dreams."

"What do you mean?" Her soul waited, anxious for the revelation she felt was coming. She wasn't sure if her heart could handle it. And yet, she couldn't stop the tingling that traveled down her arm.

A small shock popped between their hands. She tried to pull back, but Asher's grip intensified. As if he liked her shock. Her electricity.

"Are you ready?" Asher asked.

She gave him a puzzled look. "Ready for what?" she breathed.

"You asked me before about why I didn't use a nickname for you. I told you I did. And no, it's not 'Little Raccoon.' That was silly."

"I kinda liked it." Quill gave a sly smile. It was all she could muster, but she wanted Asher to keep going. To heal at least a part of her wounded soul.

"Ask me again." The mischievous look in his eye was all Asher, but she sensed the seriousness of the moment. She was vulnerable. Another attack, another "joke" from him would only mess her up further.

And yet she couldn't let this opportunity go. "Asher Stillfield," she said, her voice raspy. "What do you call me in secret?"

"You are the thorns I wear for protection. The reason I put myself in danger is to keep you safe. You're the needle that has sewn the pieces of my broken heart back together. You're the feather that gives me pause to calm my soul." He shifted so their bodies faced each other. "Without you, my world is chaos. You brought calm, showed me how to be human. You are my good thing. You are my Quill. Writing the actions I take day by day. They are for you. Every last one. For you."

His words, although lacking in true poetry, were completely him. And Quill was completely smitten by them.

"You know 'Quill' is my actual name, right?"

"Should I stick with 'Little Raccoon'?" Asher asked. "You do have an unhealthy obsession with potato chips."

She saw the moment in his green eyes that switched from confidence to uncertainty when she didn't respond. To be truthful, she wasn't sure what to say. This was what she wanted: him to be honest about his feelings. That his actions on the island weren't because they were trapped together, but because he truly cared about her. But she wasn't so sure about hers.

"Well," Asher said as he pulled away. "You've been through a lot the past few days. I shouldn't have put this on you right now." He stood and faced the door. "I'll give you your space to process."

He wasn't challenging her. Demanding an answer. He headed toward the door.

"Wait—" Quill reached for him, standing and putting a hand on his arm. Warmth radiated through his sleeve. If it weren't for the fabric, he'd likely leave a burn mark. He froze, his back to her.

"You're hot," she said. Her face flushed at the double meaning. "Are you angry at me?"

"I'm angry at myself," he admitted, his voice rough. "I'm selfish, and arrogant, and terrible at timing. But this shouldn't be about me." He turned to face her. "You're hurt, and I'm only putting more on your plate. I want you to know that I understand loss, even though I'm bad at showing it. I don't need an answer from you. I just want you to be happy. Which, again, is foolish of me right now—"

Quill placed a finger on his lips, stopping his rambling. "I want you," she said as she craned her neck and lifted her lips closer to his, waiting for him to close the gap and relieve the tension that'd been drawing them magnetically together since the day they'd met.

The wrinkles on his face smoothed as he stared at her. "What if I don't know how to make you happy?"

His eyes were like an endless forest, the green holding a depth that went on for unseeable lengths. This was a thought he truly struggled with. Perhaps it was her grief that intensified the mix of emotions she felt; however, it made her want him more.

"Don't worry. I can teach you." She was tired of waiting for him. She stood on her tiptoes, lifting her lips to him. Their warmth was almost too much to touch, but she didn't mind. She liked his heat, and the last little while had been so cold.

Their kisses were soft, delicate at first. Then he took over, lips pressing more aggressively as he slid his arms around her.

She followed his lead, wrapping her arms around his neck as she lifted from the ground. When her face became level with his, she didn't stop, but instead lifted him with her.

She hadn't felt this joy in so long. Her body had missed it.

His lips paused for a moment, his feet now dangling above the ground. She waited. She knew she was in control of her emotions at the moment, but she wasn't sure if he trusted her. Soon his lips began to move once more, gently opening to take in more of her. Truth was, she wanted to let go, give in to the warmth in her chest.

This felt right. This was right.

She wanted to go further, add more kindling to the fire between them. But as they closed their mouths together once more, Asher pulled away.

Quill bit her lip, resisting her urge to jump back on the man in front of her. She slowed her breathing, their feet once more resting on the ground.

"We should take things slow." Asher had moved his mouth away, but his arms still encircled her.

"And what do you call the thing we've been doing?" Quill raised an eyebrow.

That earned her a smirk. "You know what I mean. A lot is on our plates right now, and I want to make sure we do this thing right. I don't want to mess this up."

"And what exactly is this?"

"I... I think, I mean, I hope..." he stammered. "I'd like us to give this a shot."

Quill nodded. "Me too." She laid her head on his chest, listening to the beat of his heart. His body no longer burned in the literal way. The heat she now felt from him was different. Her hands gripped his shirt, holding him there. She didn't want to let him go.

His arms wrapped around her shoulders, his chin resting on the top of her. "You're already my perfect weapon. Live or die, we're in this together."

If anyone else had tried to call her that, she'd be repulsed. But not coming from Asher. Not with the weight of his confession earlier.

She rather liked holding his trigger.

Forty-Three

L ights dangled above Ben's head, blurry in his vision as he blinked awake. His head throbbed as he tried to roll over.

"Whoa there, buddy," an unfamiliar voice said as gentle hands weighted his chest in place. "I'd suggest waiting a little longer before you start moving. The medicine I gave you lessens the pain, but it increases your ability to overdo it."

A woman with curly brown hair stood over him in a room he didn't recognize. Parts of the walls were metal, others wood. Ben surmised he was laying on a table of some sort.

"Dad? Is my dad awake?" Louie came bounding next to him, his head and shoulders just above the table top.

"Louie." Ben smiled, his memory of waking up before returning. "I'm so glad you're okay." Although a sharp pain radiated through his arm, he lifted it anyway. A fresh white bandage covered its surface as he wrapped it around his son, pulling him into his chest.

Louie seemed to resist at first, likely noticing the flinching Ben had tried to hide, but he couldn't escape his father's reach.

"Don't worry," Ben said. "It doesn't hurt. Well, not much," he corrected. His son was getting older and deserved to be given the truth. At least in this matter.

At his words, Louie laid his head onto his chest. That one action relieved a deeper pain that had taken hold of Ben on the inside.

Louie still loved him. He wasn't a perfect father, but he was trying. And his son loved him despite his faults.

"Now, where are we?" Ben asked, looking around the rest of the room.

"Welcome to O.W.L. headquarters," the curly haired woman said. She was nearby, tidying up a pile of medical materials spread across a desk. "I'm Doctor Bea Everly. I've been treating your burns. They're pretty deep, but thankfully, you arrived when you did as infection was starting to set in. I've got you started on antibiotics now. Should clear that up in a few days. Your burns, however, will take a bit longer to heal properly."

So, they made it to the Outskirts. They saved his life.

Behind the doctor, in a chair near the door, sat Asher.

"Hey Ben. About time you wake up," he said as he stood. "Been babysitting your kid long enough."

Louie shot him a narrowed look.

"I'm sorry," Dr. Everly said. "You'll have to watch him a while longer. Ben is not finished healing."

Asher laughed. "It was a joke. I love the responsibility of being an uncle." He rubbed the top of Louie's head, which caused Louie to break into a smile as he pushed his hand off. "I'm also looking forward to your full recovery."

"Me too." Ben groaned as he shifted on the bed. The right side of his body was more tender than the left, although there were tight spots across his left arm as well. He'd really done damage to himself.

Burn damage.

His flame energy was back. Or at least, it had been. He'd need to be careful to keep from testing if it was back for good—he couldn't risk flambéing himself again.

"Glad to see we made it here safely. Wasn't there someone else headed this way too?" Ben remembered the other voice he heard, the one he'd been trying to place but couldn't.

"That was Vicki," Louie said. "She's with the Outskirts people. She drove the truck all the way here!"

"Oh wow. Let her know I'm grateful." So Ben didn't know her. Must have confused her voice for someone else earlier—his mind had been foggy and spinning.

"Oh, and guess what!" Louie bounced next to Ben. His movement caused little aches, but Ben didn't mind. "Quill is here!"

"Quill?" Ben asked. His heart ached for her. Quill had gone to Preen with Jemma and the others—perhaps Jemma was here as well. He'd overheard about Dunn's death. If this place was safe, perhaps they all came here. "Is Mom here too?"

Louie perked up and looked behind him at the two other adults in the room. "Mom! Is she here?"

The doctor and Asher locked eyes. "There've been some challenges," the doctor said.

Something more was going on. Ben looked at Louie and hesitated before asking his next question. But he needed to know, and he wasn't about to send Louie away. "What happened to Tobias Dunn? And where is my wife?"

As he finished his question, the door opened. A young man with black hair entered, his breathing rushed as if he'd ran there.

"I found them," he said, looking at the doctor.

"I'm not sure in front of our new guests was the best time to announce that, Teddy," the doctor responded.

Teddy's face reddened. "Urlan wanted them to know as well."

"Oh!" the doctor exclaimed. She didn't look upset by being corrected, merely surprised. She turned to Ben. "Your wife is Jemma, right?"

"Yes, that's her," he said. Louie stayed next to him, quiet as he listened.

"She's been missing for the past couple days." She turned to the young man. "Where were they found?"

"At Elmer's. One of the farmhands took them in—been hidin' them in the stables."

"Just a random farmhand?" Dr. Everly asked, raising her eyebrows.

Teddy turned red once more. Ben caught the innuendo, but he didn't have time to care about who this child's crush was.

"Why are they hiding?" Ben grunted as he tried to sit up, but Asher shook his head at him. Ben listened and lay back on the flat pillow.

"That may be a story for when little ears aren't listening," the doctor said.

Ben's pulse quickened. If it was too much for Louie to hear at this moment, it must be worse than he'd let his mind think.

"Is she okay?"

"Yes," Teddy answered. "But they're headed to the station to catch the emergency train back to Stillfield. Gwen is trying to stop them, to bring them here, but not sure if she'll make it in time. I headed back to fill in Urlan."

"She's headed back home," Asher said. "That's a good thing."

Dr. Everly shook her head. "Not with what happened to Governor Dunn. Wuslick and R.E.I. will be taking over Stillfield's leadership for the time being. If Beecher has reported them, they won't have anywhere to hide."

The amount of information floating in Ben's mind tangled together. Mackie was back in Stillfield with Margaret and Dominic. Hopefully, Dominic would be able to keep them safe. As for Jemma... "Reported?" His voice croaked out.

"What?" Louie's soft voice cried out. "What happened?"

Asher put a hand on Louie's shoulder. "Bad people still exist in the world. But we're going to do what we can to fix it." He looked toward the doctor and Teddy. "We need to go get Jemma and Buran. We can't let them stay on the run by themselves."

"Urlan's working to gather a group already," Teddy said. "I'll go, to show the way. Vicki has volunteered and—-"

"I want to go," Louie said.

"I don't think that's a good idea," the doctor interjected.

Louie looked at Ben. "I want to see Mom." His face was tired. This boy had been through more than any child should ever have to.

"They're going to bring her here," Ben said.

Tears welled in Louie's gray eyes, like a cloudy day before it rained. It broke Ben's heart. "I don't want to wait. I've been waiting. I want to see her."

"I'll be going," Asher said. "She's my little sister. I've gotta watch out for her."

Teddy nodded.

"Can I go with Asher?" Louie looked again at his dad. "He'll keep me safe."

Ben met Asher's gaze. "Will you?"

"I may have messed up a little in the past—"

Ben narrowed his eyes.

"Okay, messed up big time," Asher said. "But I promise I won't let him out of my sight. We'll stay back from the group if needed, and if there's any sign of him being in danger, we'll get out of there."

Looking at the pleading in Louie's eyes, an uneasiness filled Ben's chest. He didn't want to let his boy go, but at the same time, he didn't want to upset him again. Louie simply wanted his mother, and Ben wanted Jemma back. He didn't want her ending up in a more dangerous circumstance by returning home.

"There is a safe house in Preen," Dr. Everly said. "It could be a good place to wait."

"I can handle going all the way," Louie whined.

"I know buddy," Ben said. "But we can't risk you being hurt. The safe house would allow you to see mom sooner while also staying safe, which is my biggest concern."

"Okay," he said. He didn't look fully happy but agreed to the compromise.

"I promise I'll keep him safe," Asher said.

Louie gave Ben another hug, pressing on the burn on his side. Ben held his breath until Louie backed away. He smiled at his boy as he grabbed Asher's hand, and the two of them followed Teddy out the door.

He was letting his son go, but this time on terms they'd agreed on together. That made him a good father, right?

And soon Jemma would be back.

"Try not to worry," Dr. Everly said. "The safe house in Preen is secure. They'll be back by tonight. For now, you try and get some rest."

Ben closed his eyes once she left the room. He tried to sleep, but on the other side of his eyelids were images of the burning fire he'd created, the island consumed in his rage. Sleep would be difficult to find.

Forty-Four

Being surrounded by cement walls reminded Asher of his time on Lucky Island. Except on the island, he wasn't deep underground. The more he thought about the tons of pounds of dirt pressing down on the enclosure they trusted to hold it at bay, the more nervous he became.

"How much farther do we have to go?" he asked Teddy, who led the group.

"Not much," Teddy said.

Two other members of the Outskirts gang had volunteered to accompany Teddy, Vicki, Asher, and Louie. Quill had offered to go with, but Asher told her to stay. She needed to help her aunt care for Ben. Her time with the medical doctor on Lucky Island gave her unique insight on burns.

As he hiked through empty, hollow hallways, Asher almost wished he'd insisted she came with them. They'd just been reunited, and being apart again so soon reminded his heart of its ache for her.

"Why are these tunnels here?" Louie asked.

That's right. He was only six years old; he hadn't learned about the wars of the past. "People built them for safety," Asher said.

Louie wrinkled his nose. "What's safe about living under dirt?"

"Well, there were threats above ground," Asher continued. "They built these bunkers as a place to hide when bombs were dropped."

Louie's eyes widened. The gray in them matched the color of the walls. "By bad guys?"

Asher nodded.

"I hope the good guys won," Louie said.

"That depends on which side you're on," Vicki said, joining them. "Those who sent the bombs would say they were the good guys."

Asher looked at her like she was delusional. "Killing people isn't a good thing."

She met his gaze. "You forget everyone in the war used bombs, and they each thought they were using them for right. The difference is, only the survivors got to tell their story and that became history. And do you know where the survivors came from? The country that killed the most."

A pit sank in Asher's stomach. "It's not always easy knowing the truth, but I like to think the ones who fought for freedom had a valiant cause."

"But their freedom came at a cost." Vicki tucked a strand of blonde hair behind her ear. "We all know there were no winners in the war."

"What happened to the bear?" Louie asked.

Asher wrinkled his forehead. "There wasn't a bear—"

Vicki wrapped an arm around Louie's shoulders. "The bear returned stronger than ever for the girls."

"What is this?" Asher asked.

Louie shushed him. "Did he hurt them? I hope he didn't."

"No," Vicki said. "He didn't hurt them. The elf had warned the sisters about the bear, telling them he was dangerous. Yet, when the younger sister started to welcome the bear in, she was surprised to find that he wasn't as scary as the elf had taught. In fact, she started to think that perhaps it was the elf that caused her mother's death."

"The elf?" Louie gasped. "Did they stop him?"

Vicki shook her head. "The oldest sister didn't want to listen to her younger one. She didn't believe that the bear could be controlled. When the elf found out about the younger sister's chats with the bear, he sent her away. And the older sister went with her, determined to save her from the bear that might not be a threat."

Asher listened to this story Vicki weaved. Louie was young and likely didn't understand that there was more underneath her words, but Asher picked up on it. "I believe the bear can be a way to accomplish good," he said.

Vicki looked his way. "I've been hesitant, but I'm coming to believe that as well."

Asher tilted his head. If the bear was a metaphor for Disparate energy, it seemed Vicki had struggled with accepting her powers in the past. Then again, if she'd been on Lucky Island as a prisoner, that wouldn't be surprising. Asher had held a grudge against his own energy for years.

"Jim, you got the key?" Teddy asked as they approached a large metal door.

Jim, an Outskirter with a bald head, rushed forward and unlocked the door. It opened to a large room.

As Asher stepped inside, he caught sight of a ladder ascending to the darkness above. He looked at Louie, who had craned his neck to see where the ladder ended.

"Perhaps we should wait here?" Asher asked.

"No!" Louie said. "I want to find Mom."

Asher rubbed his brown hair. "I know you want to find her, but she would also want to keep you safe."

"Is the safe house close by?" Vicki asked.

Teddy nodded. "It's above our heads. A little bit of a climb, or if your air energy is prepared, that'd make it faster."

Vicki nodded. "It would be my pleasure." She placed her hands out in front of her.

"Whoa," Louie said as his small body shook and rose above the ground.

Asher pushed his arms out as if to catch himself as his own feet lifted off the cement floor. Glancing around, Teddy, Jim, and the third Outskirter also floated in the air. Vicki lifted five people at once.

As they levitated into the darkness, Asher's pulse increased. "Louie," he said.

"Uncle Asher?"

The voice came from his side. Asher reached out, tilting toward it. His hand touched a small arm, clasping hold of it.

"Hold us here!" Teddy's voice echoed down.

Their movement stopped, suspended in the dark air. Asher would've preferred the climb.

A scratching sounded near where Teddy had last spoken. With a screech, a sliver of light snuck through a round opening.

"Alright, raise us slowly," Teddy said. The light grew as Teddy flew through a round opening. The others followed behind him, Asher holding tight to Louie and pushing him through the opening first.

"Clear!" Jim yelled into the hole.

The three Outskirters fell onto a rug atop the wooden floor of a small room, not much bigger than Asher's cell on the island. A cot laid sideways attached to the hatch opening, coverage for when it was closed. A lone chair sat in the corner next to a fireplace.

Asher shot Louie a look.

Louie smirked, then let out a breath as the two of them placed their feet onto the ground.

"Did you have us the whole time?" Asher asked.

Louie laughed. "I tricked you."

Vicki floated through the opening to join them. "I felt your lightness there at the end, Louie. Were you worried I'd drop you?"

"No," Louie said. "I just wanted to practice."

"You did great." Vicki beamed.

Asher shook his head, happy to have his feet planted solidly above ground. Now to find his sister. "So, you said Jemma was heading to the train station?"

Teddy nodded. "The northern train is unloading, but we've made it before the emergency train. So they should still be here.

We need to find them and bring them to the Outskirts. We don't need them going back to Stillfield and getting caught by Responders to face charges for Governor Dunn's death. We need their witness."

"If Preen already believes they're murderers," Vicki said, "then who will believe their witness?"

Jim stepped forward. "Other Disparates tired of being treated like walking nuclear bombs and blamed for the misdeeds of the world. We're ready to fight, and having them on our side would be a symbol of what we can do."

"Fight who?" Asher said.

"The Seven Republics," the other Outskirter said. His dark eyes narrowed. "They've been containing and destroying us for decades because they're scared of our powers. It's time we show them what they have to be scared of."

"I thought the Outskirts was a safe place for Disparates to live," Asher said. "Certainly you don't have the numbers to attack the Republics."

"You don't need the numbers when you are the weapon," Teddy said, lighting a flame in the palm of his hand.

The flame danced in Asher's eyes as the information sank in. The Outskirts wasn't just a community built to thrive in the wild—it was a battle camp preparing for war.

A war where there may be no winner.

Yet Disparates deserved the freedom to feel. They deserved the freedom to be who they truly were. And Asher was tired of waiting around for the Republics to change on their own. O.W.L. might have a point.

Perhaps the best way for change to happen was by creating it.

A train whistle blew in the background.

"Time to go," Jim said. He turned to Asher. "This safe house will be a good place to lay low with the kid. Any sign of danger, drop into the bunker below. Close the top to hide."

Asher nodded, putting an arm around Louie.

"I'll stay with you both," Vicki said. "In case you need a ride back to the bunker floor."

Asher released a breath. Having Vicki to help them back down was a relief.

"Keep this with you." Teddy held a two-way radio out to Asher. "That way we can get ahold of each other if there's any trouble. Though, hopefully, there won't be."

Asher accepted it, clipping it onto the top of his jeans.

The three Outskirters left through the front door of the small shack.

"So I guess we wait," Asher said, sitting in the small chair in the corner.

"How long will it take?" Louie asked. He went to the window next to the door and looked out.

"Careful; we wouldn't want to be seen," Asher said.

Vicki moved next to Louie. "I doubt any Responders would be looking for a child. Besides, we can see the train smoke in the distance. It'll help us know if they've left or not."

"That's where my mom is, right?" Louie asked.

Vicki nodded. "Yep. At least, that's where she was headed."

Louie watched out the window silently as Asher stared at the small fire pit across from him. He shot a flame nonchalantly into the middle of it.

Vicki looked at him. "Getting cold?"

Asher shook his head. "Just needed to release some of my built-up energy."

"Feeling some anger?" She raised an eyebrow.

"Always." He sighed and got up to put the small flame he'd started out with the poker next to it. Starting a fire in this place wasn't the best idea.

He pulled coals on top of the fire, extinguishing the flame with a puff of smoke.

Louie's small body popped up from where he still watched out the window. "Hey!" he yelled.

"Who are you calling to?" Asher asked.

"Um…" Vicki put an arm around Louie's shoulders. "Maybe we should move you away from the wind—"

"Oli!" Louie shouted.

Asher rubbed the back of his neck as he stood and neared Louie. "You see someone you know?"

His face was pressed against the dirty glass. "I did… he ran around the edge of the house."

"It was probably a mistake," Vicki said. "How would you know anyone in Preen?"

Something didn't feel right. "Who did you say you saw?" Asher asked.

"One of my dad's friends," Louie said. "Oliver. They used to work together."

The name boiled a quick response inside of Asher. He knew the story behind Oliver's betrayal on Lucky Island. "Are you sure that's who you saw?" He had to be mistaken.

"Yeah," Louie said. "It was definitely him."

Asher locked eyes with Vicki. "We need to get out of here. Now." He headed toward the ladder that led to the bunker below. It was still open, the fabric of the rug that hid it gathered behind it. "Louie, come on. It's not safe for yo—" The lid fell in front of him, blocking off the path below. Asher grabbed on the handle. "Vicki, a little help? This won't budge."

Vicki moved next to him and put her hands out, trying to use her energy to pull it. When it didn't move, she used her hands by grabbing the raised edge next to Asher. It still wouldn't open.

"It's stuck," Vicki said.

Asher locked eyes with her. "We can't stay here. We have to go. Do you know of anywhere else that is safe?"

Vicki bit her lip and nodded. "I know of some place nearby. Another bunker entrance."

Asher moved to the window and searched for signs of people outside. The street—or more like alleyway—was empty of life. Louie could have been mistaken, but then again, with what Asher had heard about Oliver and the way he turned on Ben on the island, it was better not to risk it.

"Lead the way," Asher said, motioning Vicki toward the door.

She went out first, stopping to look side to side before heading to the left.

"Louie, hold my hand," Asher said. Louie listened, his little hand cool against Asher's heated skin. They followed Vicki.

"Are we in danger?" Louie asked.

Asher didn't want to scare him. "Are you sure that was Oliver you saw?"

Louie nodded. "I-I'm pretty sure. But he didn't answer when I said his name."

"We're probably fine," Vicki said, "but want to make sure no one knows where we are."

Tears welled in Louie's eyes. His lip trembled. "I'm sorry."

"It's okay, Hawk," Asher said. "We need someone with good eyes to keep a lookout. You did good."

Louie's face brightened. "I'm Hawk? Did I get a nickname?"

Asher smiled. "You earned it." He rubbed the top of his nephew's head.

"Come on, this way." Vicki turned a sharp corner into a smaller walkway. The end of it in the distance seemed to open into fields.

"Where are we going, exactly?" Asher asked. Something gnawed at the back of his mind.

Vicki glanced to her left as she exited the end of the walkway. "I told you. It's another safehouse bunker."

"How many does O.W.L. have?"

"Not a lot."

Asher hesitated at the opening, putting a hand out to stop Louie. "How do you know about another O.W.L. bunker? Didn't you join them on Lucky Island?"

Vicki turned to look at them, a smile on her face. "I wondered how long you were going to let those thoughts marinate in your mind before you got the guts to ask out loud."

Asher wrinkled his brow. Could she read his mind?

"Yes." Vicki smirked.

"But, how?"

Louie tightened his grip. "What's going on?"

"Don't get hung up on the details," Vicki said. "I wasn't lying about another bunker. Too bad you won't get to see it."

A sharp prick stabbed into Asher's upper arm. He grabbed at the area, his hand wrapping around another man's, who was pressing the end of a needle-tipped syringe into Asher. Warm liquid spread through his veins. Tingling filled Asher's body as he pushed against the man's hand, causing the needle to leave his skin.

However, the liquid had fully drained into his bloodstream.

"Oliver..." Louie's voice trickled off as his wide eyes stared at the scene.

"Yes, oh, hi Louie." Oliver gave a small wave.

Asher punched him in the face with all the strength he had left. Blood splattered from Oliver's nose.

Asher was in charge of Louie. He was looking after Louie. He wasn't going to let a simple chemical stop him from protecting Louie. He breathed a sharp breath through his nose, turning the tingling from the tranquilizer into fuel for his flames.

"Oh! That wasn't very nice," Vicki yelled. "Are you okay, Oliver, dear?"

Louie stepped back as fire danced around Asher. He focused on Vicki, still a few feet away. Her feet were planted on the ground, hands up. Lightning escaped from them—which was unexpected. He thought she was only an Air Disparate. Asher didn't have time to wait. His flames reflected in her eyes as they shot toward her, hungry.

A burst of air from the side blew the lightning and fire away, the strikes and flames dispersing into smoke as if they were never there.

Asher twisted to see Louie with his hands out in front of him.

"No!" Louie yelled. "These powers are not for hurting people!"

The world around Asher blurred as his stance wavered. "She's not... safe..."

Oliver, with blood streaming from his nose down his chin, pushed Asher's shoulder, causing him to completely lose his balance and fall to the ground. "I'm fine, Vicki, my love," Oliver said.

"Leave... him alone..." Asher's breath was heavy. He focused on brewing more flames, but Louie had blown away the last of his accumulated flame energy. He was a young boy. He didn't understand.

"What's happening?" Louie asked, rushing toward him.

"Asher's going to take a little nap," Oliver said, wrapping an arm across Louie and pulling him away.

"Wait! We can't leave him!" Louie shouted, pushing against Oliver.

It was no use.

Asher caught Vicki in his vision once more. The color on her face had drained as she looked at him. She took a step to stand by his side. "Let Ben know I'll take care of his boy. He's very special."

Asher swung his arm from his body to grab Vicki, but she'd already taken a step back to dodge it, as if knowing it was coming.

With a flick of her wrist, she pushed Asher's frail body into the bushes nearby. He barely felt the branches scratching him.

"There," Vicki said. "Now you'll be out of the way."

Louie's screams rang out as Vicki followed Oliver's trail, but Asher couldn't keep his focus on her for long. Spots blocked his view.

With the last of his energy, he moved his hand to the two-way radio on his hip. He pressed down on the top button, but he didn't have enough strength to call for help. His hand slipped.

A beep sounded. "I don't believe we got your message." Teddy's voice came through the speaker. "Is everything alright at the safe house?"

Asher's world went black, as if coals were placed across his eyesight to extinguish his flame.

FORTY-FIVE

Jemma's back ached as she stretched. Someone was shaking her awake. Sleeping on the ground, and then in a horse stall last night, did not give the best sleep. Her body yearned for a soft bed.

"Time to wake up," Buran said, handing her an apple. "You ready to head home today?"

Jemma straightened, rubbing her eyes. She'd been tossing and turning all night worried they'd miss waking up in time. Of course, she'd finally passed out right before. Perhaps an apple for breakfast would give her energy.

Lightning's tail swished in front of them. The good boy had kept her safe throughout the night. She patted his side before leaving. "Thank you for providing me a safe place for the night."

Lightning gave a deep nicker, the sound vibrating through his body.

"Let's go," Buran said, heading to the front doors.

As much as Jemma enjoyed being around the horses, her nose begged her to leave. The smell in the barn was still as pungent as when they'd first entered, despite her hope that she'd get over it after a few hours. Jemma took in a deep breath as she escaped into the cool, fresh, morning air.

It was dark outside, but morning light was threatening to arrive on the horizon. They needed to be quick.

A train whistled from a distance. Jemma shot Buran a sharp look.

"It's probably the northern supply train," he said. Poppy had mentioned that was arriving today as well when she was talking with Gwen.

"Do we know that for sure?" Jemma asked.

Buran shuffled and shook his head. "That's why we need to get going."

"How long do we have?"

"The first horn is a fifteen minute warning, then two sound for five minutes, and three signify one minute before they leave. We should be able to make it in time."

It was early enough in the day that the farm hands had risen, yet late enough that they would be out in the fields. Gwen had taken over horse stall duties for the week and would likely arrive soon, but not soon enough for them to say goodbye.

"Should we leave a note?" Jemma asked Buran.

"Do you see any paper?" He shrugged.

She didn't. However, the ground was covered in hay and dirt. There were other ways to leave a message. She bent down, tracing the outline of a thank you with a heart on the floor. That should be enough to let Gwen know they left by their own choice and weren't caught.

They stepped out the doors and headed in the direction of the train station. Thankfully, they saw no other signs of life near the stables. In the distance, farm hands worked between rows of crops.

"Shoot," Buran said. He looked around and picked up two small shovels nearby. "Take this. If we look like we belong, they won't question it. Especially with the distance between us."

Jemma held the cold metal handle. Her heart beat hard, but they had little other choice at the moment.

They clomped between rows of wheat, making their way toward the station. It was in view, a train parked behind the building.

They didn't need to make it all the way to realize the train was facing the opposite direction of Stillfield. This was the northern supply drop.

Buran continued ahead as Jemma quickened her steps. "Buran," she said, her breath heavy.

He didn't stop.

"Buran," Jemma said louder. "The train."

"I see it."

"It's facing the wrong way." She couldn't understand why he wasn't stopping.

"I see that. We don't have many other choices, though, do we?"

Jemma stopped. Buran stepped forward a few more feet, then sighed and turned to face her.

"We're wanted criminals here, Jemma. We need to get out of Preen."

"We need to get home. An emergency train is on its way."

"Okay, we'll wait at the station. We need to be ready when it arrives, as the emergency one won't stick around. It doesn't take long to load up a body."

Governor Dunn's body. A chill ran down Jemma's spine. Buran was right; they needed to be prepared to hop on as quickly as possible.

"I know you want to get home," Buran said. "At the station, we can hide out. Maybe grab some breakfast that's not an apple."

"Okay," Jemma agreed. "I just need to be with my babies."

Blood rushed to her head. In her tired state, she hadn't taken Enertin for two days. The thought popped into her mind to take one now, but she resisted.

The risk wasn't worth it.

The train whistle blew twice as they approached the station. Five minutes. Jemma felt her blood rush and reminded herself that they weren't taking this train. It was heading the wrong way.

But where would they hide?

For now, they stood behind a pillar. People were busy loading crates into the backs of trucks. Jemma suspected the people who stood watch were trained Responders. They'd need to avoid being seen.

Jemma's stomach growled. Inside the station was a small convenience store. She had a few dollars inside her bag, enough to get herself breakfast.

The group of people lifted a large crate that looked to be from Vespher into the truck bed. Seemed they didn't listen to Preen's request for less clothing.

Buran seized the chance to dart into the station, Jemma right behind. As they entered, the man at the register glanced up briefly before returning his attention back to the newspaper in his hand.

There was another couple looking at the selection of reading material available to purchase. Jemma noticed a small pharmacy area, and next to it, some snacks. It sparked a thought she wanted to ignore, but she felt doing so would be more dangerous.

She slipped her hand into Buran's arm, which immediately earned her a confused look. "Honey, why don't you check the schedule while I grab us some travel snacks?" she said sweetly.

Buran caught on quickly as his confusion turned to a smile. "Of course. Get whatever you need."

She smiled back as she headed to the corner. She picked up a bag of chips, moving slowly toward the pharmaceutical area. Beef sticks... trail mix... there. She grabbed a small box and slipped it into her bag then turned to head to the register, her snacks in hand.

She hoped purchasing these small items would hide the one she was stealing.

She spread her treasures onto the desk as Buran moved to join her. "Looks like the train we need will be here this afternoon."

Jemma smiled. She didn't know what train was scheduled to arrive later that day, but she knew the one they were taking wouldn't be on the printed schedule.

The cashier scrunched his nose as he scanned the few items Jemma had grabbed.

After paying, Jemma held her purse close as they headed out the doors at the same time as the other couple that had been shopping.

Jemma eyed the machines that lined the entrance to prevent shoplifting. Buran motioned for the other couple to go ahead and Jemma followed close behind them.

The alarm caused Jemma to jump. The couple moved to the side and began looking through their shopping bags. The final three blows of a whistle sounded, masking the alarm for a moment.

Jemma locked eyes with Buran, who was focused forward, panic written across his face. Jemma followed his gaze to the unmarked Responder they'd passed earlier, his red hair bright in the morning sunlight. He headed their way.

"Act calm," Buran said as he grabbed Jemma's arm and moved toward the side of the building.

"Hold up there," the Responder yelled. "We need to check all persons."

Buran's steps quickened as the Responder's friends turned their attention to the chaos. "I think that's who Beecher wanted us to watch for, Flannan," one of them yelled.

"Stop where you are!" The red headed Responder pulled a gun from his waist as Buran and Jemma turned the corner and ran.

"Where do we go?" Jemma huffed. They were heading toward the trainyard.

"We need somewhere to hide." They darted behind the station building and caught sight of a dumpster.

Jemma hesitated for a moment, but her pause quickly disappeared as she heard more shouting and the sound of boots running across the cement. Buran hopped into the large container of trash first, then held out his hand to pull Jemma inside.

With the lid shut, Jemma hardly caught her breath. Buran threw a trash bag over her body, and a strange liquid splashed out the top.

She placed a hand over her mouth to keep from gagging as they waited for the sound of Responders to lessen.

"Did you see which way they went?" a voice said.

"I'm not sure. I'll take this direction, you head that way."

Footsteps passed by their hiding spot. Jemma prayed they wouldn't open the dumpster lid. Although they'd hidden beneath the trash around them, if the Responders did any digging, they would easily be caught.

As the hustling sound faded, Jemma bent over. She couldn't hold her disgust any longer as she added her own insides of undigested apples to the mix of trash. She'd tried to do so quietly, but Buran's raised eyebrows told her she hadn't.

He lifted the lid and peeked out. "We need to go," he said as he threw it open and pulled Jemma up. Thankfully, no Responders were in view.

She wiped old wrappers and a piece of gum off her clothing as they hurried toward the end of the building. Before they arrived, a Responder turned the corner, a gun held between his hands. "They're over here!" he yelled.

A bolt of electricity jumped from Jemma's hands into the ground in front of them, causing the Responder to stumble backwards.

Buran and Jemma took advantage of the distraction, turning around as they picked up their pace. Another Responder emerged from the other side. They shifted their path toward the trainyard, and Buran shot a shield of ice between them and the new Responder. He shouted as a shot rang out, cracking the ice.

They ran past the front of the loading train, hopping over the tracks. Empty train carts littered the unused portions of the yard. Buran ran to the doors of one and tugged. It wouldn't open.

As a Responder came back into view, they took off once more, passing open carts they didn't dare try to hide in. They'd be seen climbing inside.

A long whistle blew, followed by two short ones. The volume pierced Jemma's ears as the sound of wheels clacking began. The train was pulling out of the station.

"This way," Jemma said as she tugged on Buran. They disappeared between stacked crates and shifted back onto their heels as the moving train stood before them. It was picking up speed as the sound of Responders followed them.

"They went this way!" they yelled.

Buran glanced at Jemma. "Are we doing this?" he asked.

Jemma nodded, her focus on the train cart at the back that was moving toward them. One with open doors. This train may be heading the wrong way, but if they stayed and were caught, they'd only make it back to Stillfield in chains. She took a deep breath as the wheels turned faster, the chugging of the train matching the speeding up of her heart.

Buran grabbed her hand. "On the count of three."

"One—"

"They're over there!" a Responder's voice echoed.

"Two—"

The click of a gun being loaded.

"Three!" Buran and Jemma jumped as a gunshot rang out. They rolled into the moving cart, the hard metal meeting with Jemma's shoulder. Pain shot through it as wind swirled around her. She sat up, Buran on all fours nearby.

"I think—" she took a deep breath, "we made it."

Buran turned his head to her. "Looks like we did. Are you hurt at all?"

Jemma shook her head, although where they were headed next loomed in her mind.

It wasn't going to be Stillfield.

Without being able to stop them, tears welled in Jemma's eyes.

"Oh," Buran said, moving toward her. "We're okay. We got away."

"But we're going the wrong way." A tear slid down her cheek.

"I know," Buran said. "But we'll circle around. Catch a train to Stillfield at the next stop, although it'll probably be faster to stay on this train all the way around at this point."

That would take days, with stops where they would need to keep hidden so as to not get caught. Not that they had many choices at the moment.

She clutched her bag tight to her chest, the bag of chips crinkling under the pressure. They were likely all smashed already.

The train cart was mostly empty, only a few broken crates lining the back.

"I'm gonna inspect over here," Jemma yelled over the increasing sound of the train picking up speed.

"Sounds good." Buran headed toward the train doors.

Inside the crates that were still partially together were old packing materials. She headed behind a couple that were stacked together, out of sight of Buran. Here, she opened her bag and pulled out the smashed box of a pregnancy test. Hopefully it wasn't broken.

She let out a sigh of relief. The contents inside were still in one piece. She placed the end of the test against her finger and pressed, releasing the small needle into her skin.

It took only a few seconds for her blood to pool inside the glass vial body.

She placed her wounded finger into her mouth as she held the test still, waiting for the small screen to read her results.

The sound of the train door sliding shut, the smell of musty wood, and the taste of her dry mouth were her companions as she learned her life would change in a big way once more.

The word on the dark screen read:

Pregnant.

End of Book Two

ACKNOWLEDGEMENTS

Book two. The messy middle of the series. The book that takes all the good that happened in the first one and turns it upside-down. Well, maybe not all of it. I think there's still lots of good in this one—despite how it ends. Sorry for that.

I drafted this book before publishing One Spark. So much has changed from that first draft to this final draft, and it's all the better for it. A huge part of this books' transformation is due to Kimberleigh Dixon—my brainstorm partner, alpha reader, beta reader, everything reader, and best friend. When we met in 7th grade, we didn't know our friendship would last decades. I'm so glad that it has. I never would have written a book without your encouragement. I love your stories and love that we're doing this author thing together.

Being a mom to four kids makes life full of distractions. Without my husband Jeremy, I would have a difficulty finding the time to work on my books. I appreciate his support and willingness to give me time to create this world. Plus, his map making skills are impressive. Like the dedication says—I love you *all ways.*

Speaking of those kiddos, I love each and every one of them. Their individualities add so much joy to our family. K's curiosity about the world and wanting to know how things work. R's creativity and quiet but observant self. M's outgoing personality and ability to make friends. A's imagination and big heart. Although Ben and Jemma only have two kids (soon to be more), a part of each of you helped develop both Louie and Mackie.

A huge part of the writing process is revising, which can be a gruesome process. However, receiving feedback from talented friends and authors makes it so much better. They've helped the story grow into what it is. Thank you to TJ Lundin, A.M. Yeager, Jen Woodrum, and Haley Bono for giving your thoughts and feelings to let me know how to help my story improve. I appreciate every bit of thought and time you put into beta reading. Also, an honorary shout-out to AJ Monroe, I know life can get in the way, but your love for my story raised my confidence to keep working on it.

Speaking of others who helped encourage met to get this story out—shout out to the Spark Squad!! Grateful for my street team hyping me up and helping to spread the word about the Disparate Energy Novels. You all rock!! Or maybe I should say you help me fly. You know, because joy makes Disparates float.

I also want to give a special thanks to my cover designer Benita Thompson, my artist EFA_finearts, and my editor Angela Morse. I've loved working with each of you again on this second book. The final look is more than I could ask for, you've each gone above and beyond!

My final thanks go to my Kickstarter backers and my READERS. Your support helps this indie author continue to create. I appreciate you for picking up this series and giving it

a shot. I hope you've found your time in this story worthwhile.
Happy reading!

About the Author

Holly D. Morgan is a wife and mother of four. She has a Bachelor's Degree in Elementary Education and taught fourth graders they were mathematicians, scientists, historians, and writers. It wasn't until after she left teaching that she realized she, too, was a writer (with some motivation from a friend leading her to accept the call).

Although her short mystery stories have been published in anthologies, *One Spark* and *Two Flames* are her first novels. She can be found typing away from her home in San Tan Valley, Arizona.

Follow along for updates:

Instagram: @hollydmorganbooks

Facebook: Author Holly D. Morgan

Website: https://hollydmorganbooks.company.site/